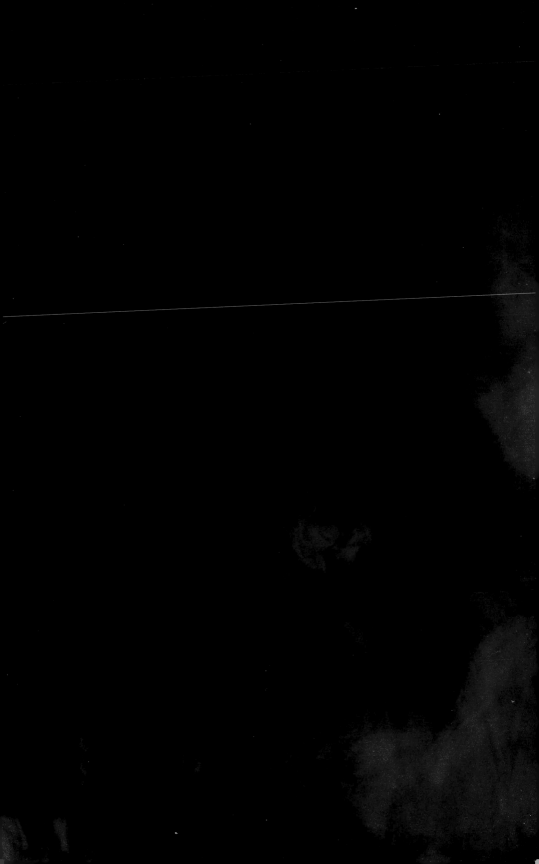

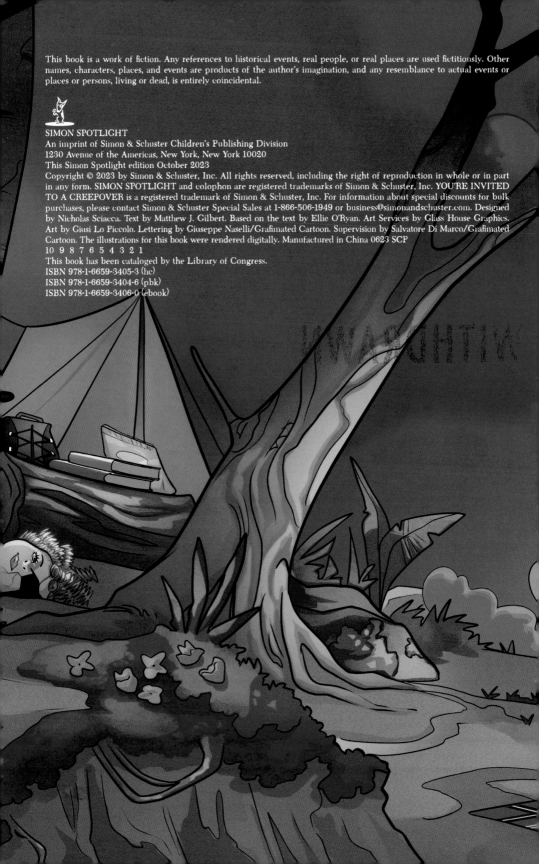

SIMON SPOTLIGHT
An imprint of Simon & Schuster Children's Publishing Division
1230 Avenue of the Americas, New York, New York 10020
This Simon Spotlight edition October 2023
Copyright © 2023 by Simon & Schuster, Inc. All rights reserved, including the right of reproduction in whole or in part in any form. SIMON SPOTLIGHT and colophon are registered trademarks of Simon & Schuster, Inc. YOU'RE INVITED TO A CREEPOVER is a registered trademark of Simon & Schuster, Inc. For information about special discounts for bulk purchases, please contact Simon & Schuster Special Sales at 1-866-506-1949 or business@simonandschuster.com. Designed by Nicholas Sciacca. Text by Matthew J. Gilbert. Based on the text by Ellie O'Ryan. Art Services by Glass House Graphics. Art by Giusi Lo Piccolo. Lettering by Giuseppe Naselli/Grafimated Cartoon. Supervision by Salvatore Di Marco/Grafimated Cartoon. The illustrations for this book were rendered digitally. Manufactured in China 0623 SCP
10 9 8 7 6 5 4 3 2 1
This book has been cataloged by the Library of Congress.
ISBN 978-1-6659-3405-3 (hc)
ISBN 978-1-6659-3404-6 (pbk)
ISBN 978-1-6659-3406-0 (ebook)

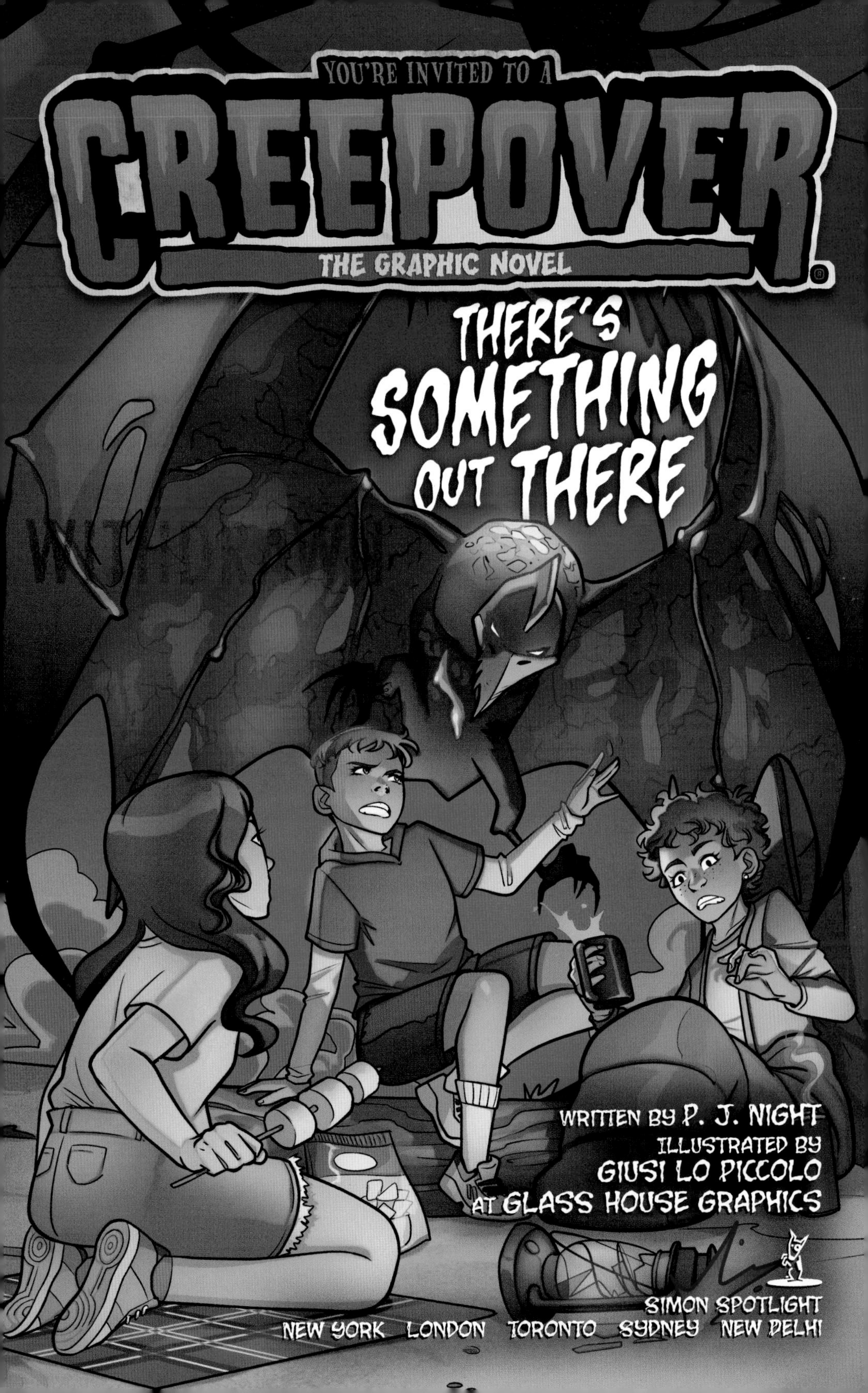

YOU'RE INVITED TO A

CREEPOVER®

THE GRAPHIC NOVEL

THERE'S SOMETHING OUT THERE

WRITTEN BY P. J. NIGHT

ILLUSTRATED BY GIUSI LO PICCOLO AT GLASS HOUSE GRAPHICS

SIMON SPOTLIGHT

NEW YORK LONDON TORONTO SYDNEY NEW DELHI

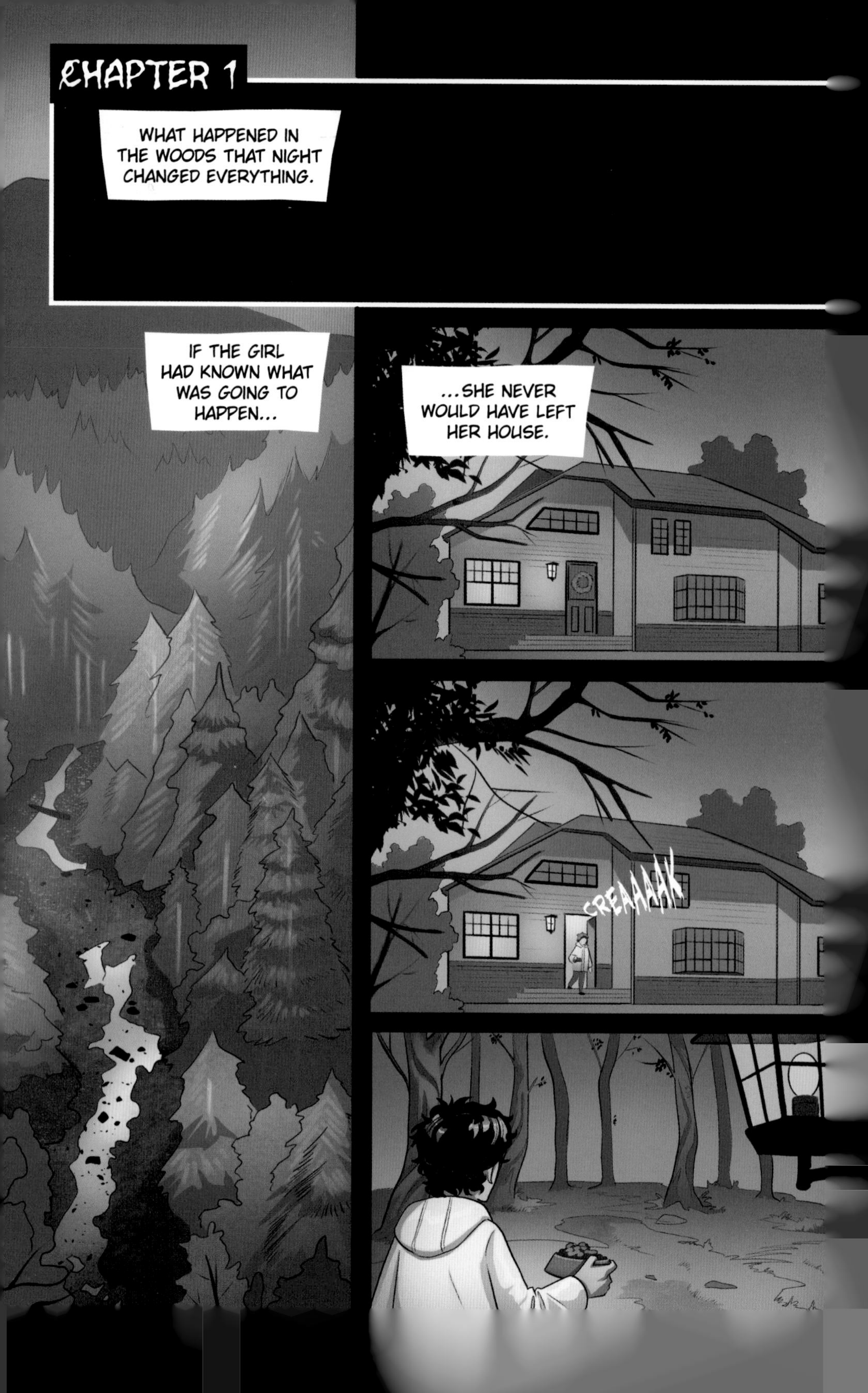
CHAPTER 1
WHAT HAPPENED IN THE WOODS THAT NIGHT CHANGED EVERYTHING.
IF THE GIRL HAD KNOWN WHAT WAS GOING TO HAPPEN...
...SHE NEVER WOULD HAVE LEFT HER HOUSE.
CREAAAAK

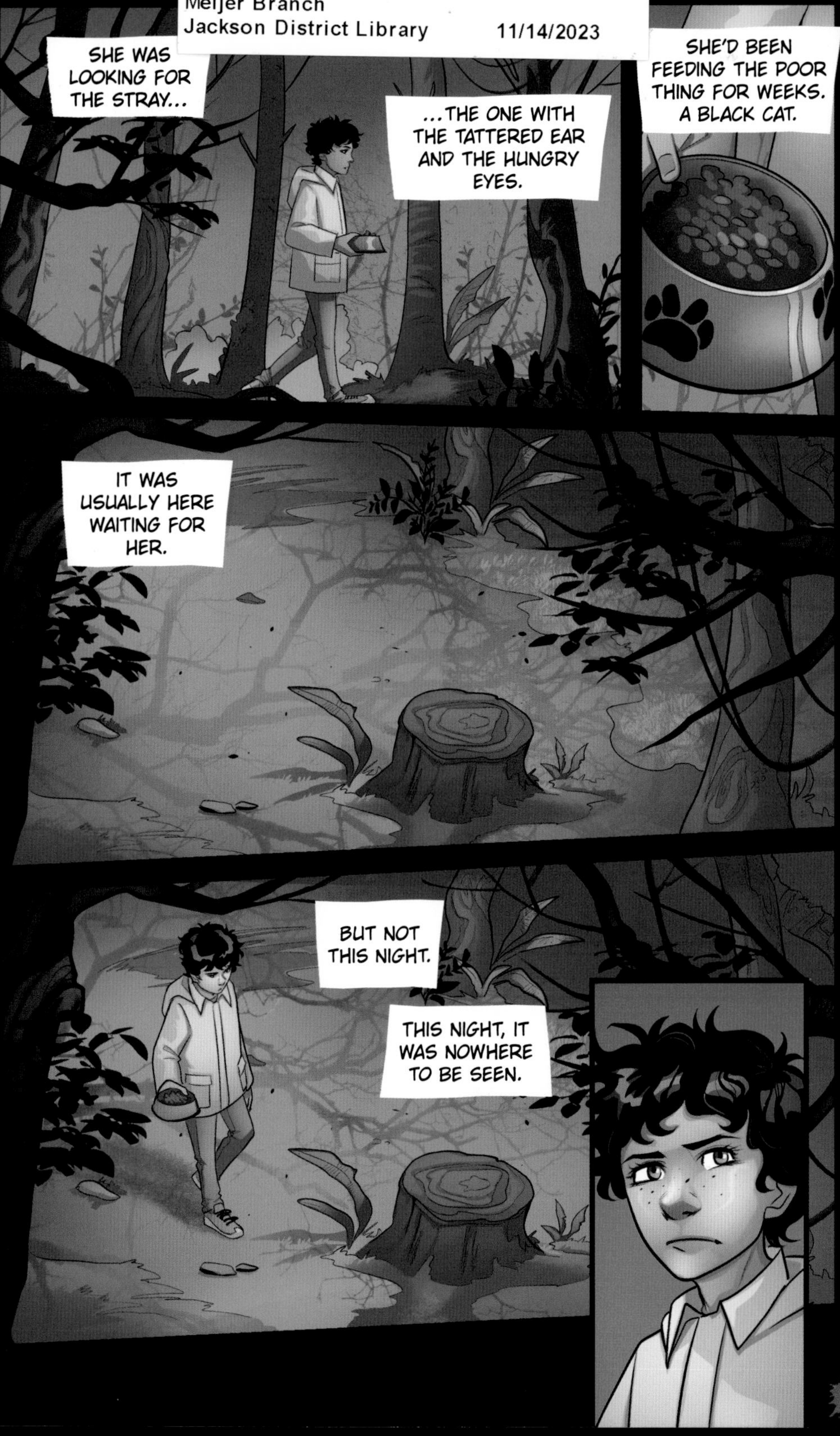
SHE WAS LOOKING FOR THE STRAY...
...THE ONE WITH THE TATTERED EAR AND THE HUNGRY EYES.
SHE'D BEEN FEEDING THE POOR THING FOR WEEKS. A BLACK CAT.
IT WAS USUALLY HERE WAITING FOR HER.
BUT NOT THIS NIGHT.
THIS NIGHT, IT WAS NOWHERE TO BE SEEN.

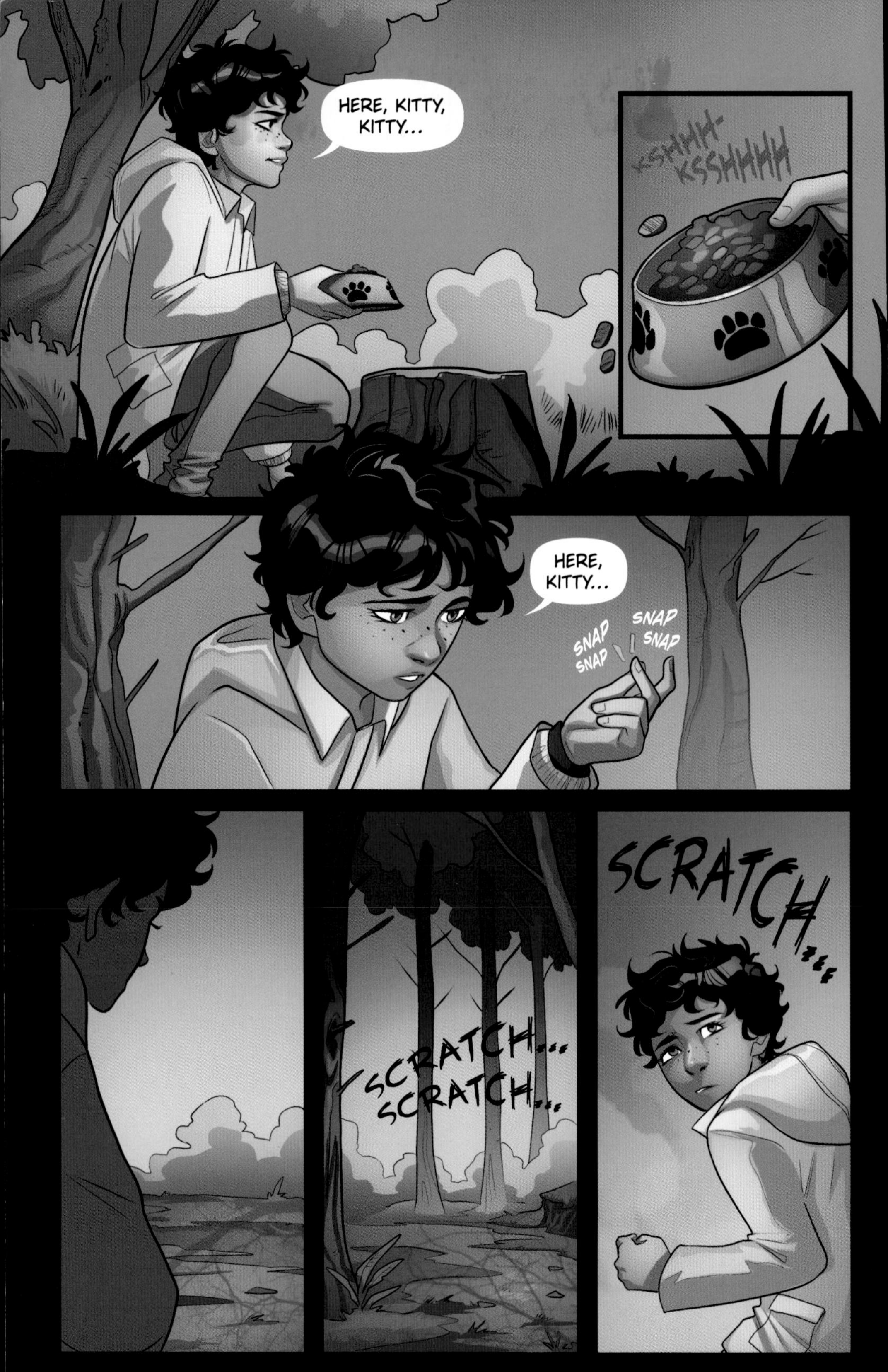
HERE, KITTY, KITTY...
KSHHH-KSSHHHH
HERE, KITTY...
SNAP SNAP
SNAP SNAP
SCRATCH... SCRATCH...
SCRATCH...

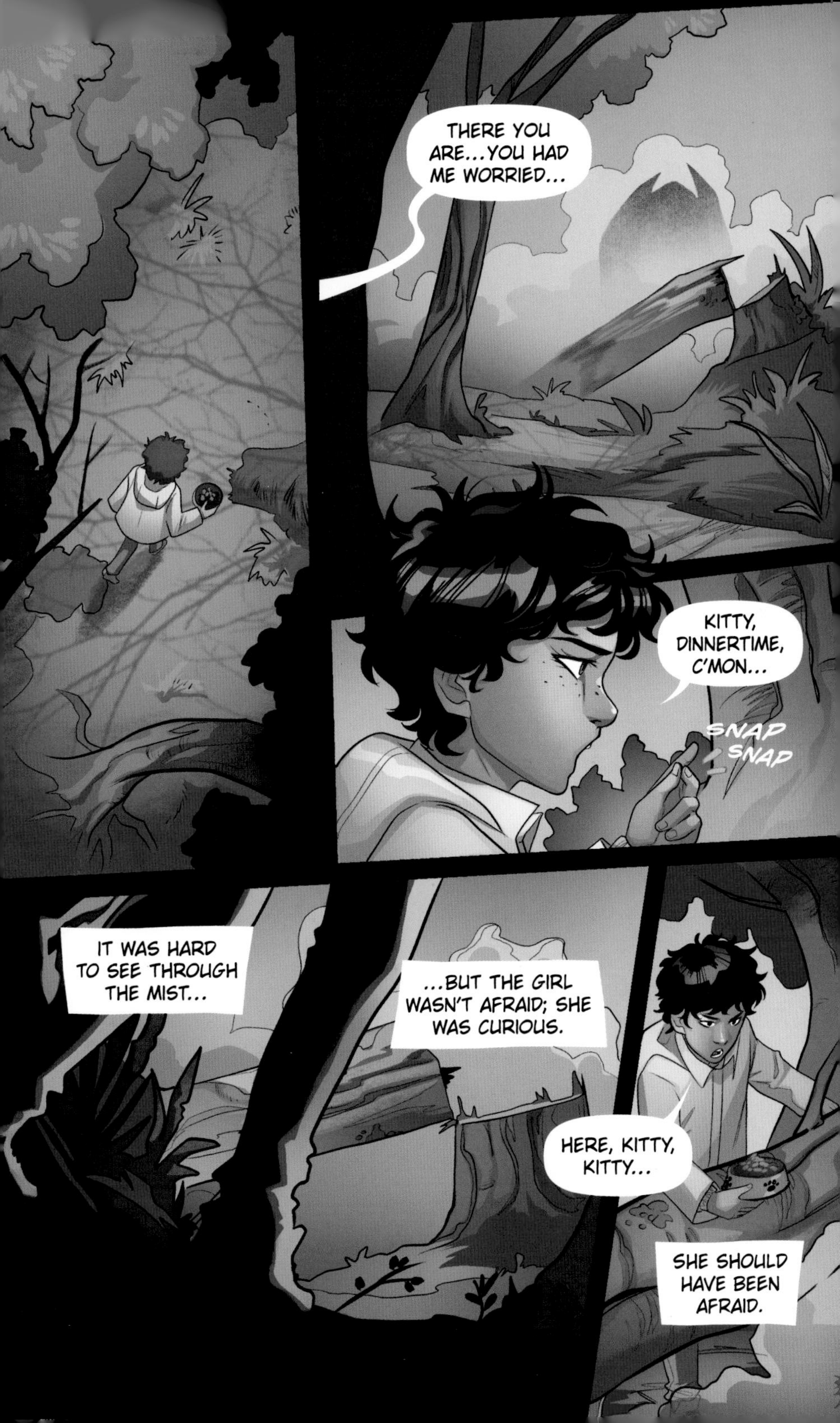
THERE YOU ARE...YOU HAD ME WORRIED...
KITTY, DINNERTIME, C'MON...
SNAP SNAP
IT WAS HARD TO SEE THROUGH THE MIST...
...BUT THE GIRL WASN'T AFRAID; SHE WAS CURIOUS.
HERE, KITTY, KITTY...
SHE SHOULD HAVE BEEN AFRAID.

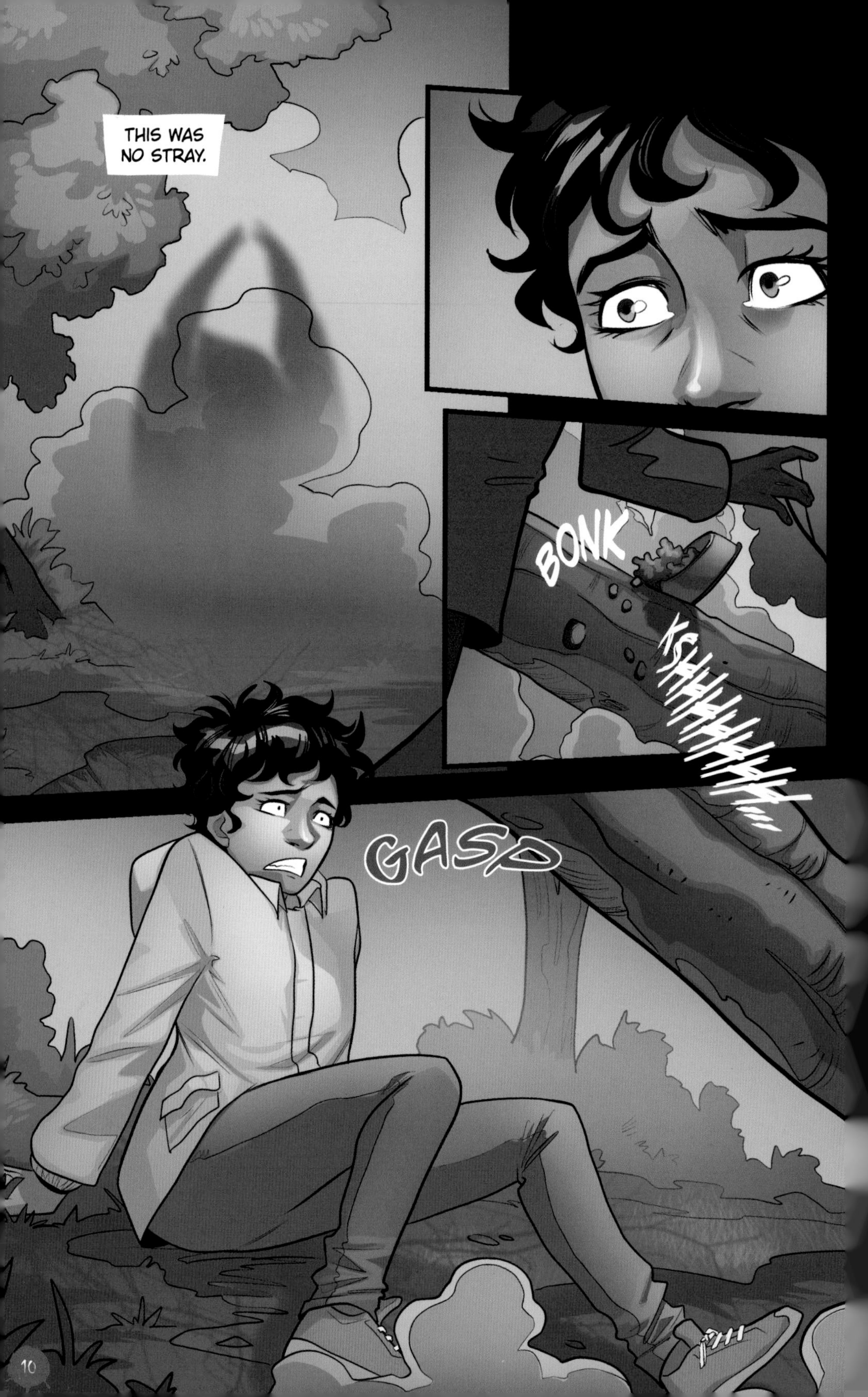
THIS WAS NO STRAY.
BONK
KSHHHHHHHHH...
GASP

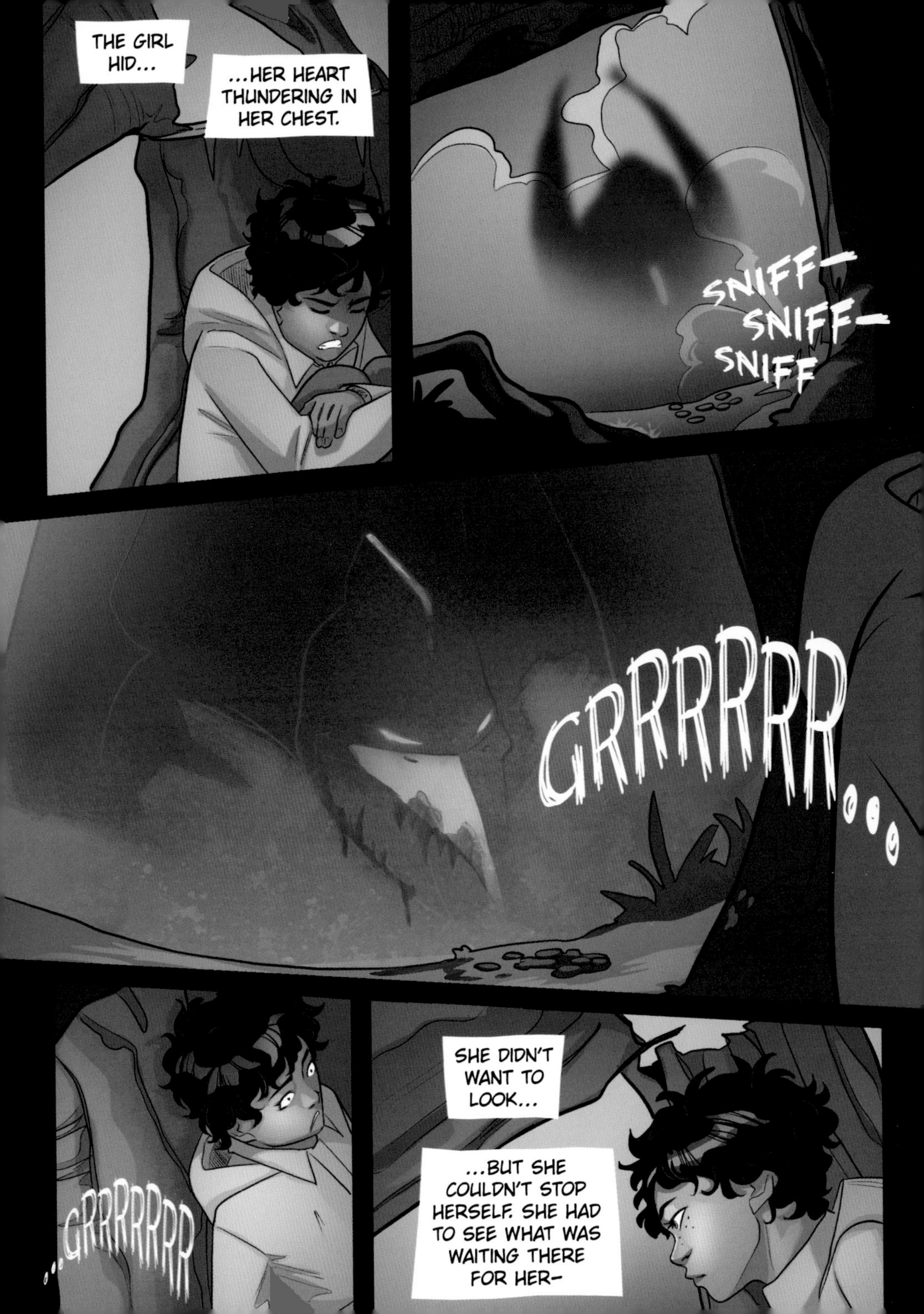
THE GIRL HID...
...HER HEART THUNDERING IN HER CHEST.
SNIFF-
SNIFF-
SNIFF
GRRRRRRR...
...GRRRRRRR
SHE DIDN'T WANT TO LOOK...
...BUT SHE COULDN'T STOP HERSELF. SHE HAD TO SEE WHAT WAS WAITING THERE FOR HER-

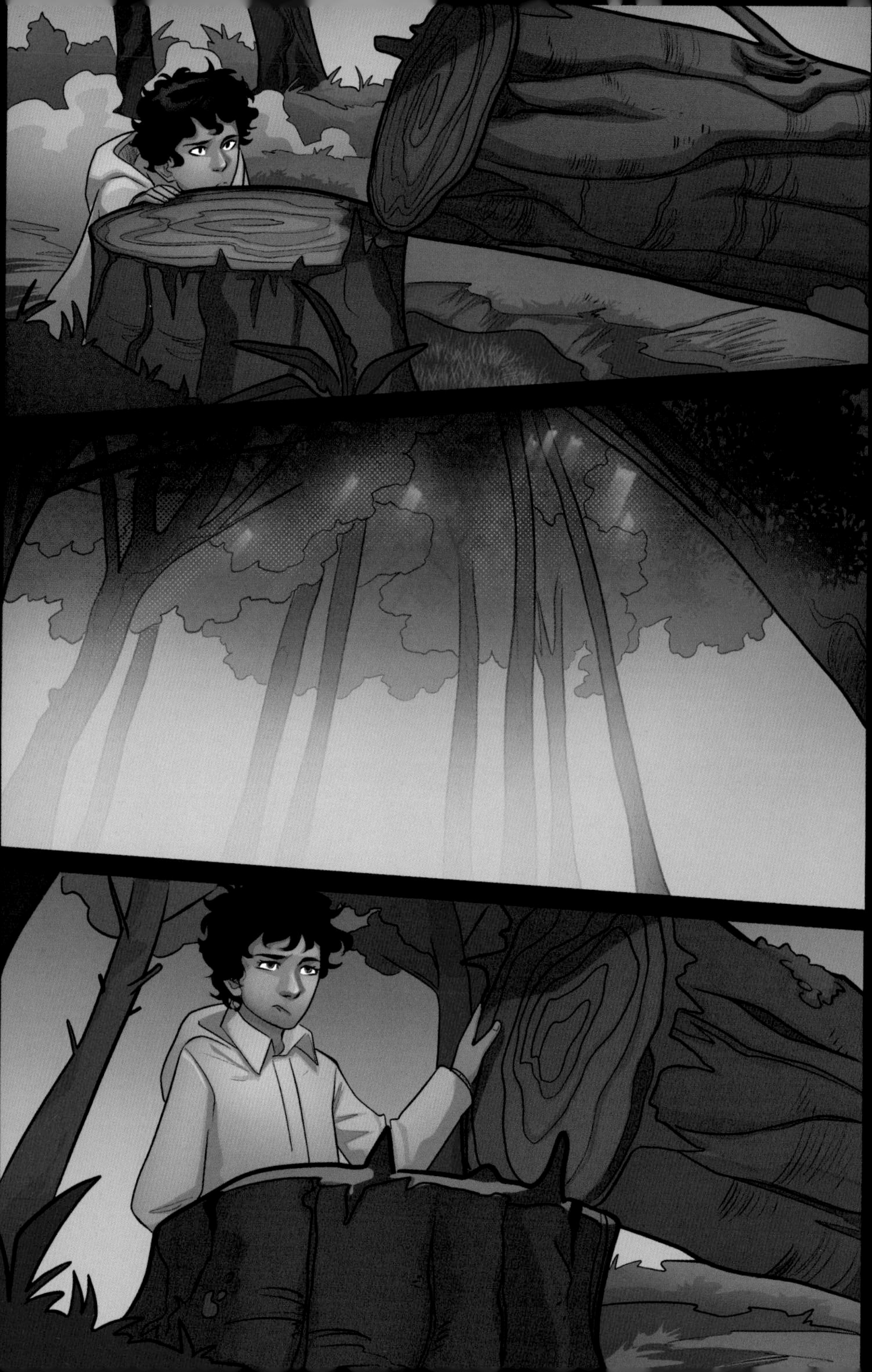

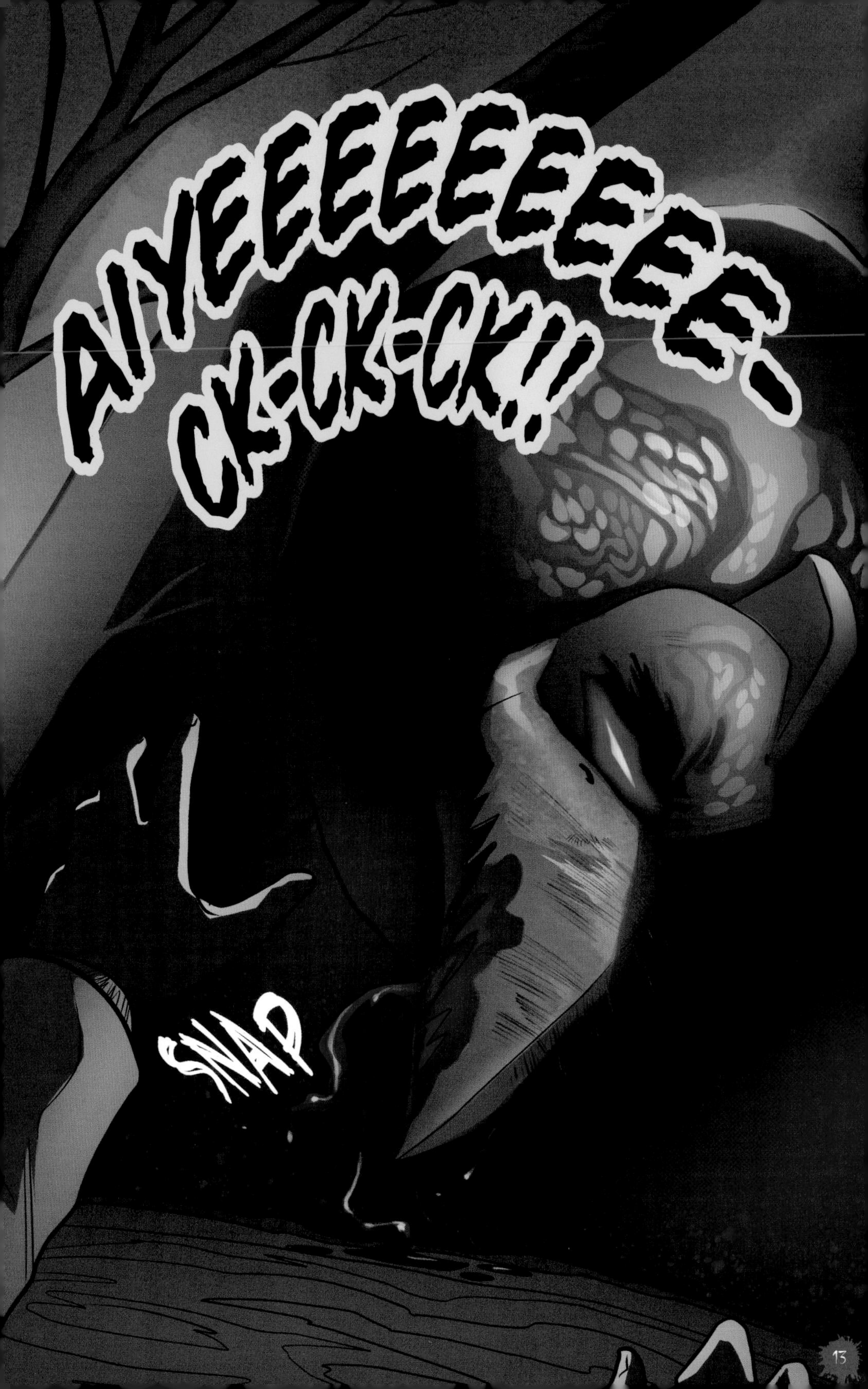
AIYEEEEEEEEE-
CK-CK-CK!!
SNAP

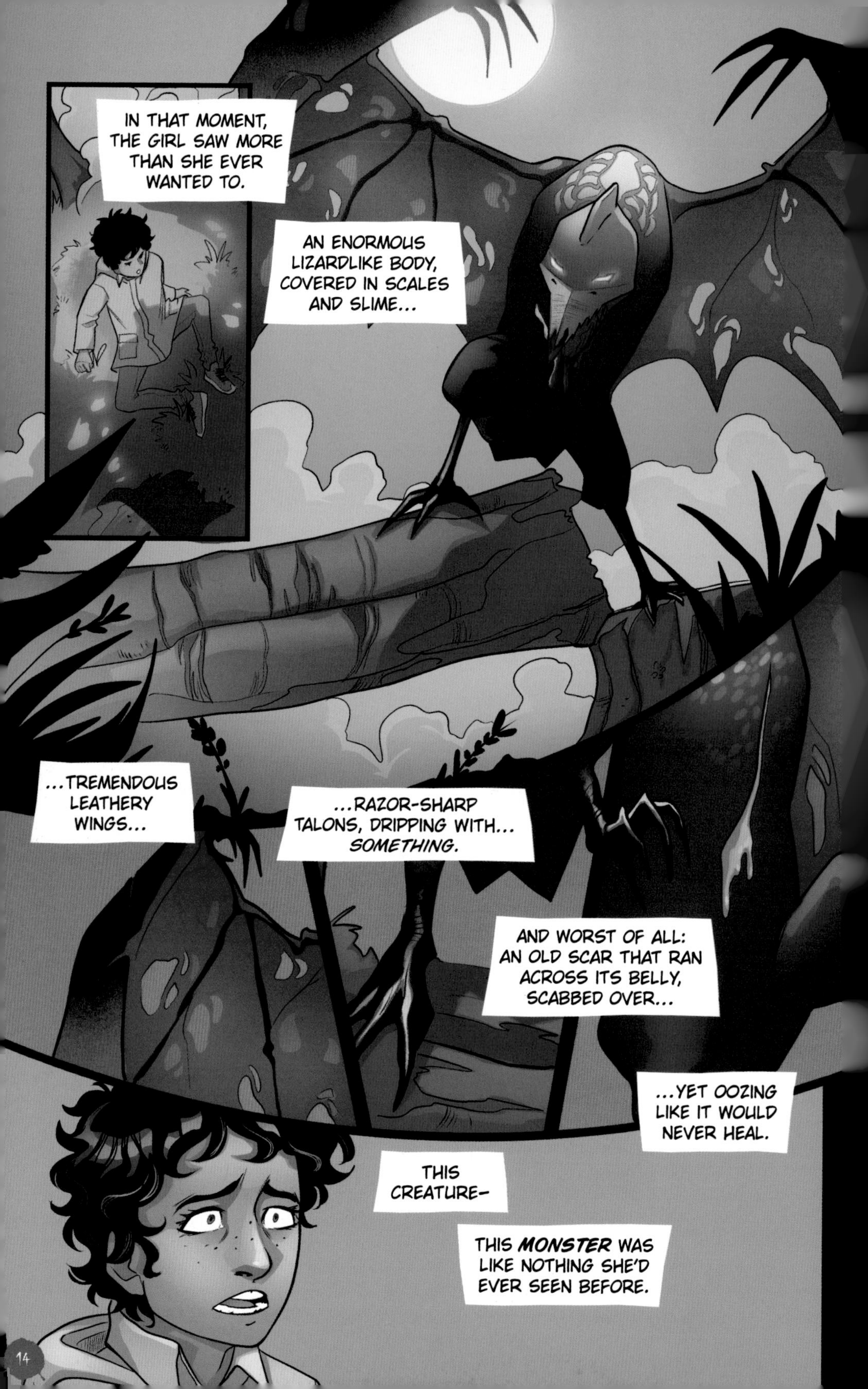
IN THAT MOMENT, THE GIRL SAW MORE THAN SHE EVER WANTED TO.
AN ENORMOUS LIZARDLIKE BODY, COVERED IN SCALES AND SLIME...
...TREMENDOUS LEATHERY WINGS...
...RAZOR-SHARP TALONS, DRIPPING WITH... *SOMETHING.*
AND WORST OF ALL: AN OLD SCAR THAT RAN ACROSS ITS BELLY, SCABBED OVER...
...YET OOZING LIKE IT WOULD NEVER HEAL.
THIS CREATURE–
THIS ***MONSTER*** WAS LIKE NOTHING SHE'D EVER SEEN BEFORE.

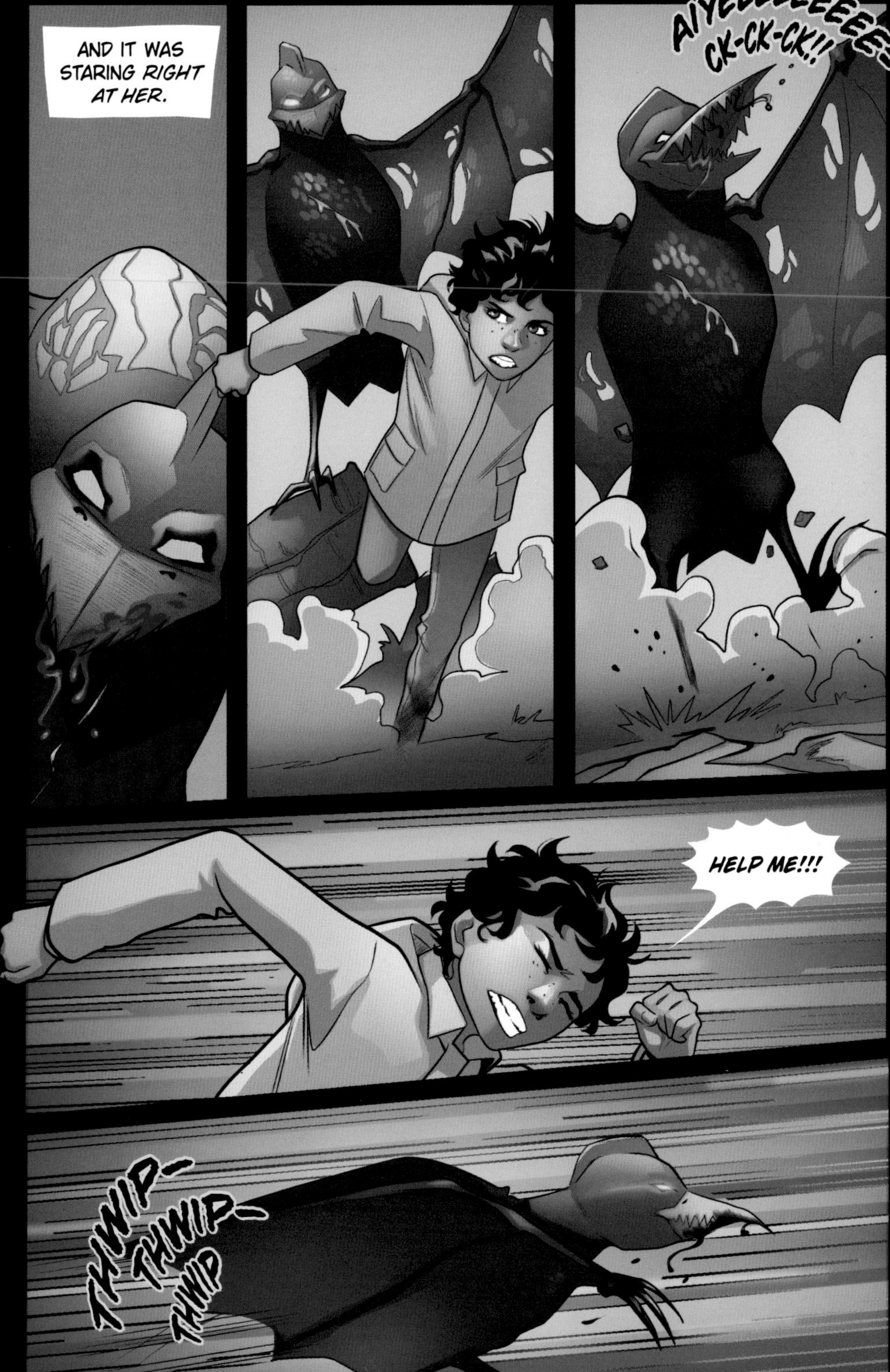
AND IT WAS STARING *RIGHT* AT HER.
AIYEEEEEEEEE-CK-CK-CK!!
HELP ME!!!
THWIP-THWIP-THWIP

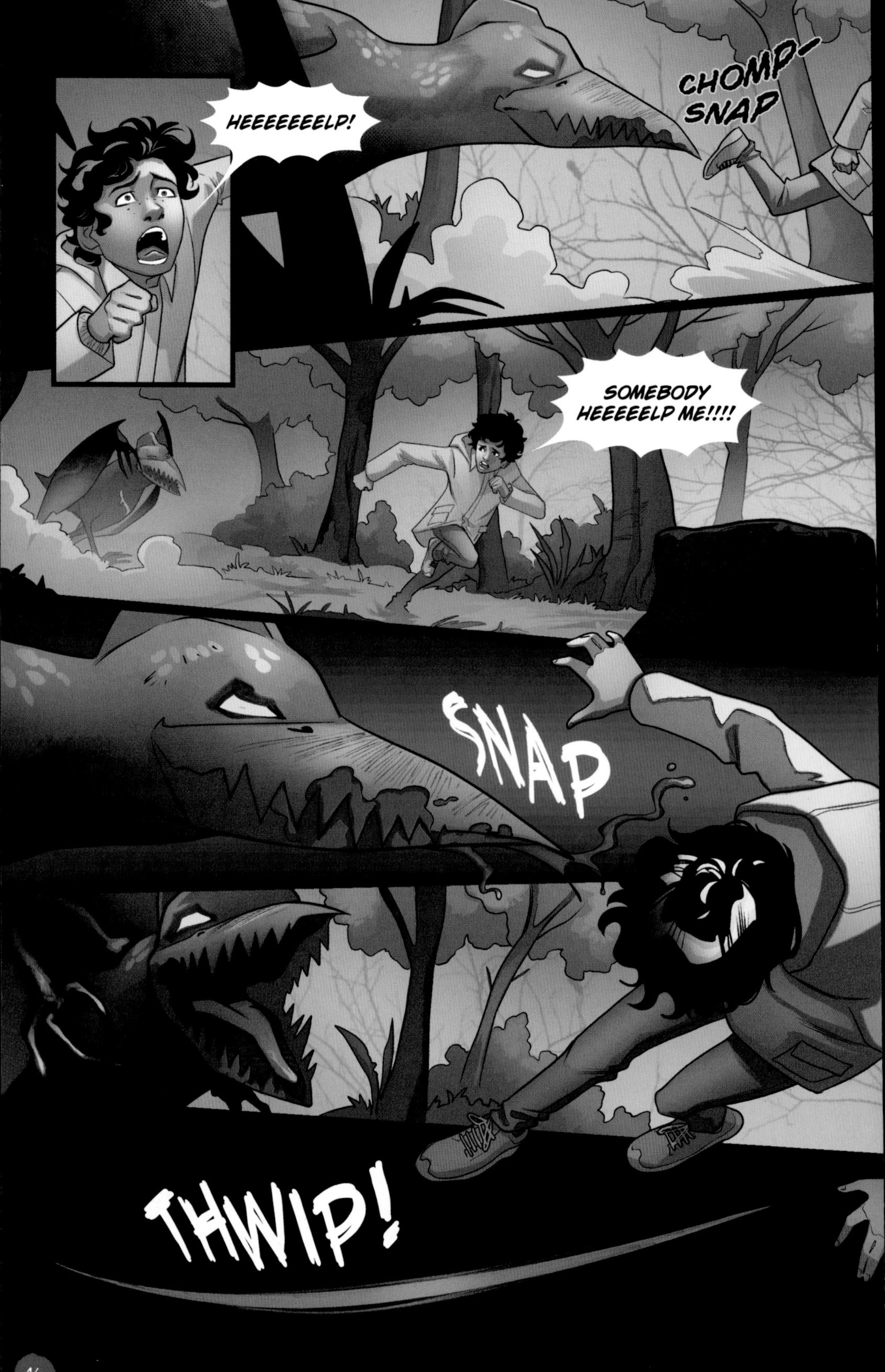
HEEEEEEELP!
CHOMP-
SNAP
SOMEBODY
HEEEEELP ME!!!!
SNAP
THWIP!

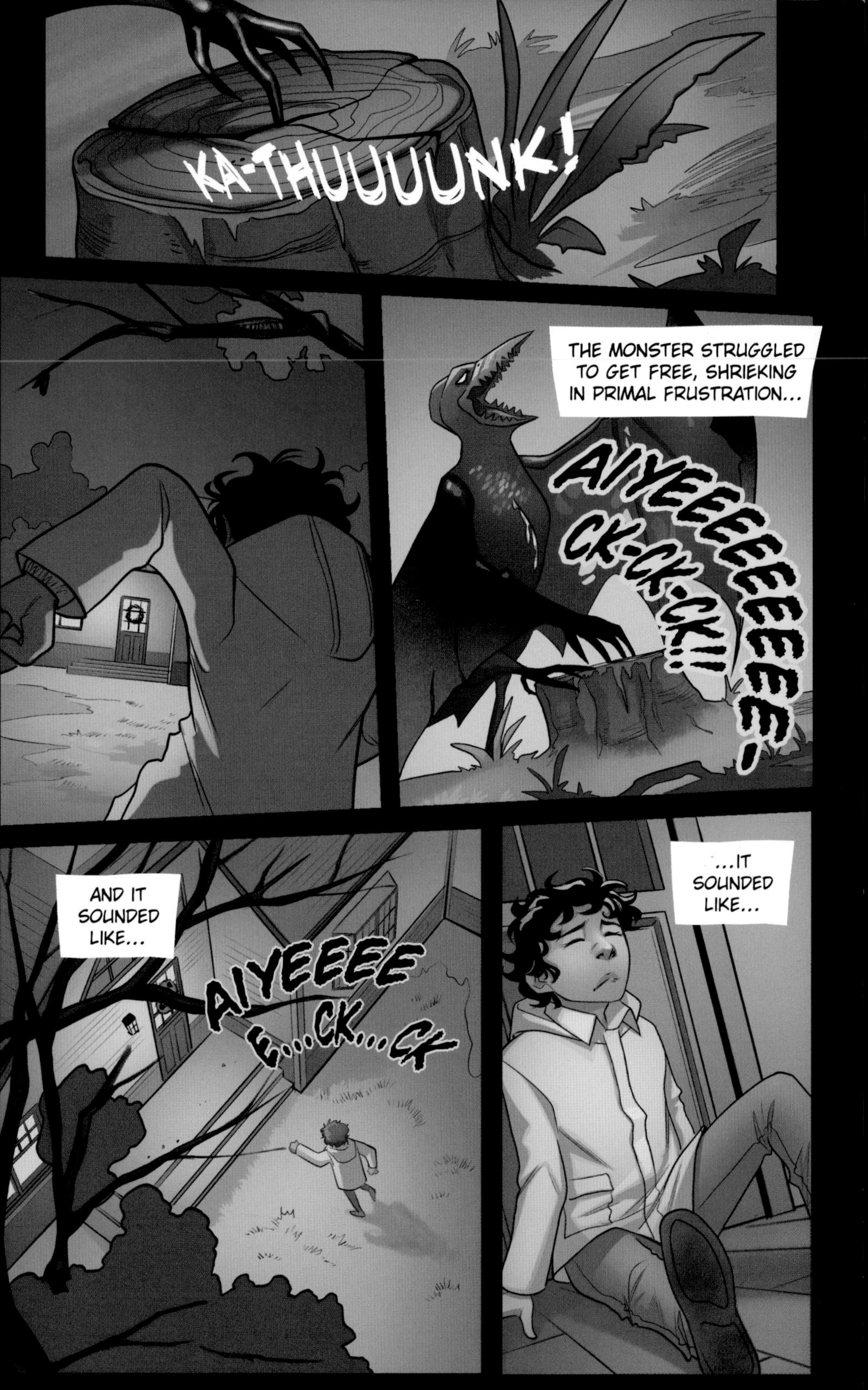
KA-THUUUUUNK!
THE MONSTER STRUGGLED TO GET FREE, SHRIEKING IN PRIMAL FRUSTRATION...
AIYEEEEEEEEEEEEE-CK-CK-CK!!
AND IT SOUNDED LIKE...
AIYEEEEE E...CK...CK
...IT SOUNDED LIKE...

CHAPTER 2

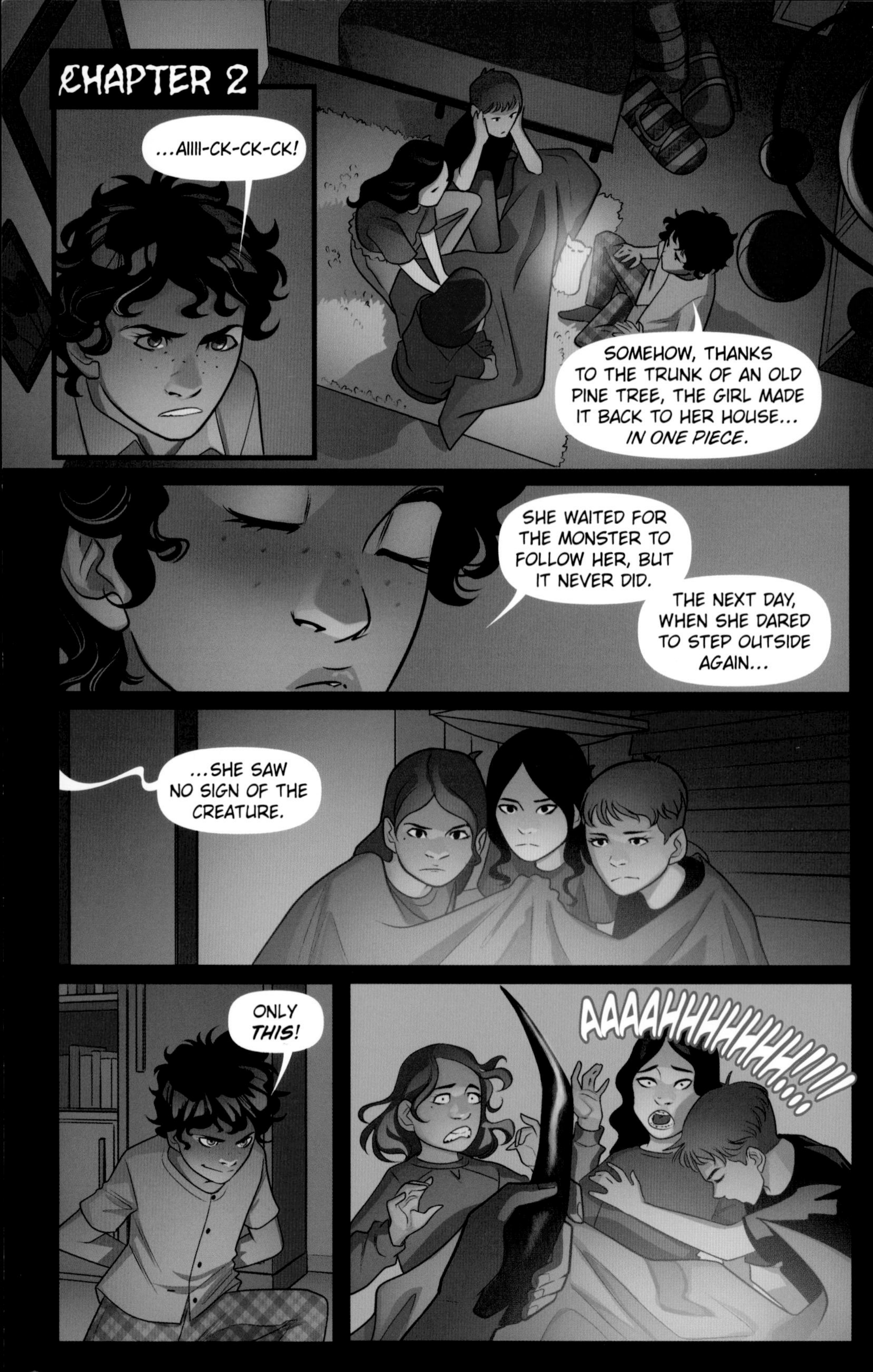
...AIIII-CK-CK-CK!
SOMEHOW, THANKS TO THE TRUNK OF AN OLD PINE TREE, THE GIRL MADE IT BACK TO HER HOUSE... *IN ONE PIECE*.
SHE WAITED FOR THE MONSTER TO FOLLOW HER, BUT IT NEVER DID.
THE NEXT DAY, WHEN SHE DARED TO STEP OUTSIDE AGAIN...
...SHE SAW NO SIGN OF THE CREATURE.
ONLY *THIS*!
AAAAHHHHHHHH!!!!!...

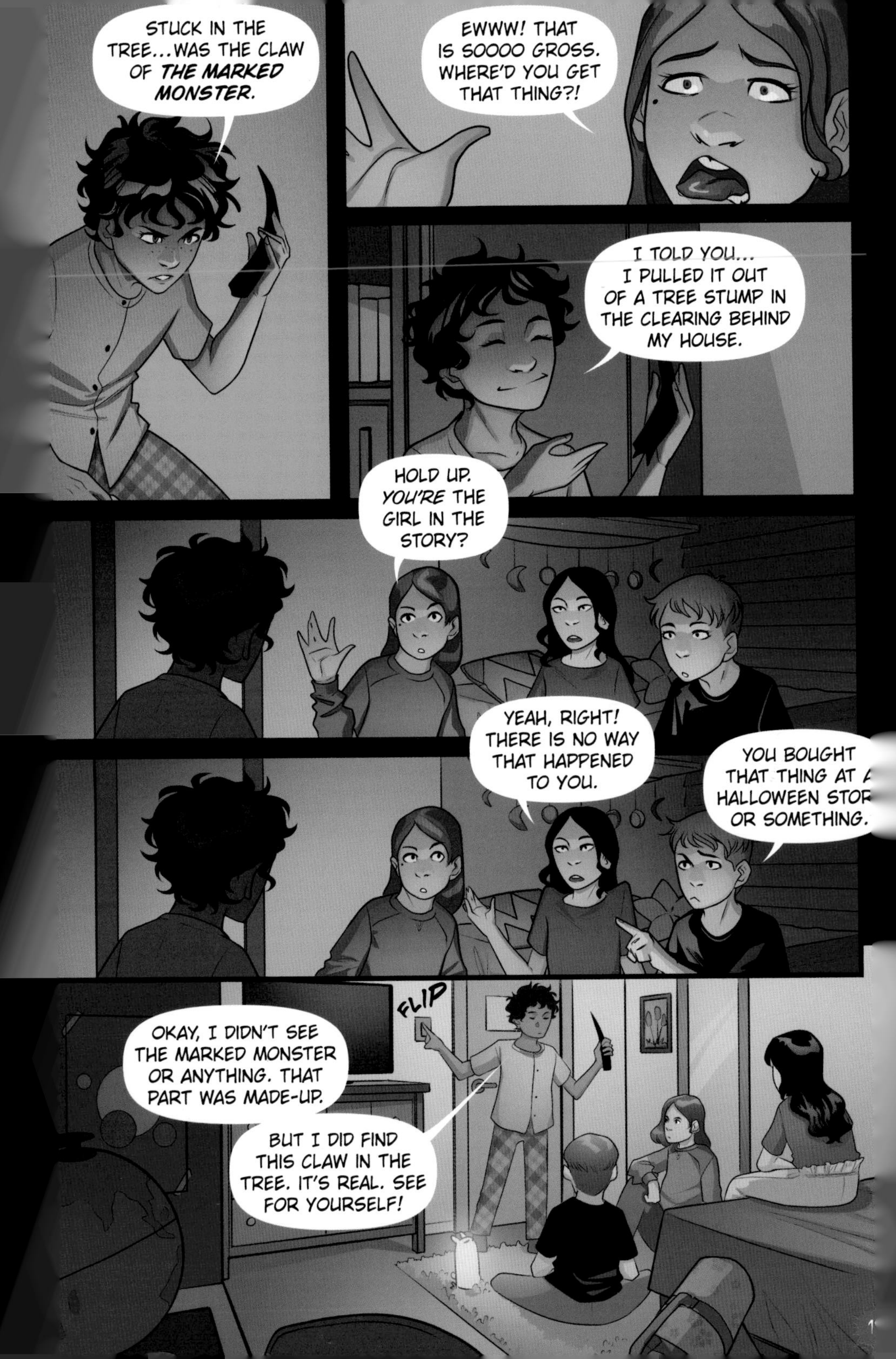
STUCK IN THE TREE...WAS THE CLAW OF ***THE MARKED MONSTER***.
EWWW! THAT IS SOOOO GROSS. WHERE'D YOU GET THAT THING?!
I TOLD YOU... I PULLED IT OUT OF A TREE STUMP IN THE CLEARING BEHIND MY HOUSE.
HOLD UP. *YOU'RE* THE GIRL IN THE STORY?
YEAH, RIGHT! THERE IS NO WAY THAT HAPPENED TO YOU.
YOU BOUGHT THAT THING AT A HALLOWEEN STOR OR SOMETHING.
FLIP
OKAY, I DIDN'T SEE THE MARKED MONSTER OR ANYTHING. THAT PART WAS MADE-UP.
BUT I DID FIND THIS CLAW IN THE TREE. IT'S REAL. SEE FOR YOURSELF!

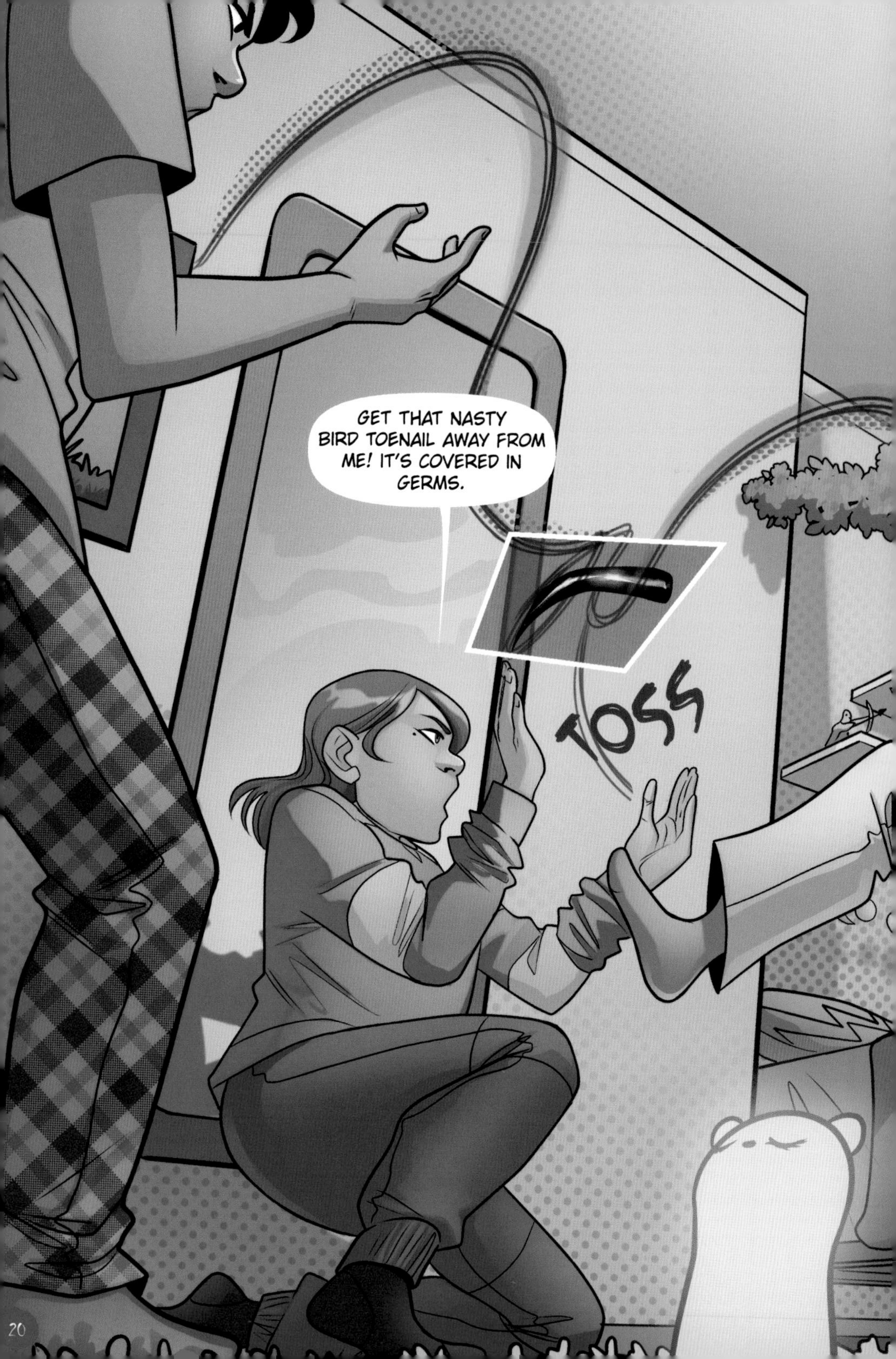
GET THAT NASTY BIRD TOENAIL AWAY FROM ME! IT'S COVERED IN GERMS.
TOSS

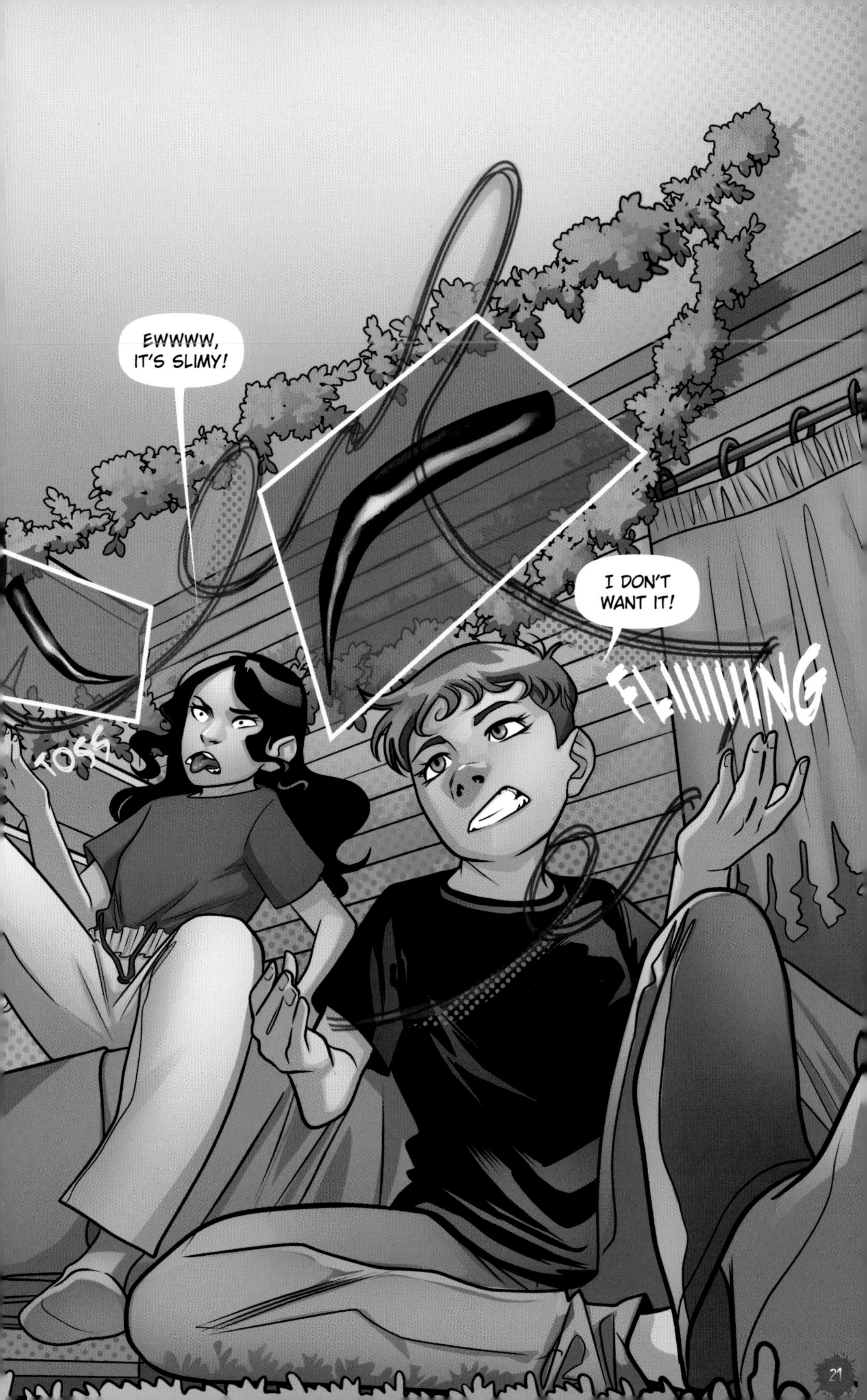
EWWWW, IT'S SLIMY!
TOSS
I DON'T WANT IT!
FLIIIIIING

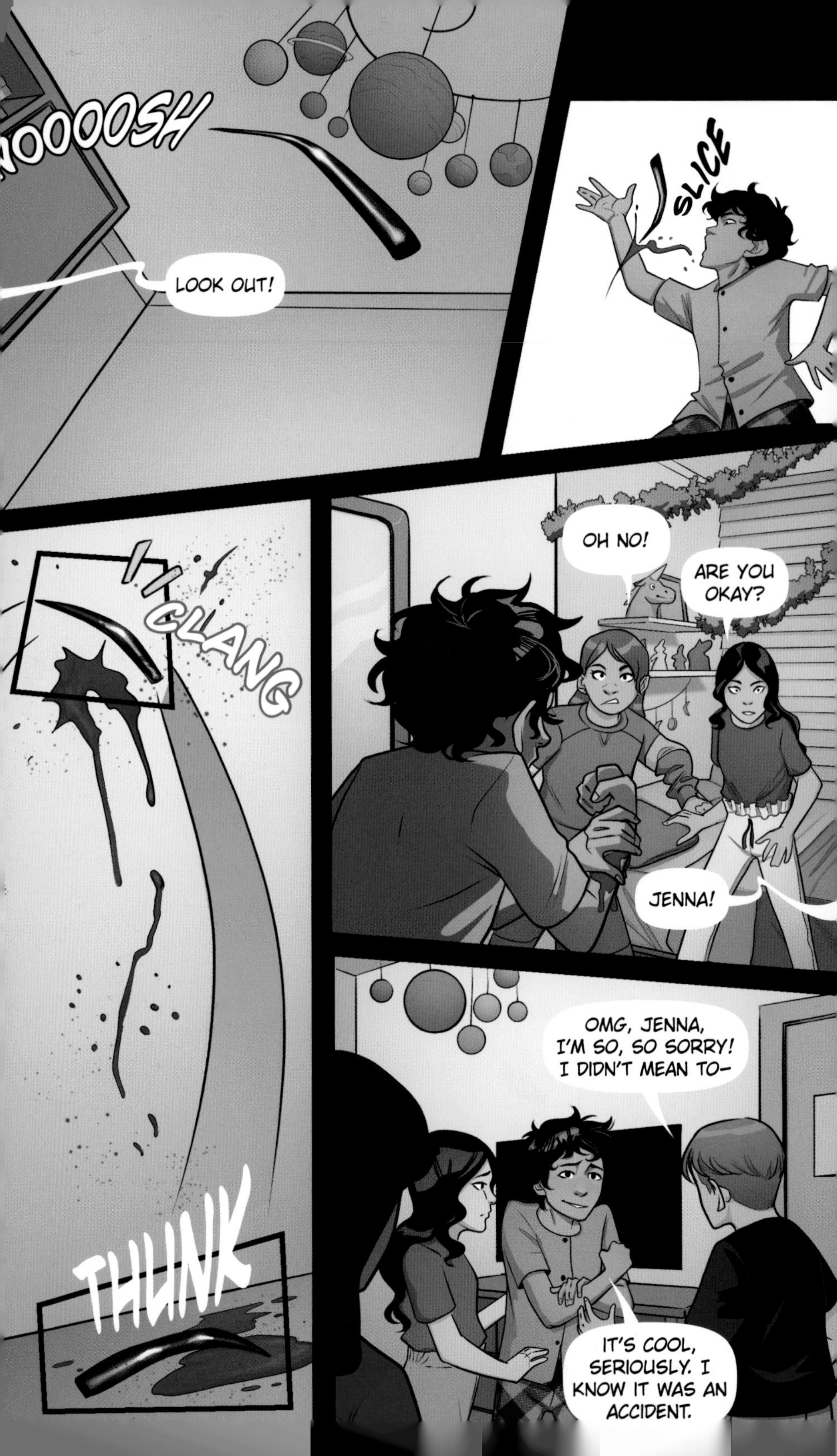

WHOOOOOSH
LOOK OUT!
SLICE
CLANG
THUNK
OH NO!
ARE YOU OKAY?
JENNA!
OMG, JENNA, I'M SO, SO SORRY! I DIDN'T MEAN TO—
IT'S COOL, SERIOUSLY. I KNOW IT WAS AN ACCIDENT.

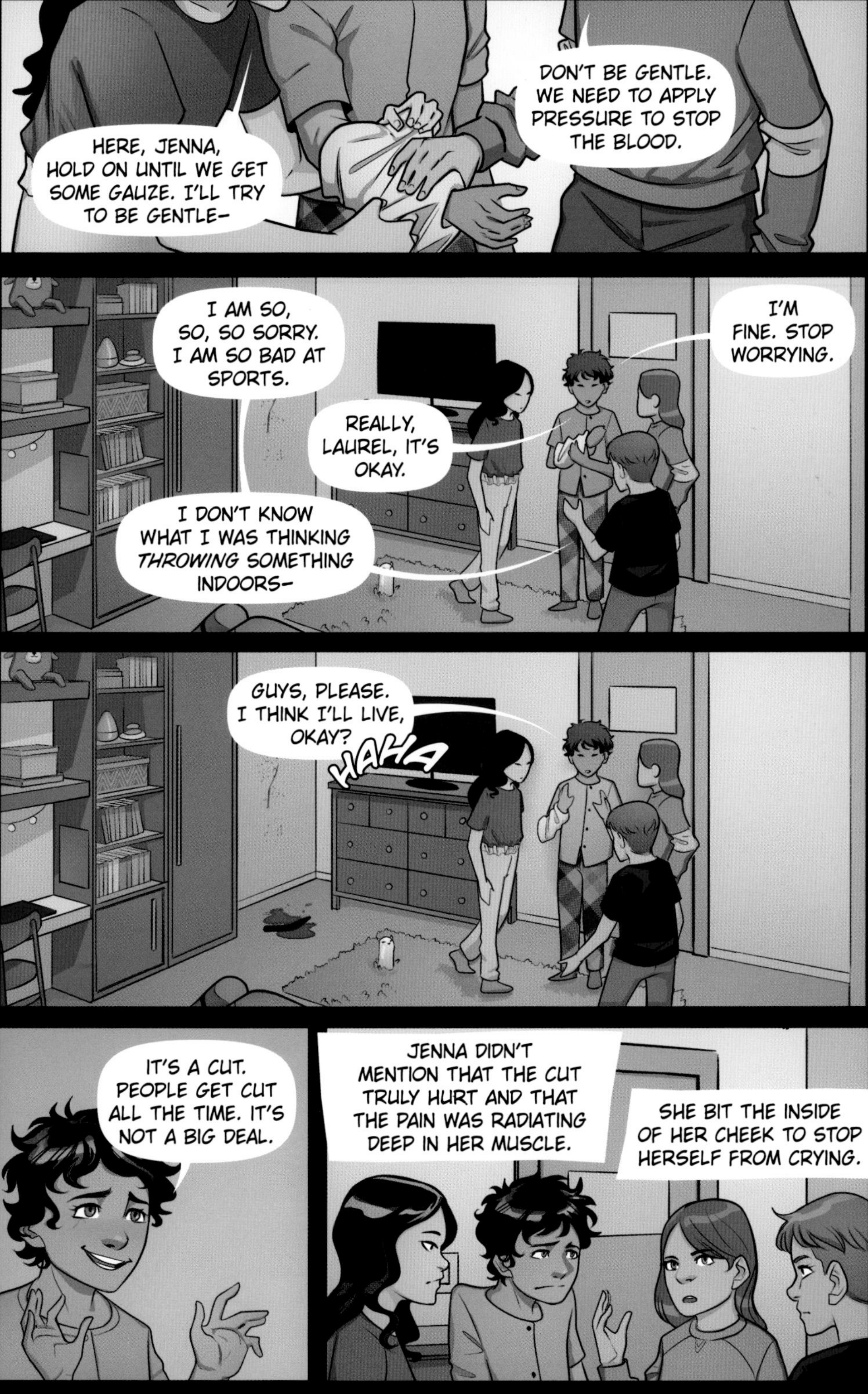

HERE, JENNA, HOLD ON UNTIL WE GET SOME GAUZE. I'LL TRY TO BE GENTLE—
DON'T BE GENTLE. WE NEED TO APPLY PRESSURE TO STOP THE BLOOD.
I AM SO, SO, SO SORRY. I AM SO BAD AT SPORTS.
I'M FINE. STOP WORRYING.
REALLY, LAUREL, IT'S OKAY.
I DON'T KNOW WHAT I WAS THINKING *THROWING* SOMETHING INDOORS—
GUYS, PLEASE. I THINK I'LL LIVE, OKAY?
HAHA
IT'S A CUT. PEOPLE GET CUT ALL THE TIME. IT'S NOT A BIG DEAL.
JENNA DIDN'T MENTION THAT THE CUT TRULY HURT AND THAT THE PAIN WAS RADIATING DEEP IN HER MUSCLE.
SHE BIT THE INSIDE OF HER CHEEK TO STOP HERSELF FROM CRYING.

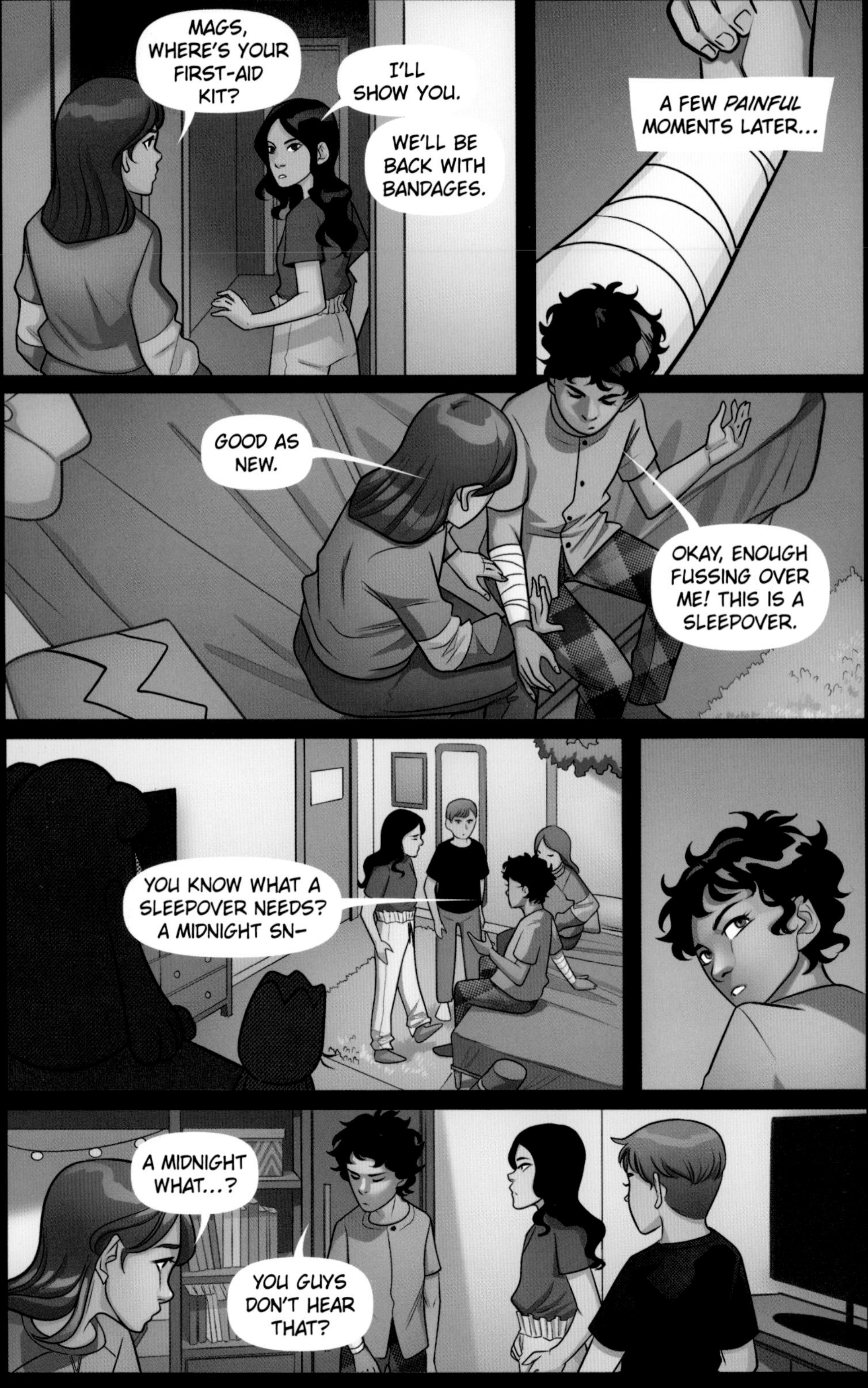
MAGS, WHERE'S YOUR FIRST-AID KIT?
I'LL SHOW YOU.
WE'LL BE BACK WITH BANDAGES.
A FEW *PAINFUL* MOMENTS LATER...
GOOD AS NEW.
OKAY, ENOUGH FUSSING OVER ME! THIS IS A SLEEPOVER.
YOU KNOW WHAT A SLEEPOVER NEEDS? A MIDNIGHT SN–
A MIDNIGHT WHAT...?
YOU GUYS DON'T HEAR THAT?

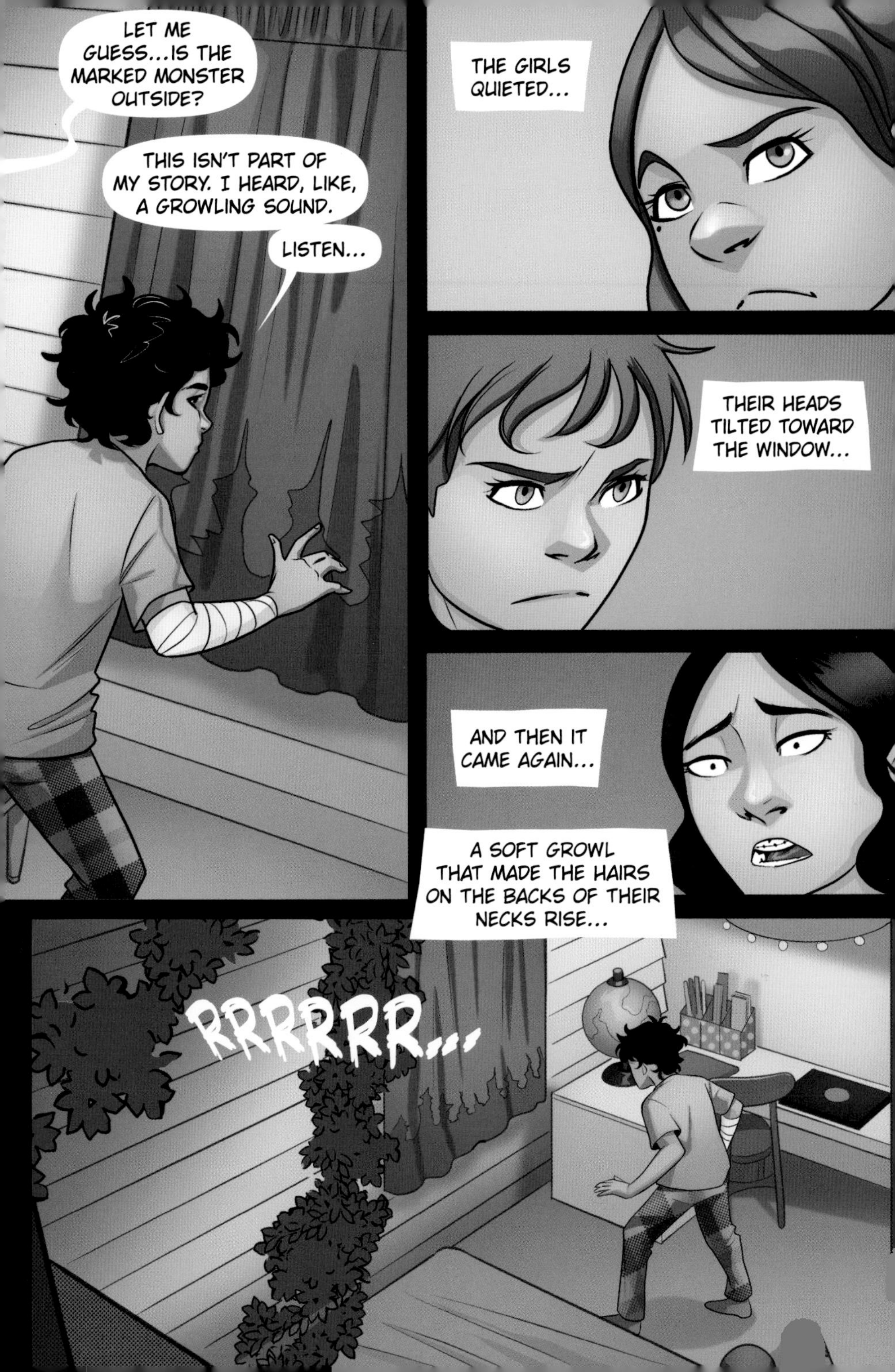
LET ME GUESS...IS THE MARKED MONSTER OUTSIDE?
THIS ISN'T PART OF MY STORY. I HEARD, LIKE, A GROWLING SOUND.
LISTEN...
THE GIRLS QUIETED...
THEIR HEADS TILTED TOWARD THE WINDOW...
AND THEN IT CAME AGAIN...
A SOFT GROWL THAT MADE THE HAIRS ON THE BACKS OF THEIR NECKS RISE...
RRRRRR...

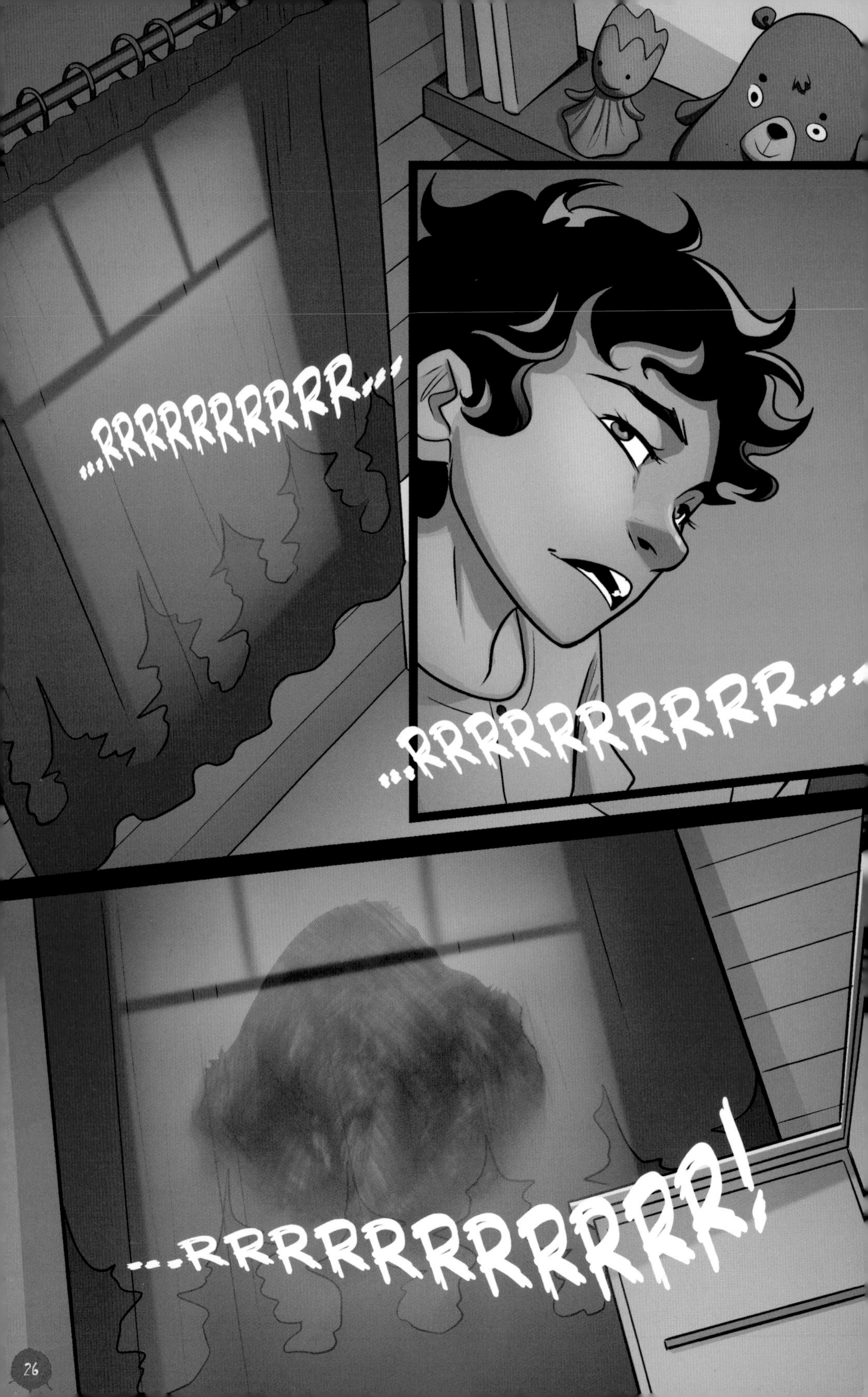
..RRRRRRRRRR...
..RRRRRRRRRR...
...RRRRRRRRRRRR!

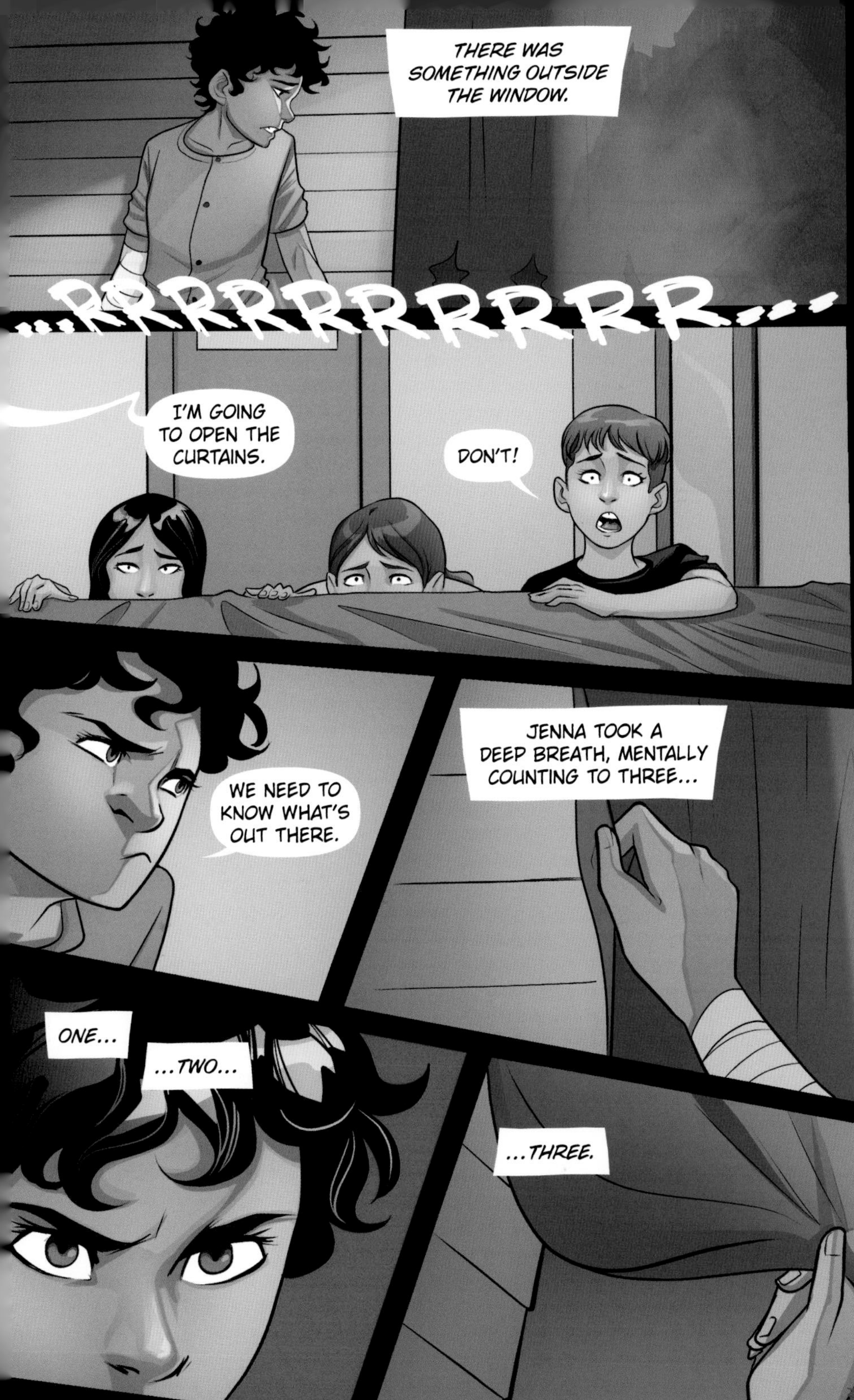
THERE WAS SOMETHING OUTSIDE THE WINDOW.
...RRRRRRRRRRRR...
I'M GOING TO OPEN THE CURTAINS.
DON'T!
WE NEED TO KNOW WHAT'S OUT THERE.
JENNA TOOK A DEEP BREATH, MENTALLY COUNTING TO THREE...
ONE...
...TWO...
...THREE.

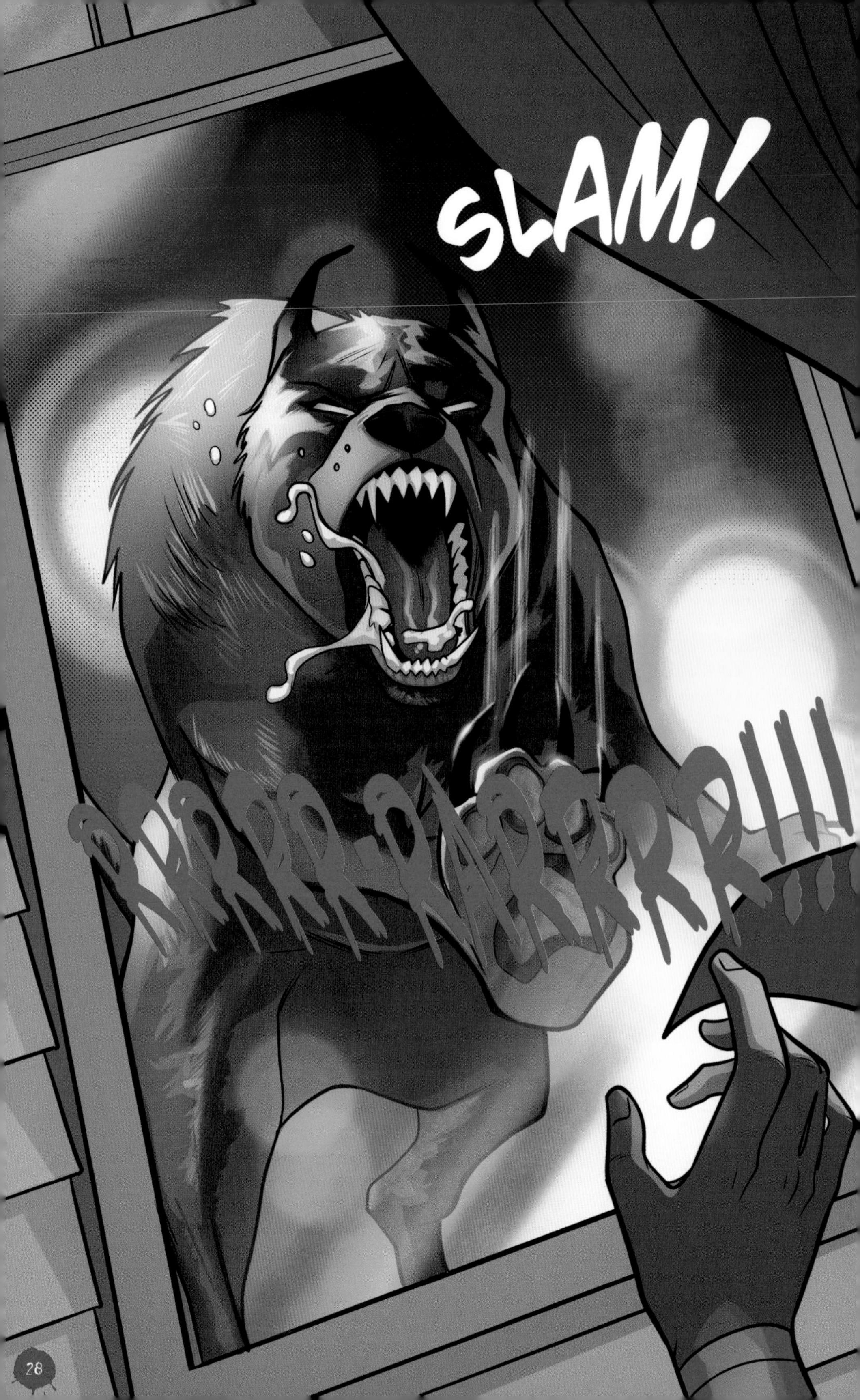
SLAM!
RRRRR-RARRRR!!!!

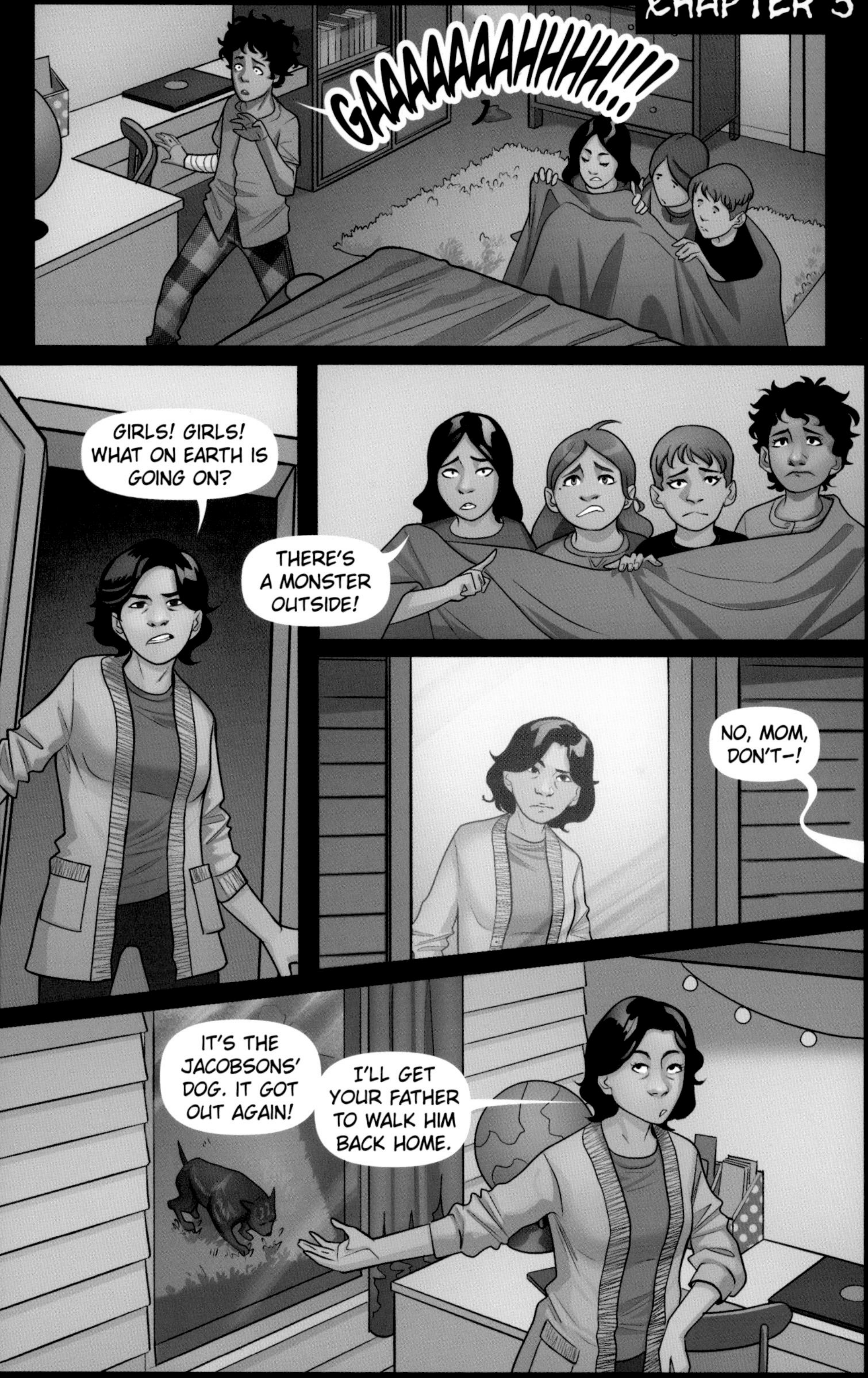
GAAAAAAAHHHH!!!
GIRLS! GIRLS! WHAT ON EARTH IS GOING ON?
THERE'S A MONSTER OUTSIDE!
NO, MOM, DON'T–!
IT'S THE JACOBSONS' DOG. IT GOT OUT AGAIN!
I'LL GET YOUR FATHER TO WALK HIM BACK HOME.

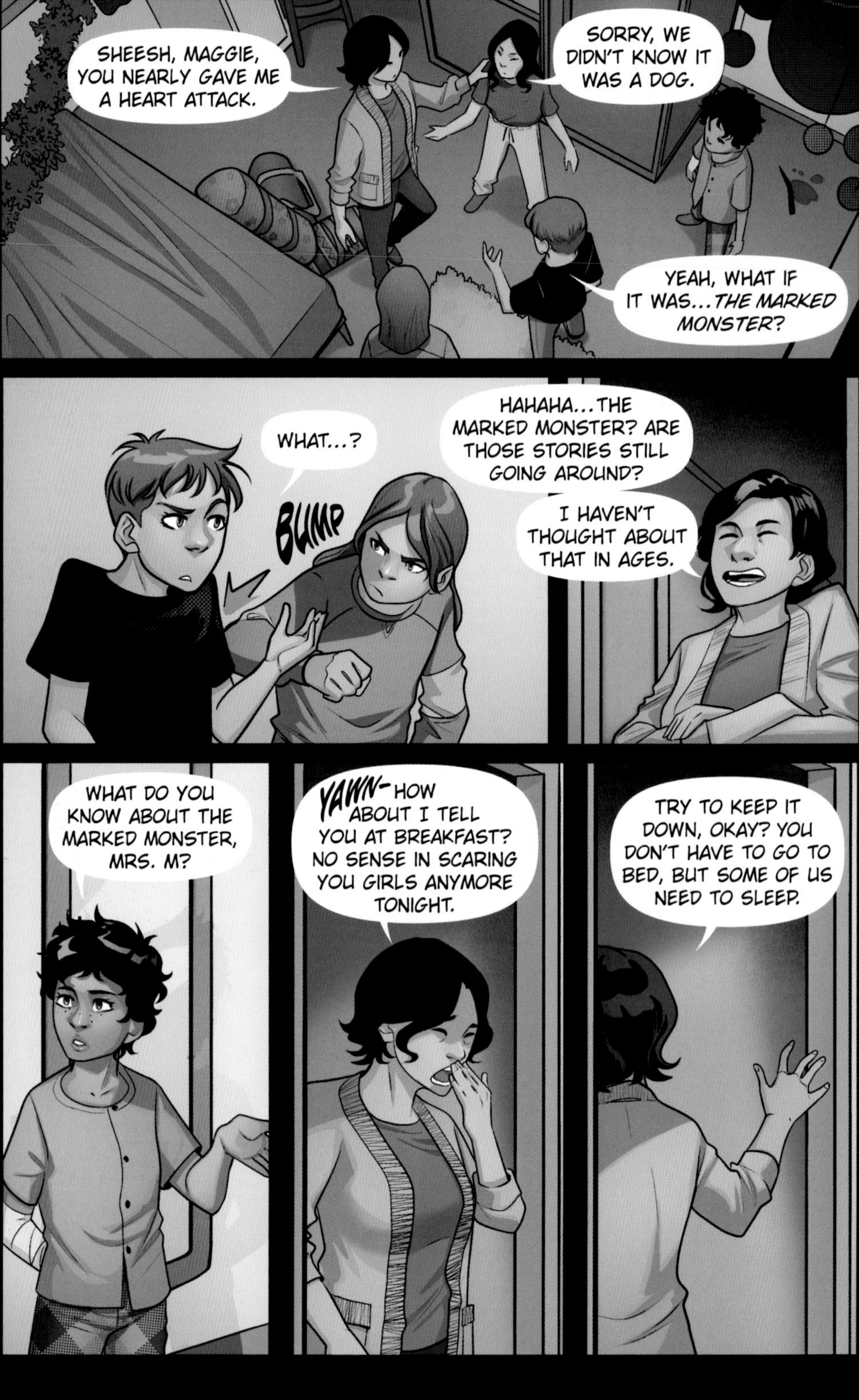
SHEESH, MAGGIE, YOU NEARLY GAVE ME A HEART ATTACK.
SORRY, WE DIDN'T KNOW IT WAS A DOG.
YEAH, WHAT IF IT WAS...*THE MARKED MONSTER*?
WHAT...?
BUMP
HAHAHA...THE MARKED MONSTER? ARE THOSE STORIES STILL GOING AROUND?
I HAVEN'T THOUGHT ABOUT THAT IN AGES.
WHAT DO YOU KNOW ABOUT THE MARKED MONSTER, MRS. M?
YAWN- HOW ABOUT I TELL YOU AT BREAKFAST? NO SENSE IN SCARING YOU GIRLS ANYMORE TONIGHT.
TRY TO KEEP IT DOWN, OKAY? YOU DON'T HAVE TO GO TO BED, BUT SOME OF US NEED TO SLEEP.

SO, WHAT NOW? MORE SCARY STORIES?

NO, THANKS. I'M SCARED ENOUGH. HOW ABOUT WE-

JENNA, YOUR ARM!

UGH, NOT AGAIN.

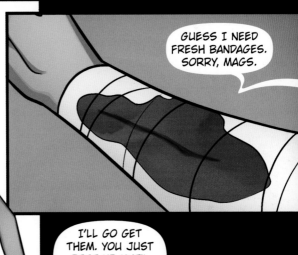

GUESS I NEED FRESH BANDAGES. SORRY, MAGS.

I'LL GO GET THEM. YOU JUST REST UP UNTIL YOUR CUT STOPS BLEEDING.

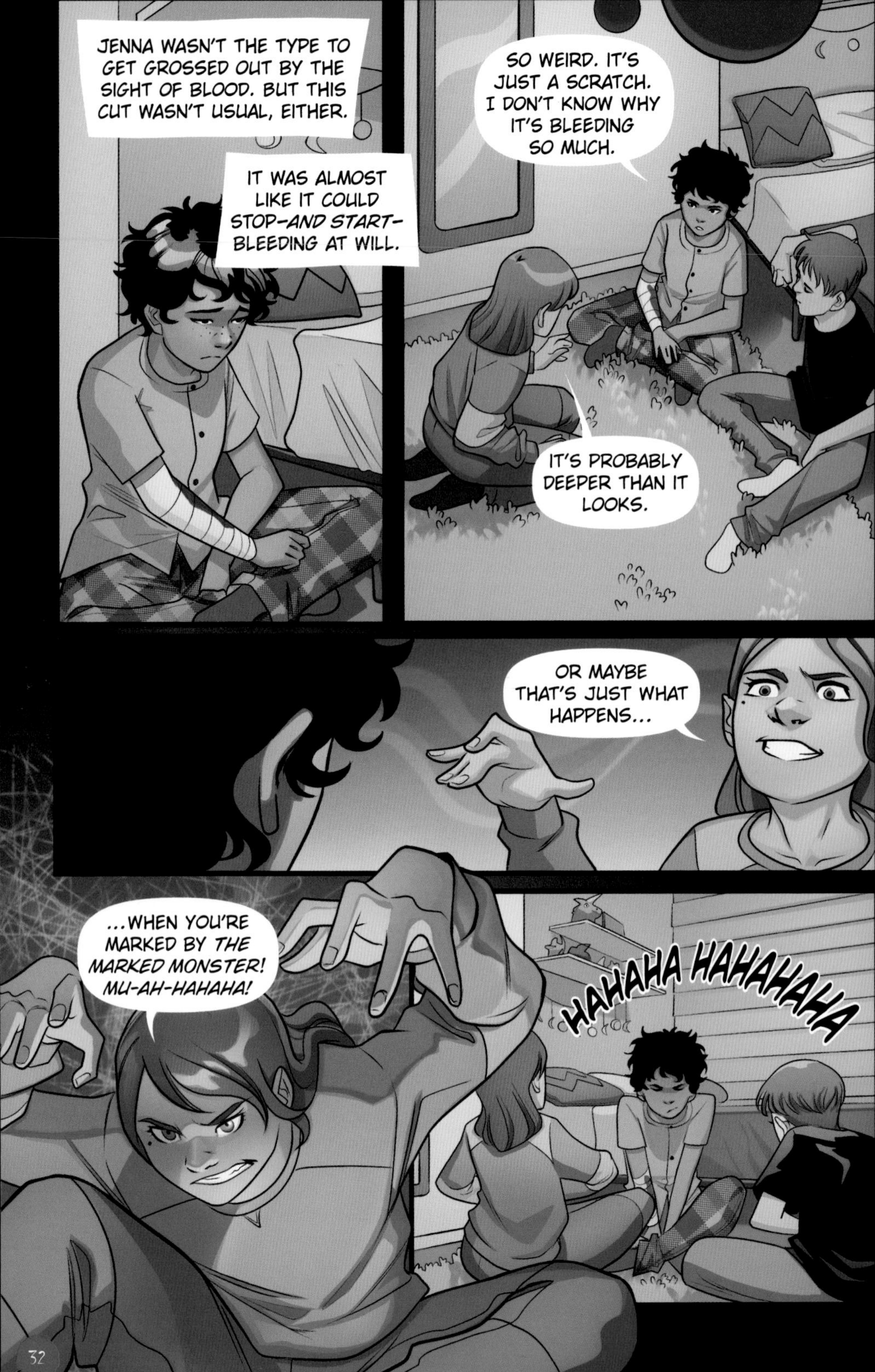
JENNA WASN'T THE TYPE TO GET GROSSED OUT BY THE SIGHT OF BLOOD. BUT THIS CUT WASN'T USUAL, EITHER.
IT WAS ALMOST LIKE IT COULD STOP—AND START—BLEEDING AT WILL.
SO WEIRD. IT'S JUST A SCRATCH. I DON'T KNOW WHY IT'S BLEEDING SO MUCH.
IT'S PROBABLY DEEPER THAN IT LOOKS.
OR MAYBE THAT'S JUST WHAT HAPPENS...
...WHEN YOU'RE MARKED BY THE MARKED MONSTER! MU-AH-HAHAHA!
HAHAHA HAHAHAHA

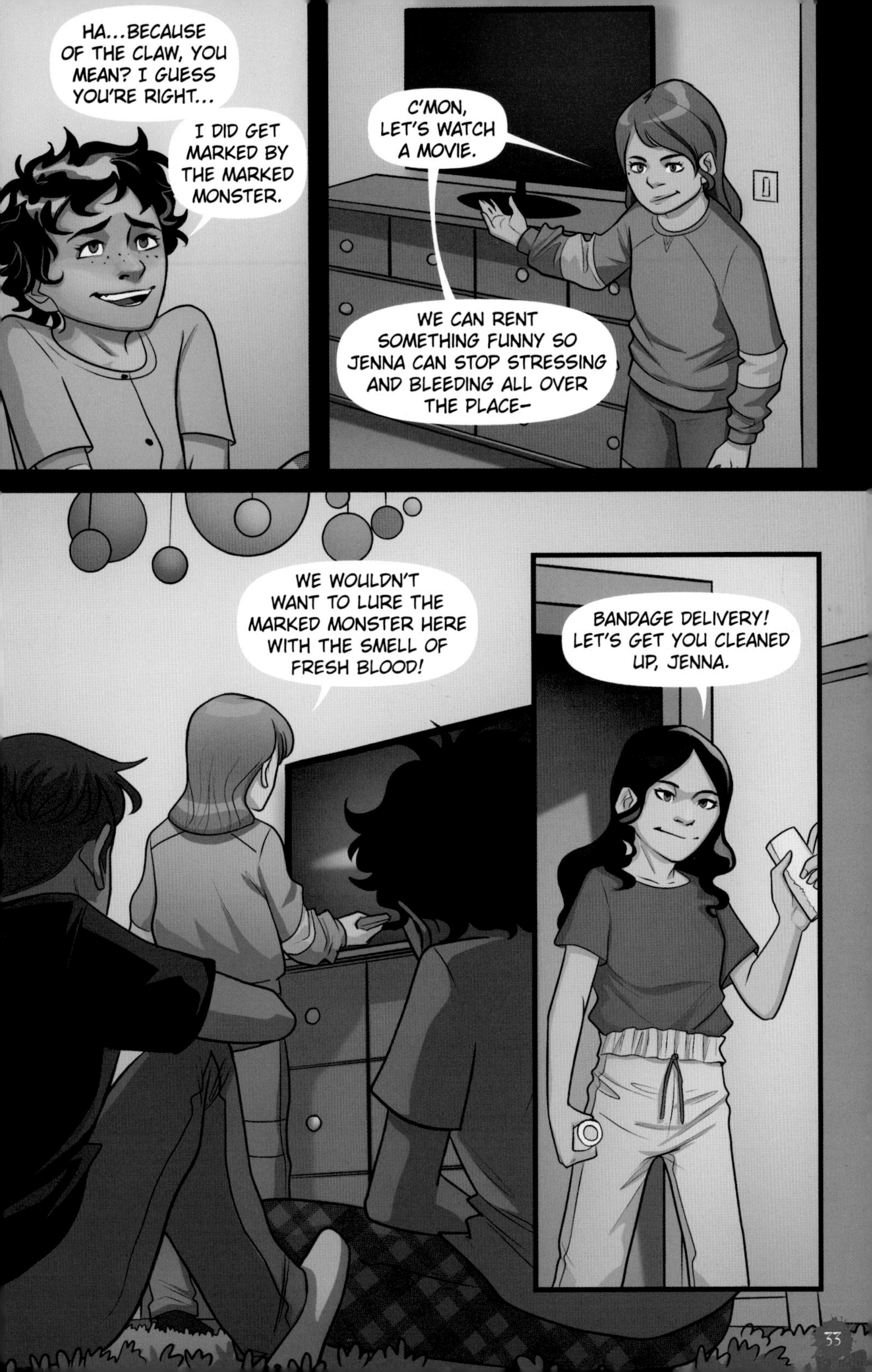
HA...BECAUSE OF THE CLAW, YOU MEAN? I GUESS YOU'RE RIGHT...
I DID GET MARKED BY THE MARKED MONSTER.
C'MON, LET'S WATCH A MOVIE.
WE CAN RENT SOMETHING FUNNY SO JENNA CAN STOP STRESSING AND BLEEDING ALL OVER THE PLACE-
WE WOULDN'T WANT TO LURE THE MARKED MONSTER HERE WITH THE SMELL OF FRESH BLOOD!
BANDAGE DELIVERY! LET'S GET YOU CLEANED UP, JENNA.

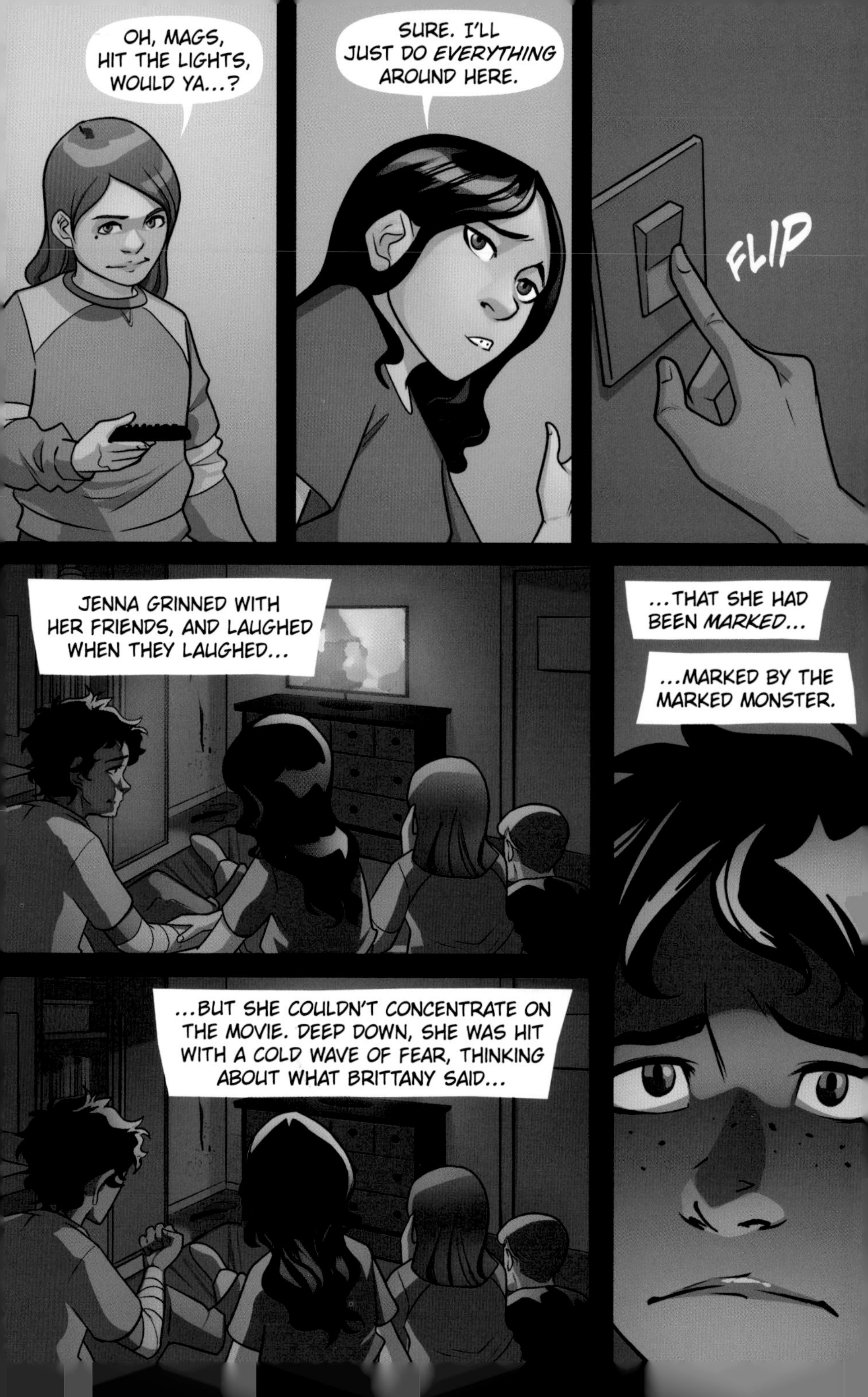
OH, MAGS, HIT THE LIGHTS, WOULD YA...?
SURE. I'LL JUST DO *EVERYTHING* AROUND HERE.
FLIP
JENNA GRINNED WITH HER FRIENDS, AND LAUGHED WHEN THEY LAUGHED...
...BUT SHE COULDN'T CONCENTRATE ON THE MOVIE. DEEP DOWN, SHE WAS HIT WITH A COLD WAVE OF FEAR, THINKING ABOUT WHAT BRITTANY SAID...
...THAT SHE HAD BEEN *MARKED*...
...MARKED BY THE MARKED MONSTER.

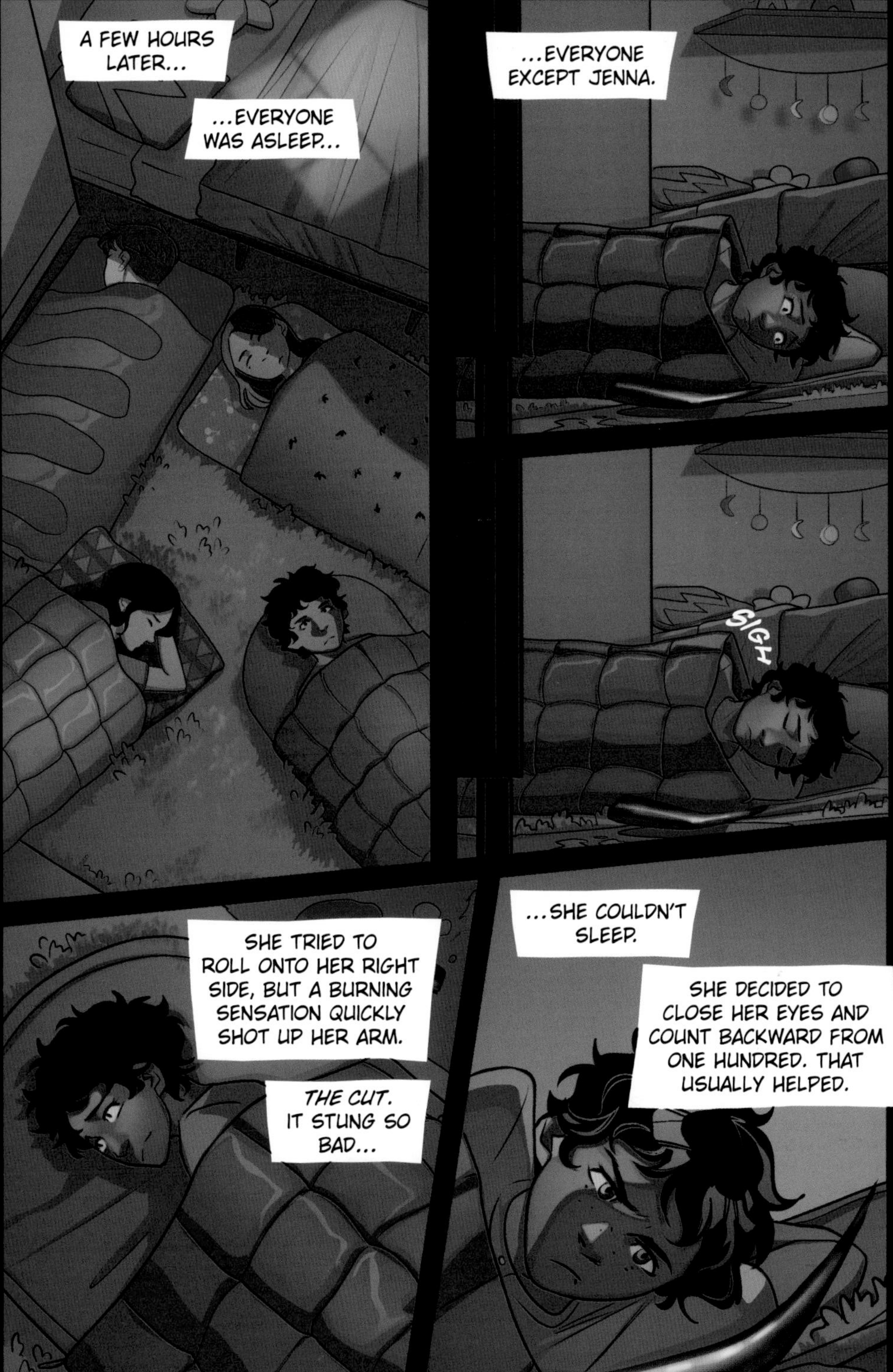
A FEW HOURS LATER...
...EVERYONE WAS ASLEEP...
...EVERYONE EXCEPT JENNA.
SIGH
SHE TRIED TO ROLL ONTO HER RIGHT SIDE, BUT A BURNING SENSATION QUICKLY SHOT UP HER ARM.
THE CUT. IT STUNG SO BAD...
...SHE COULDN'T SLEEP.
SHE DECIDED TO CLOSE HER EYES AND COUNT BACKWARD FROM ONE HUNDRED. THAT USUALLY HELPED.

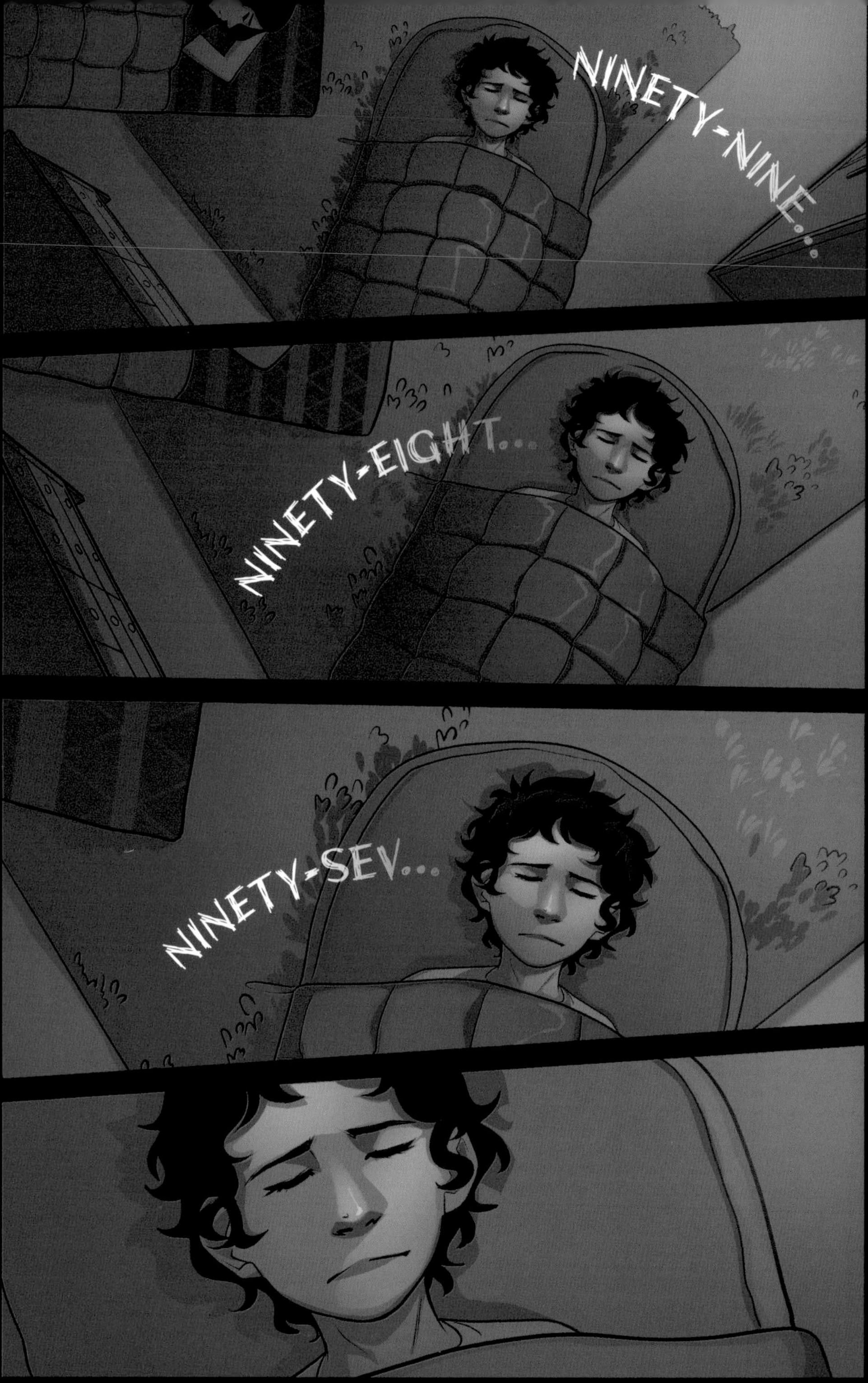
NINETY-NINE...
NINETY-EIGHT...
NINETY-SEV...

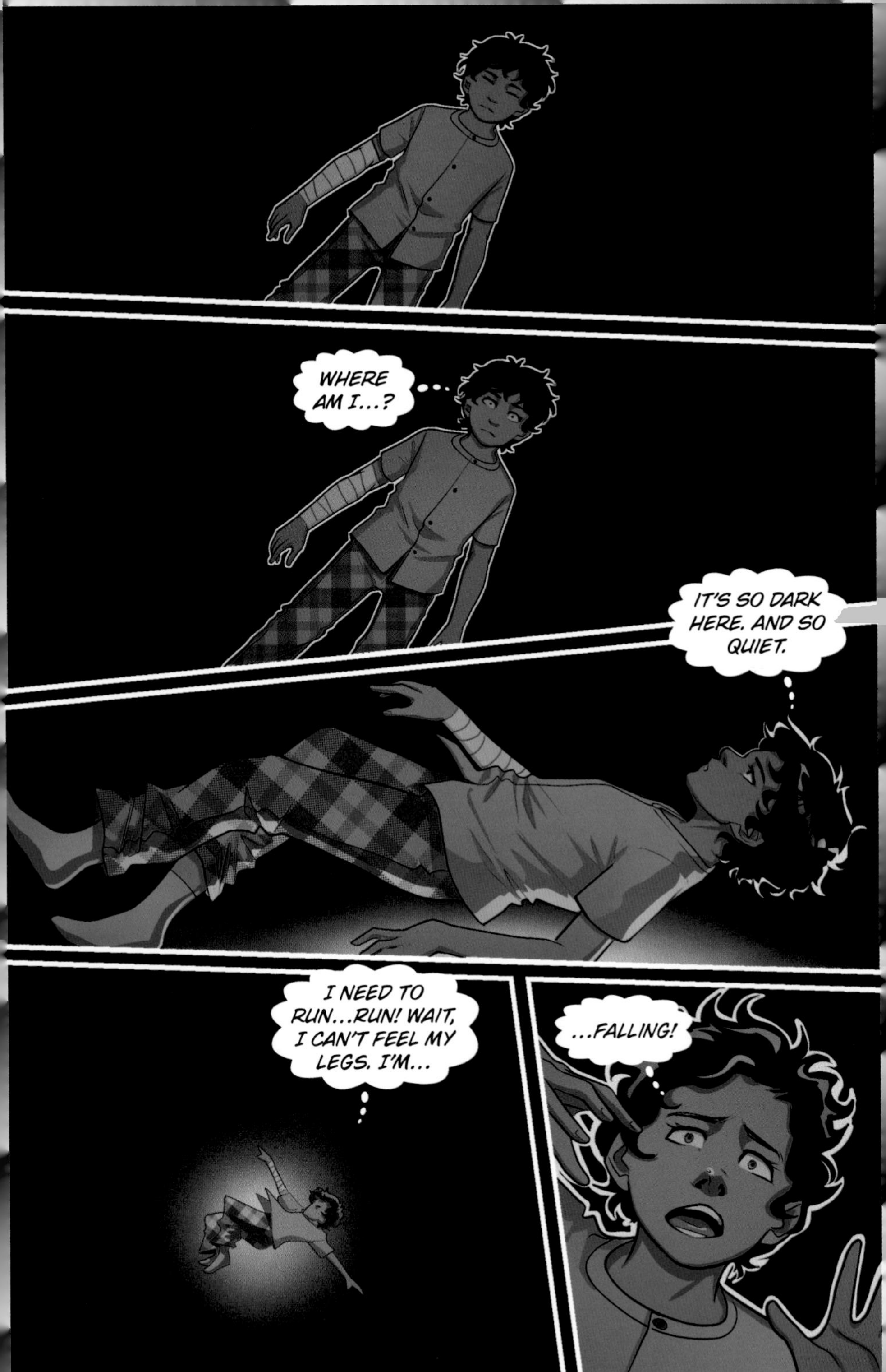

WHERE AM I...?
IT'S SO DARK HERE. AND SO QUIET.
I NEED TO RUN...RUN! WAIT, I CAN'T FEEL MY LEGS. I'M...
...FALLING!

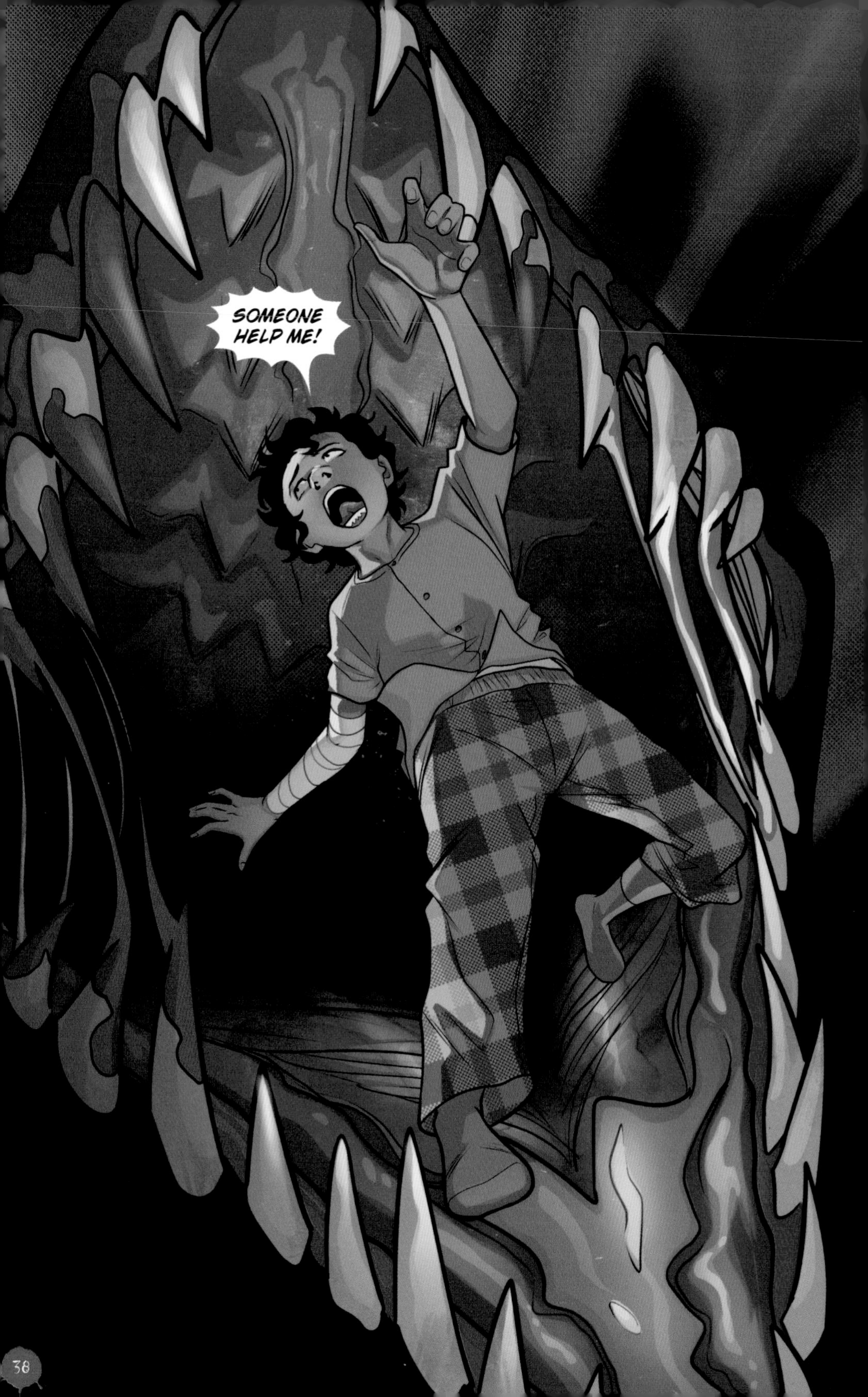
SOMEONE HELP ME!

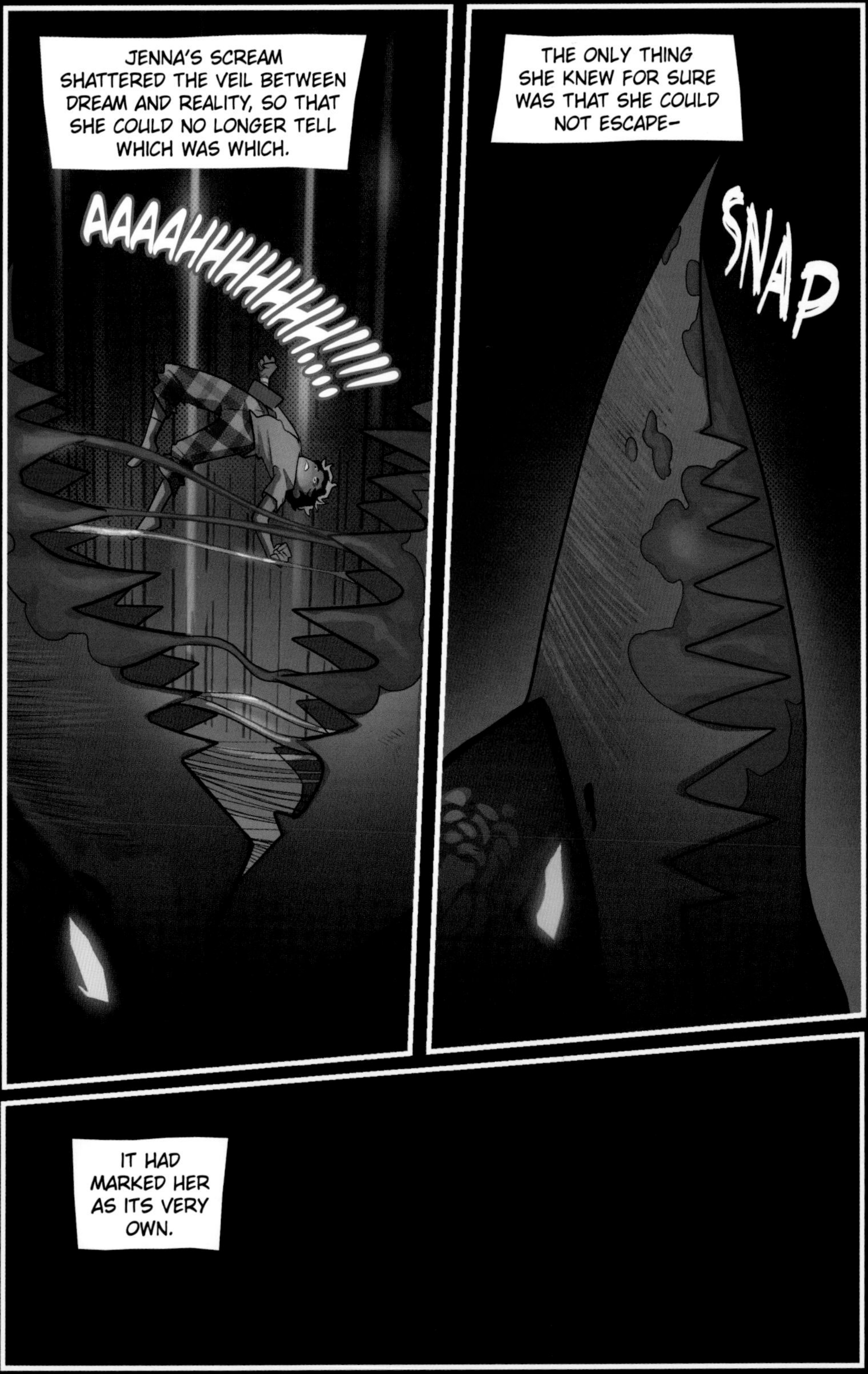
JENNA'S SCREAM SHATTERED THE VEIL BETWEEN DREAM AND REALITY, SO THAT SHE COULD NO LONGER TELL WHICH WAS WHICH.
AAAAHHHHHHH!!!!!!
THE ONLY THING SHE KNEW FOR SURE WAS THAT SHE COULD NOT ESCAPE–
SNAP
IT HAD MARKED HER AS ITS VERY OWN.

CHAPTER 4

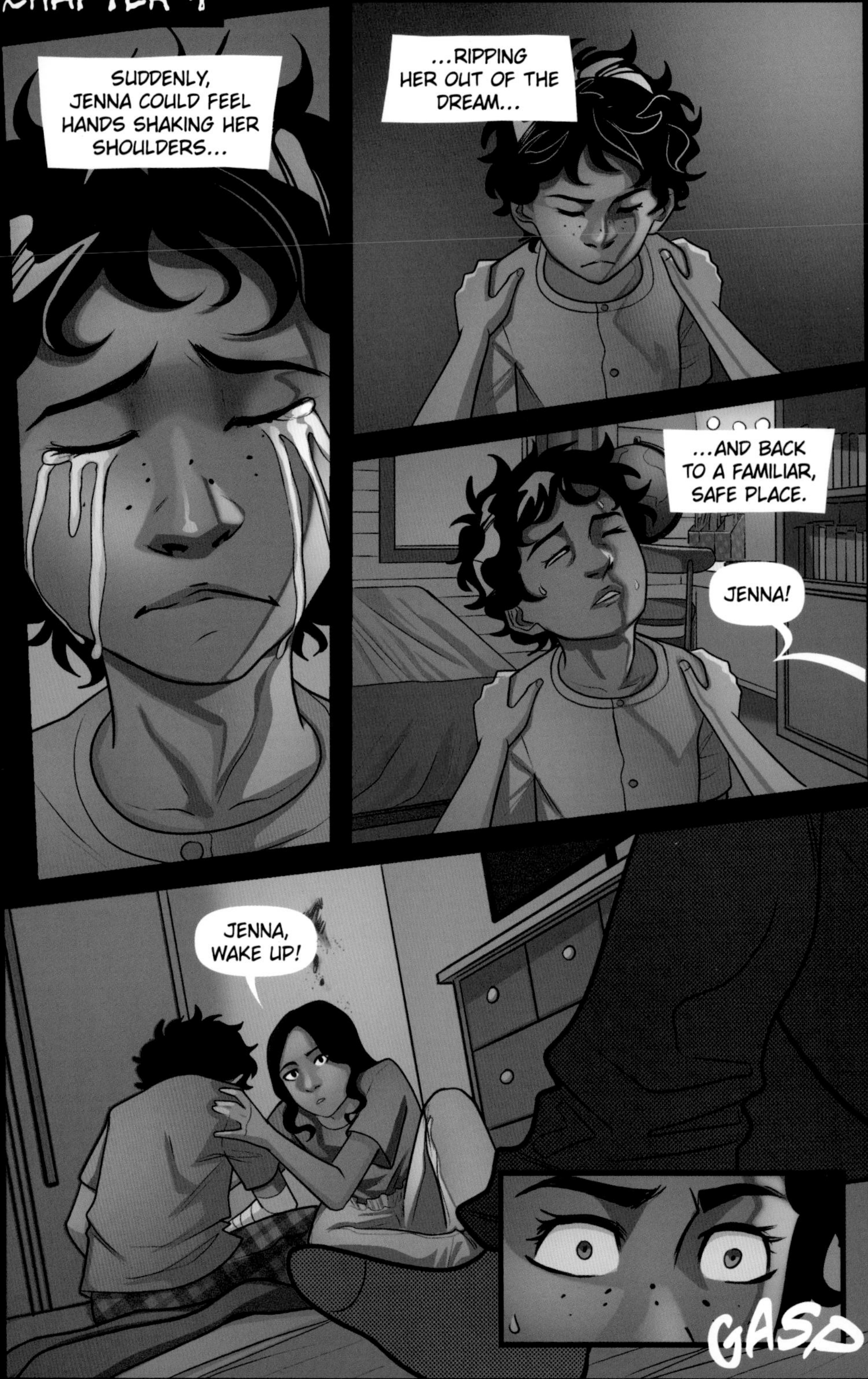

SUDDENLY, JENNA COULD FEEL HANDS SHAKING HER SHOULDERS...
...RIPPING HER OUT OF THE DREAM...
...AND BACK TO A FAMILIAR, SAFE PLACE.
JENNA!
JENNA, WAKE UP!
GASP

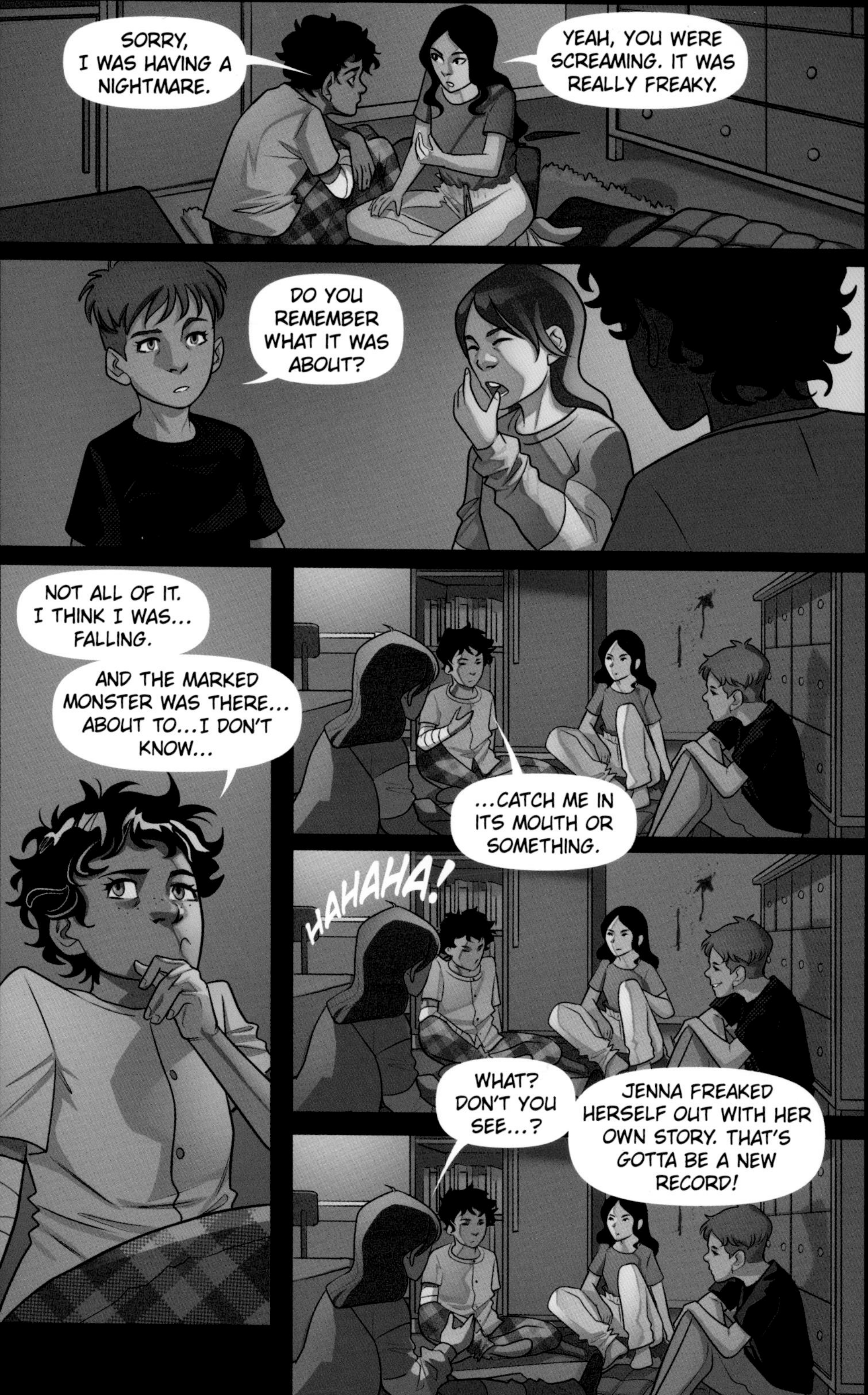

SORRY, I WAS HAVING A NIGHTMARE.
YEAH, YOU WERE SCREAMING. IT WAS REALLY FREAKY.
DO YOU REMEMBER WHAT IT WAS ABOUT?
NOT ALL OF IT. I THINK I WAS... FALLING.
AND THE MARKED MONSTER WAS THERE... ABOUT TO...I DON'T KNOW...
...CATCH ME IN ITS MOUTH OR SOMETHING.
HAHAHA!
WHAT? DON'T YOU SEE...?
JENNA FREAKED HERSELF OUT WITH HER OWN STORY. THAT'S GOTTA BE A NEW RECORD!

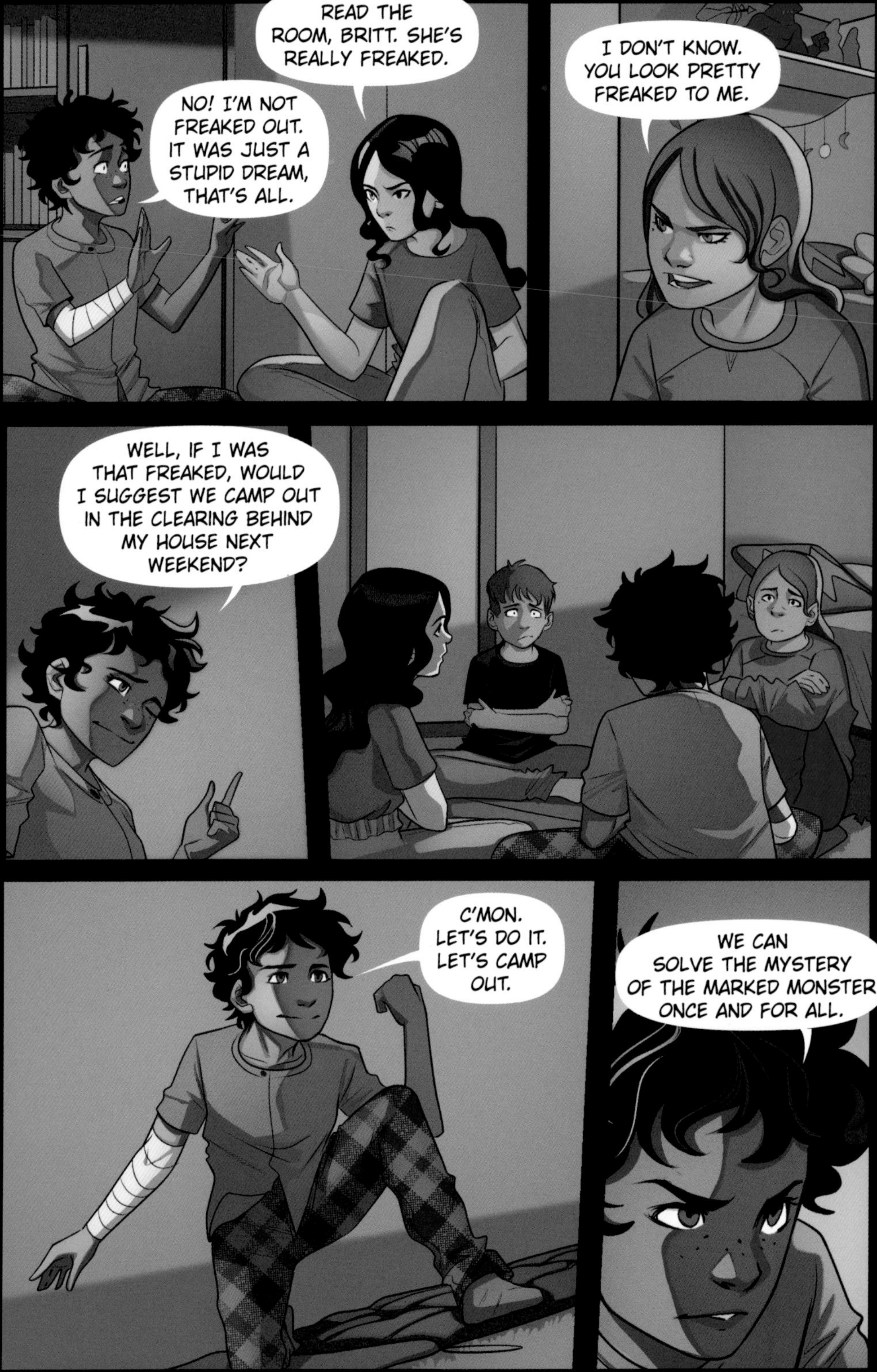
NO! I'M NOT FREAKED OUT. IT WAS JUST A STUPID DREAM, THAT'S ALL.
READ THE ROOM, BRITT. SHE'S REALLY FREAKED.
I DON'T KNOW. YOU LOOK PRETTY FREAKED TO ME.
WELL, IF I WAS THAT FREAKED, WOULD I SUGGEST WE CAMP OUT IN THE CLEARING BEHIND MY HOUSE NEXT WEEKEND?
C'MON. LET'S DO IT. LET'S CAMP OUT.
WE CAN SOLVE THE MYSTERY OF THE MARKED MONSTER ONCE AND FOR ALL.

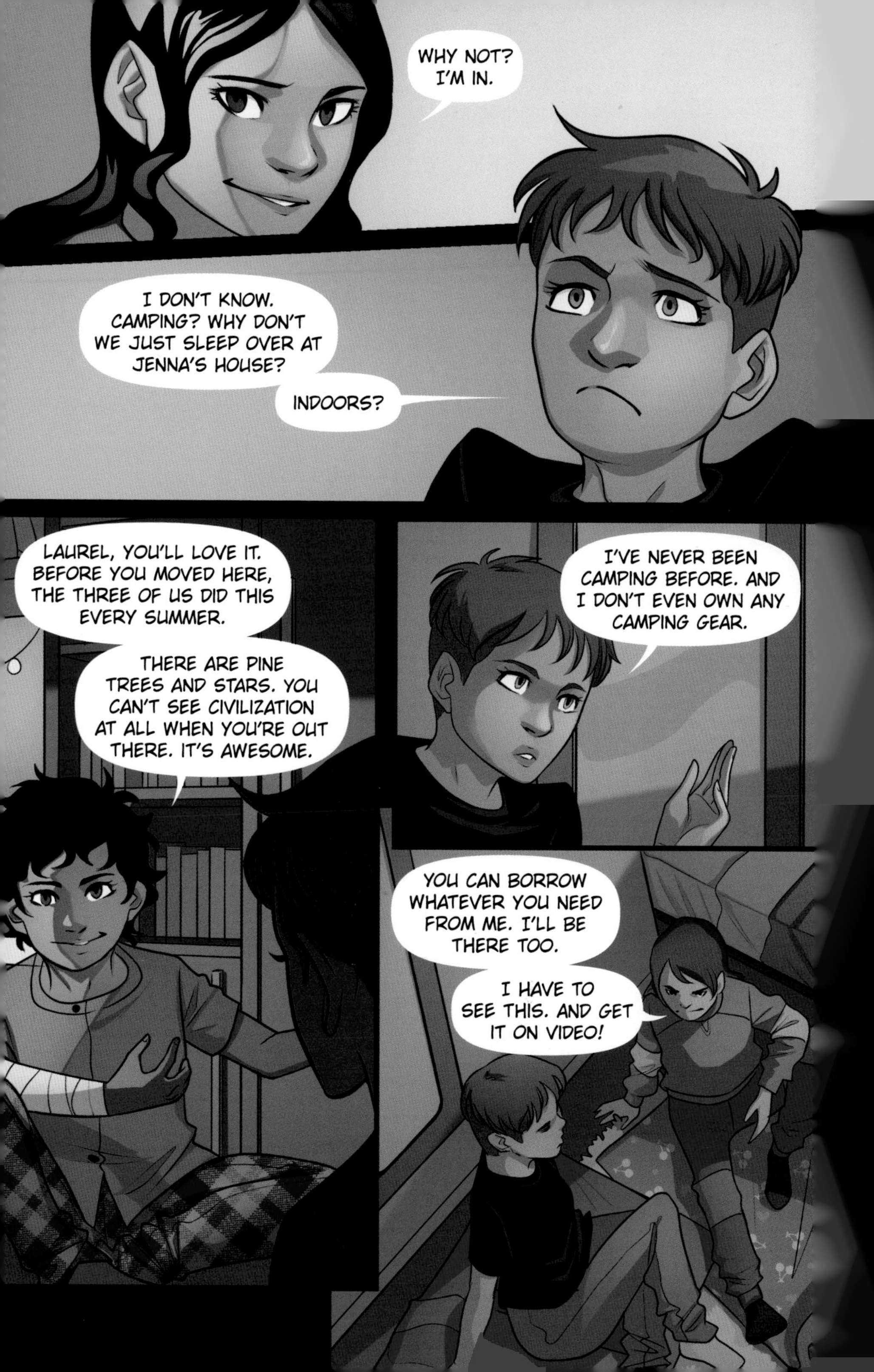
WHY NOT? I'M IN.
I DON'T KNOW. CAMPING? WHY DON'T WE JUST SLEEP OVER AT JENNA'S HOUSE?
INDOORS?
LAUREL, YOU'LL LOVE IT. BEFORE YOU MOVED HERE, THE THREE OF US DID THIS EVERY SUMMER.
THERE ARE PINE TREES AND STARS. YOU CAN'T SEE CIVILIZATION AT ALL WHEN YOU'RE OUT THERE. IT'S AWESOME.
I'VE NEVER BEEN CAMPING BEFORE. AND I DON'T EVEN OWN ANY CAMPING GEAR.
YOU CAN BORROW WHATEVER YOU NEED FROM ME. I'LL BE THERE TOO.
I HAVE TO SEE THIS. AND GET IT ON VIDEO!

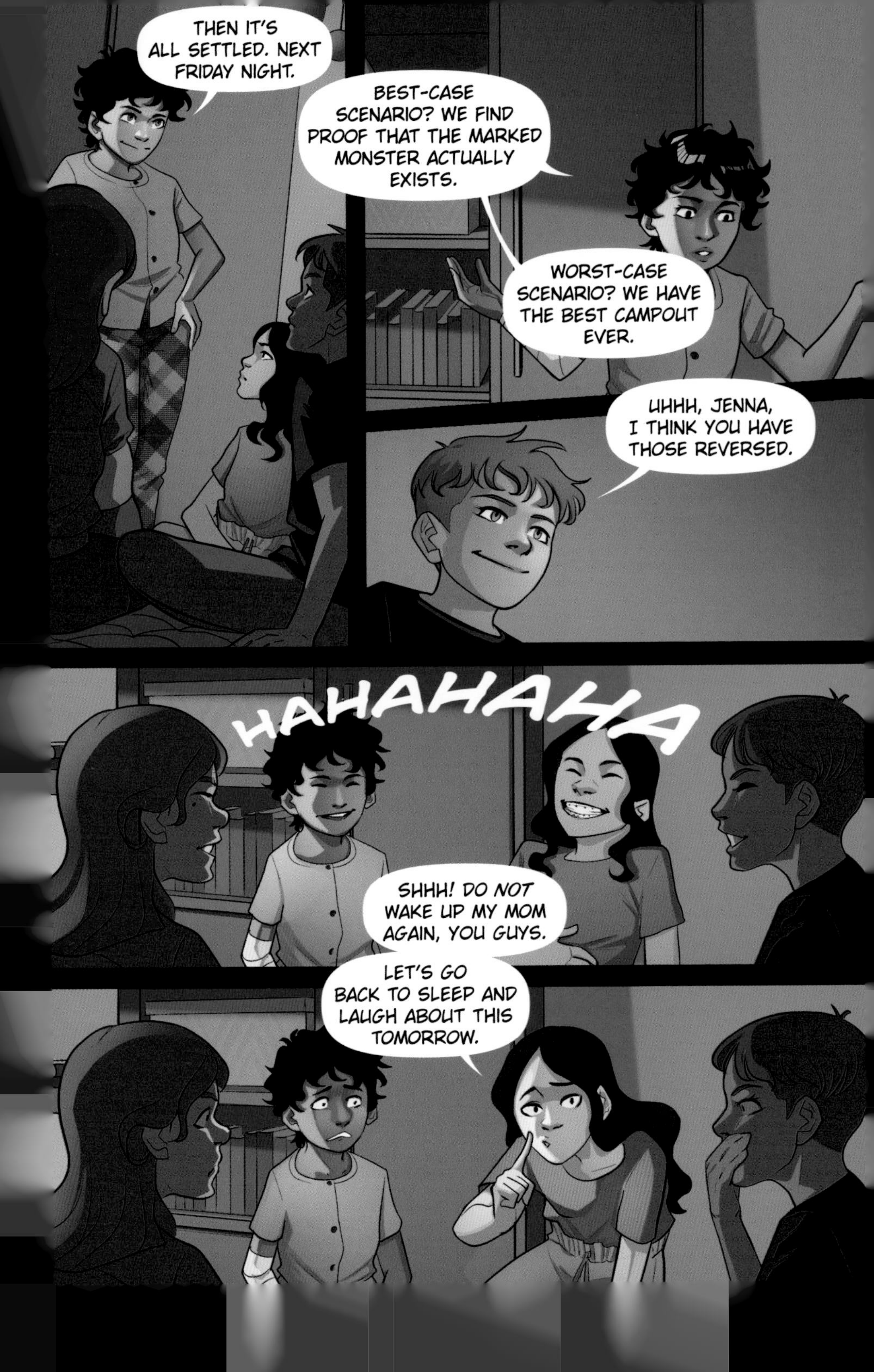
THEN IT'S ALL SETTLED. NEXT FRIDAY NIGHT.
BEST-CASE SCENARIO? WE FIND PROOF THAT THE MARKED MONSTER ACTUALLY EXISTS.
WORST-CASE SCENARIO? WE HAVE THE BEST CAMPOUT EVER.
UHHH, JENNA, I THINK YOU HAVE THOSE REVERSED.
HAHAHAHA
SHHH! DO *NOT* WAKE UP MY MOM AGAIN, YOU GUYS.
LET'S GO BACK TO SLEEP AND LAUGH ABOUT THIS TOMORROW.

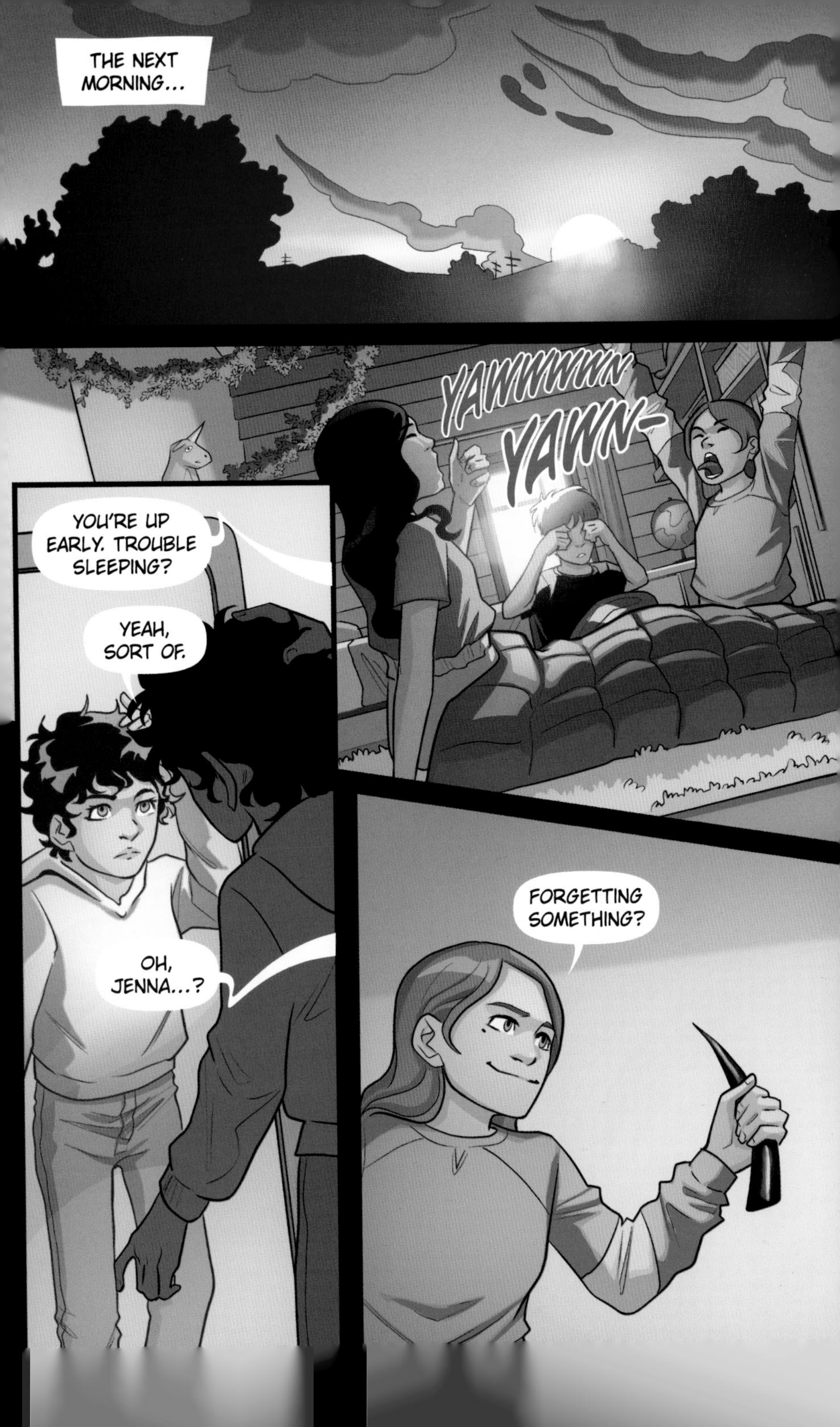
THE NEXT MORNING...
YAWWWWN
YAWN-
YOU'RE UP EARLY. TROUBLE SLEEPING?
YEAH, SORT OF.
OH, JENNA...?
FORGETTING SOMETHING?

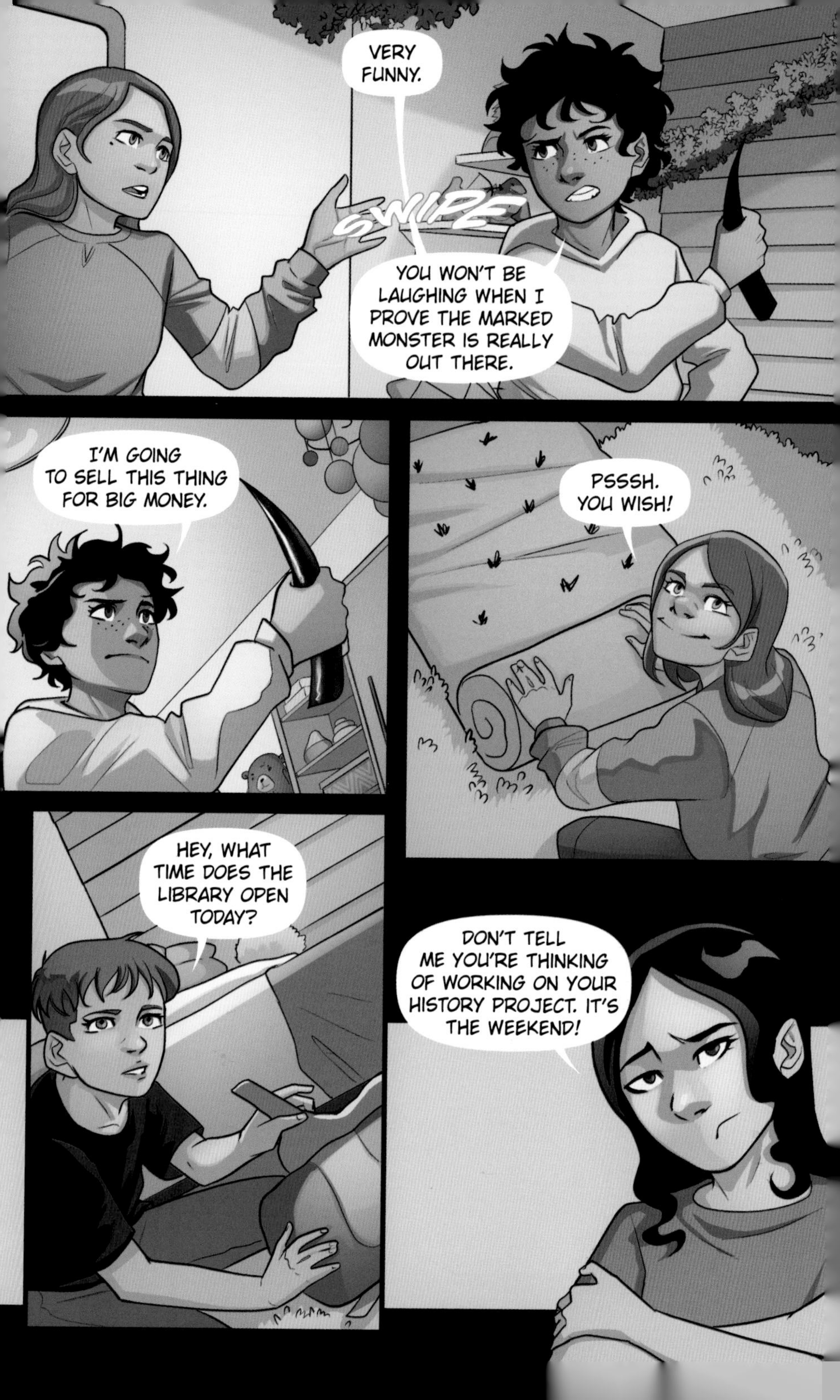
VERY FUNNY.
SWIPE
YOU WON'T BE LAUGHING WHEN I PROVE THE MARKED MONSTER IS REALLY OUT THERE.
I'M GOING TO SELL THIS THING FOR BIG MONEY.
PSSSH. YOU WISH!
HEY, WHAT TIME DOES THE LIBRARY OPEN TODAY?
DON'T TELL ME YOU'RE THINKING OF WORKING ON YOUR HISTORY PROJECT. IT'S THE WEEKEND!

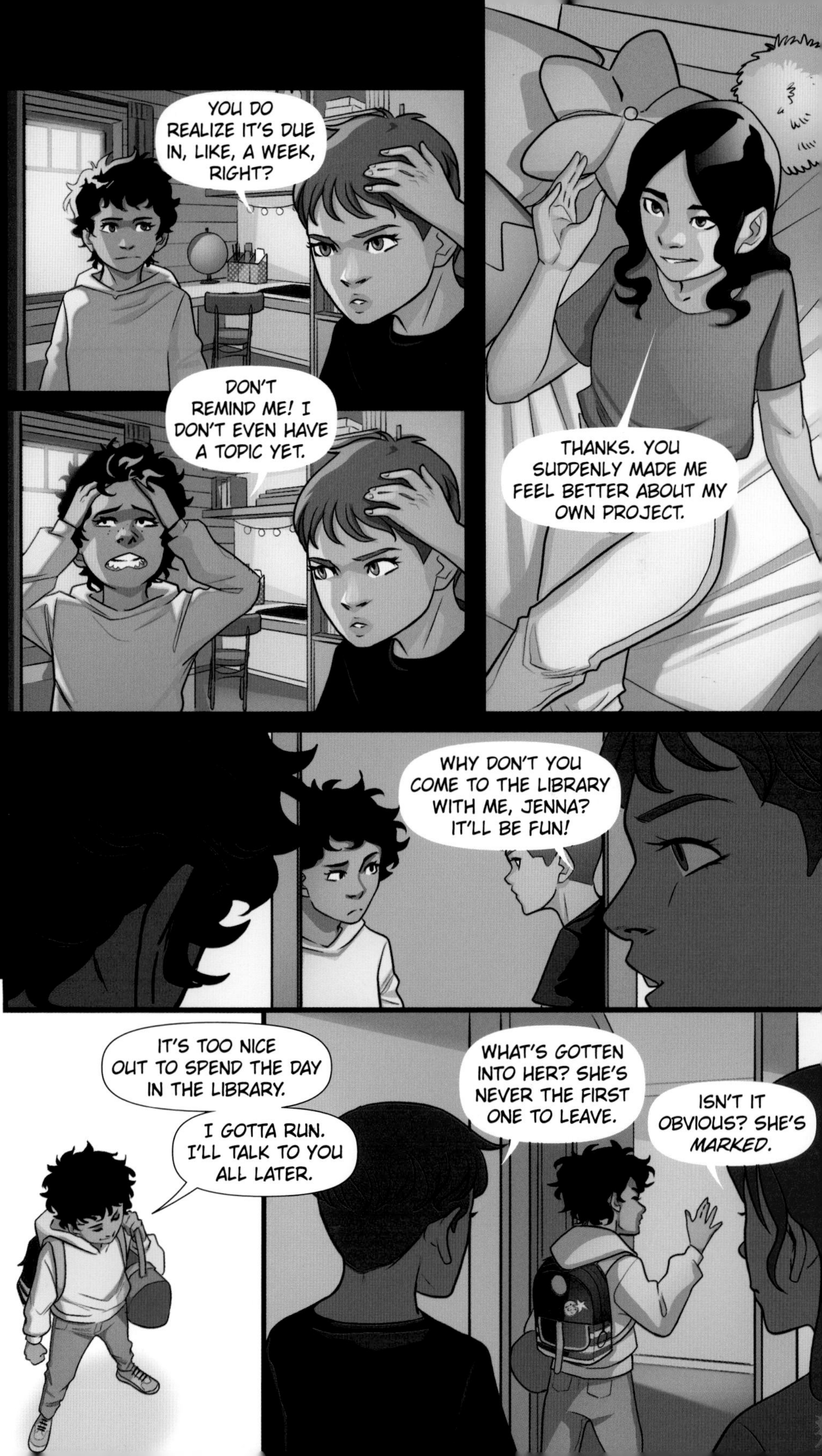
YOU DO REALIZE IT'S DUE IN, LIKE, A WEEK, RIGHT?
DON'T REMIND ME! I DON'T EVEN HAVE A TOPIC YET.
THANKS. YOU SUDDENLY MADE ME FEEL BETTER ABOUT MY OWN PROJECT.
WHY DON'T YOU COME TO THE LIBRARY WITH ME, JENNA? IT'LL BE FUN!
IT'S TOO NICE OUT TO SPEND THE DAY IN THE LIBRARY.
I GOTTA RUN. I'LL TALK TO YOU ALL LATER.
WHAT'S GOTTEN INTO HER? SHE'S NEVER THE FIRST ONE TO LEAVE.
ISN'T IT OBVIOUS? SHE'S *MARKED.*

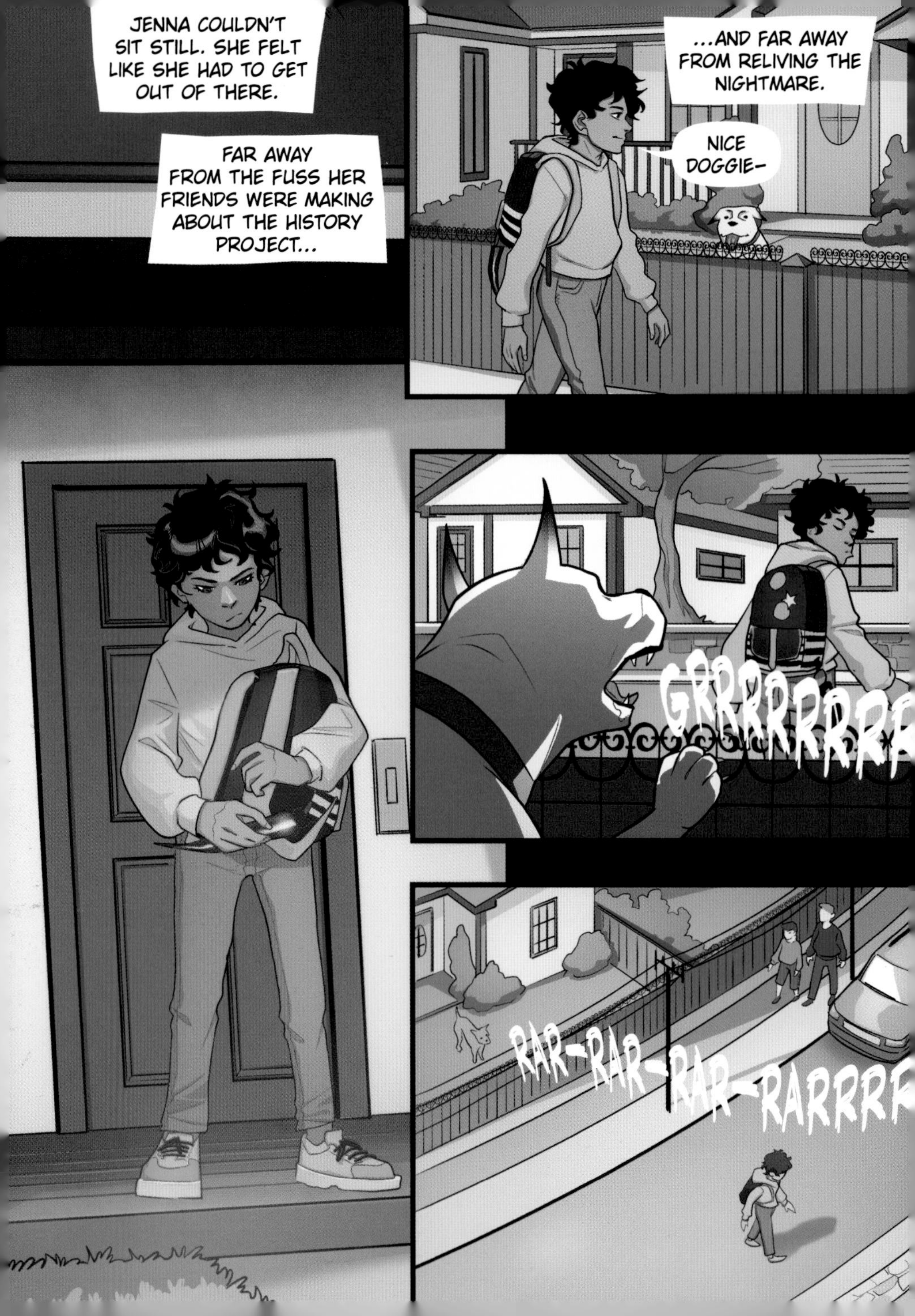
JENNA COULDN'T SIT STILL. SHE FELT LIKE SHE HAD TO GET OUT OF THERE.
FAR AWAY FROM THE FUSS HER FRIENDS WERE MAKING ABOUT THE HISTORY PROJECT...
...AND FAR AWAY FROM RELIVING THE NIGHTMARE.
NICE DOGGIE—
GRRRRRRRR
RAR-RAR-RAR-RARRRR

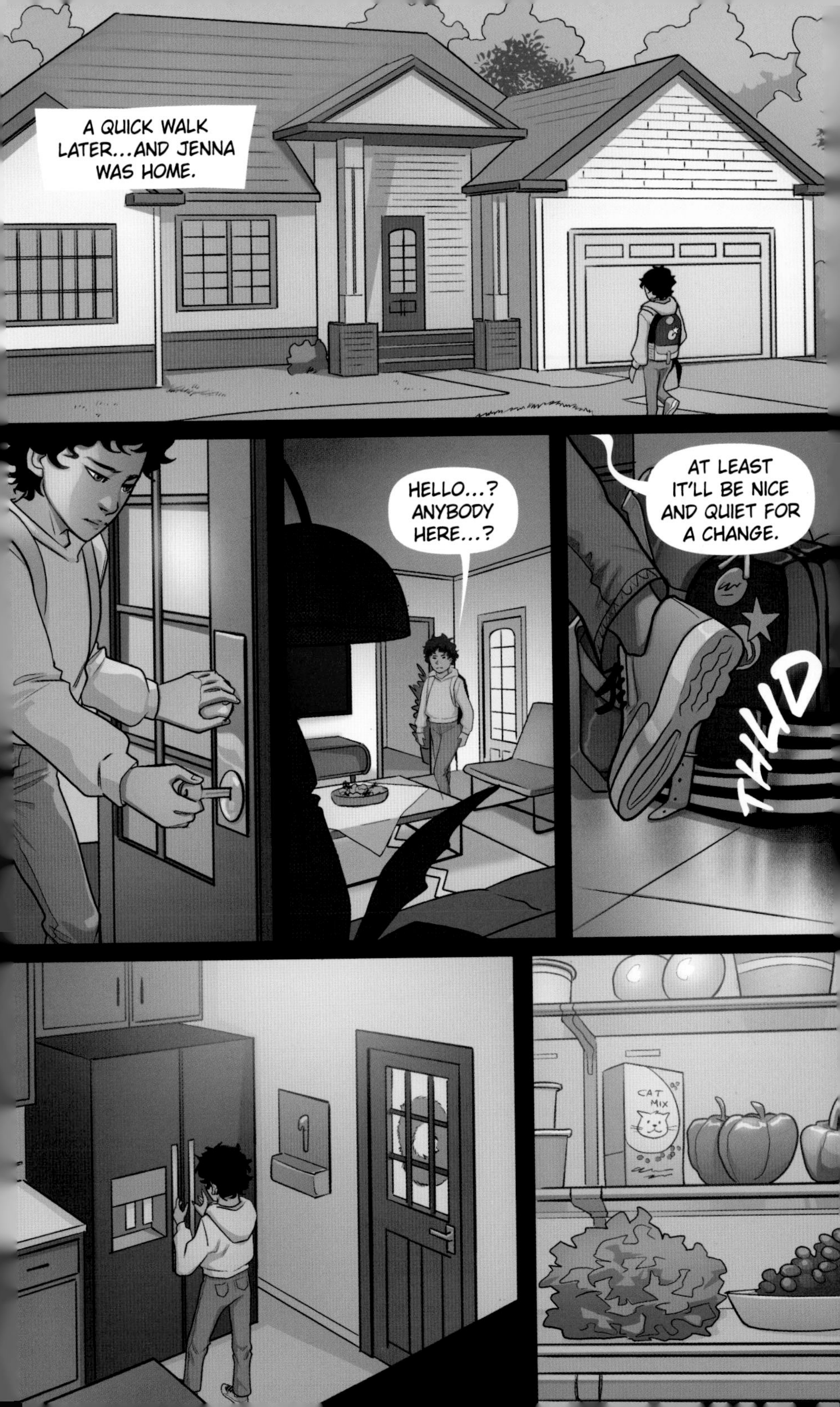
A QUICK WALK LATER...AND JENNA WAS HOME.
HELLO...? ANYBODY HERE...?
AT LEAST IT'LL BE NICE AND QUIET FOR A CHANGE.
THUD
CAT MIX

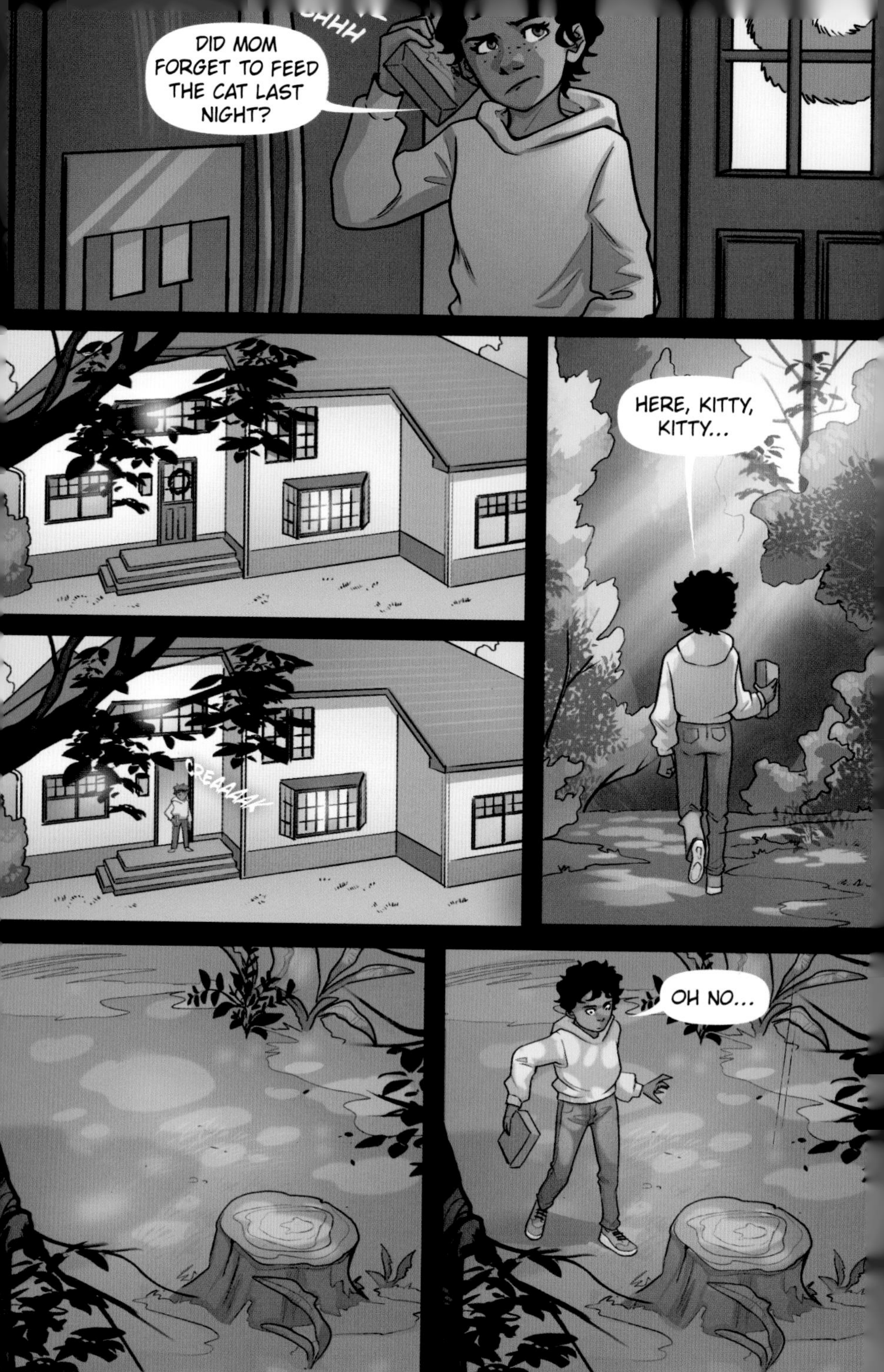

DID MOM FORGET TO FEED THE CAT LAST NIGHT?
HERE, KITTY, KITTY...
CREAAAAK
OH NO...

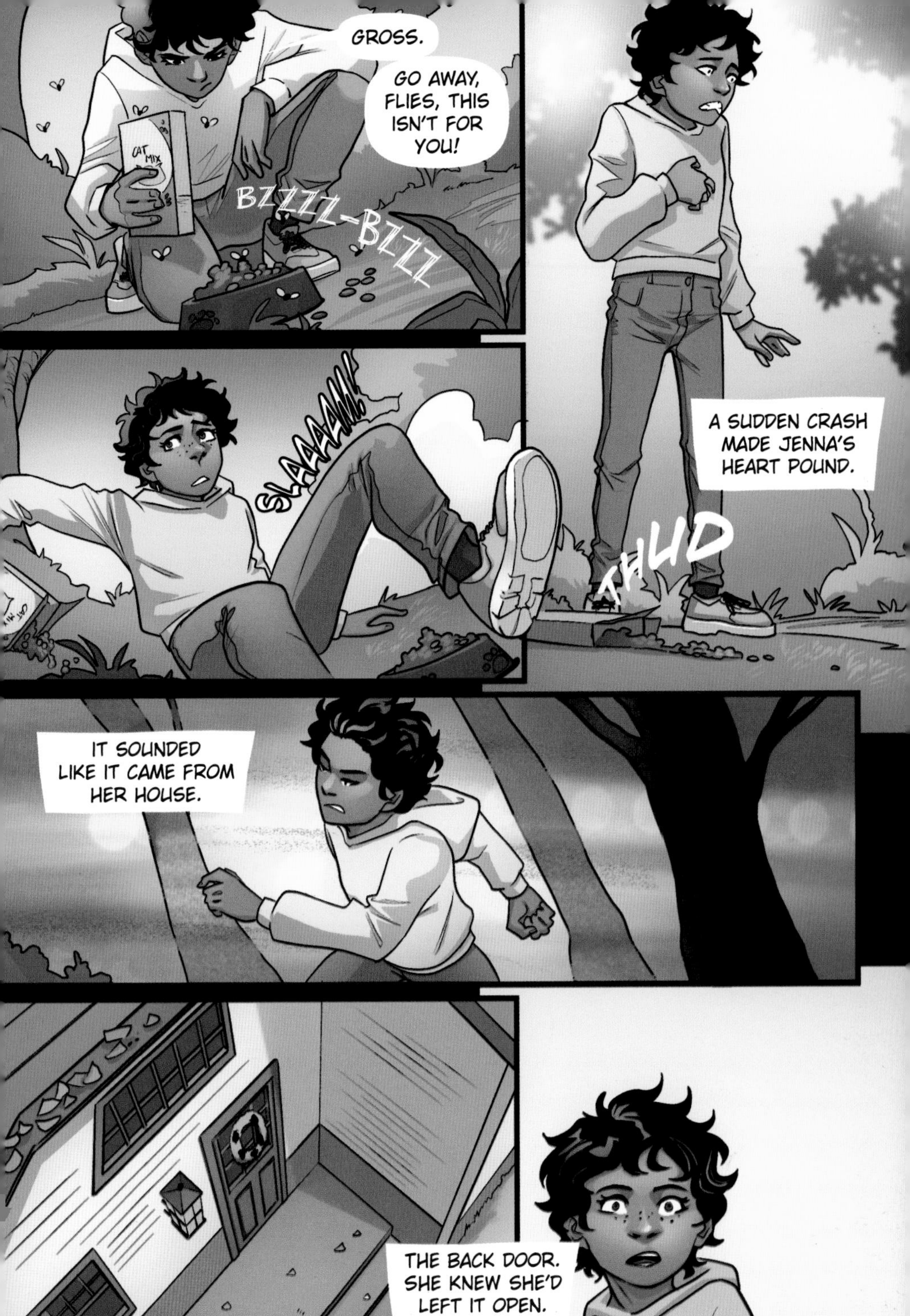
GROSS.
GO AWAY, FLIES, THIS ISN'T FOR YOU!
BZZZZ-BZZZ
CAT MIX
A SUDDEN CRASH MADE JENNA'S HEART POUND.
SLAAAAM!
THUD
IT SOUNDED LIKE IT CAME FROM HER HOUSE.
THE BACK DOOR. SHE KNEW SHE'D LEFT IT OPEN.

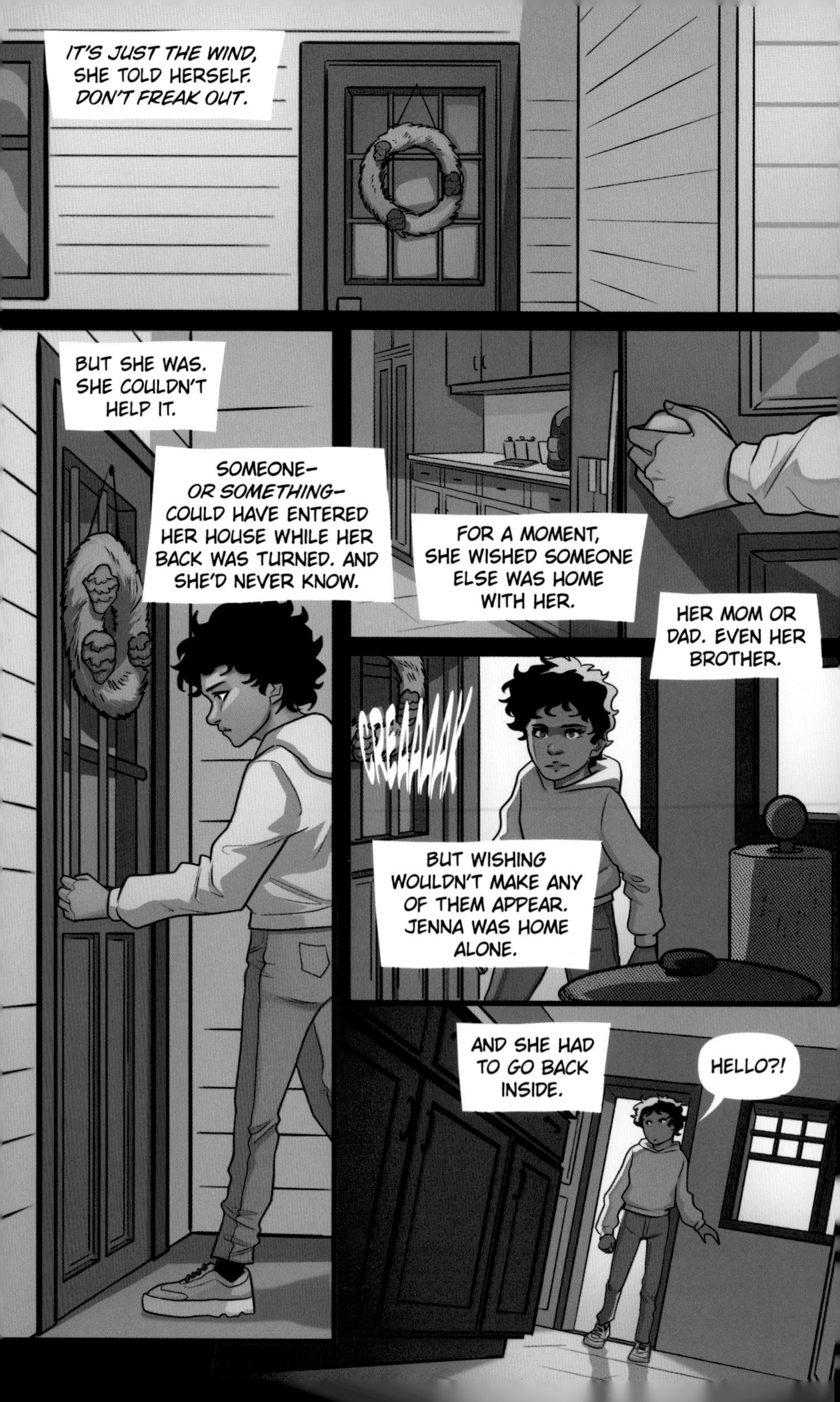
IT'S JUST THE WIND, SHE TOLD HERSELF. DON'T FREAK OUT.
BUT SHE WAS. SHE COULDN'T HELP IT.
SOMEONE– OR SOMETHING– COULD HAVE ENTERED HER HOUSE WHILE HER BACK WAS TURNED. AND SHE'D NEVER KNOW.
FOR A MOMENT, SHE WISHED SOMEONE ELSE WAS HOME WITH HER.
HER MOM OR DAD. EVEN HER BROTHER.
CREAAAAK
BUT WISHING WOULDN'T MAKE ANY OF THEM APPEAR. JENNA WAS HOME ALONE.
AND SHE HAD TO GO BACK INSIDE.
HELLO?!

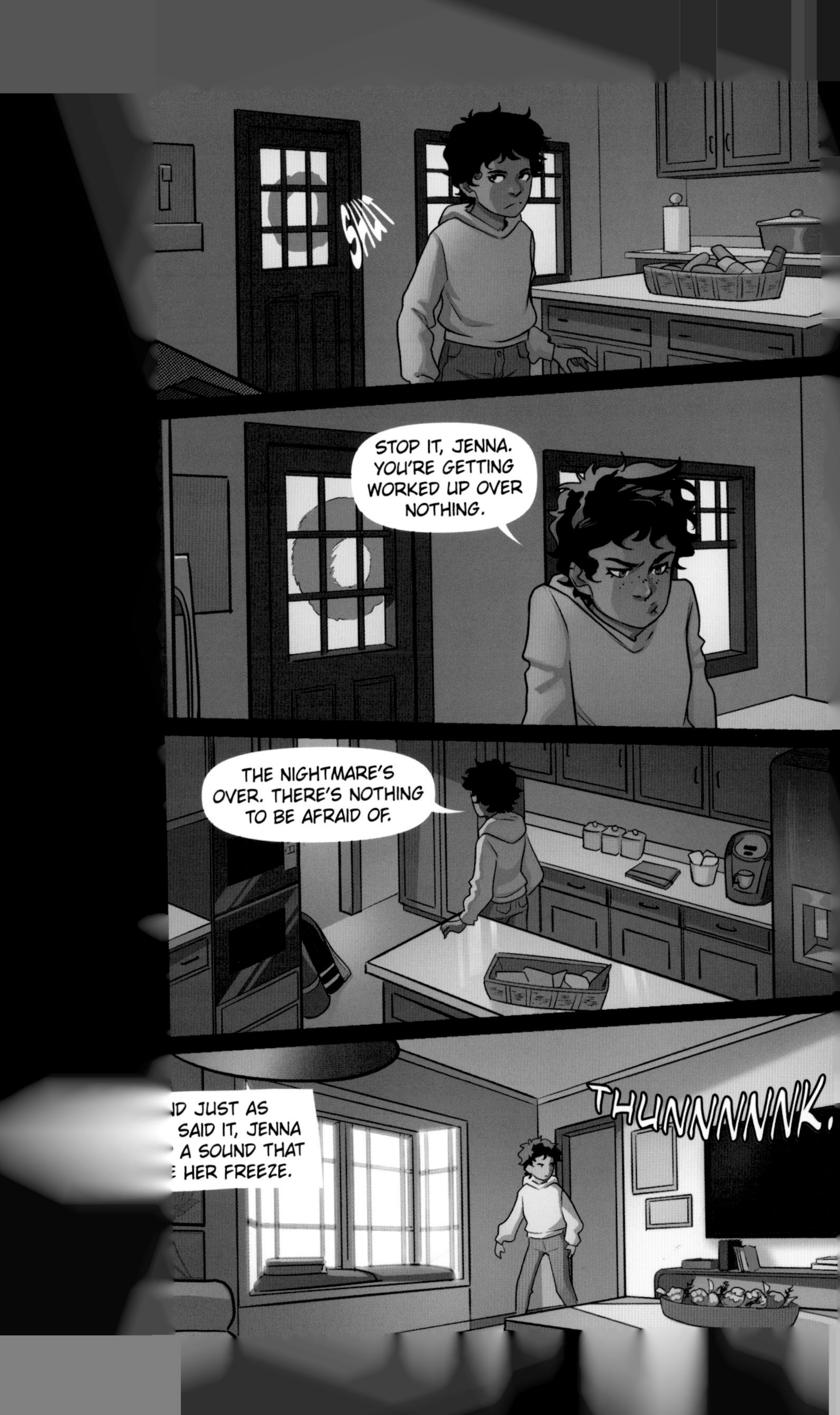
SHUT
STOP IT, JENNA. YOU'RE GETTING WORKED UP OVER NOTHING.
THE NIGHTMARE'S OVER. THERE'S NOTHING TO BE AFRAID OF.
ND JUST AS
SAID IT, JENNA
A SOUND THAT
E HER FREEZE.
THUNNNNNNK.

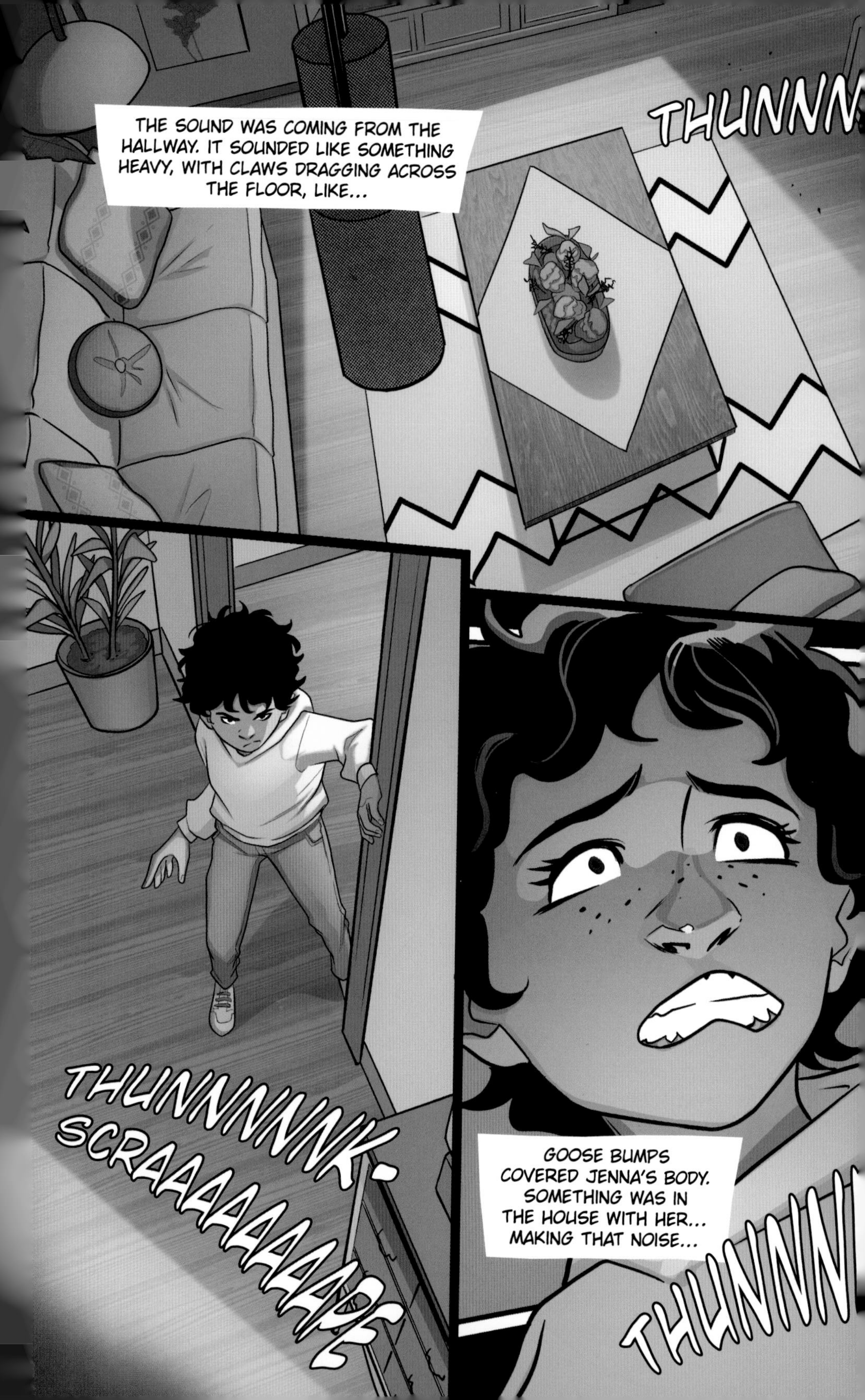
THE SOUND WAS COMING FROM THE HALLWAY. IT SOUNDED LIKE SOMETHING HEAVY, WITH CLAWS DRAGGING ACROSS THE FLOOR, LIKE...
THUNNN
THUNNNNNNK-SCRAAAAAAAAPE
GOOSE BUMPS COVERED JENNA'S BODY. SOMETHING WAS IN THE HOUSE WITH HER... MAKING THAT NOISE...
THUNNN

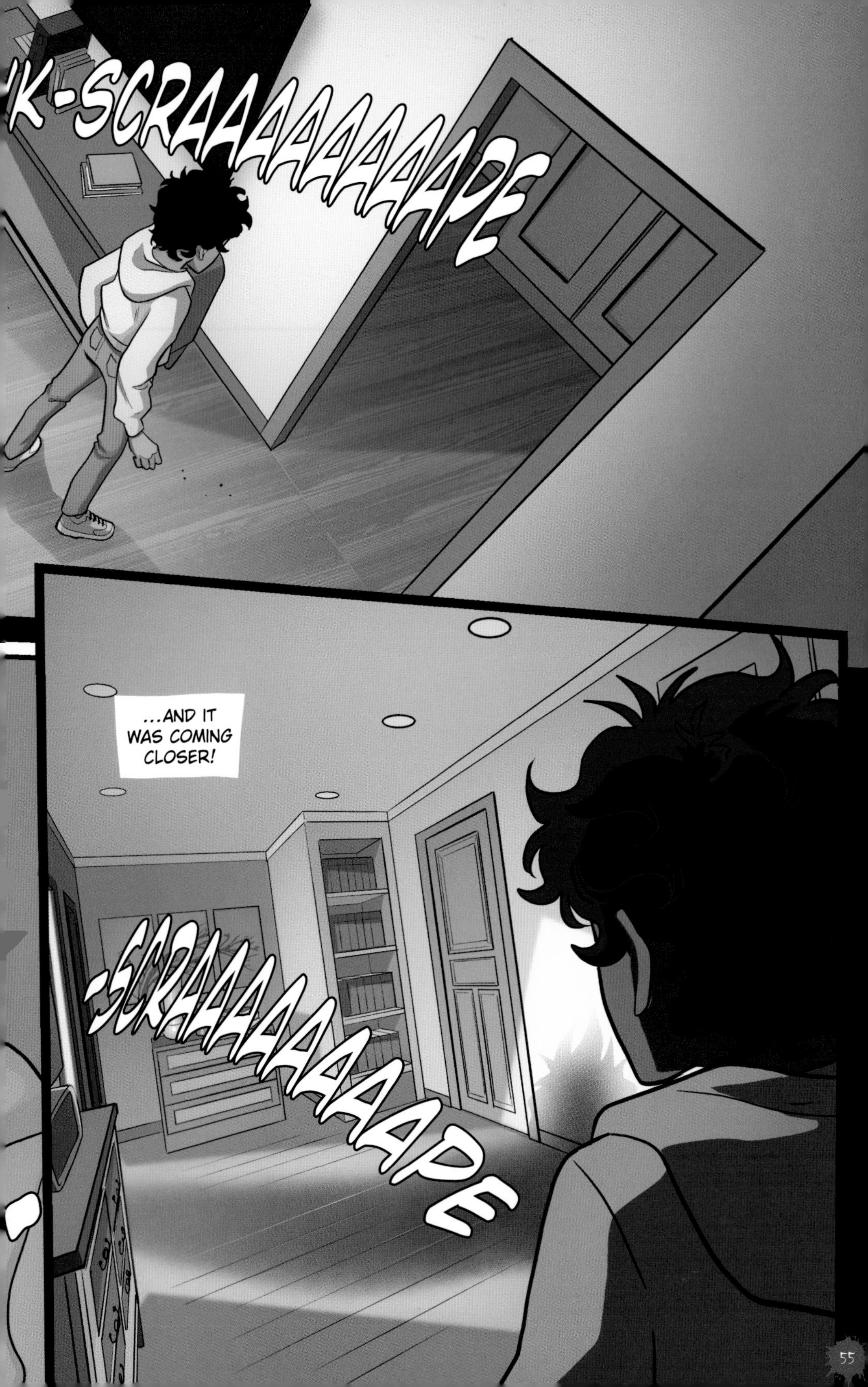
K-SCRAAAAAAAAAAPE
...AND IT WAS COMING CLOSER!
-SCRAAAAAAAAAAAPE

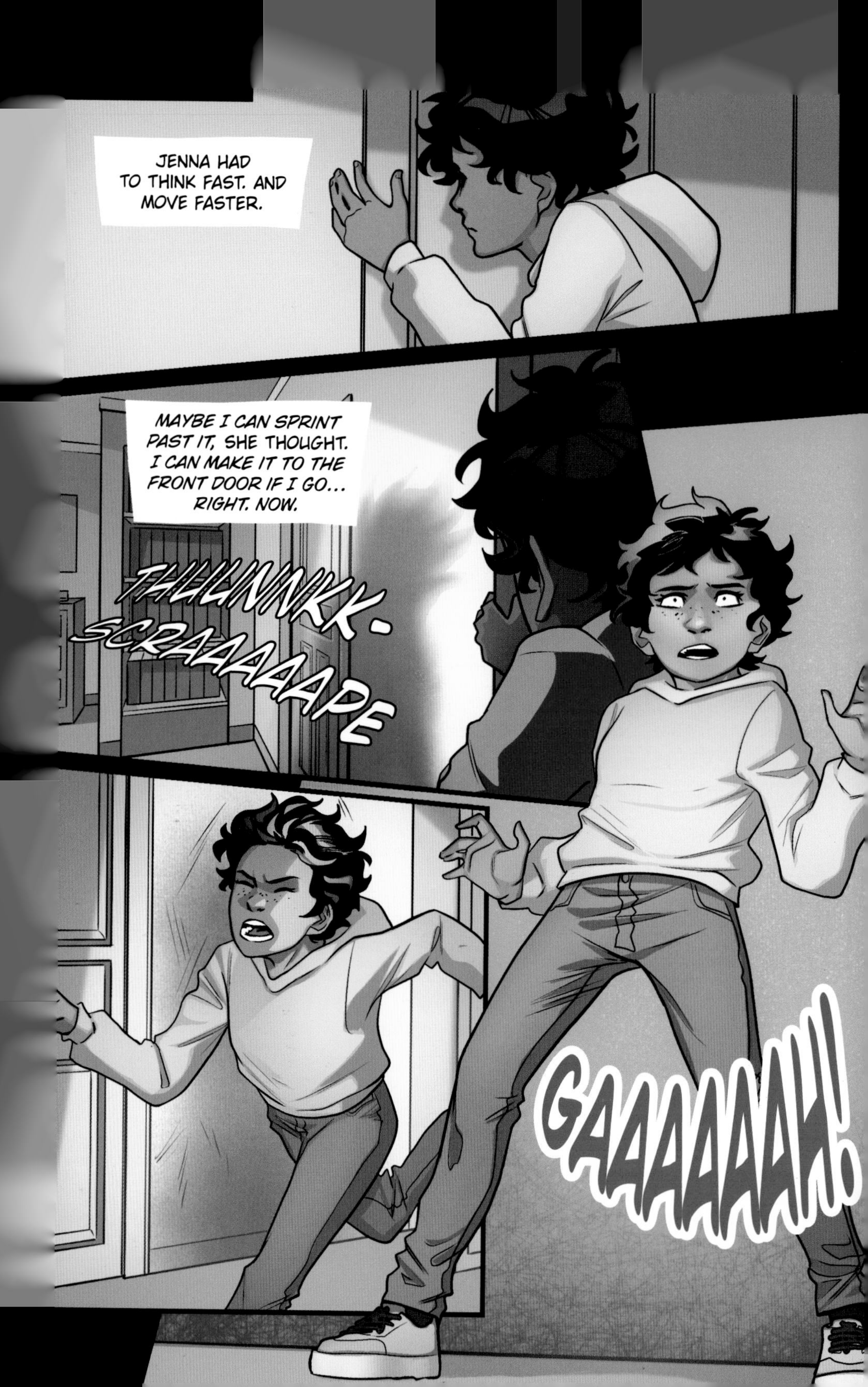
JENNA HAD TO THINK FAST. AND MOVE FASTER.
MAYBE I CAN SPRINT PAST IT, SHE THOUGHT. I CAN MAKE IT TO THE FRONT DOOR IF I GO... RIGHT. NOW.
THUUNNKK-SCRAAAAAAPE
GAAAAAH!

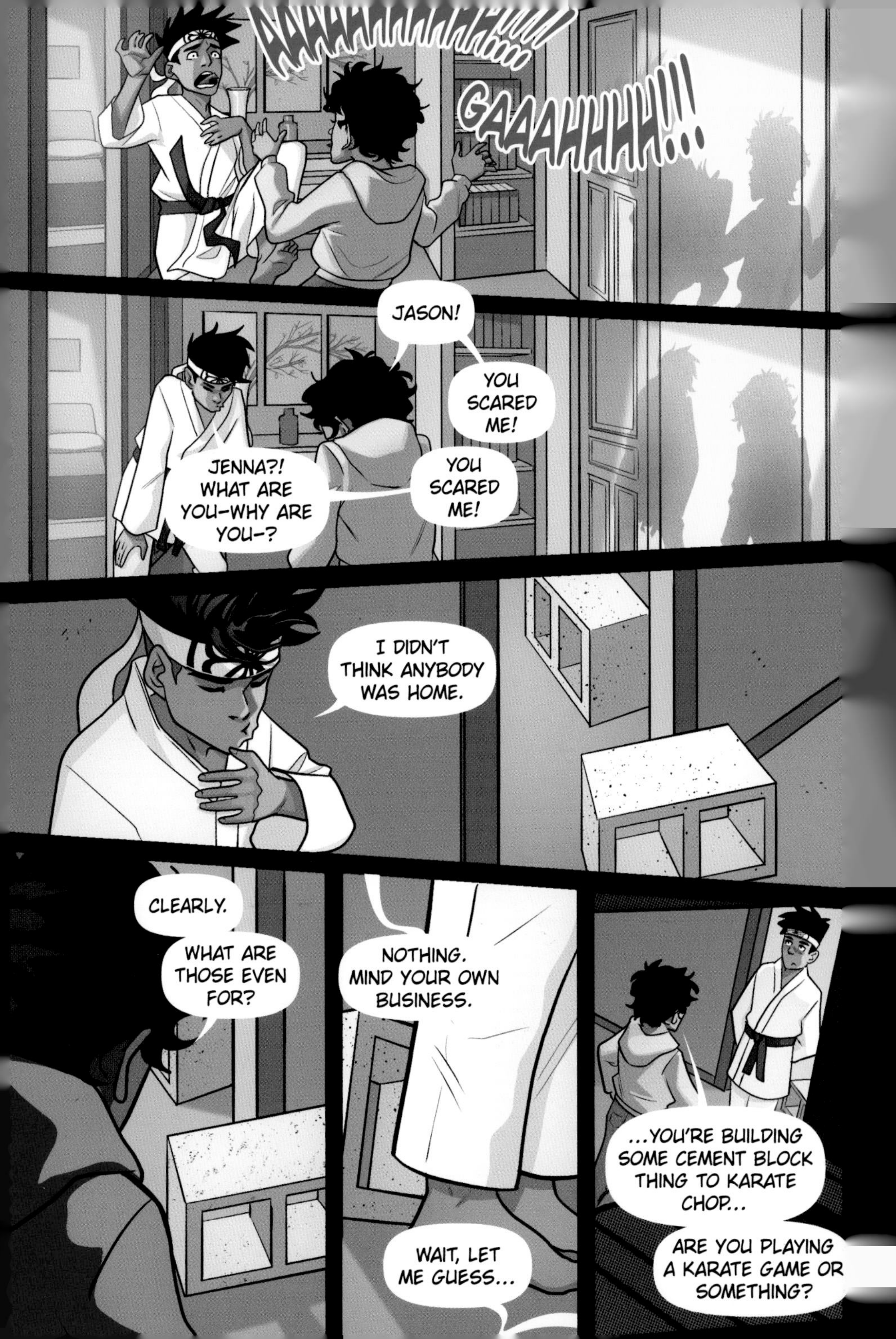
AAAAHHHHHHH...!!!
GAAAHHHH!!!
JASON!
YOU SCARED ME!
JENNA?! WHAT ARE YOU–WHY ARE YOU–?
YOU SCARED ME!
I DIDN'T THINK ANYBODY WAS HOME.
CLEARLY.
WHAT ARE THOSE EVEN FOR?
NOTHING. MIND YOUR OWN BUSINESS.
WAIT, LET ME GUESS...
...YOU'RE BUILDING SOME CEMENT BLOCK THING TO KARATE CHOP...
ARE YOU PLAYING A KARATE GAME OR SOMETHING?

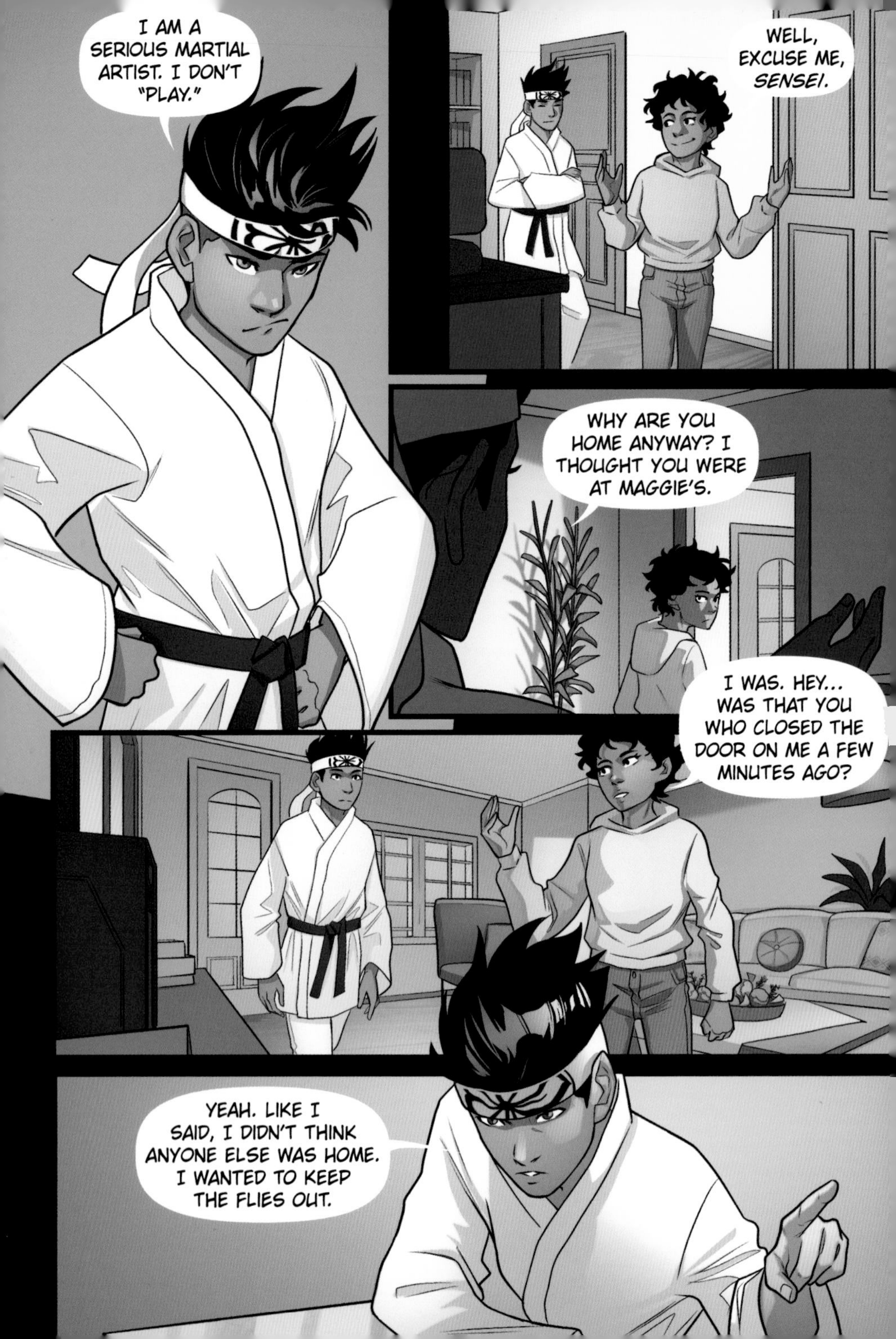
I AM A SERIOUS MARTIAL ARTIST. I DON'T "PLAY."
WELL, EXCUSE ME, *SENSEI*.
WHY ARE YOU HOME ANYWAY? I THOUGHT YOU WERE AT MAGGIE'S.
I WAS. HEY... WAS THAT YOU WHO CLOSED THE DOOR ON ME A FEW MINUTES AGO?
YEAH. LIKE I SAID, I DIDN'T THINK ANYONE ELSE WAS HOME. I WANTED TO KEEP THE FLIES OUT.

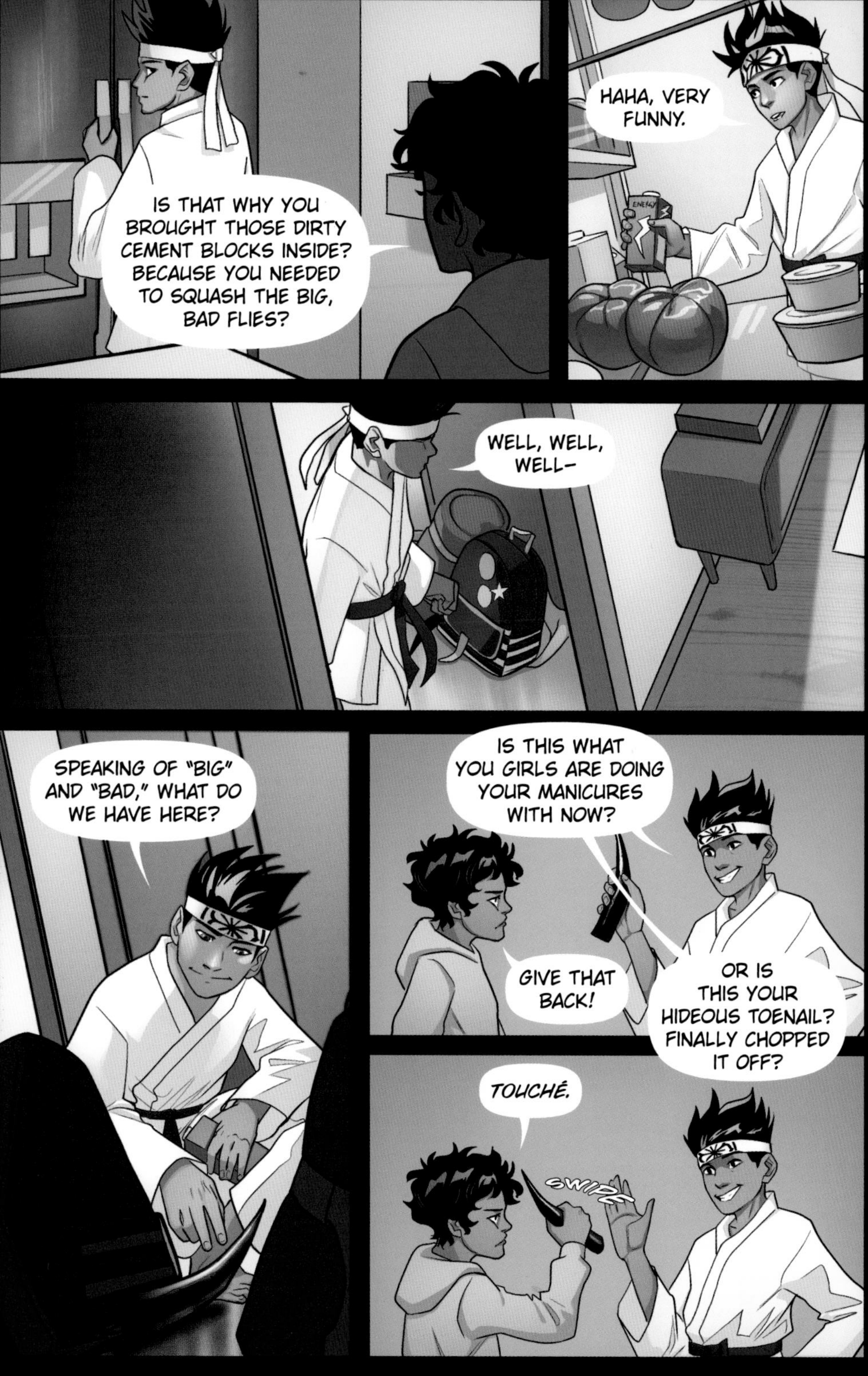
IS THAT WHY YOU BROUGHT THOSE DIRTY CEMENT BLOCKS INSIDE? BECAUSE YOU NEEDED TO SQUASH THE BIG, BAD FLIES?
HAHA, VERY FUNNY.
WELL, WELL, WELL—
SPEAKING OF "BIG" AND "BAD," WHAT DO WE HAVE HERE?
IS THIS WHAT YOU GIRLS ARE DOING YOUR MANICURES WITH NOW?
GIVE THAT BACK!
OR IS THIS YOUR HIDEOUS TOENAIL? FINALLY CHOPPED IT OFF?
TOUCHÉ.
SWIPE

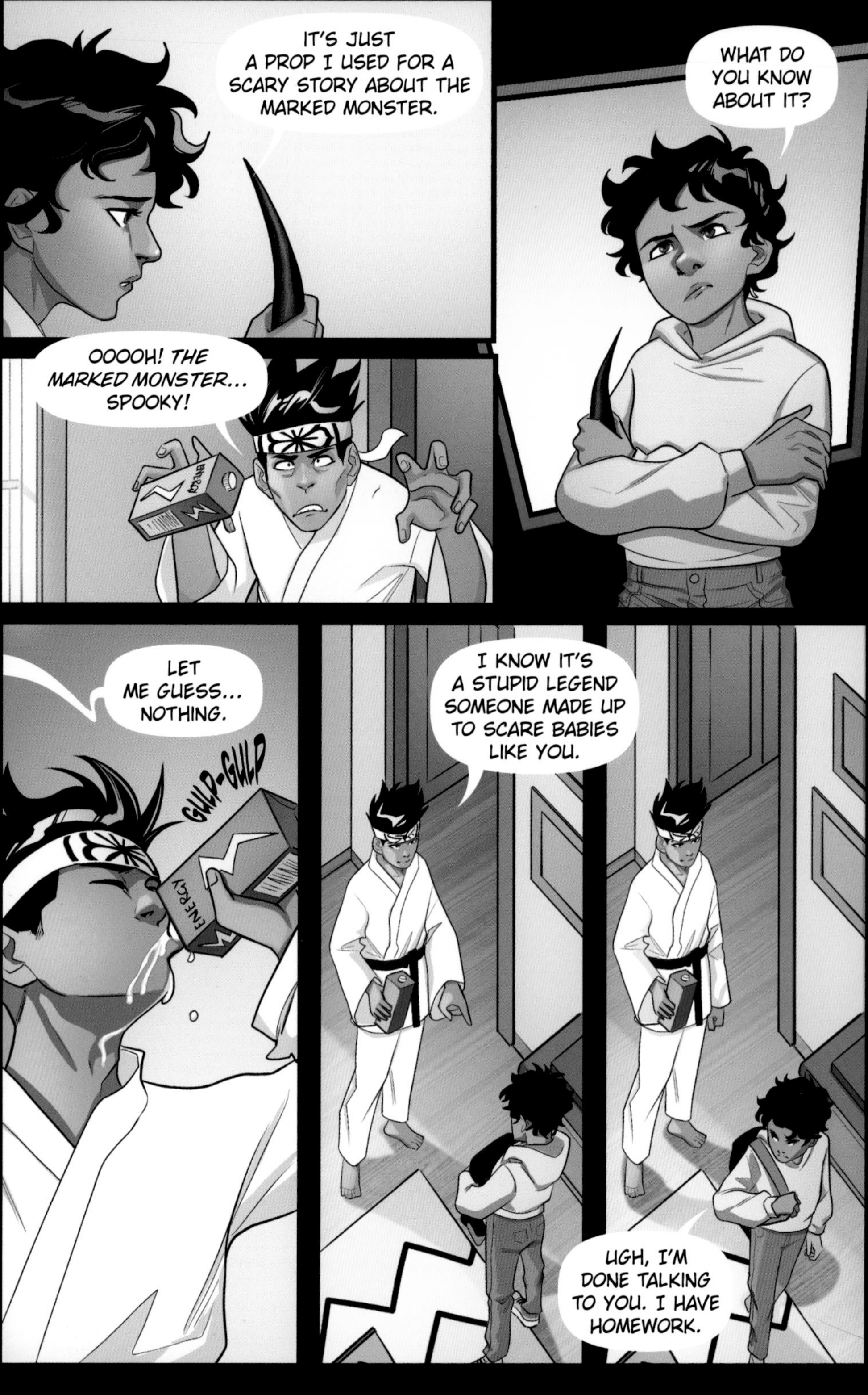

IT'S JUST A PROP I USED FOR A SCARY STORY ABOUT THE MARKED MONSTER.
WHAT DO YOU KNOW ABOUT IT?
OOOOH! THE MARKED MONSTER... SPOOKY!
ENERGY
LET ME GUESS... NOTHING.
GULP-GULP
ENERGY
I KNOW IT'S A STUPID LEGEND SOMEONE MADE UP TO SCARE BABIES LIKE YOU.
UGH, I'M DONE TALKING TO YOU. I HAVE HOMEWORK.

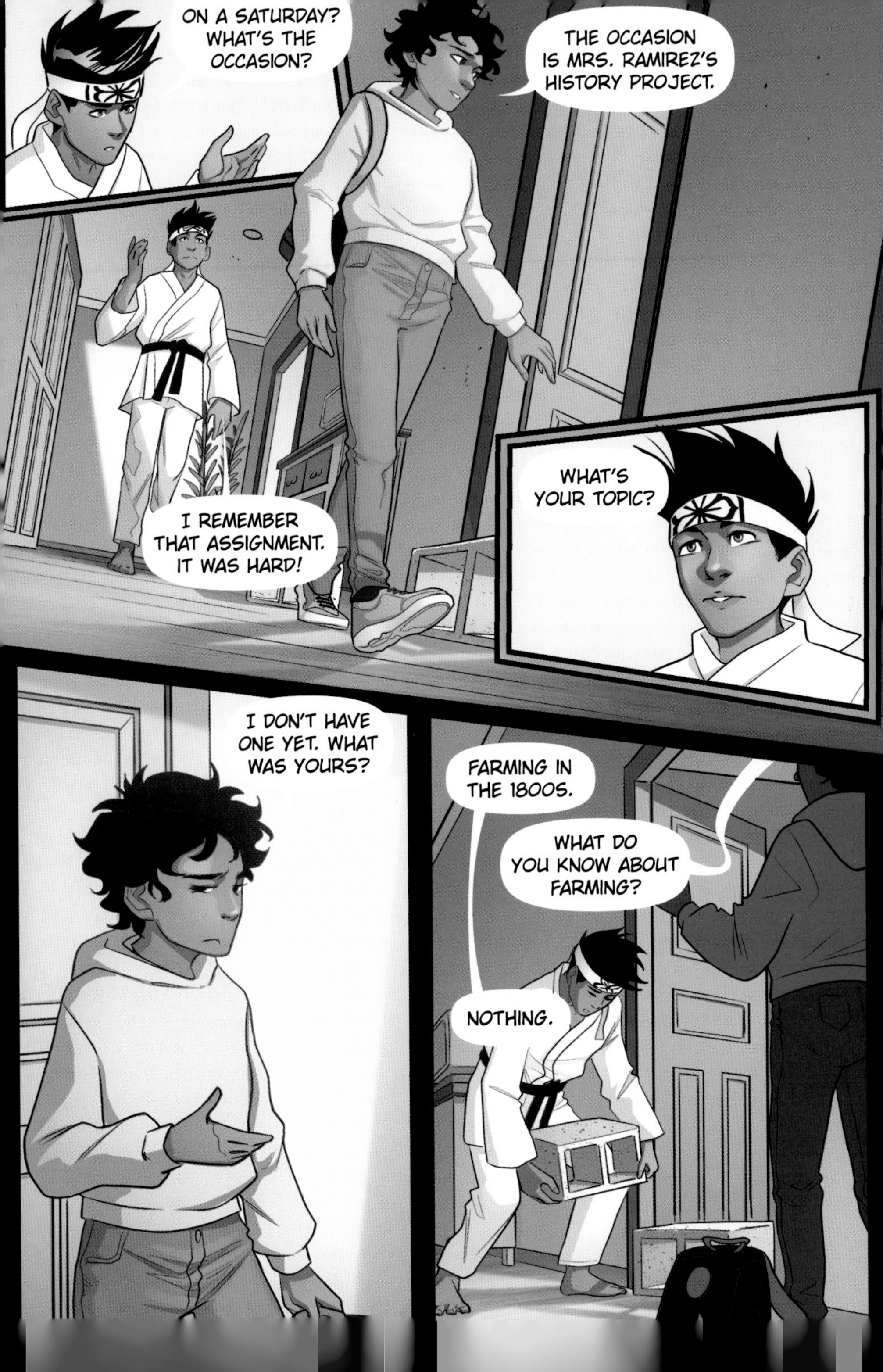
ON A SATURDAY? WHAT'S THE OCCASION?
THE OCCASION IS MRS. RAMIREZ'S HISTORY PROJECT.
I REMEMBER THAT ASSIGNMENT. IT WAS HARD!
WHAT'S YOUR TOPIC?
I DON'T HAVE ONE YET. WHAT WAS YOURS?
FARMING IN THE 1800S.
WHAT DO YOU KNOW ABOUT FARMING?
NOTHING.

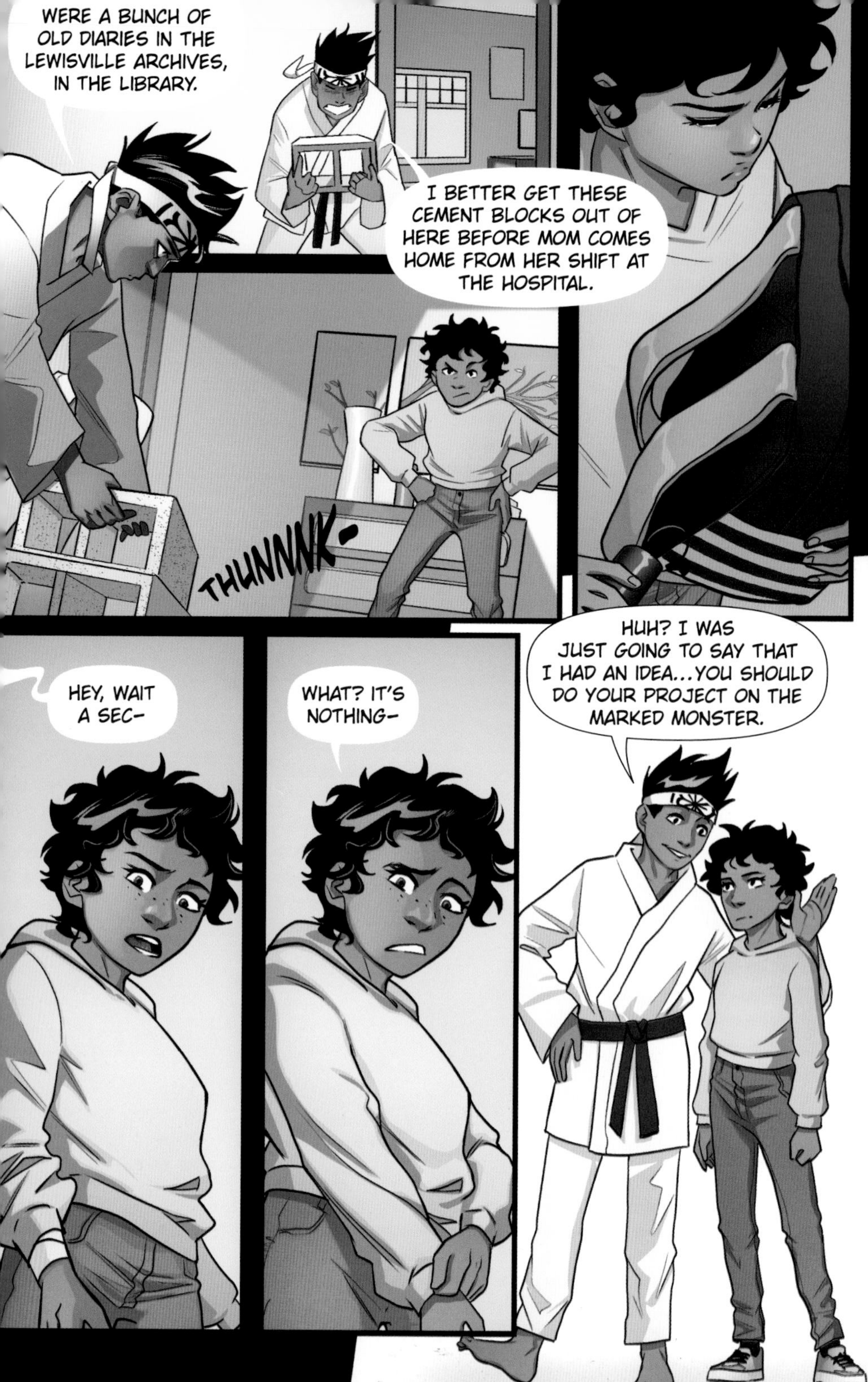
WERE A BUNCH OF OLD DIARIES IN THE LEWISVILLE ARCHIVES, IN THE LIBRARY.
I BETTER GET THESE CEMENT BLOCKS OUT OF HERE BEFORE MOM COMES HOME FROM HER SHIFT AT THE HOSPITAL.
THUNNNK-
HEY, WAIT A SEC-
WHAT? IT'S NOTHING-
HUH? I WAS JUST GOING TO SAY THAT I HAD AN IDEA...YOU SHOULD DO YOUR PROJECT ON THE MARKED MONSTER.

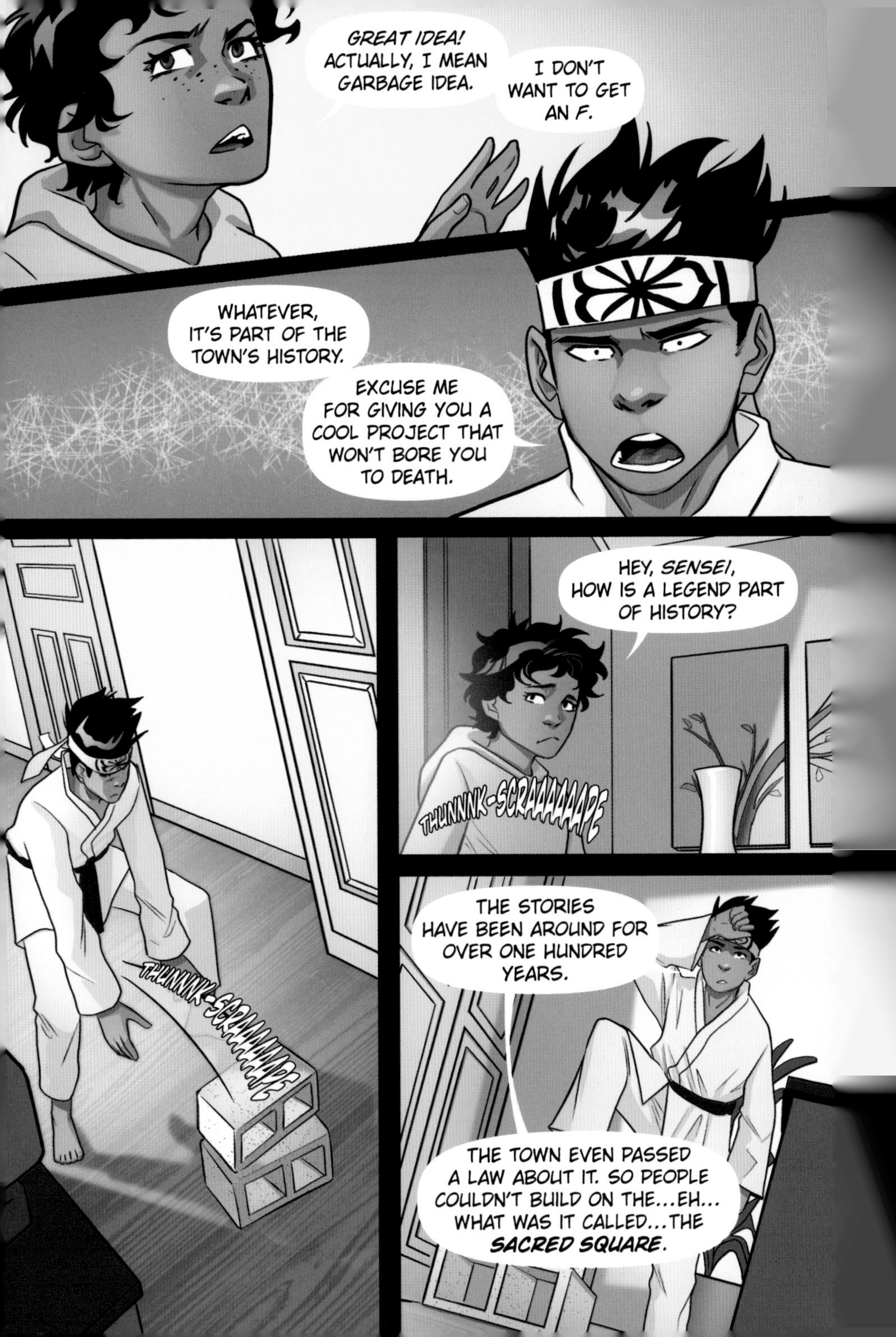
GREAT IDEA! ACTUALLY, I MEAN GARBAGE IDEA.
I DON'T WANT TO GET AN F.
WHATEVER, IT'S PART OF THE TOWN'S HISTORY.
EXCUSE ME FOR GIVING YOU A COOL PROJECT THAT WON'T BORE YOU TO DEATH.
THUNNNK-SCRAAAAAAPE
HEY, SENSEI, HOW IS A LEGEND PART OF HISTORY?
THUNNNK-SCRAAAAAAPE
THE STORIES HAVE BEEN AROUND FOR OVER ONE HUNDRED YEARS.
THE TOWN EVEN PASSED A LAW ABOUT IT. SO PEOPLE COULDN'T BUILD ON THE...EH... WHAT WAS IT CALLED...THE SACRED SQUARE.

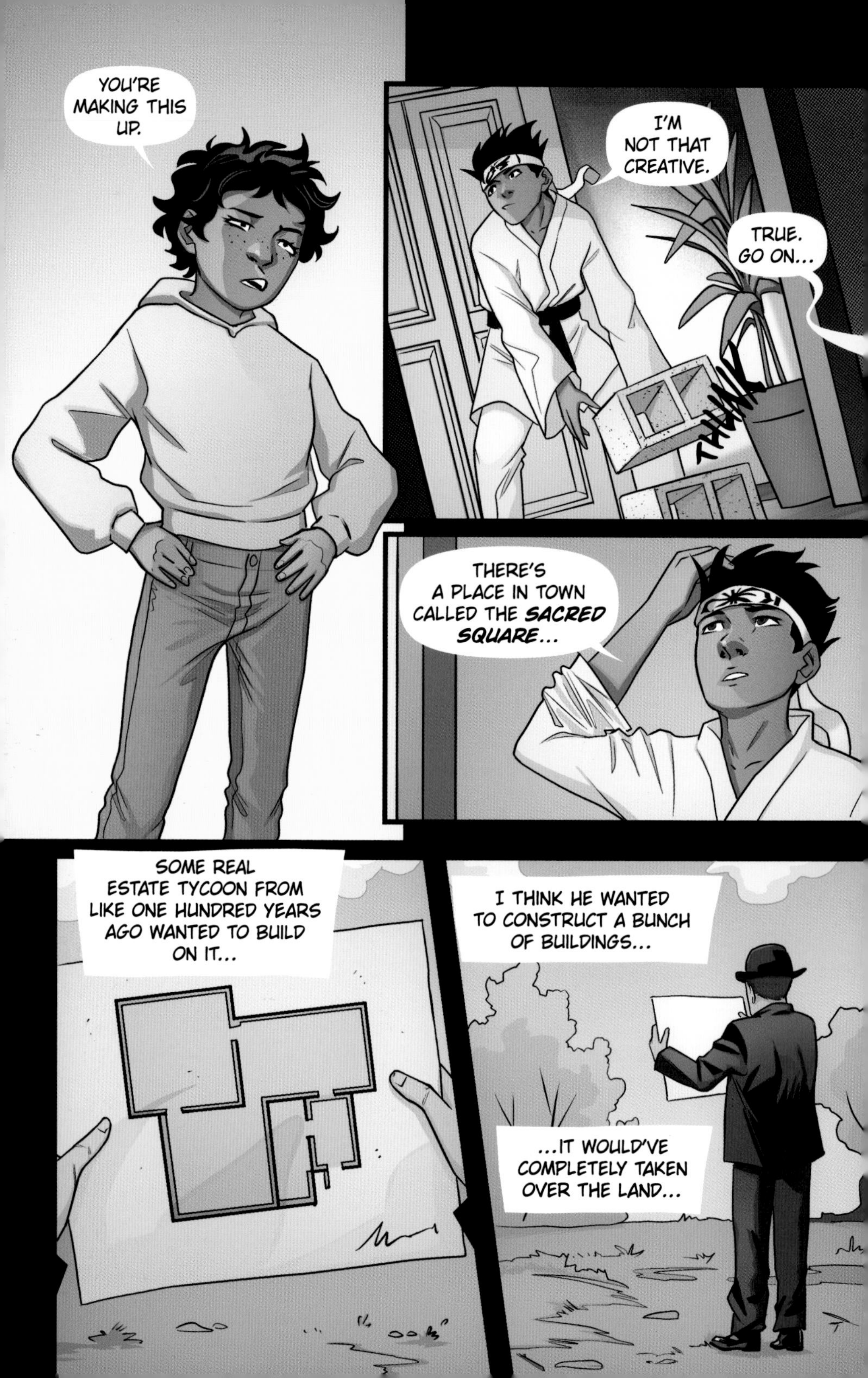
YOU'RE MAKING THIS UP.
I'M NOT THAT CREATIVE.
TRUE. GO ON...
THUNK
THERE'S A PLACE IN TOWN CALLED THE SACRED SQUARE...
SOME REAL ESTATE TYCOON FROM LIKE ONE HUNDRED YEARS AGO WANTED TO BUILD ON IT...
I THINK HE WANTED TO CONSTRUCT A BUNCH OF BUILDINGS...
...IT WOULD'VE COMPLETELY TAKEN OVER THE LAND...

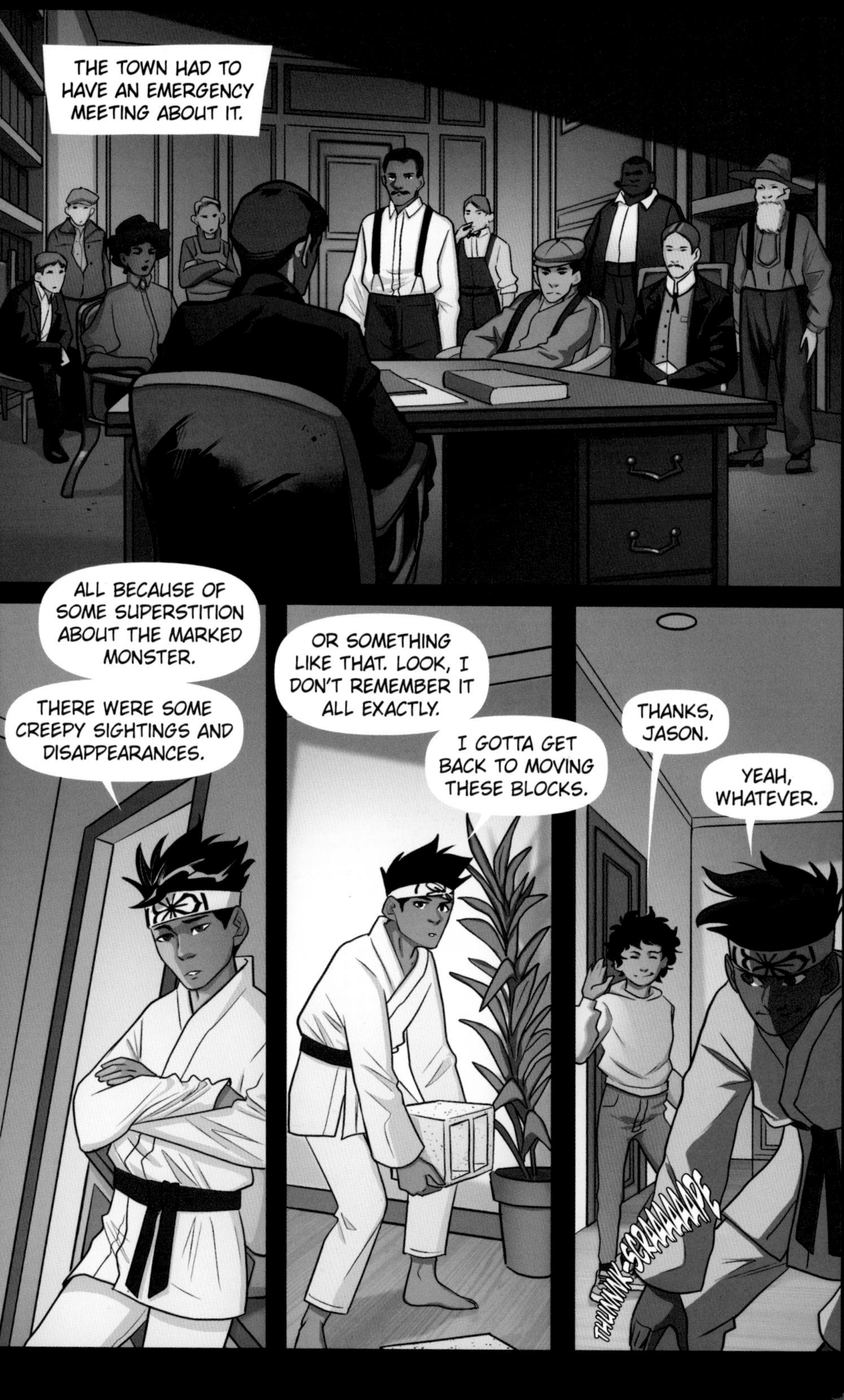

THE TOWN HAD TO HAVE AN EMERGENCY MEETING ABOUT IT.
ALL BECAUSE OF SOME SUPERSTITION ABOUT THE MARKED MONSTER.
THERE WERE SOME CREEPY SIGHTINGS AND DISAPPEARANCES.
OR SOMETHING LIKE THAT. LOOK, I DON'T REMEMBER IT ALL EXACTLY.
I GOTTA GET BACK TO MOVING THESE BLOCKS.
THANKS, JASON.
YEAH, WHATEVER.
THUNNK-SCRAAAAAPE

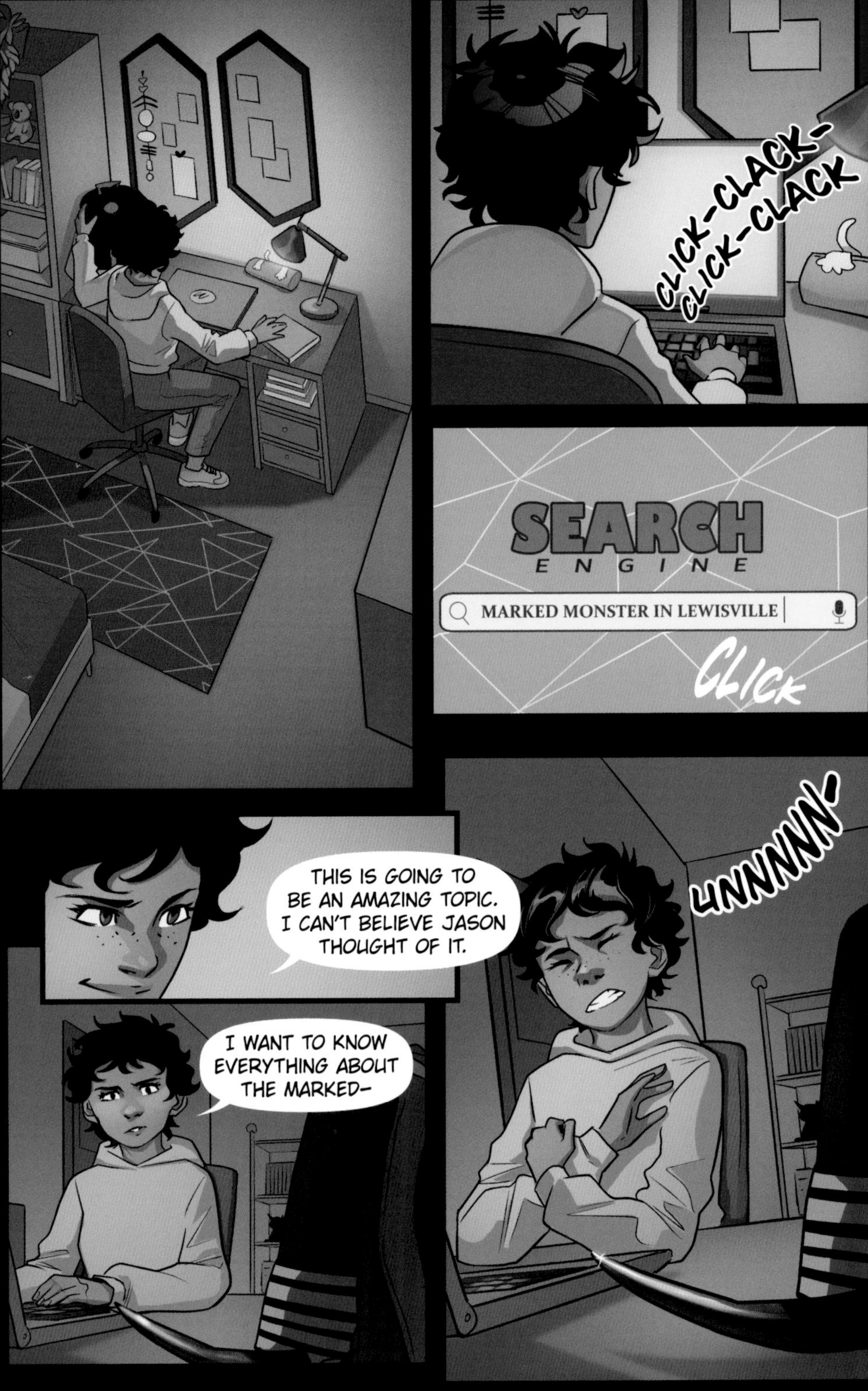
CLICK-CLACK-
CLICK-CLACK
SEARCH
ENGINE
MARKED MONSTER IN LEWISVILLE
CLICK
THIS IS GOING TO BE AN AMAZING TOPIC. I CAN'T BELIEVE JASON THOUGHT OF IT.
I WANT TO KNOW EVERYTHING ABOUT THE MARKED-
UNNNNN-

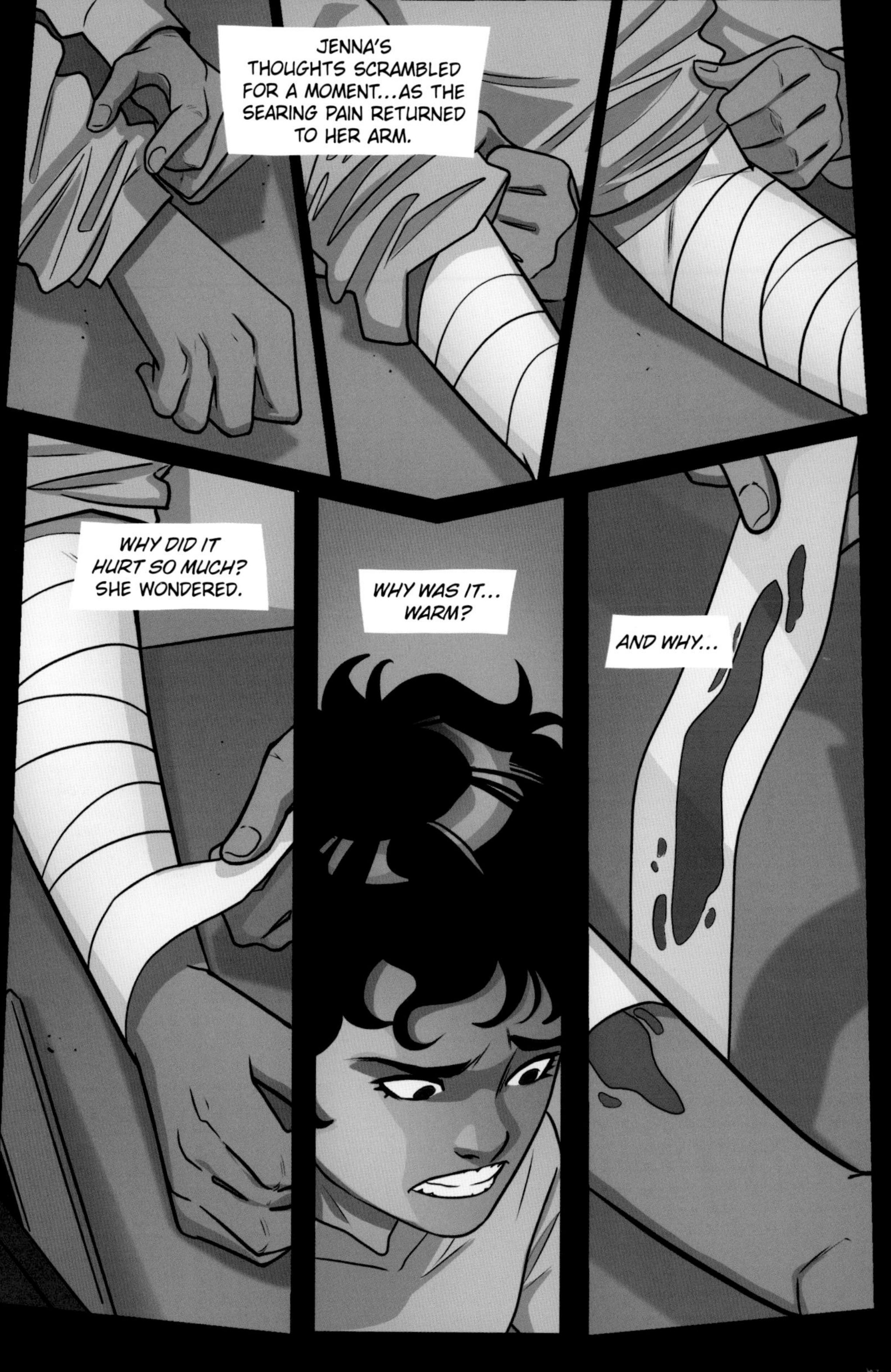
JENNA'S THOUGHTS SCRAMBLED FOR A MOMENT...AS THE SEARING PAIN RETURNED TO HER ARM.
WHY DID IT HURT SO MUCH? SHE WONDERED.
WHY WAS IT... WARM?
AND WHY...

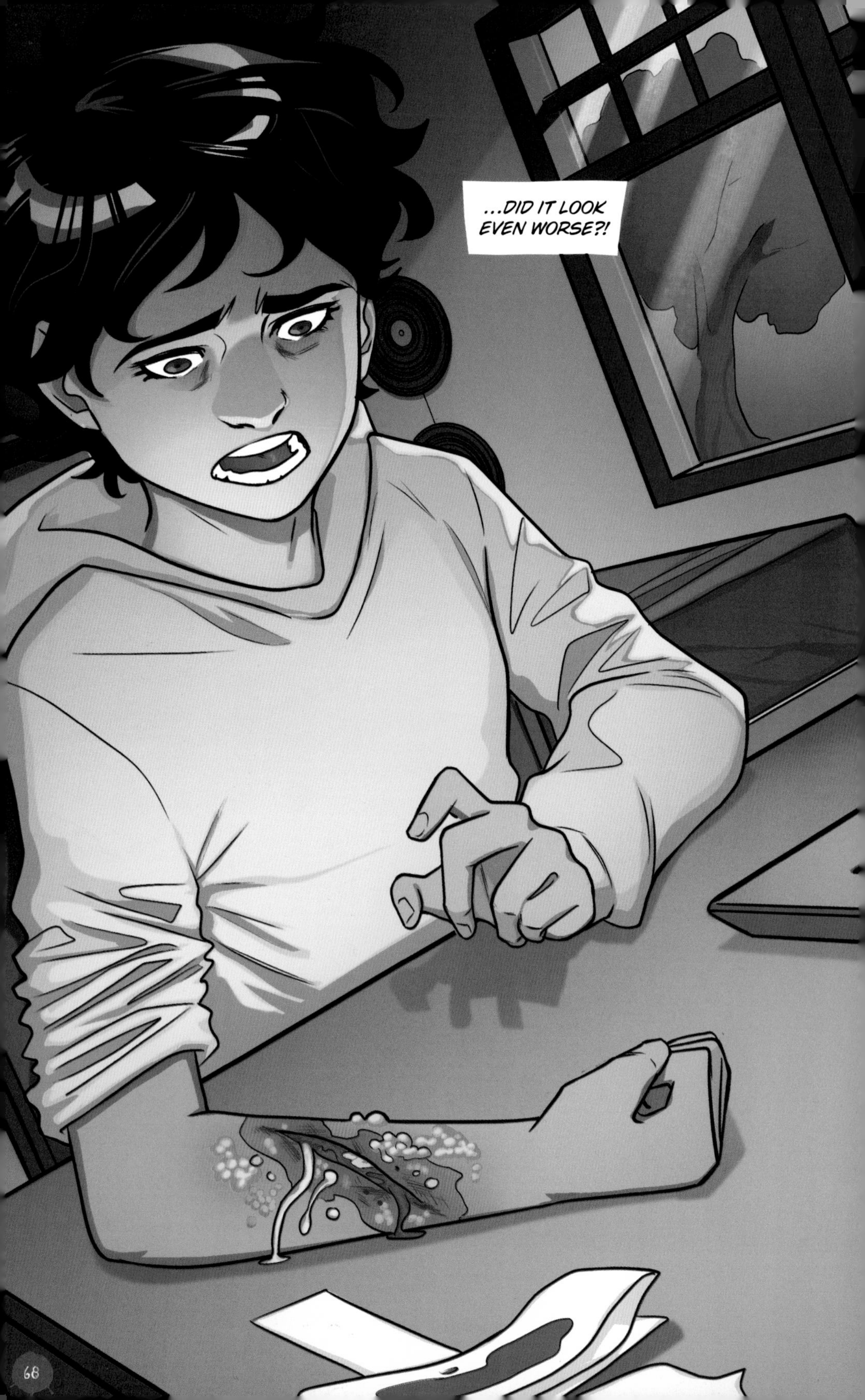
...DID IT LOOK
EVEN WORSE?!

CHAPTER 6

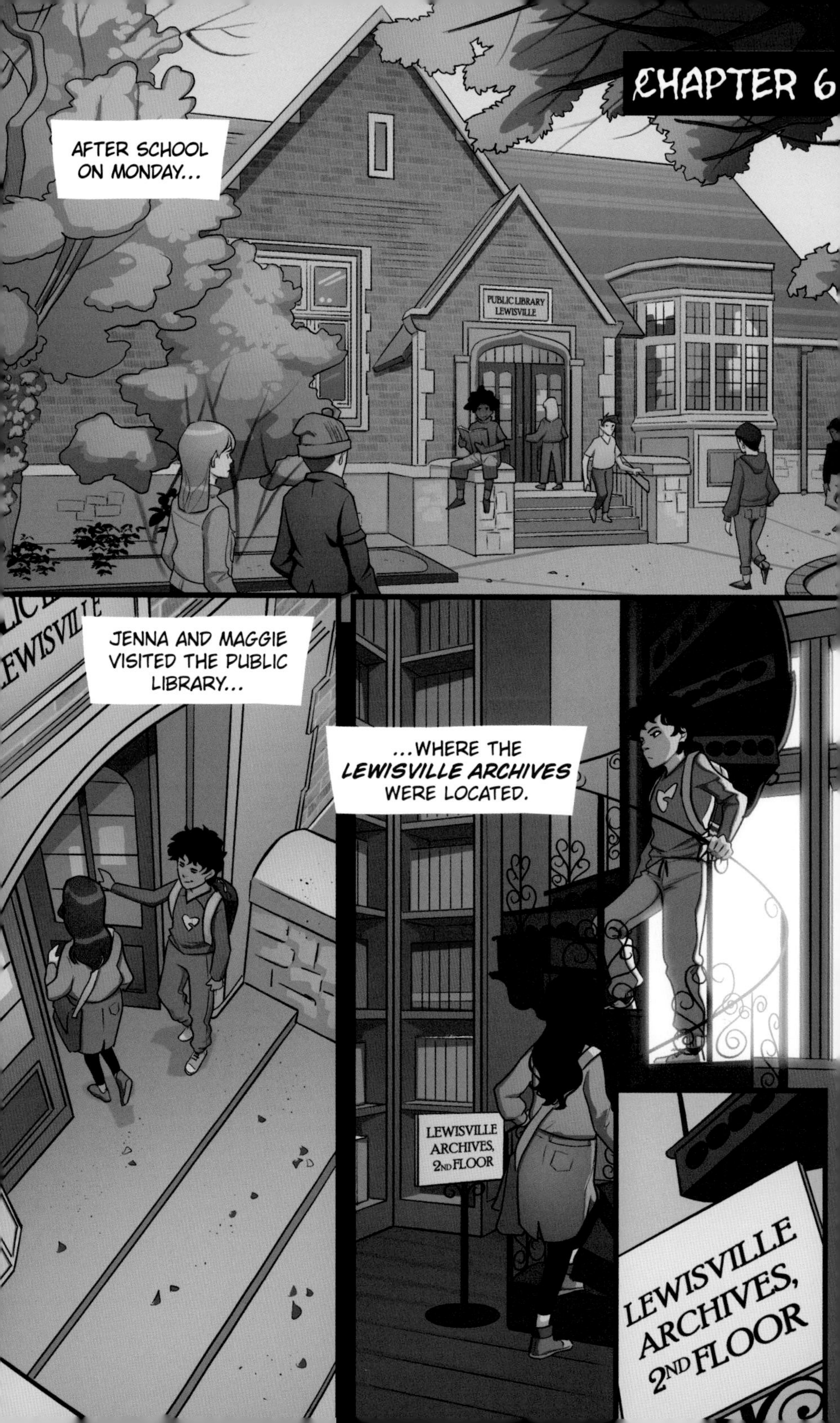
AFTER SCHOOL ON MONDAY...
PUBLIC LIBRARY LEWISVILLE
JENNA AND MAGGIE VISITED THE PUBLIC LIBRARY...
...WHERE THE *LEWISVILLE ARCHIVES* WERE LOCATED.
LEWISVILLE ARCHIVES, 2ND FLOOR
LEWISVILLE ARCHIVES, 2ND FLOOR

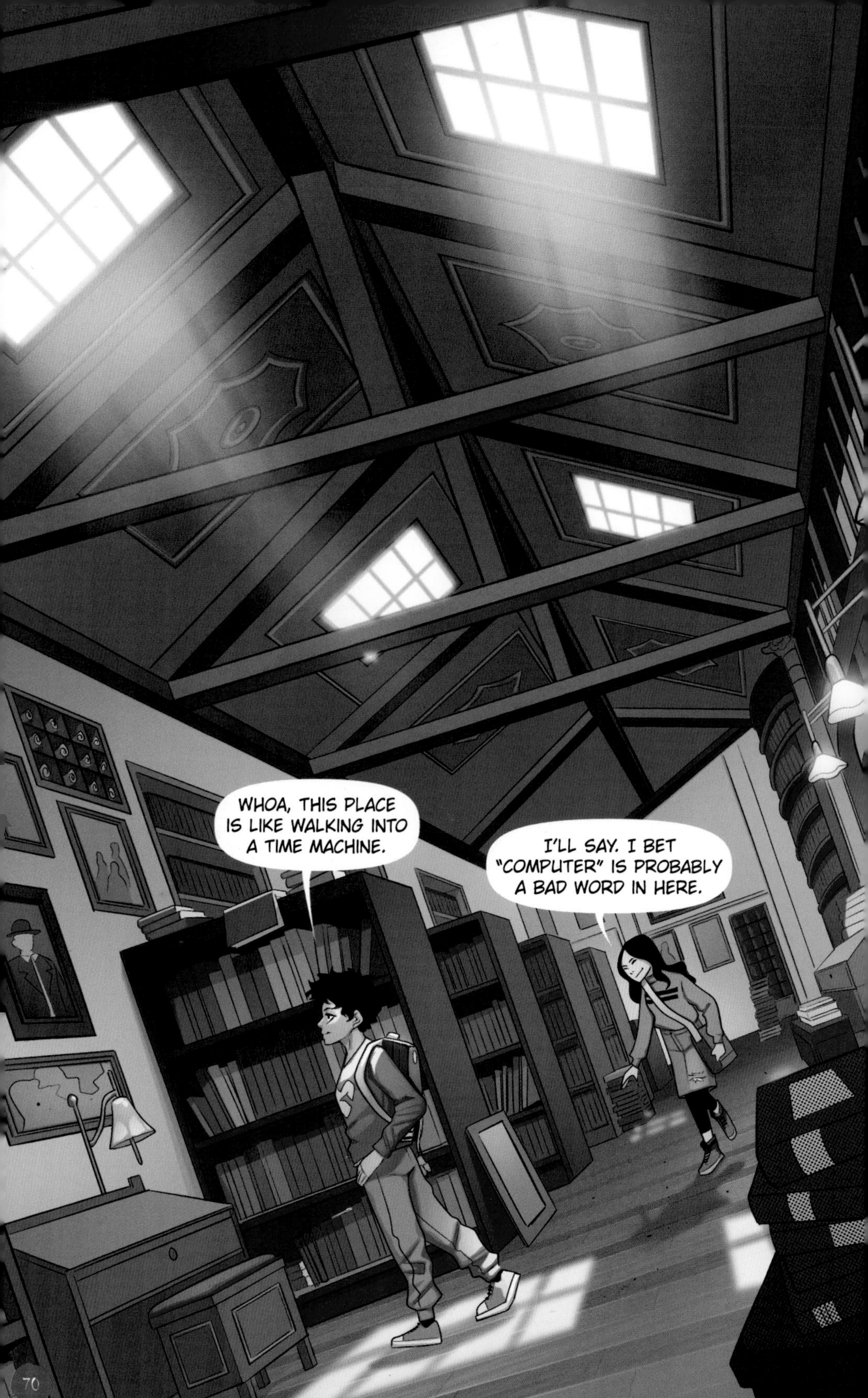
WHOA, THIS PLACE IS LIKE WALKING INTO A TIME MACHINE.
I'LL SAY. I BET "COMPUTER" IS PROBABLY A BAD WORD IN HERE.

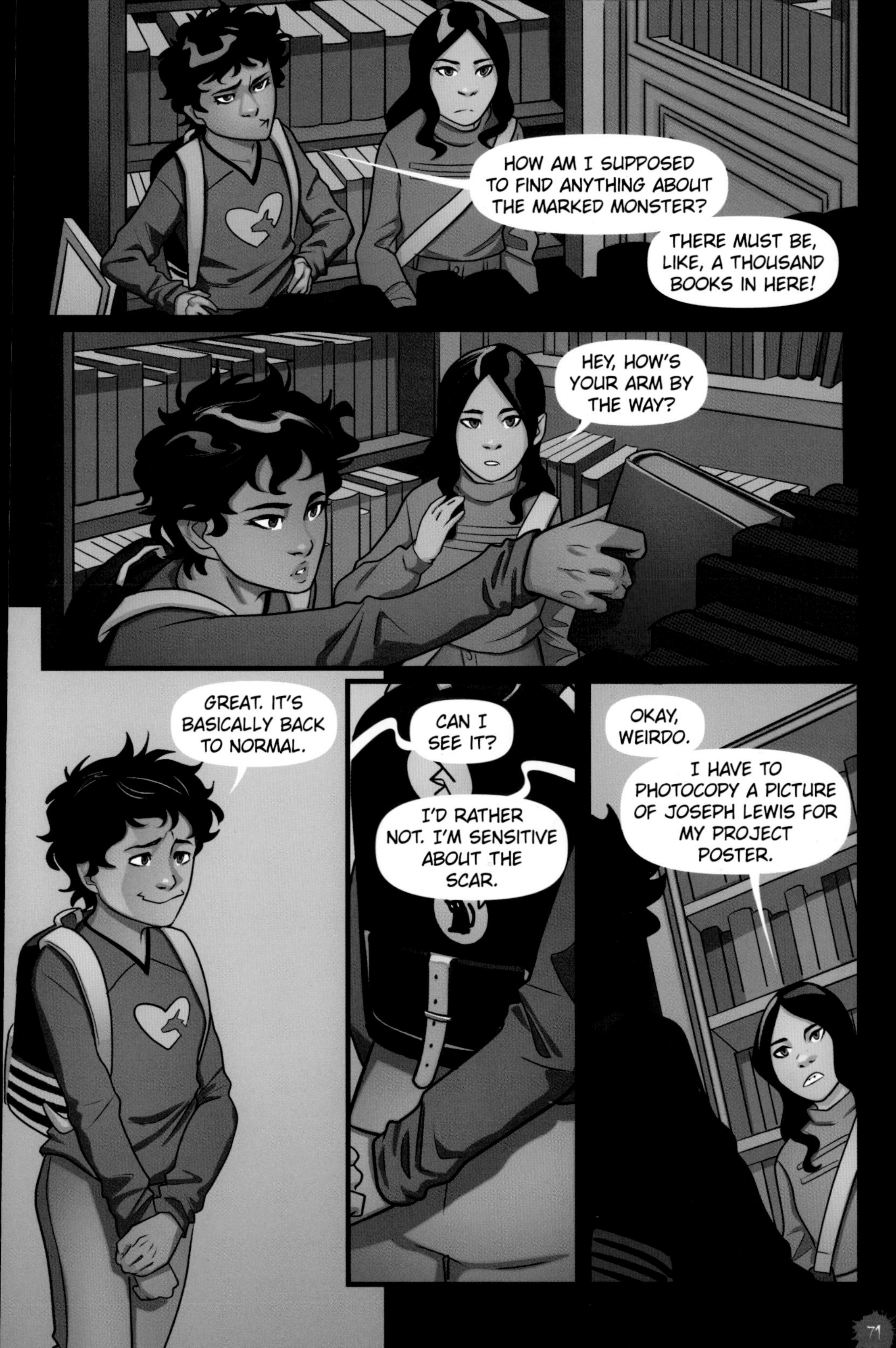
HOW AM I SUPPOSED TO FIND ANYTHING ABOUT THE MARKED MONSTER?
THERE MUST BE, LIKE, A THOUSAND BOOKS IN HERE!
HEY, HOW'S YOUR ARM BY THE WAY?
GREAT. IT'S BASICALLY BACK TO NORMAL.
CAN I SEE IT?
I'D RATHER NOT. I'M SENSITIVE ABOUT THE SCAR.
OKAY, WEIRDO.
I HAVE TO PHOTOCOPY A PICTURE OF JOSEPH LEWIS FOR MY PROJECT POSTER.

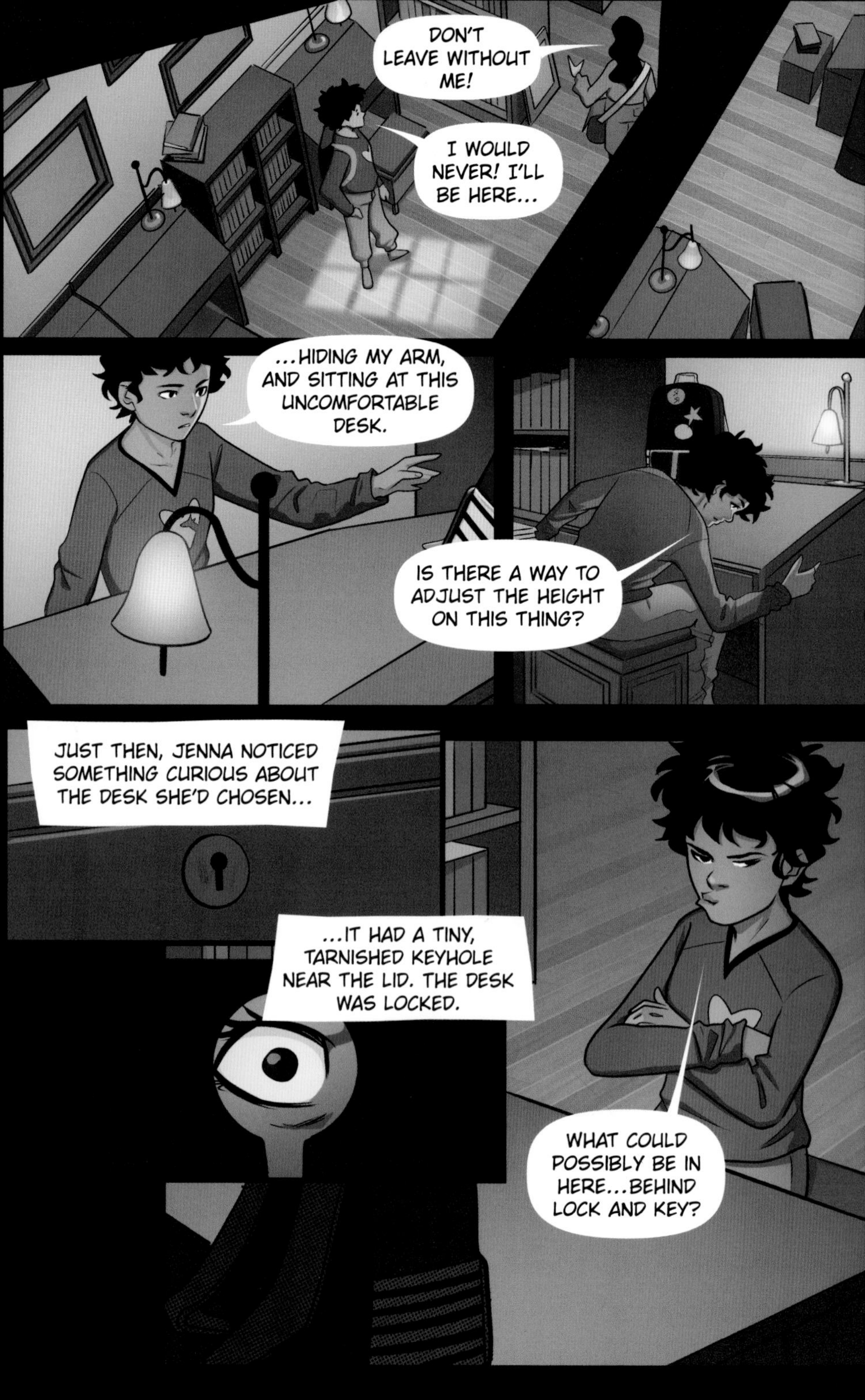
DON'T LEAVE WITHOUT ME!
I WOULD NEVER! I'LL BE HERE...
...HIDING MY ARM, AND SITTING AT THIS UNCOMFORTABLE DESK.
IS THERE A WAY TO ADJUST THE HEIGHT ON THIS THING?
JUST THEN, JENNA NOTICED SOMETHING CURIOUS ABOUT THE DESK SHE'D CHOSEN...
...IT HAD A TINY, TARNISHED KEYHOLE NEAR THE LID. THE DESK WAS LOCKED.
WHAT COULD POSSIBLY BE IN HERE...BEHIND LOCK AND KEY?

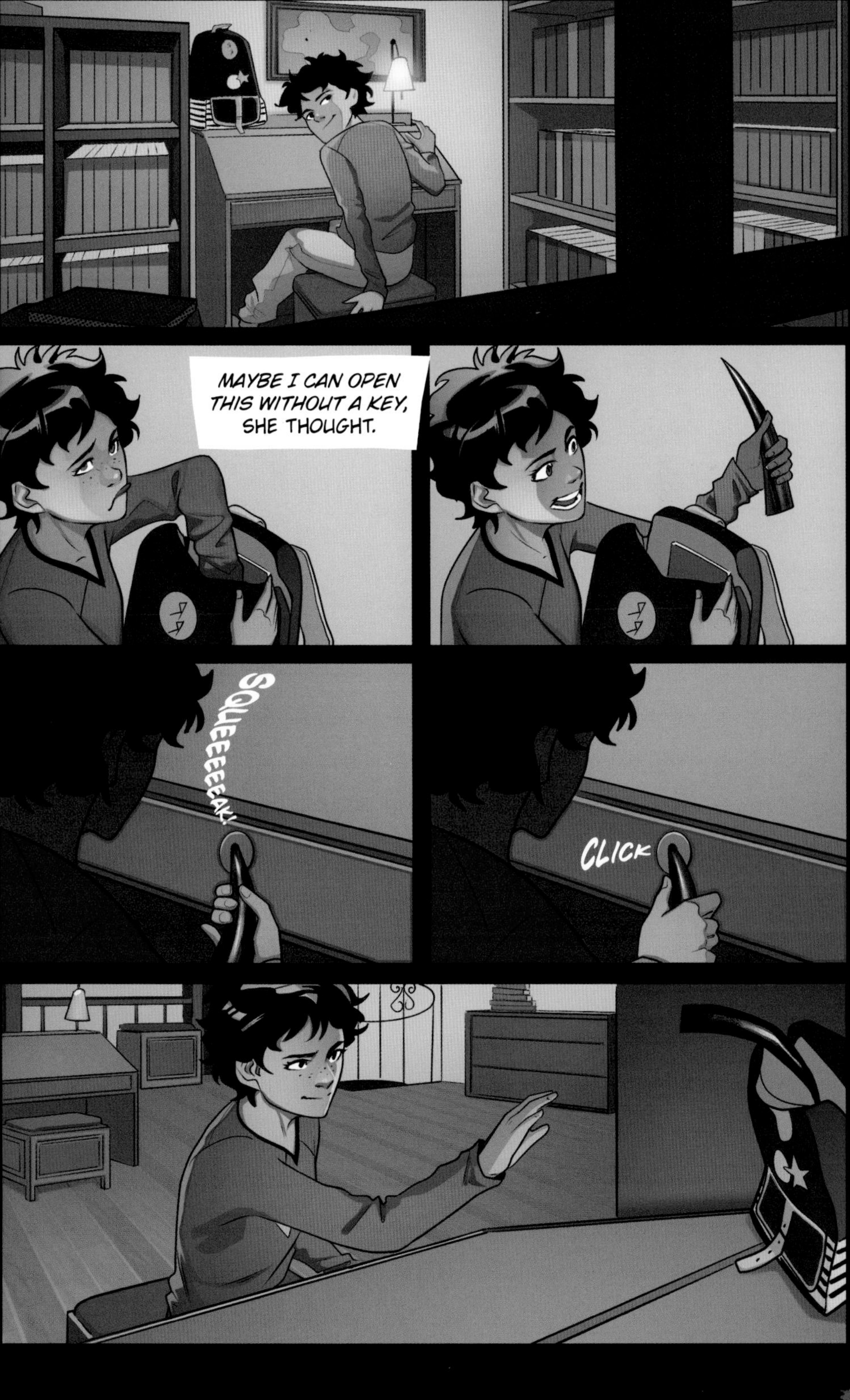
MAYBE I CAN OPEN THIS WITHOUT A KEY, SHE THOUGHT.
SQUEEEEEEAK!
CLICK

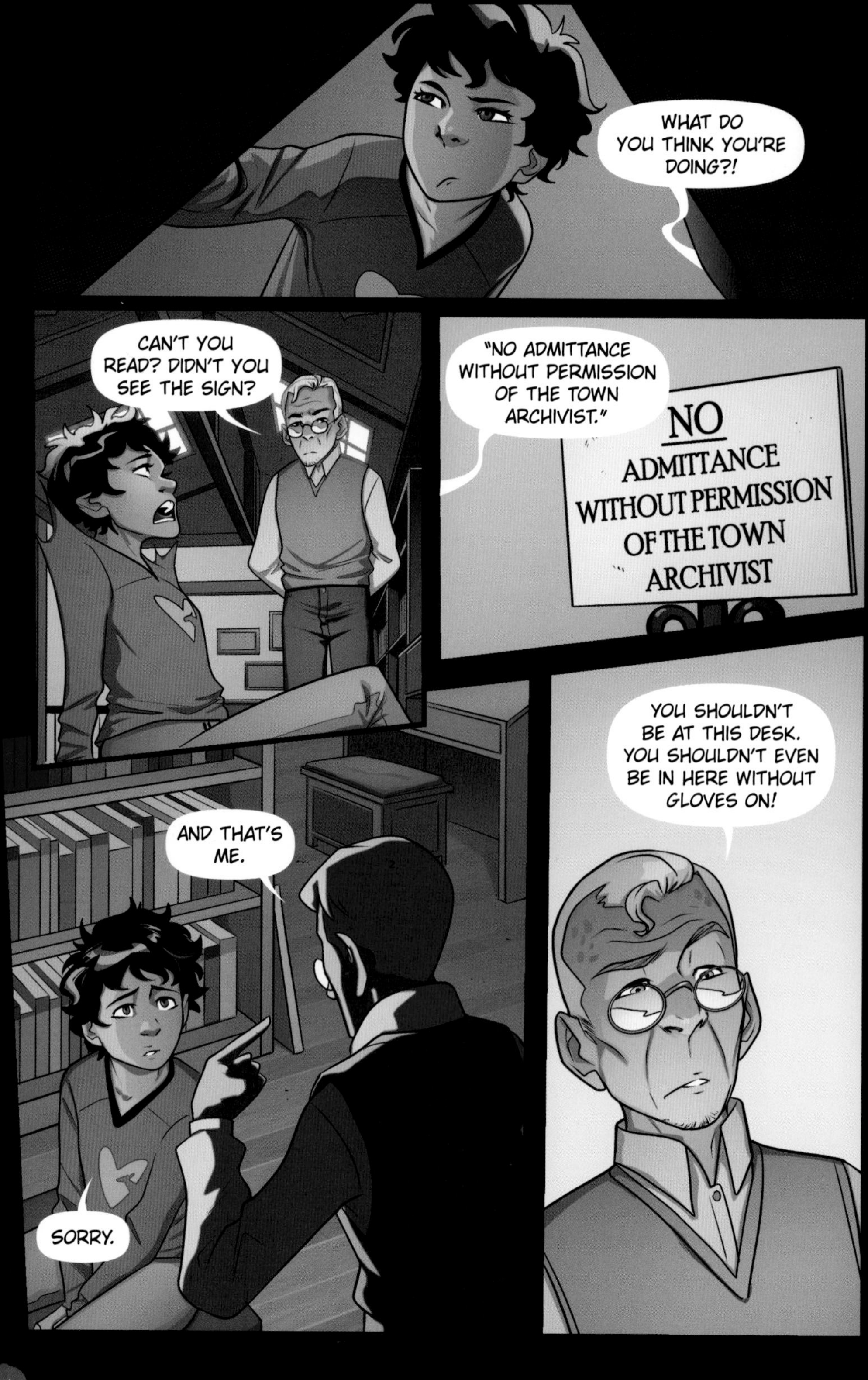
WHAT DO YOU THINK YOU'RE DOING?!
CAN'T YOU READ? DIDN'T YOU SEE THE SIGN?
"NO ADMITTANCE WITHOUT PERMISSION OF THE TOWN ARCHIVIST."
NO
ADMITTANCE
WITHOUT PERMISSION
OF THE TOWN
ARCHIVIST
AND THAT'S ME.
SORRY.
YOU SHOULDN'T BE AT THIS DESK. YOU SHOULDN'T EVEN BE IN HERE WITHOUT GLOVES ON!

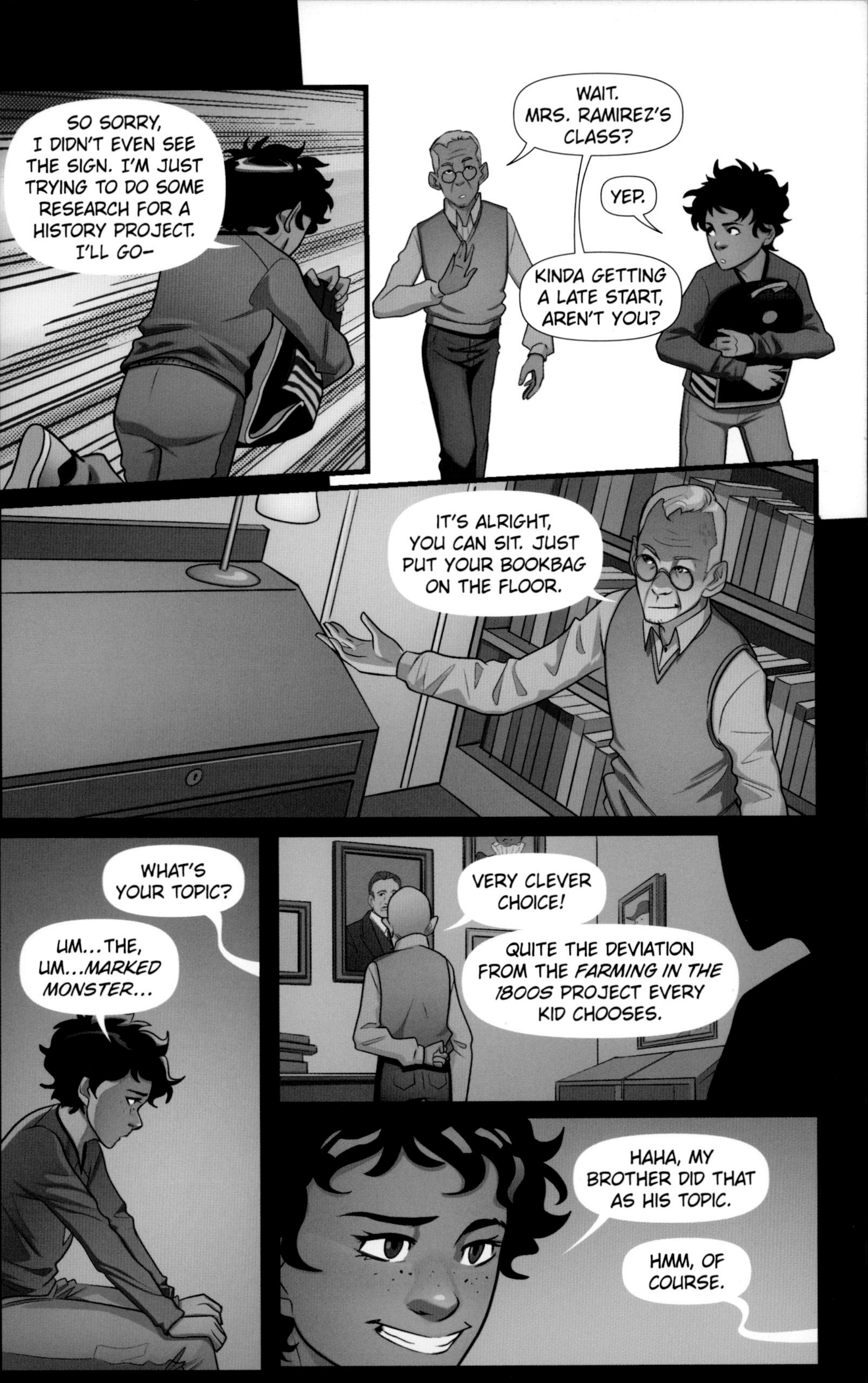
SO SORRY, I DIDN'T EVEN SEE THE SIGN. I'M JUST TRYING TO DO SOME RESEARCH FOR A HISTORY PROJECT. I'LL GO-
WAIT. MRS. RAMIREZ'S CLASS?
YEP.
KINDA GETTING A LATE START, AREN'T YOU?
IT'S ALRIGHT, YOU CAN SIT. JUST PUT YOUR BOOKBAG ON THE FLOOR.
WHAT'S YOUR TOPIC?
UM...THE, UM...*MARKED MONSTER*...
VERY CLEVER CHOICE!
QUITE THE DEVIATION FROM THE *FARMING IN THE 1800S* PROJECT EVERY KID CHOOSES.
HAHA, MY BROTHER DID THAT AS HIS TOPIC.
HMM, OF COURSE.

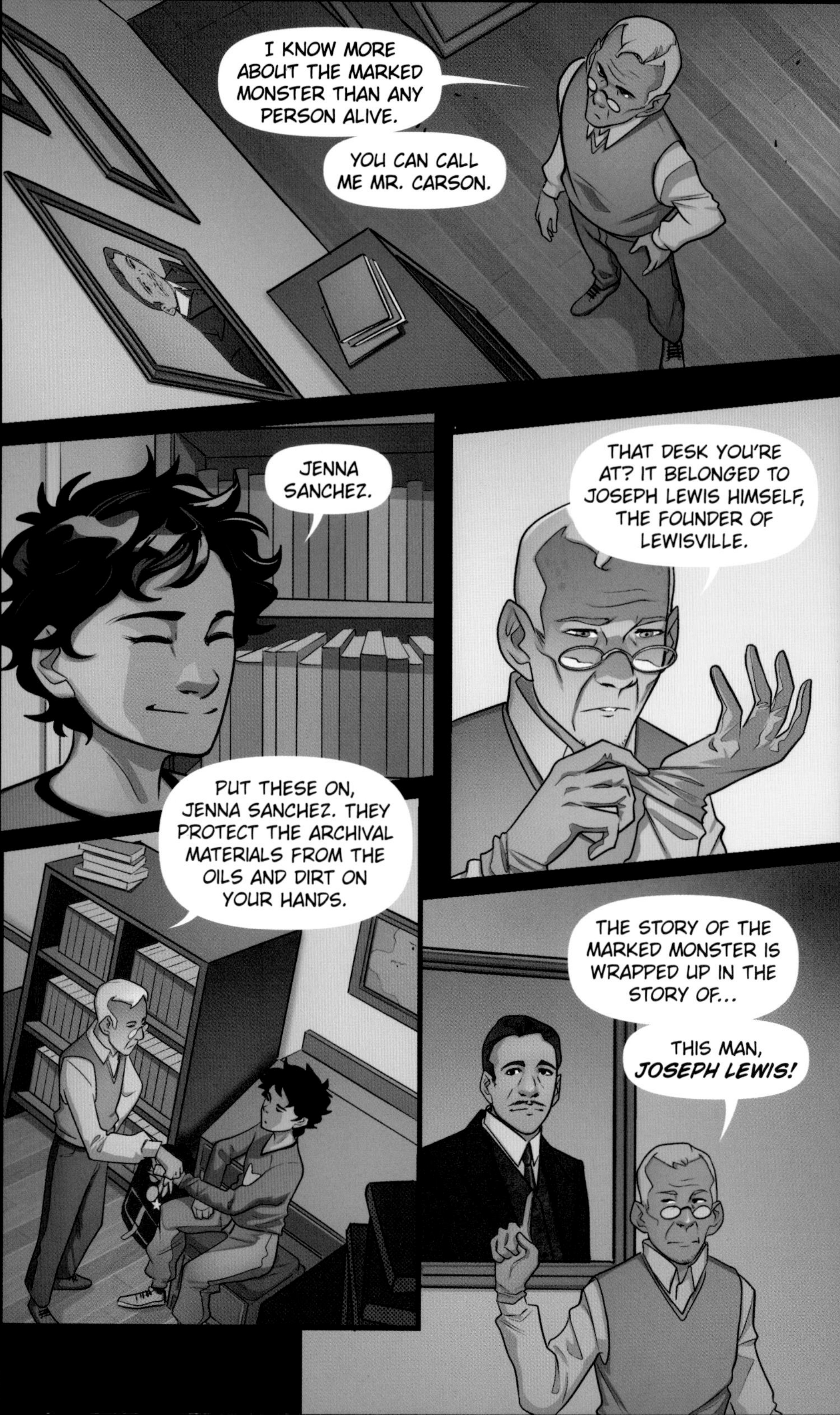
I KNOW MORE ABOUT THE MARKED MONSTER THAN ANY PERSON ALIVE.
YOU CAN CALL ME MR. CARSON.
JENNA SANCHEZ.
THAT DESK YOU'RE AT? IT BELONGED TO JOSEPH LEWIS HIMSELF, THE FOUNDER OF LEWISVILLE.
PUT THESE ON, JENNA SANCHEZ. THEY PROTECT THE ARCHIVAL MATERIALS FROM THE OILS AND DIRT ON YOUR HANDS.
THE STORY OF THE MARKED MONSTER IS WRAPPED UP IN THE STORY OF...
THIS MAN, ***JOSEPH LEWIS!***

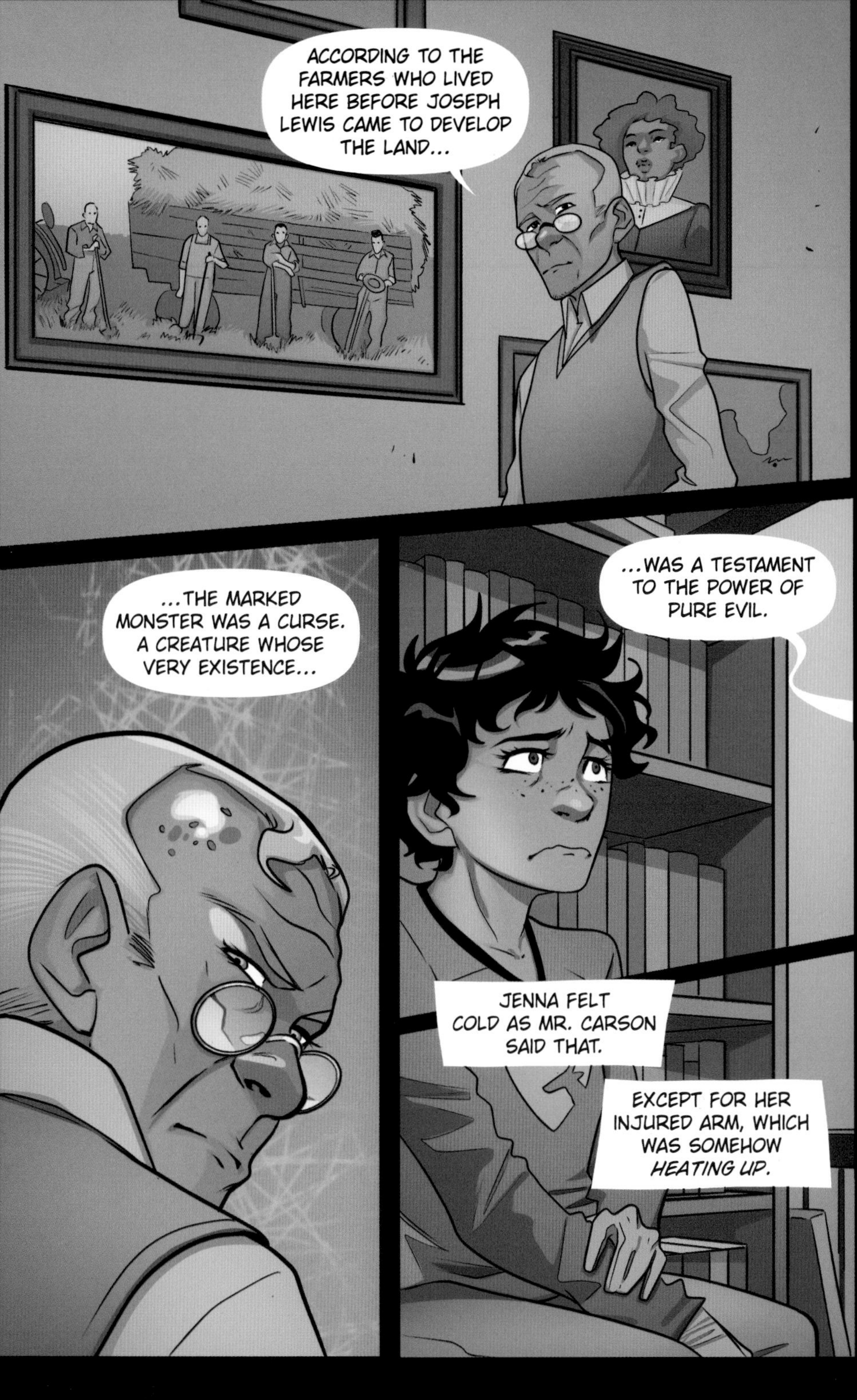
ACCORDING TO THE FARMERS WHO LIVED HERE BEFORE JOSEPH LEWIS CAME TO DEVELOP THE LAND...
...THE MARKED MONSTER WAS A CURSE. A CREATURE WHOSE VERY EXISTENCE...
...WAS A TESTAMENT TO THE POWER OF PURE EVIL.
JENNA FELT COLD AS MR. CARSON SAID THAT.
EXCEPT FOR HER INJURED ARM, WHICH WAS SOMEHOW *HEATING UP*.

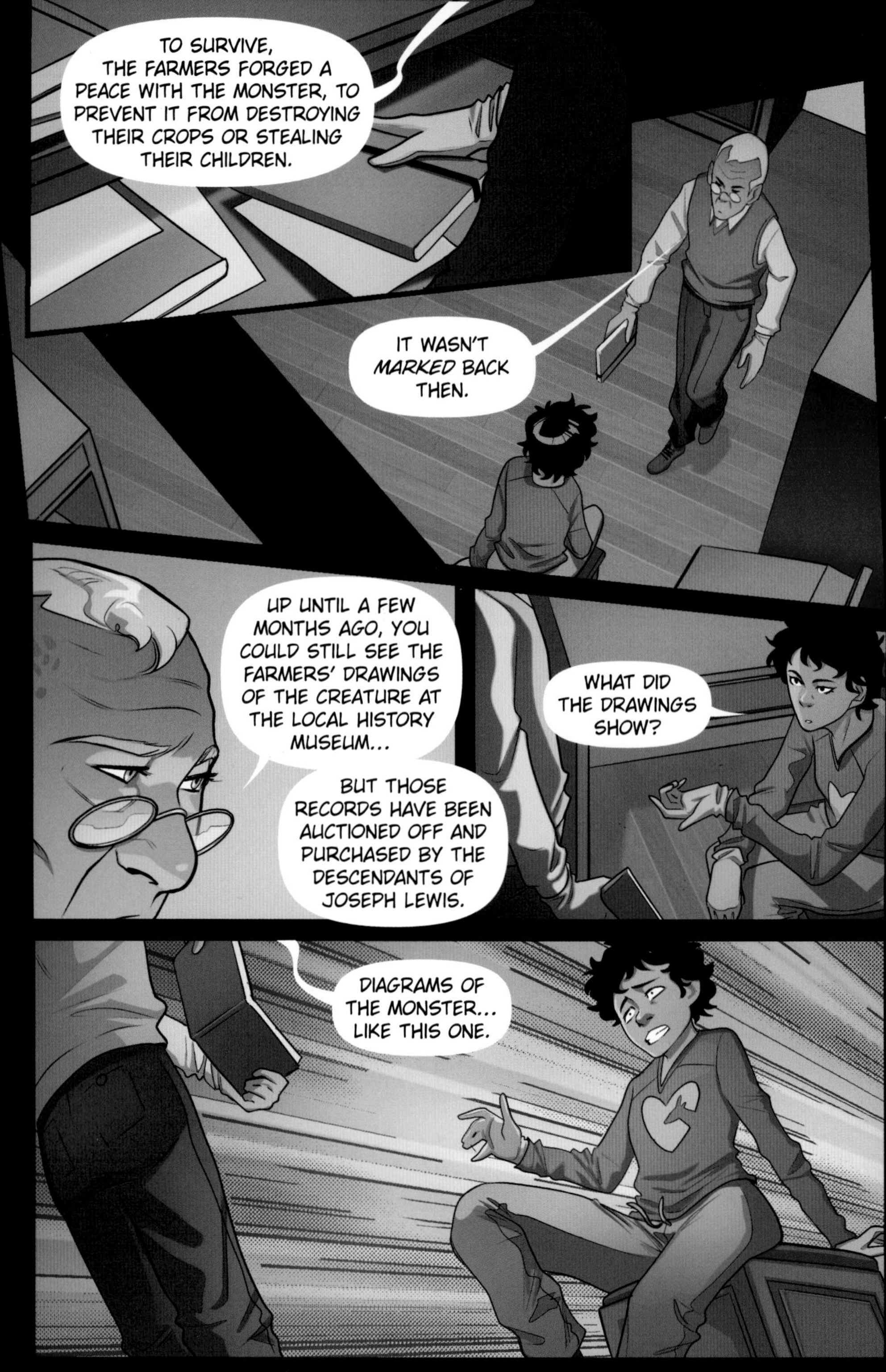
TO SURVIVE, THE FARMERS FORGED A PEACE WITH THE MONSTER, TO PREVENT IT FROM DESTROYING THEIR CROPS OR STEALING THEIR CHILDREN.
IT WASN'T *MARKED* BACK THEN.
UP UNTIL A FEW MONTHS AGO, YOU COULD STILL SEE THE FARMERS' DRAWINGS OF THE CREATURE AT THE LOCAL HISTORY MUSEUM...
BUT THOSE RECORDS HAVE BEEN AUCTIONED OFF AND PURCHASED BY THE DESCENDANTS OF JOSEPH LEWIS.
WHAT DID THE DRAWINGS SHOW?
DIAGRAMS OF THE MONSTER... LIKE THIS ONE.

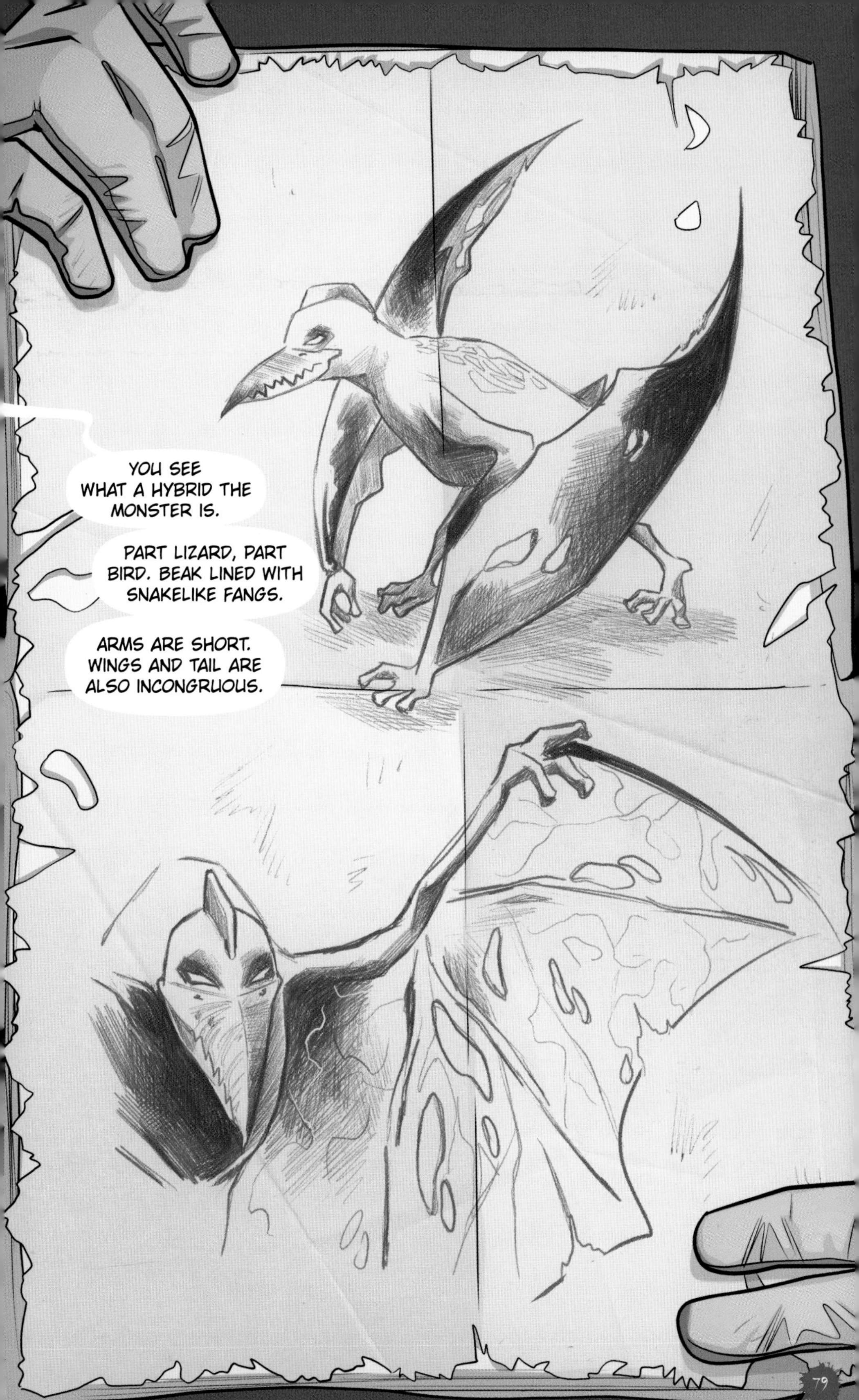
YOU SEE WHAT A HYBRID THE MONSTER IS.
PART LIZARD, PART BIRD. BEAK LINED WITH SNAKELIKE FANGS.
ARMS ARE SHORT. WINGS AND TAIL ARE ALSO INCONGRUOUS.

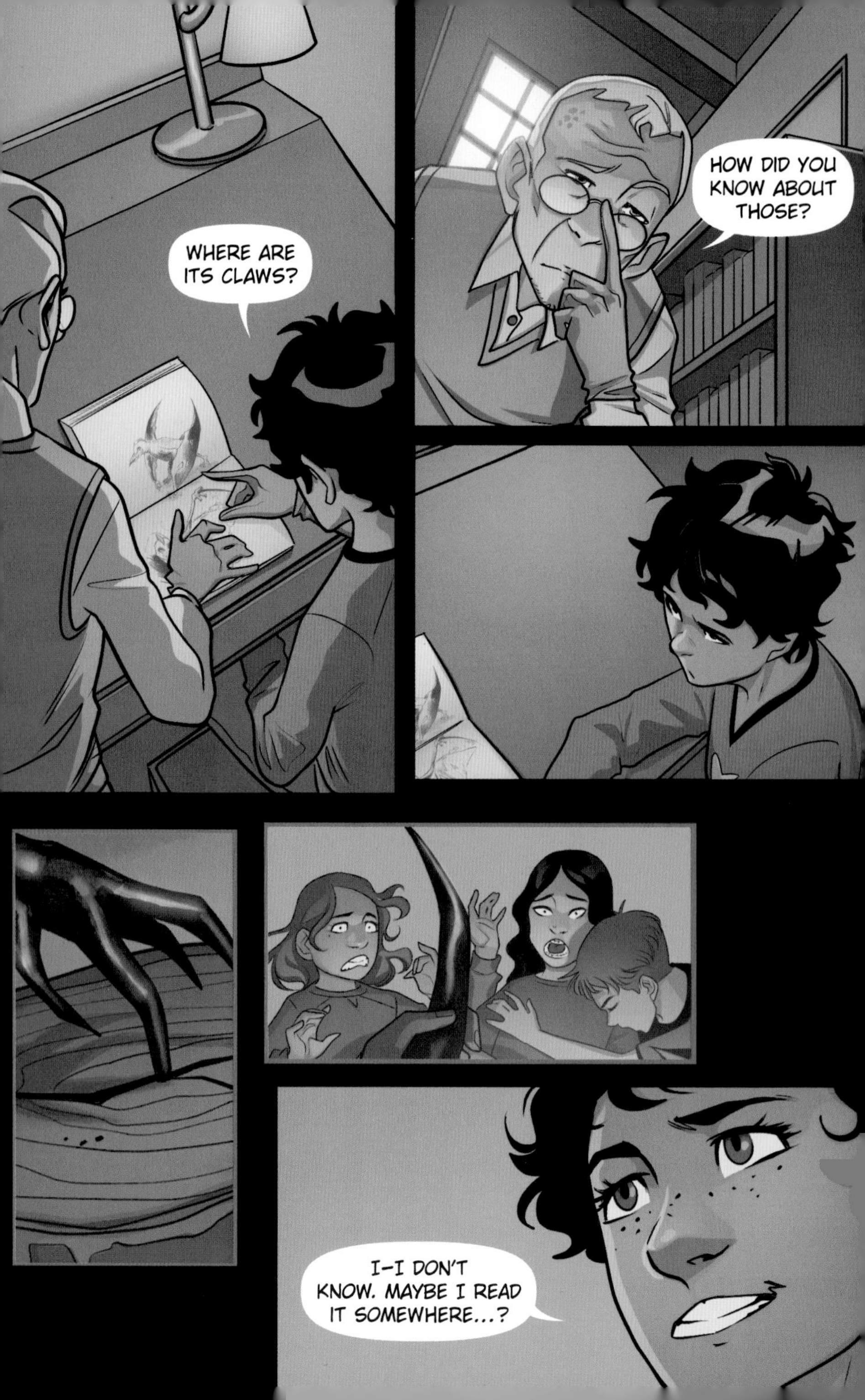
WHERE ARE ITS CLAWS?
HOW DID YOU KNOW ABOUT THOSE?
I-I DON'T KNOW. MAYBE I READ IT SOMEWHERE...?

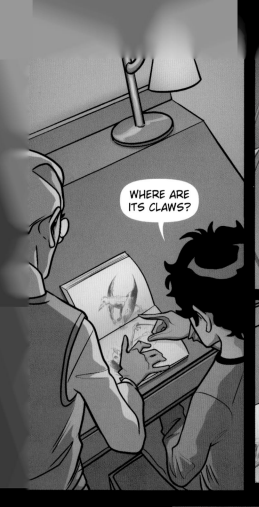

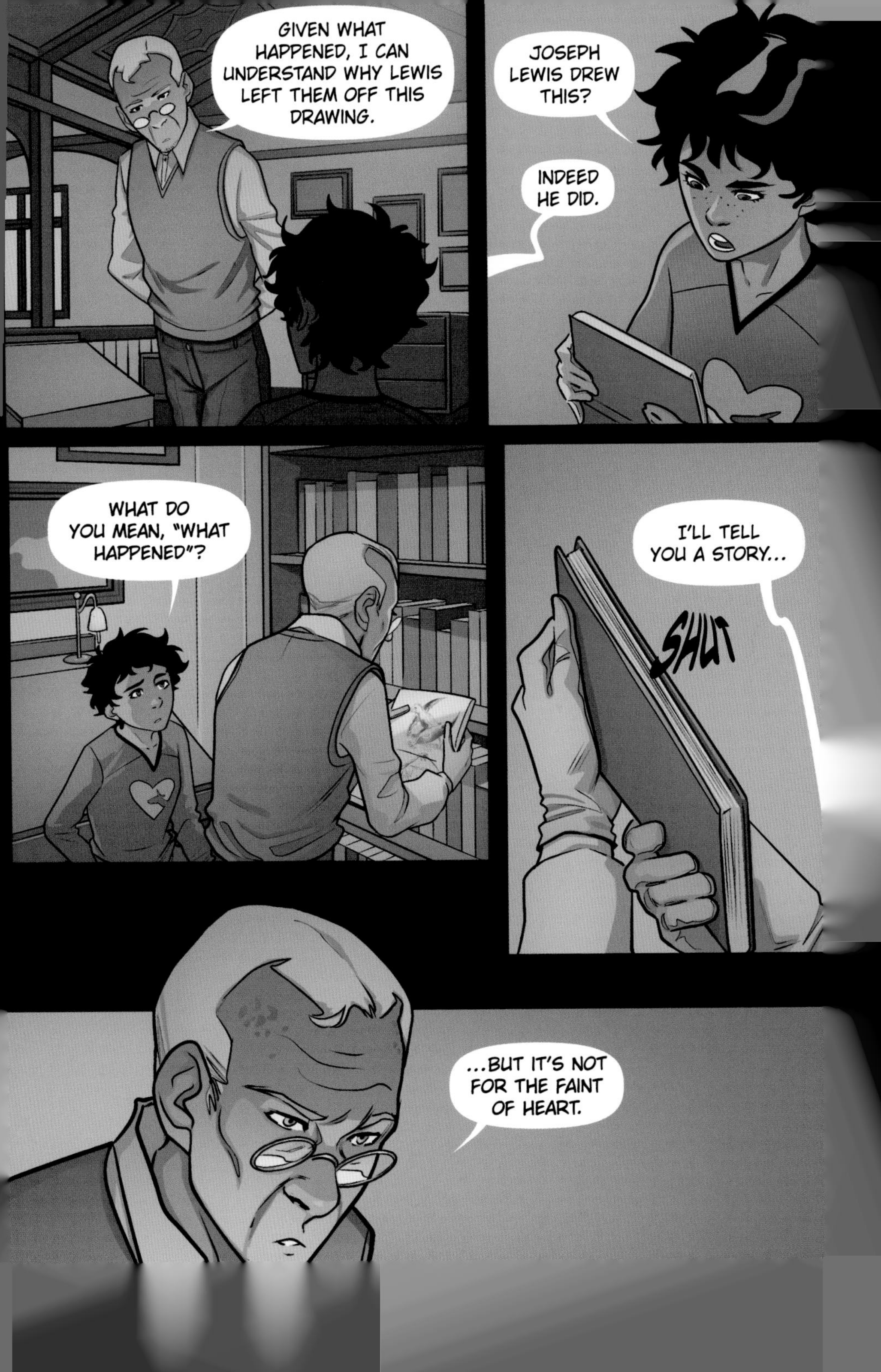
GIVEN WHAT HAPPENED, I CAN UNDERSTAND WHY LEWIS LEFT THEM OFF THIS DRAWING.
JOSEPH LEWIS DREW THIS?
INDEED HE DID.
WHAT DO YOU MEAN, "WHAT HAPPENED"?
I'LL TELL YOU A STORY...
SHUT
...BUT IT'S NOT FOR THE FAINT OF HEART.

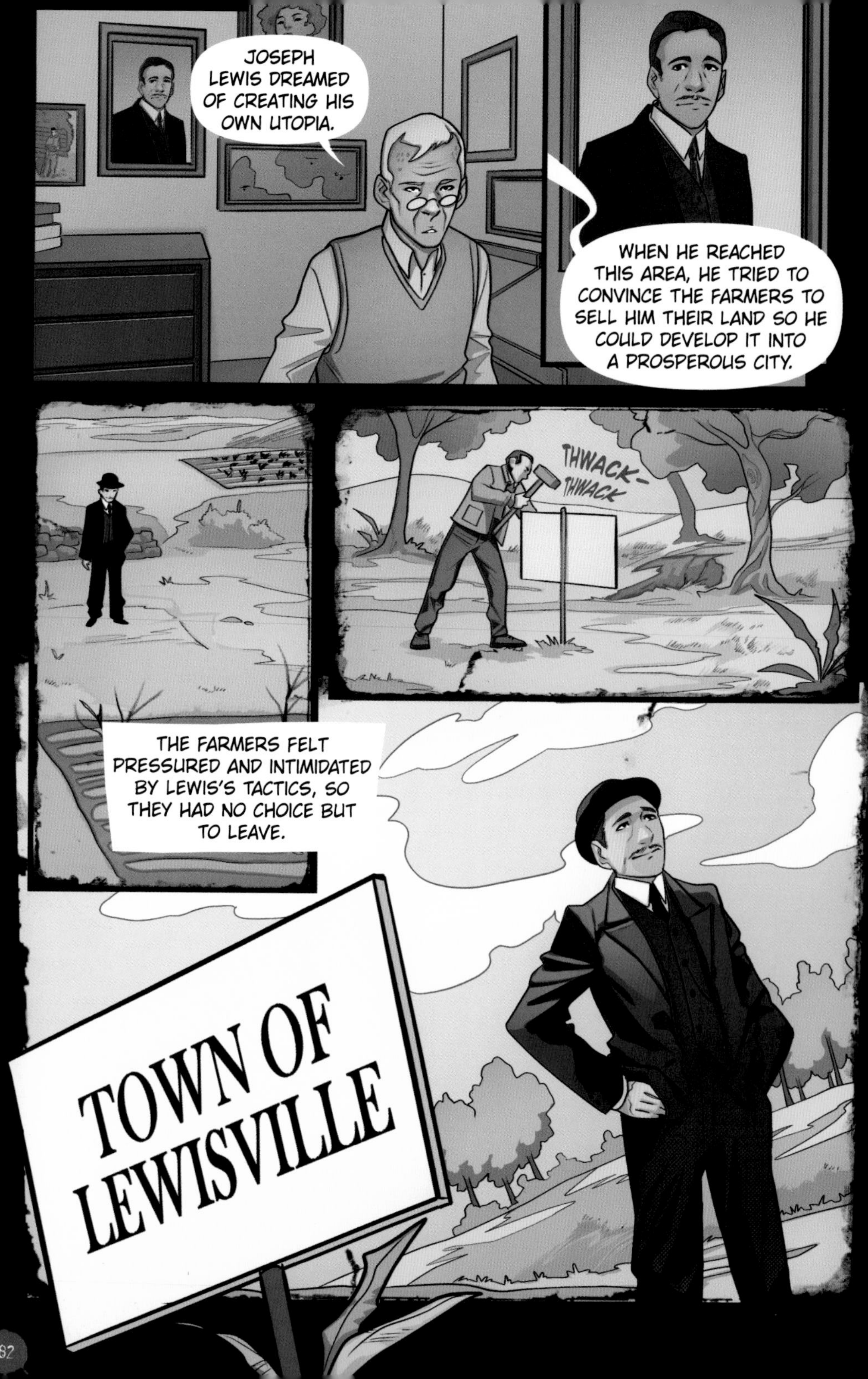
JOSEPH LEWIS DREAMED OF CREATING HIS OWN UTOPIA.
WHEN HE REACHED THIS AREA, HE TRIED TO CONVINCE THE FARMERS TO SELL HIM THEIR LAND SO HE COULD DEVELOP IT INTO A PROSPEROUS CITY.
THWACK-THWACK
THE FARMERS FELT PRESSURED AND INTIMIDATED BY LEWIS'S TACTICS, SO THEY HAD NO CHOICE BUT TO LEAVE.
TOWN OF LEWISVILLE

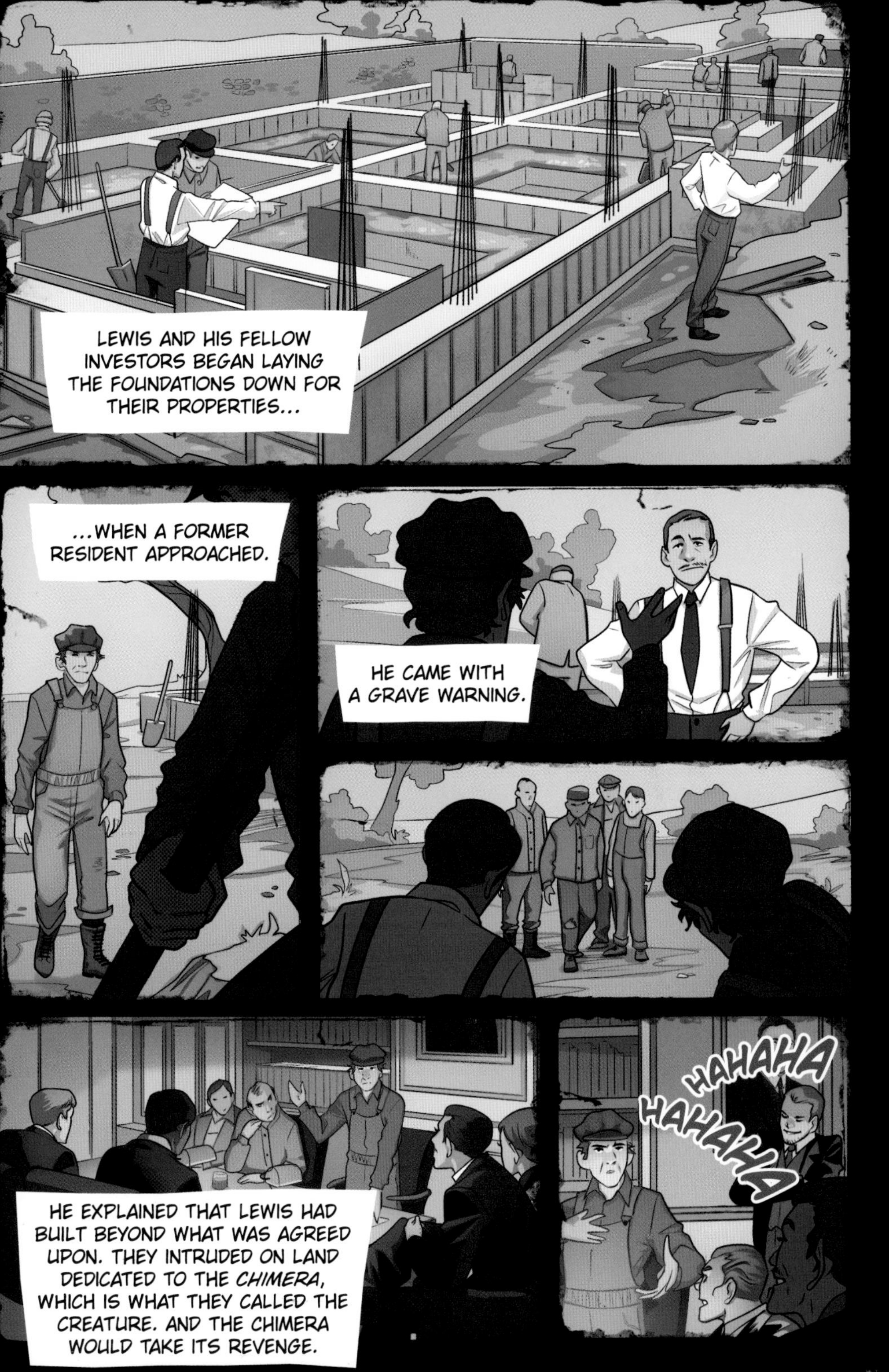

LEWIS AND HIS FELLOW INVESTORS BEGAN LAYING THE FOUNDATIONS DOWN FOR THEIR PROPERTIES...
...WHEN A FORMER RESIDENT APPROACHED.
HE CAME WITH A GRAVE WARNING.
HE EXPLAINED THAT LEWIS HAD BUILT BEYOND WHAT WAS AGREED UPON. THEY INTRUDED ON LAND DEDICATED TO THE *CHIMERA*, WHICH IS WHAT THEY CALLED THE CREATURE. AND THE CHIMERA WOULD TAKE ITS REVENGE.
HAHAHA
HAHAHA

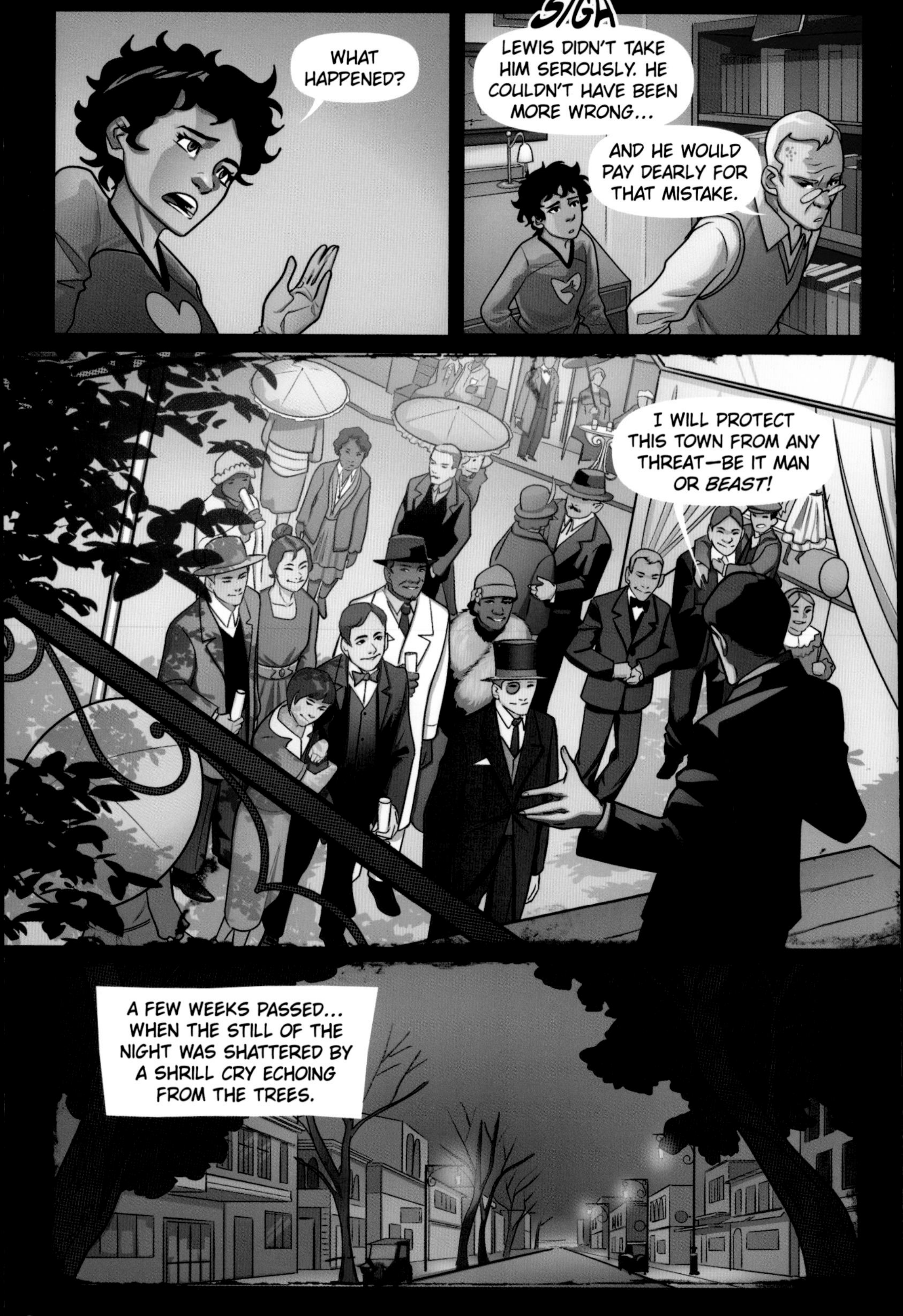
WHAT HAPPENED?
SIGH
LEWIS DIDN'T TAKE HIM SERIOUSLY. HE COULDN'T HAVE BEEN MORE WRONG...
AND HE WOULD PAY DEARLY FOR THAT MISTAKE.
I WILL PROTECT THIS TOWN FROM ANY THREAT—BE IT MAN OR *BEAST*!
A FEW WEEKS PASSED... WHEN THE STILL OF THE NIGHT WAS SHATTERED BY A SHRILL CRY ECHOING FROM THE TREES.

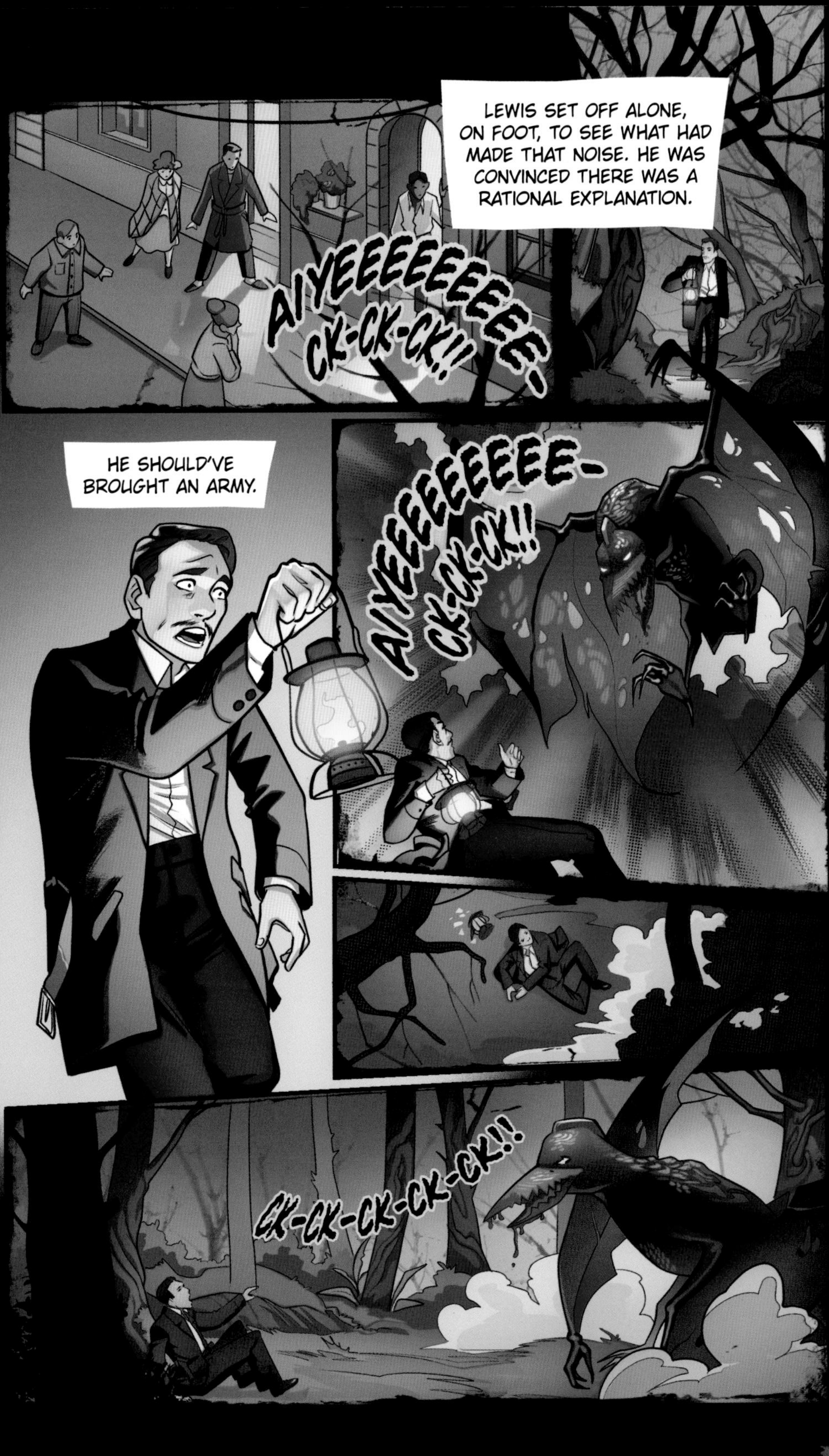
LEWIS SET OFF ALONE, ON FOOT, TO SEE WHAT HAD MADE THAT NOISE. HE WAS CONVINCED THERE WAS A RATIONAL EXPLANATION.
AIYEEEEEEEEEE-CK-CK-CK!!
HE SHOULD'VE BROUGHT AN ARMY.
AIYEEEEEEEEEE-CK-CK-CK!!
CK-CK-CK-CK-CK!!

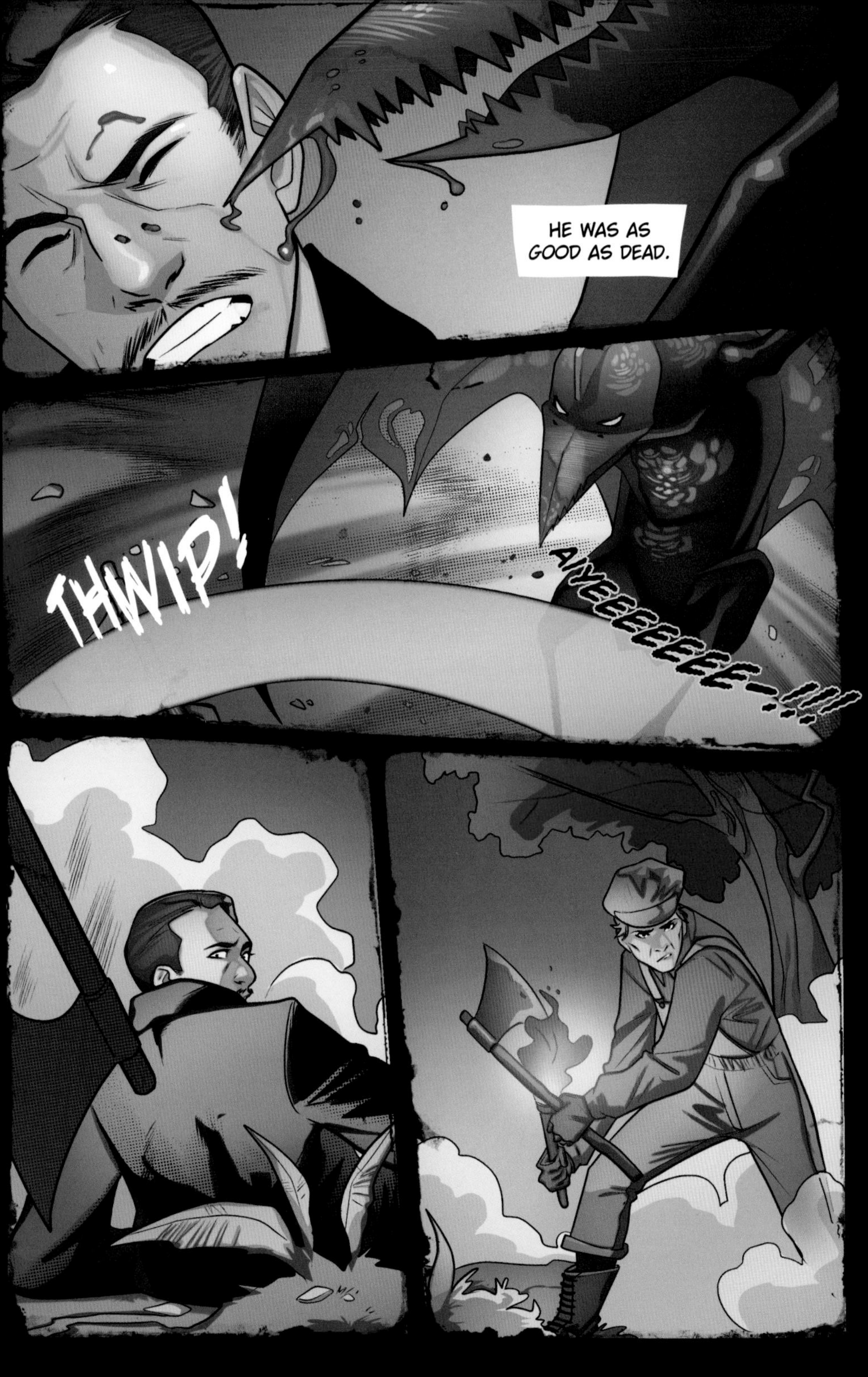
HE WAS AS GOOD AS DEAD.
THWIP!
AIYEEEEEEEE--!!!

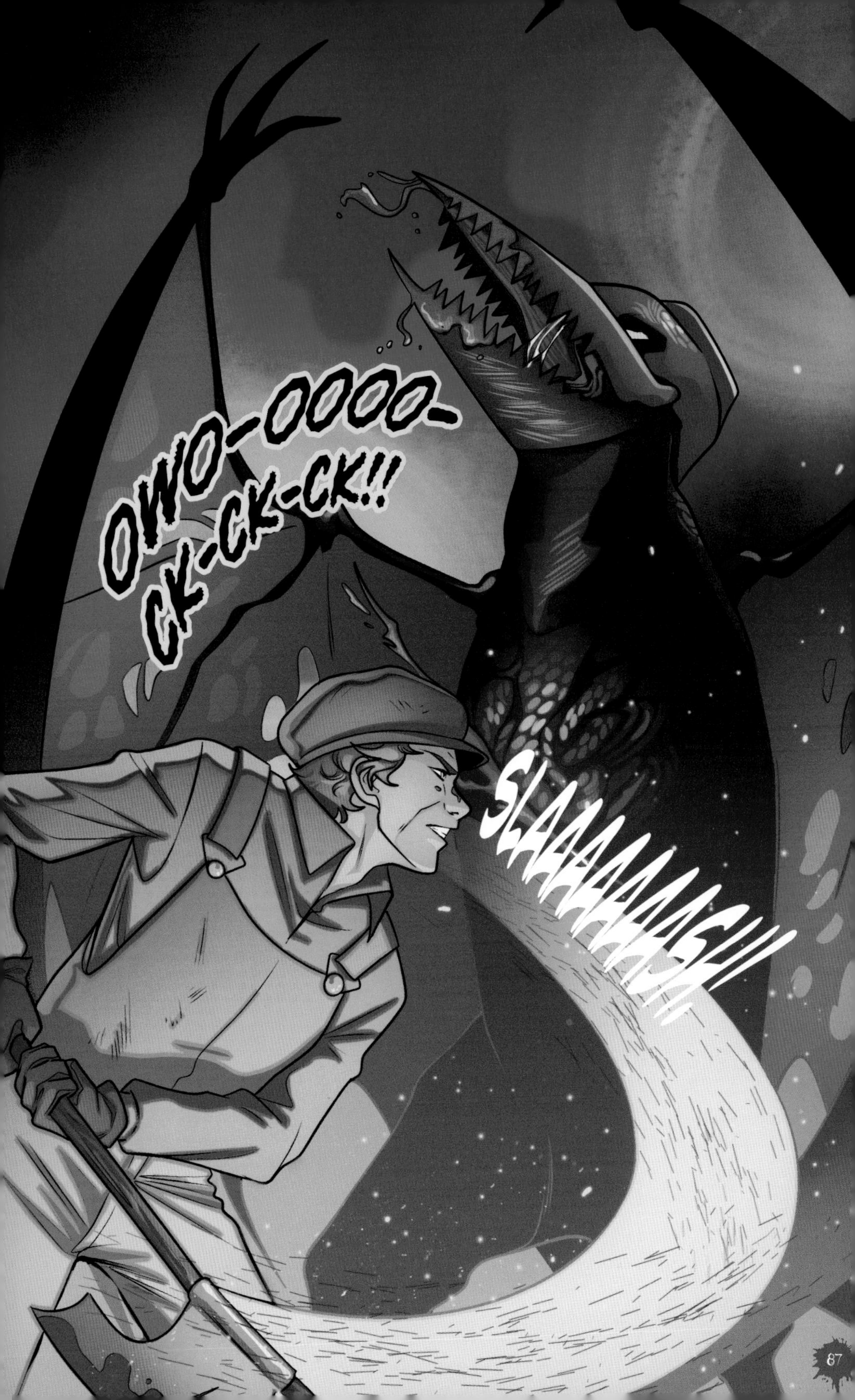
OWO-OOOO-
CK-CK-CK!!
SLAAAAAAAGH!!

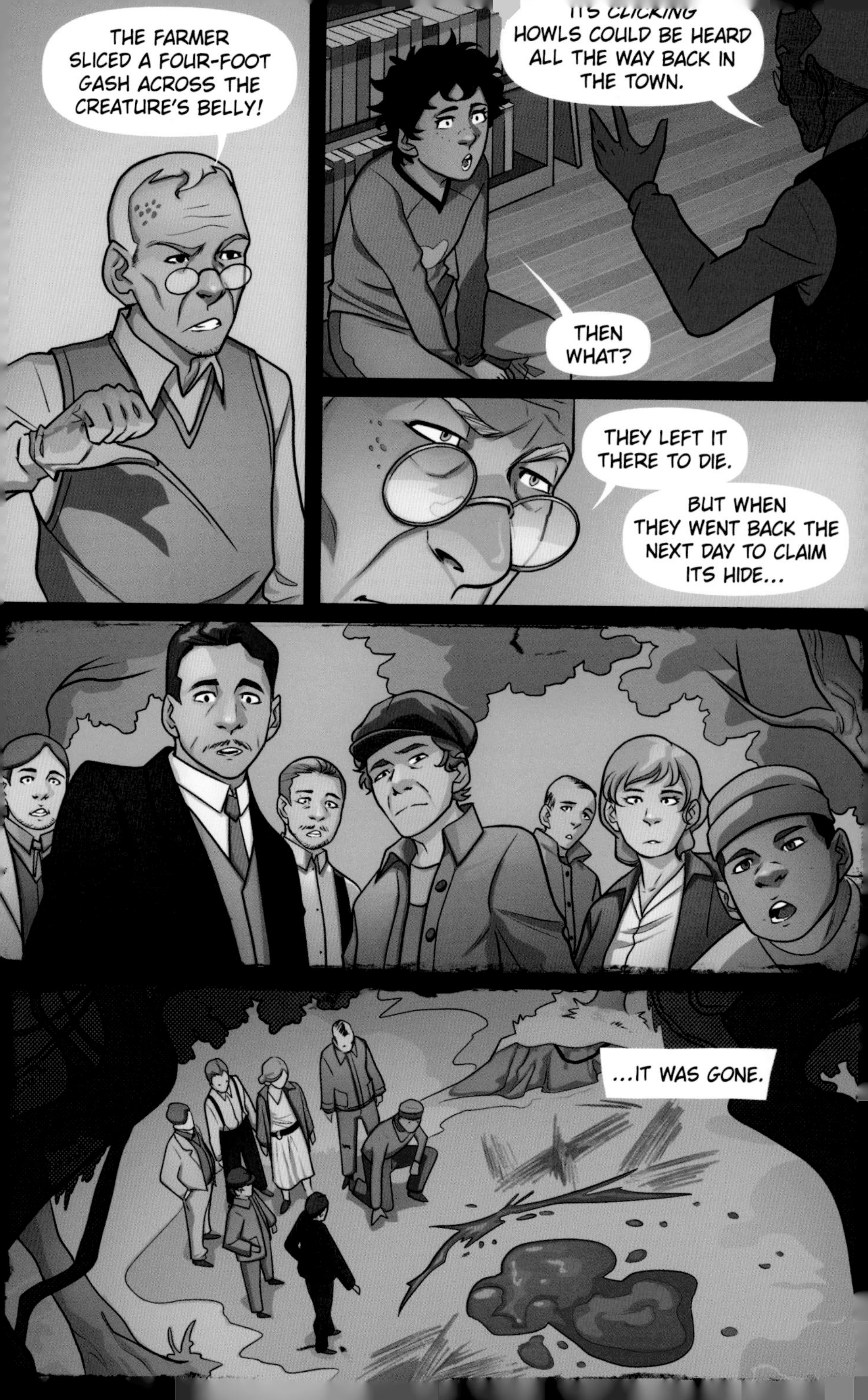
THE FARMER SLICED A FOUR-FOOT GASH ACROSS THE CREATURE'S BELLY!
IT'S CLICKING HOWLS COULD BE HEARD ALL THE WAY BACK IN THE TOWN.
THEN WHAT?
THEY LEFT IT THERE TO DIE.
BUT WHEN THEY WENT BACK THE NEXT DAY TO CLAIM ITS HIDE...
...IT WAS GONE.

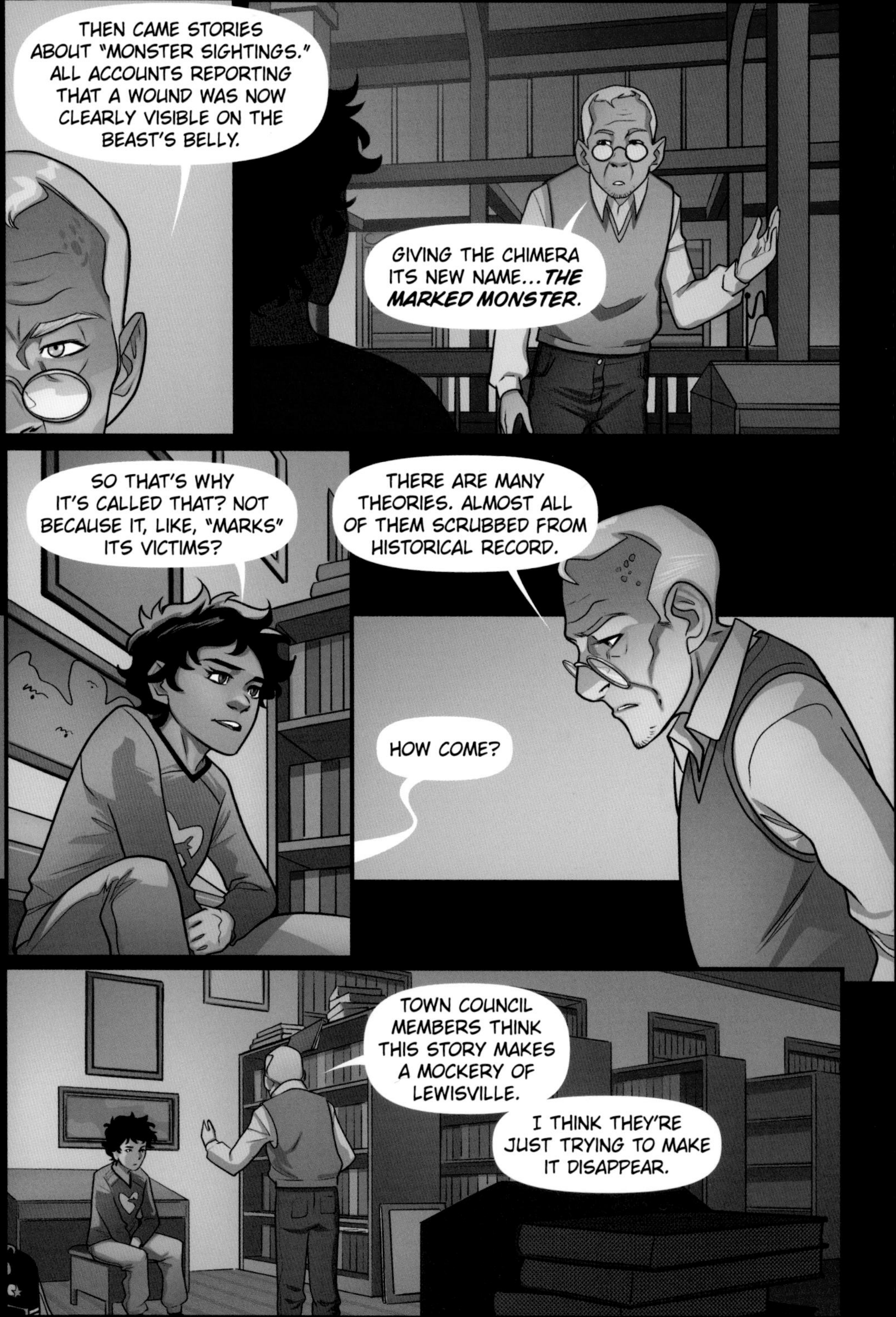
THEN CAME STORIES ABOUT "MONSTER SIGHTINGS." ALL ACCOUNTS REPORTING THAT A WOUND WAS NOW CLEARLY VISIBLE ON THE BEAST'S BELLY.
GIVING THE CHIMERA ITS NEW NAME...*THE MARKED MONSTER.*
SO THAT'S WHY IT'S CALLED THAT? NOT BECAUSE IT, LIKE, "MARKS" ITS VICTIMS?
THERE ARE MANY THEORIES. ALMOST ALL OF THEM SCRUBBED FROM HISTORICAL RECORD.
HOW COME?
TOWN COUNCIL MEMBERS THINK THIS STORY MAKES A MOCKERY OF LEWISVILLE.
I THINK THEY'RE JUST TRYING TO MAKE IT DISAPPEAR.

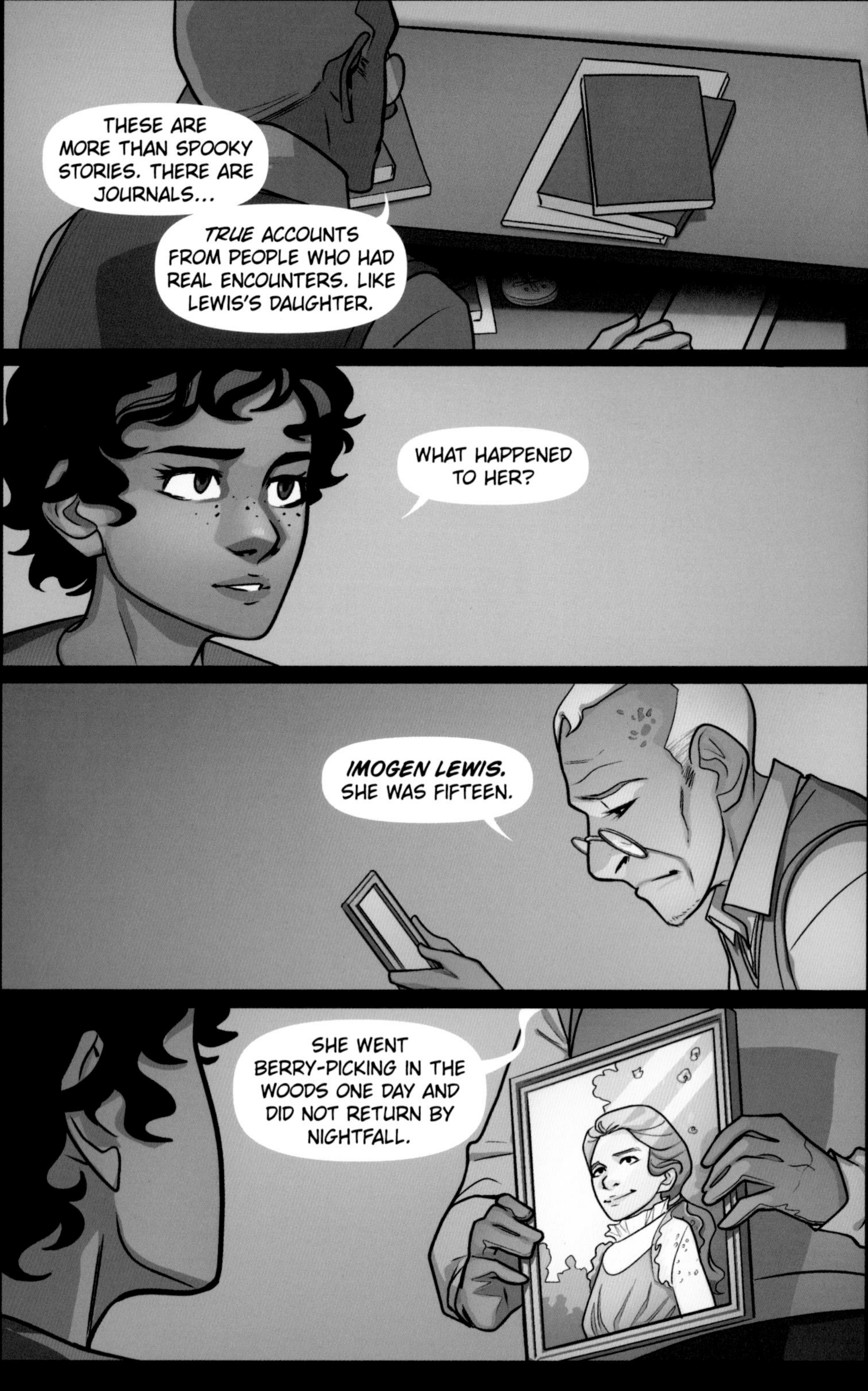
THESE ARE MORE THAN SPOOKY STORIES. THERE ARE JOURNALS...
TRUE ACCOUNTS FROM PEOPLE WHO HAD REAL ENCOUNTERS. LIKE LEWIS'S DAUGHTER.
WHAT HAPPENED TO HER?
IMOGEN LEWIS. SHE WAS FIFTEEN.
SHE WENT BERRY-PICKING IN THE WOODS ONE DAY AND DID NOT RETURN BY NIGHTFALL.

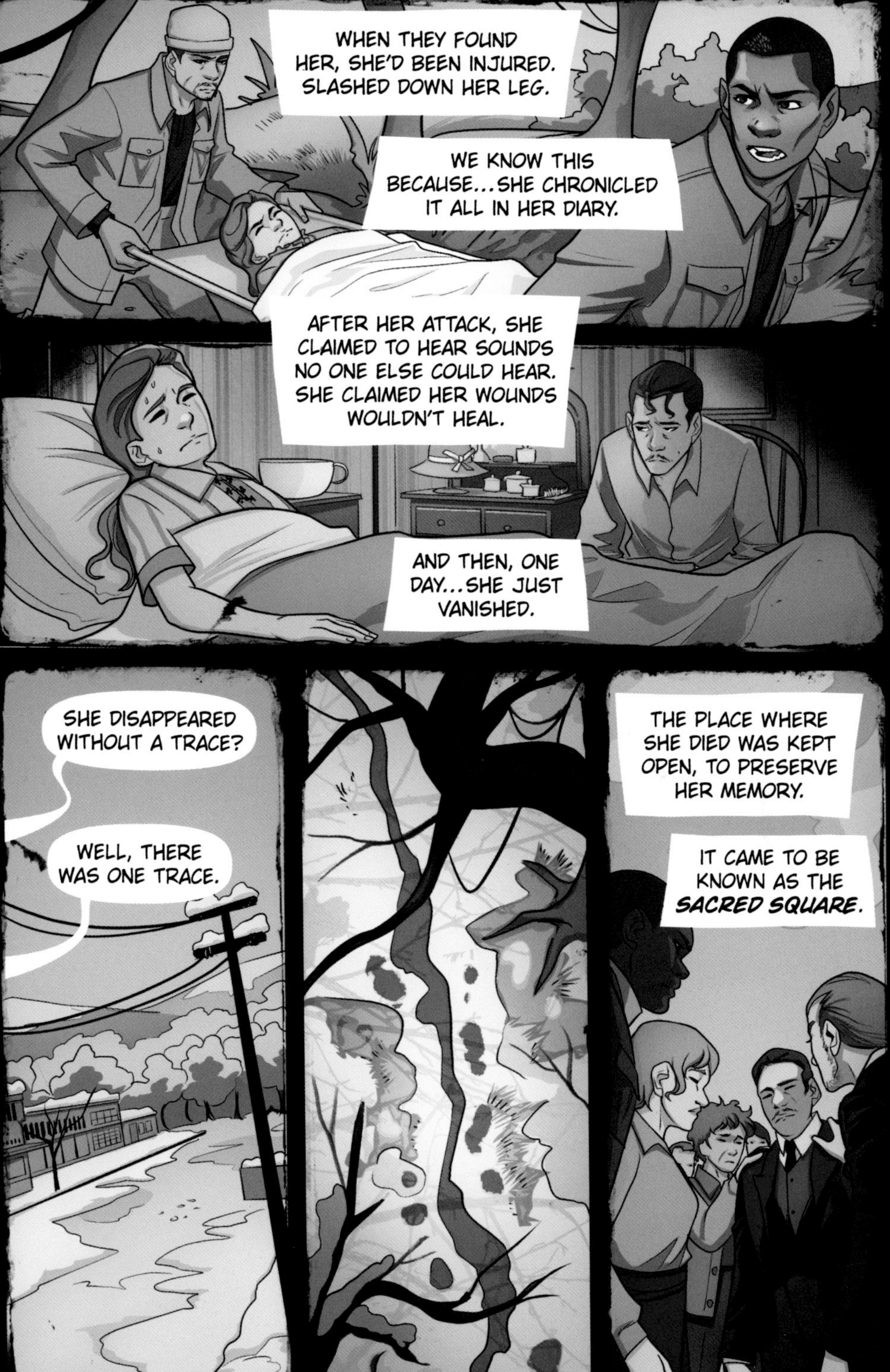
WHEN THEY FOUND HER, SHE'D BEEN INJURED. SLASHED DOWN HER LEG.
WE KNOW THIS BECAUSE...SHE CHRONICLED IT ALL IN HER DIARY.
AFTER HER ATTACK, SHE CLAIMED TO HEAR SOUNDS NO ONE ELSE COULD HEAR. SHE CLAIMED HER WOUNDS WOULDN'T HEAL.
AND THEN, ONE DAY...SHE JUST VANISHED.
SHE DISAPPEARED WITHOUT A TRACE?
WELL, THERE WAS ONE TRACE.
THE PLACE WHERE SHE DIED WAS KEPT OPEN, TO PRESERVE HER MEMORY.
IT CAME TO BE KNOWN AS THE *SACRED SQUARE*.

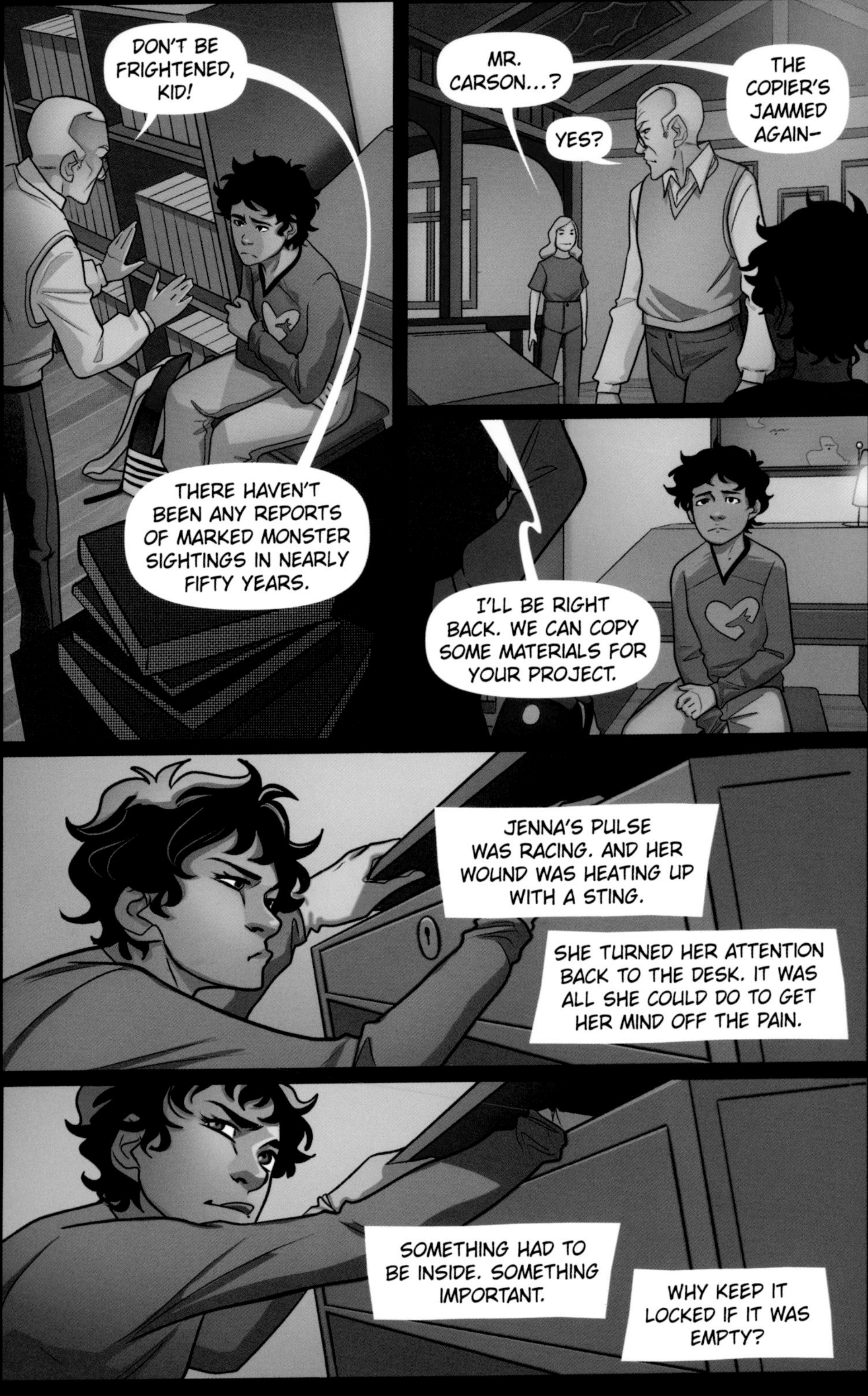
DON'T BE FRIGHTENED, KID!
THERE HAVEN'T BEEN ANY REPORTS OF MARKED MONSTER SIGHTINGS IN NEARLY FIFTY YEARS.
MR. CARSON...?
YES?
THE COPIER'S JAMMED AGAIN–
I'LL BE RIGHT BACK. WE CAN COPY SOME MATERIALS FOR YOUR PROJECT.
JENNA'S PULSE WAS RACING. AND HER WOUND WAS HEATING UP WITH A STING.
SHE TURNED HER ATTENTION BACK TO THE DESK. IT WAS ALL SHE COULD DO TO GET HER MIND OFF THE PAIN.
SOMETHING HAD TO BE INSIDE. SOMETHING IMPORTANT.
WHY KEEP IT LOCKED IF IT WAS EMPTY?

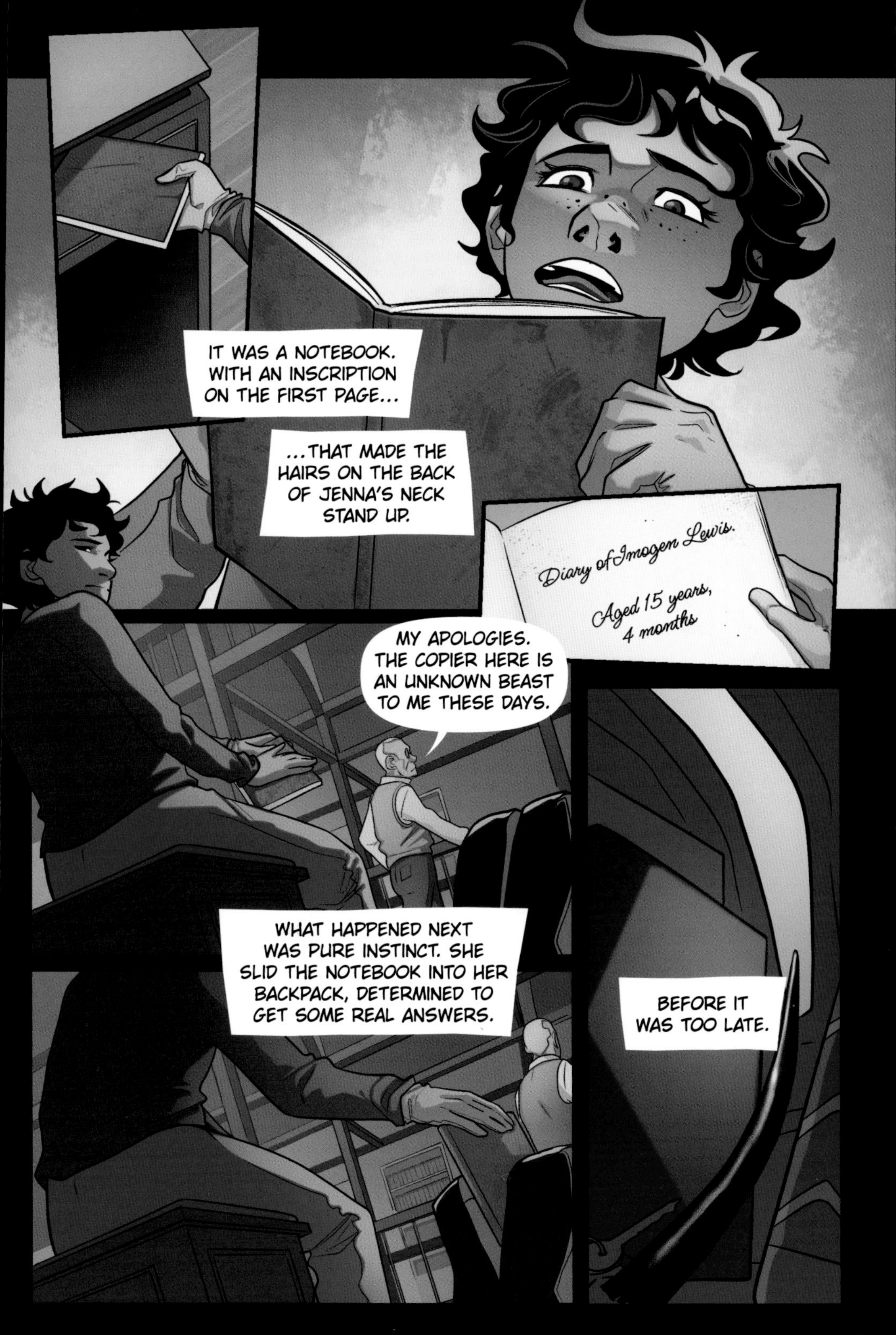
IT WAS A NOTEBOOK. WITH AN INSCRIPTION ON THE FIRST PAGE...
...THAT MADE THE HAIRS ON THE BACK OF JENNA'S NECK STAND UP.
Diary of Imogen Lewis.
Aged 15 years, 4 months
MY APOLOGIES. THE COPIER HERE IS AN UNKNOWN BEAST TO ME THESE DAYS.
WHAT HAPPENED NEXT WAS PURE INSTINCT. SHE SLID THE NOTEBOOK INTO HER BACKPACK, DETERMINED TO GET SOME REAL ANSWERS.
BEFORE IT WAS TOO LATE.

CHAPTER 8

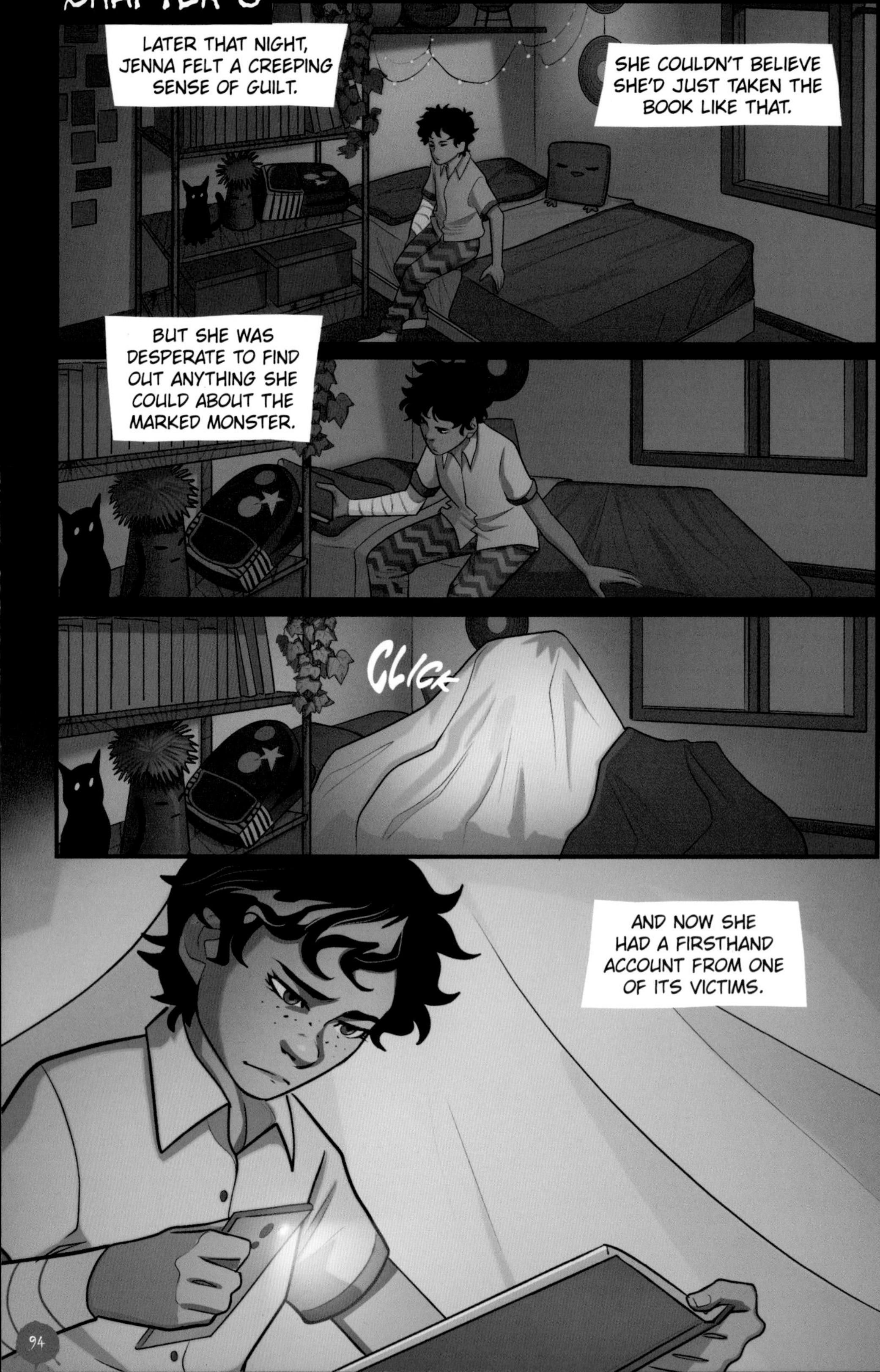

LATER THAT NIGHT, JENNA FELT A CREEPING SENSE OF GUILT.
SHE COULDN'T BELIEVE SHE'D JUST TAKEN THE BOOK LIKE THAT.
BUT SHE WAS DESPERATE TO FIND OUT ANYTHING SHE COULD ABOUT THE MARKED MONSTER.
CLICK
AND NOW SHE HAD A FIRSTHAND ACCOUNT FROM ONE OF ITS VICTIMS.

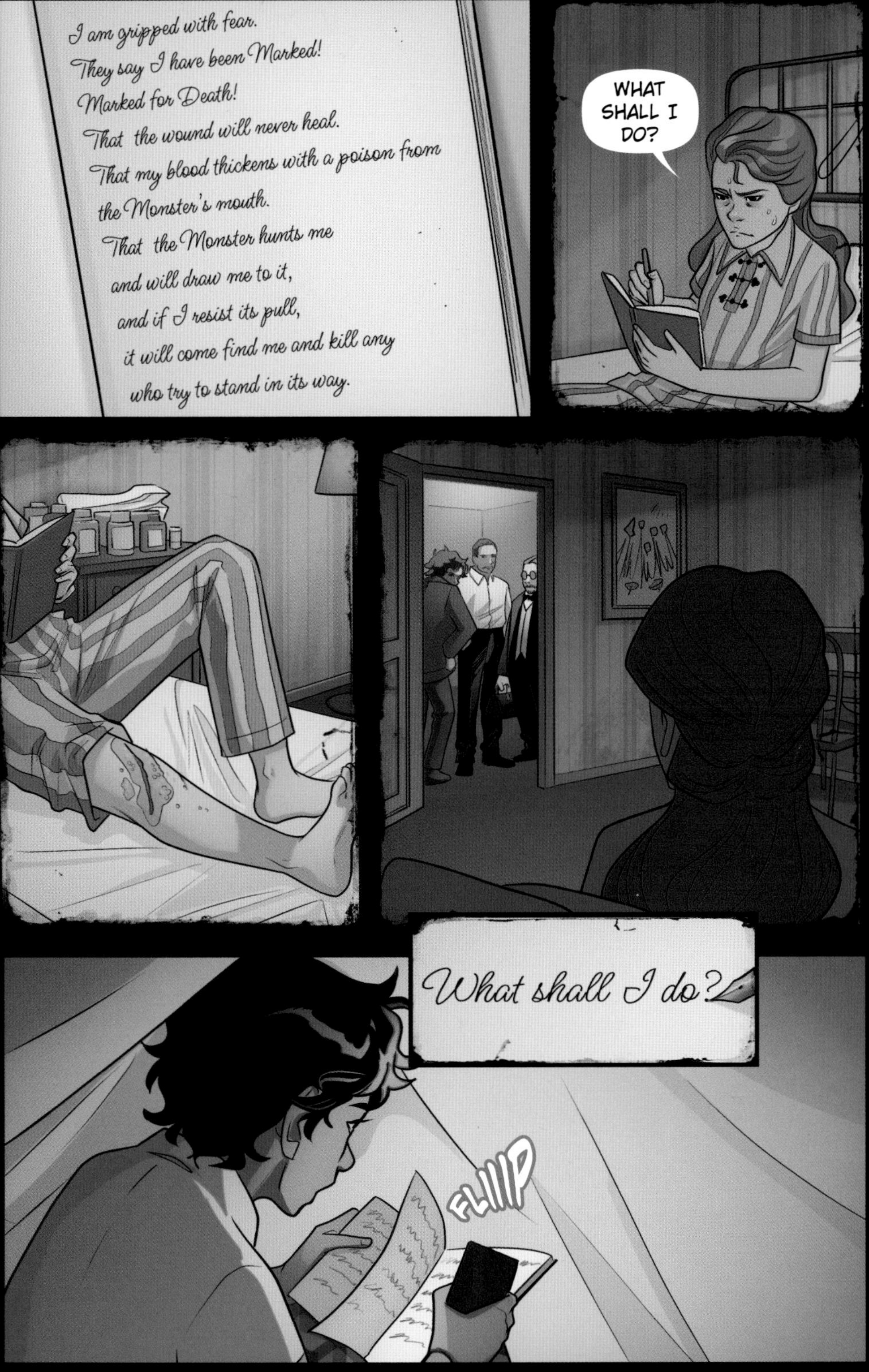
I am gripped with fear.
They say I have been Marked!
Marked for Death!
That the wound will never heal.
That my blood thickens with a poison from the Monster's mouth.
That the Monster hunts me
and will draw me to it,
and if I resist its pull,
it will come find me and kill any
who try to stand in its way.
WHAT SHALL I DO?
What shall I do?
FLIIIP

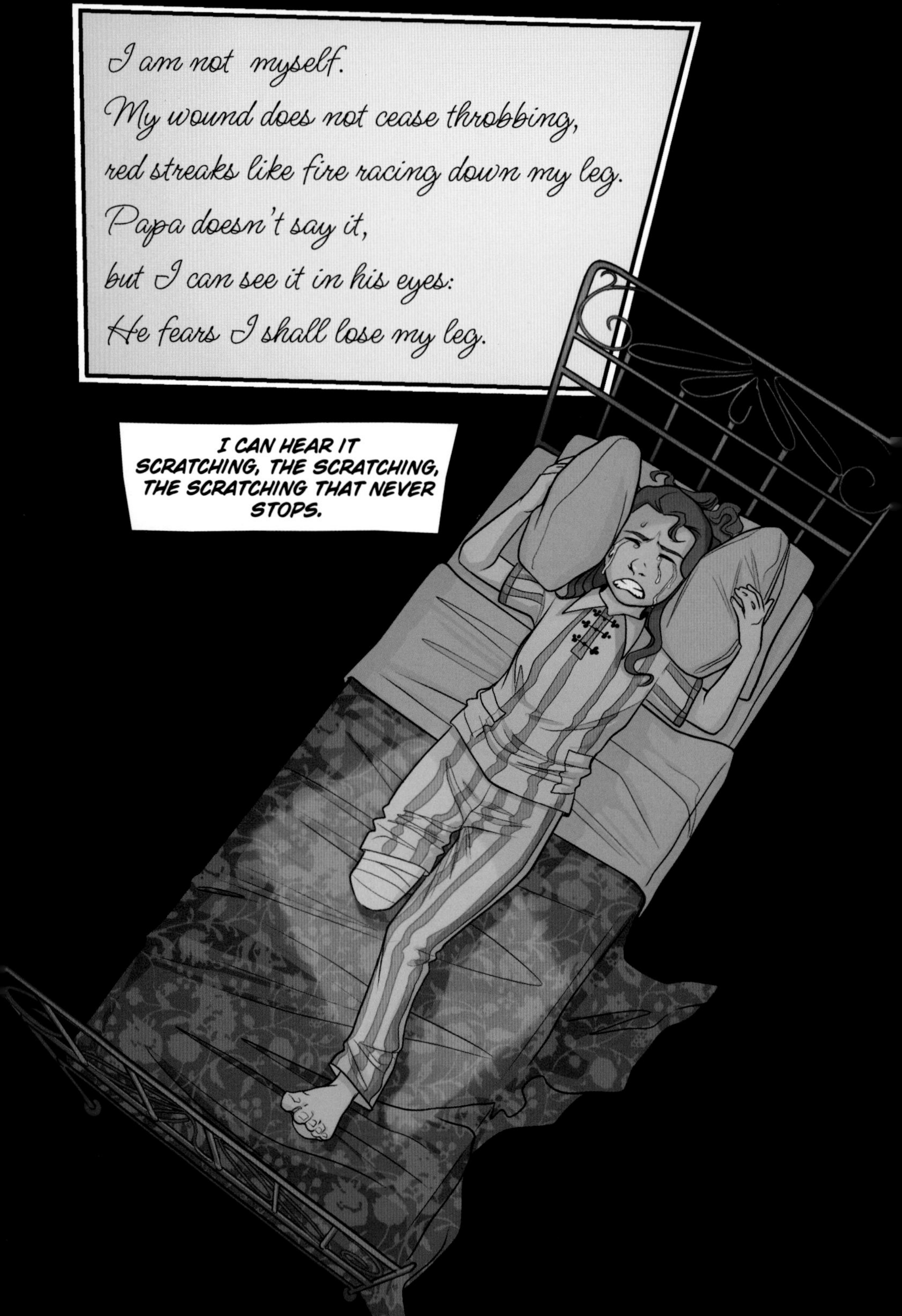
I am not myself.
My wound does not cease throbbing,
red streaks like fire racing down my leg.
Papa doesn't say it,
but I can see it in his eyes:
He fears I shall lose my leg.
I CAN HEAR IT SCRATCHING, THE SCRATCHING, THE SCRATCHING THAT NEVER STOPS.

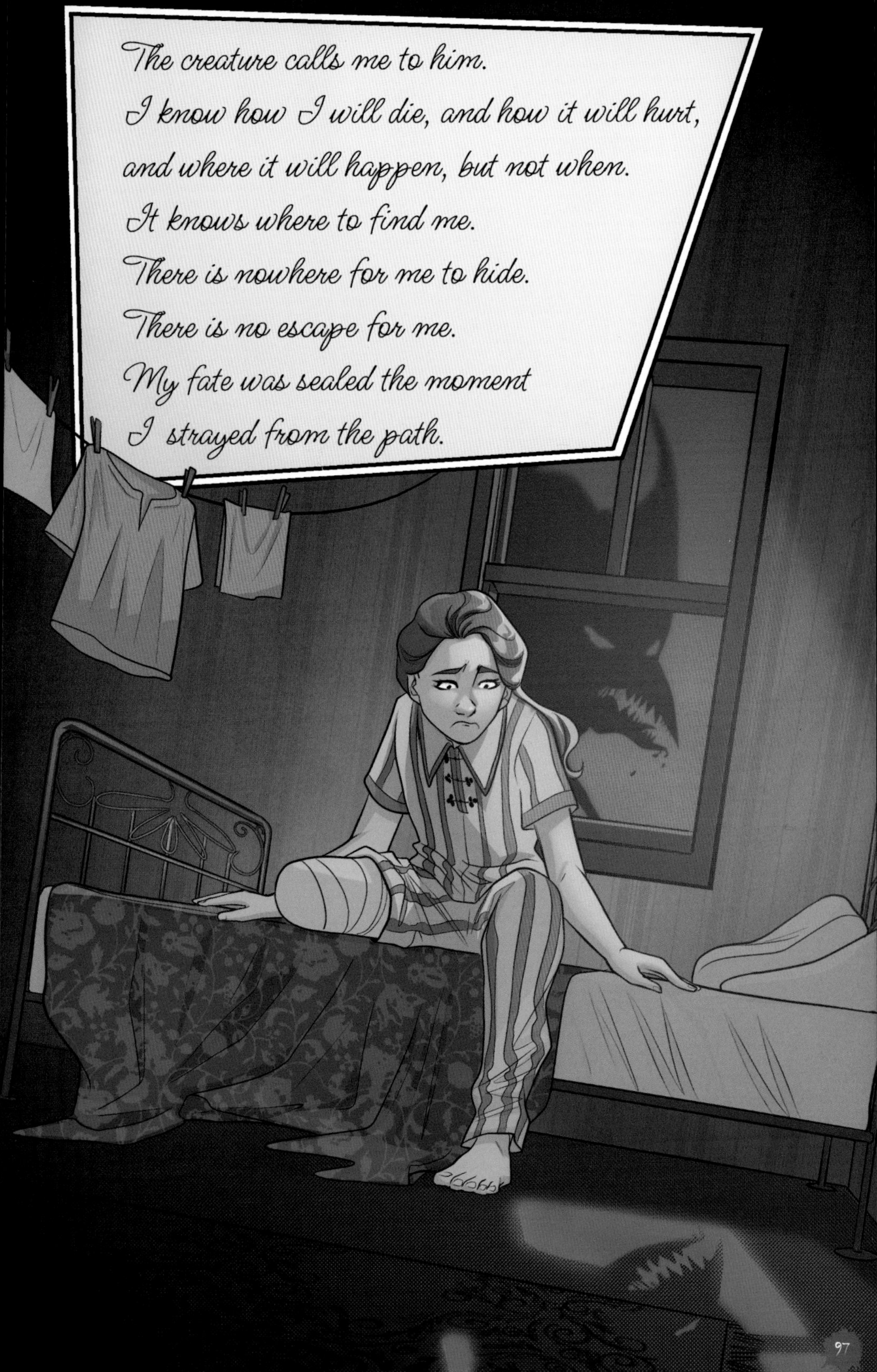
The creature calls me to him.
I know how I will die, and how it will hurt,
and where it will happen, but not when.
It knows where to find me.
There is nowhere for me to hide.
There is no escape for me.
My fate was sealed the moment
I strayed from the path.

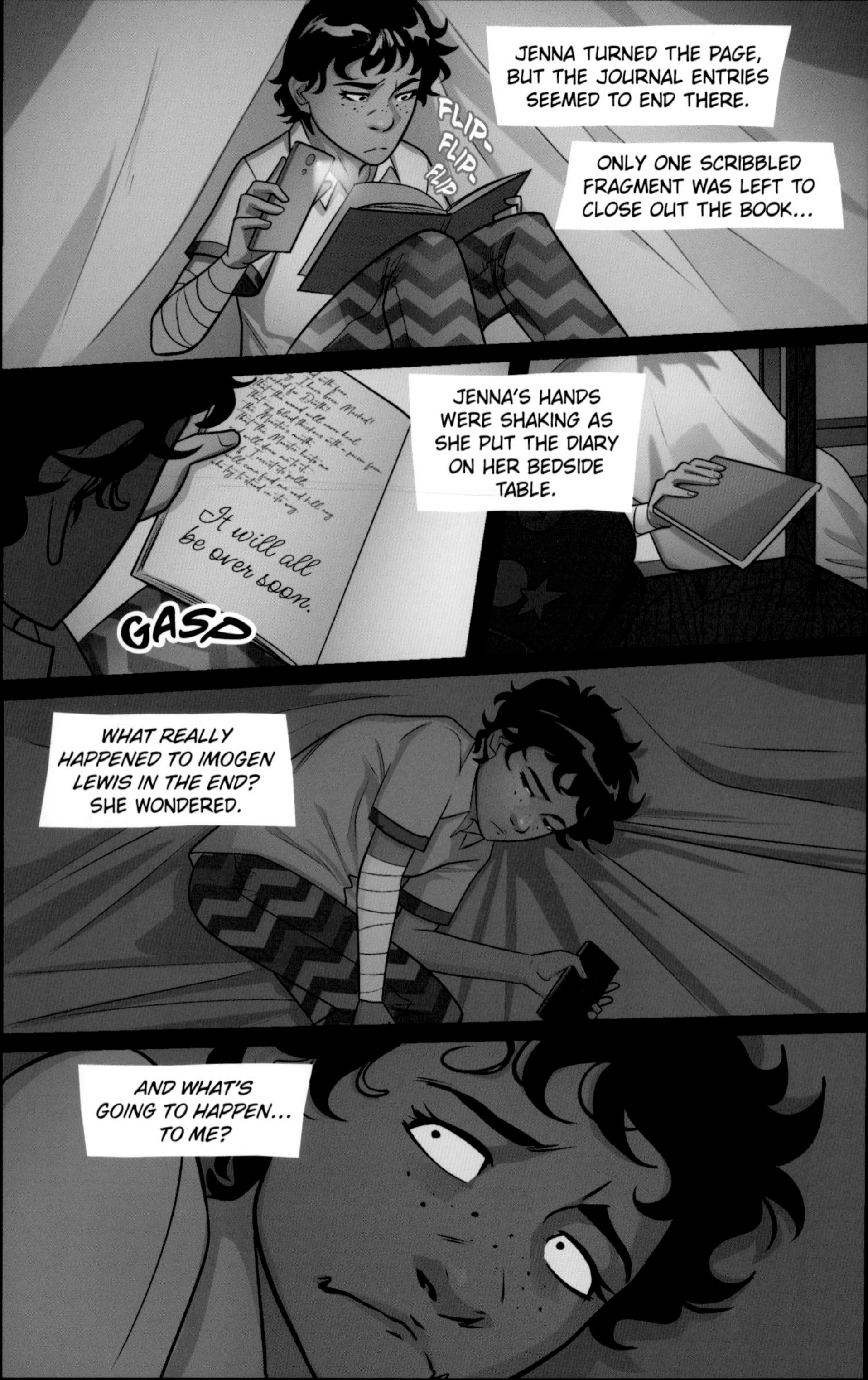
JENNA TURNED THE PAGE, BUT THE JOURNAL ENTRIES SEEMED TO END THERE.
FLIP-FLIP-FLIP
ONLY ONE SCRIBBLED FRAGMENT WAS LEFT TO CLOSE OUT THE BOOK...
It will all be over soon.
GASP
JENNA'S HANDS WERE SHAKING AS SHE PUT THE DIARY ON HER BEDSIDE TABLE.
WHAT REALLY HAPPENED TO IMOGEN LEWIS IN THE END? SHE WONDERED.
AND WHAT'S GOING TO HAPPEN... TO ME?

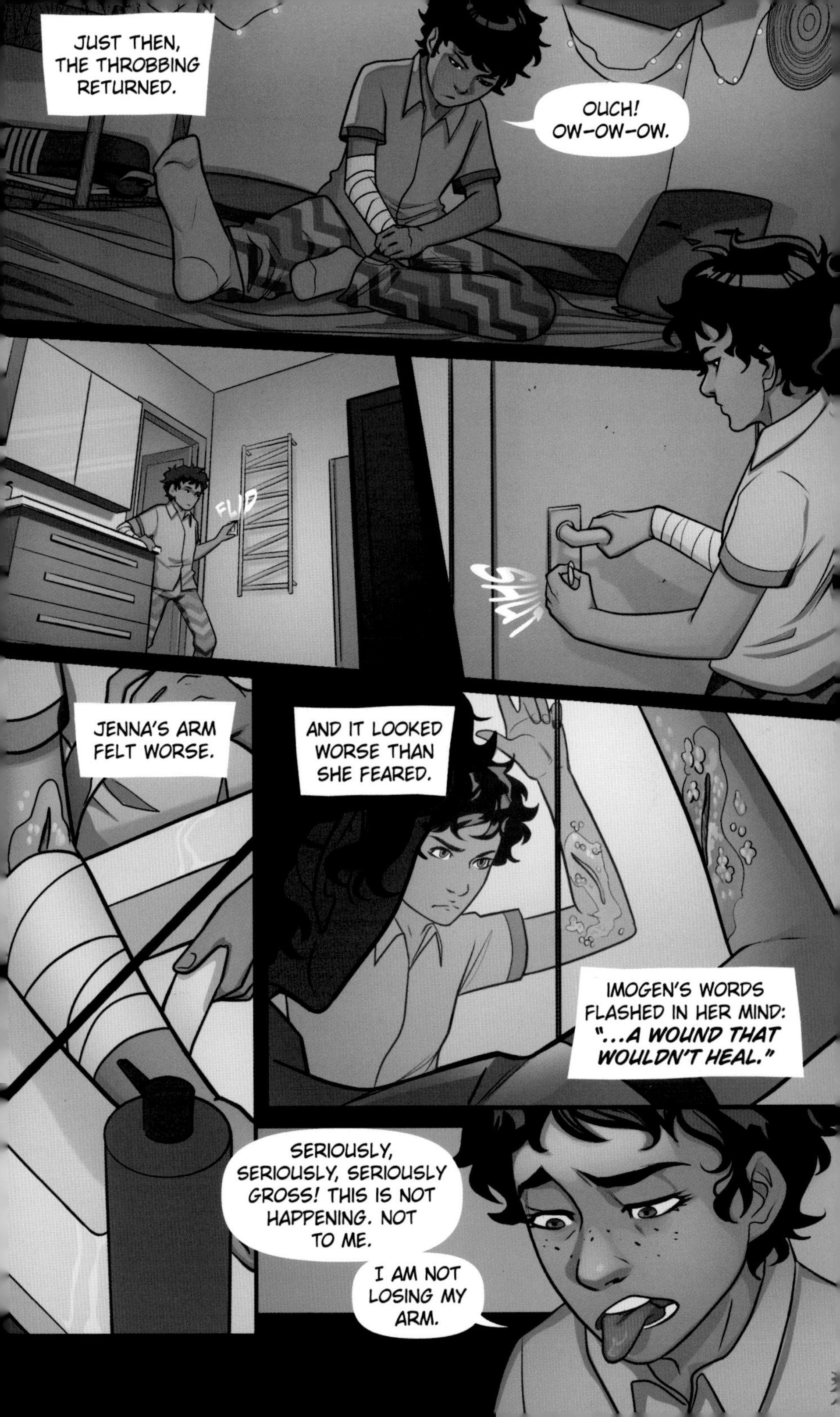
JUST THEN, THE THROBBING RETURNED.
OUCH! OW-OW-OW.
FLIP
SNAP
JENNA'S ARM FELT WORSE.
AND IT LOOKED WORSE THAN SHE FEARED.
IMOGEN'S WORDS FLASHED IN HER MIND: *"...A WOUND THAT WOULDN'T HEAL."*
SERIOUSLY, SERIOUSLY, SERIOUSLY GROSS! THIS IS NOT HAPPENING. NOT TO ME.
I AM NOT LOSING MY ARM.

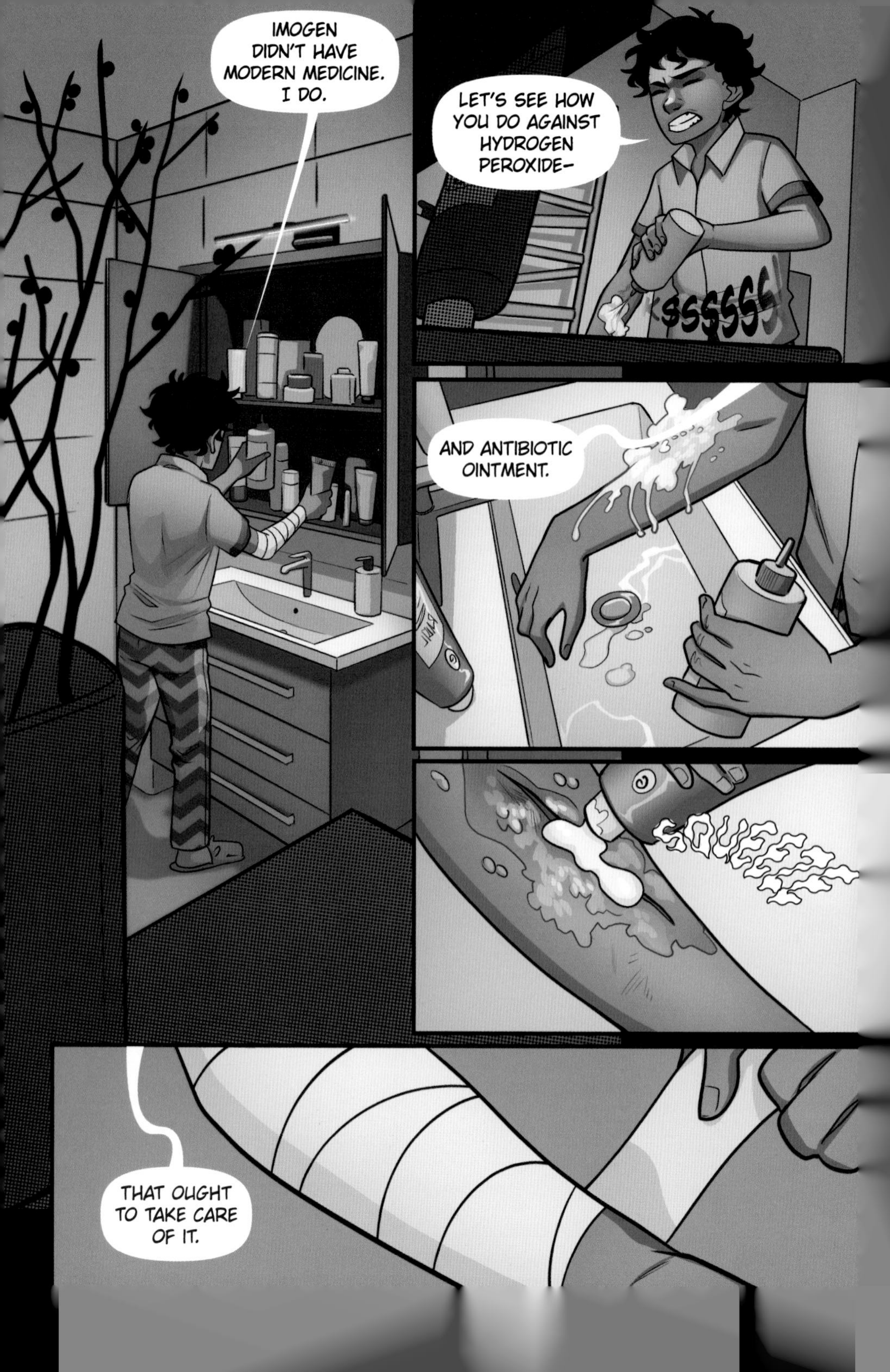
IMOGEN DIDN'T HAVE MODERN MEDICINE. I DO.
LET'S SEE HOW YOU DO AGAINST HYDROGEN PEROXIDE-
SSSSSS
AND ANTIBIOTIC OINTMENT.
SQUEEZE
THAT OUGHT TO TAKE CARE OF IT.

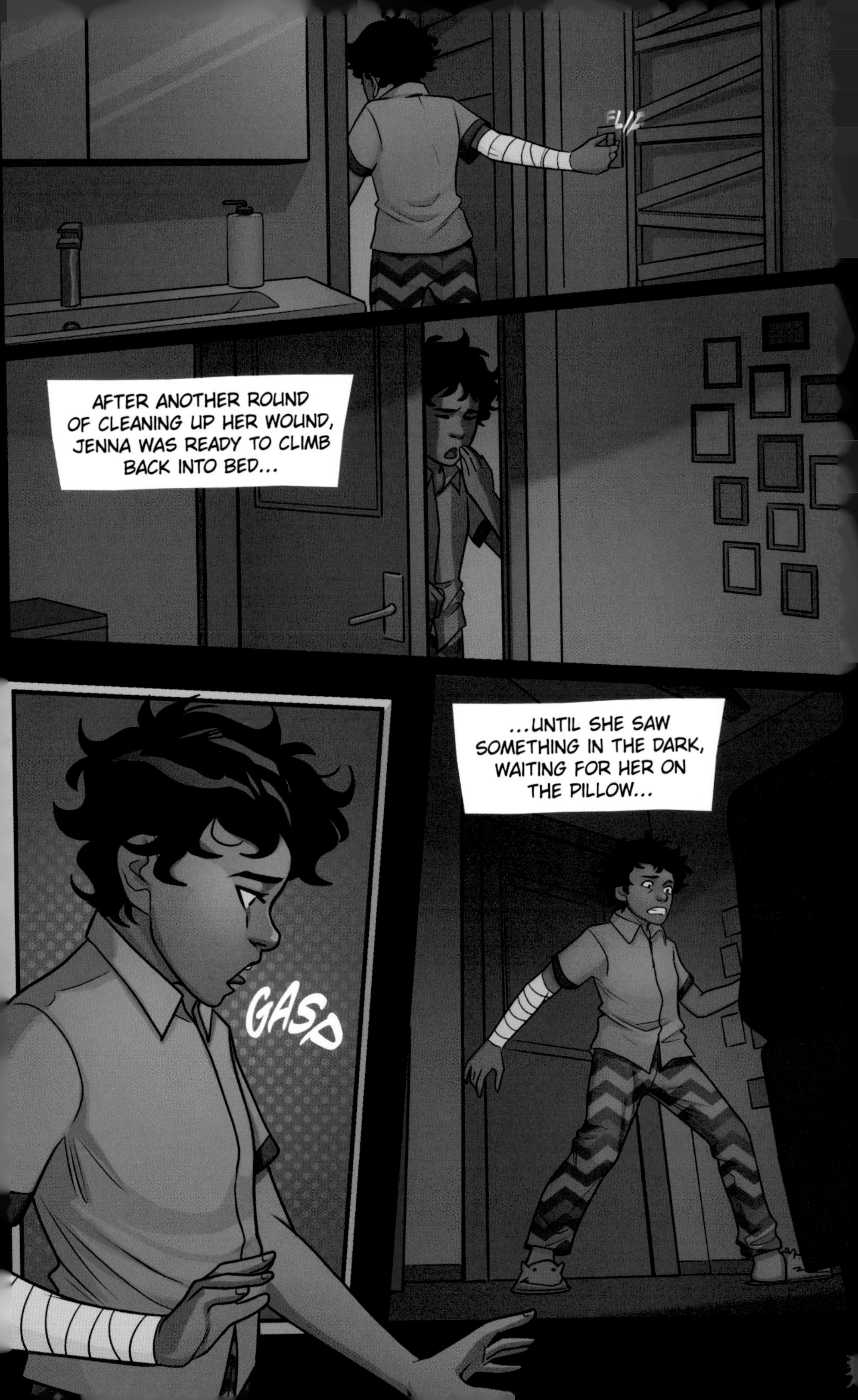
AFTER ANOTHER ROUND OF CLEANING UP HER WOUND, JENNA WAS READY TO CLIMB BACK INTO BED...
GASP
...UNTIL SHE SAW SOMETHING IN THE DARK, WAITING FOR HER ON THE PILLOW...

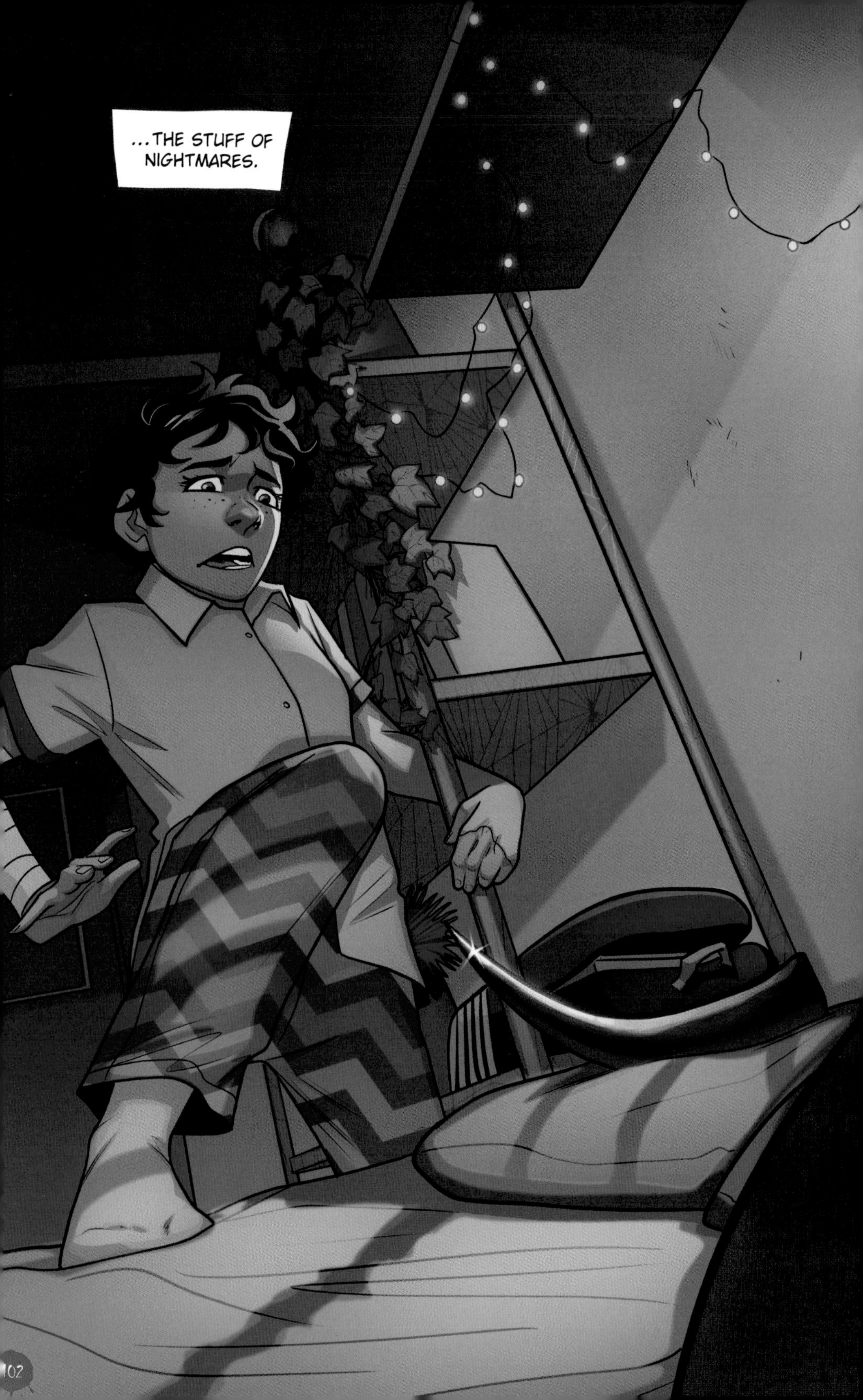
...THE STUFF OF NIGHTMARES.

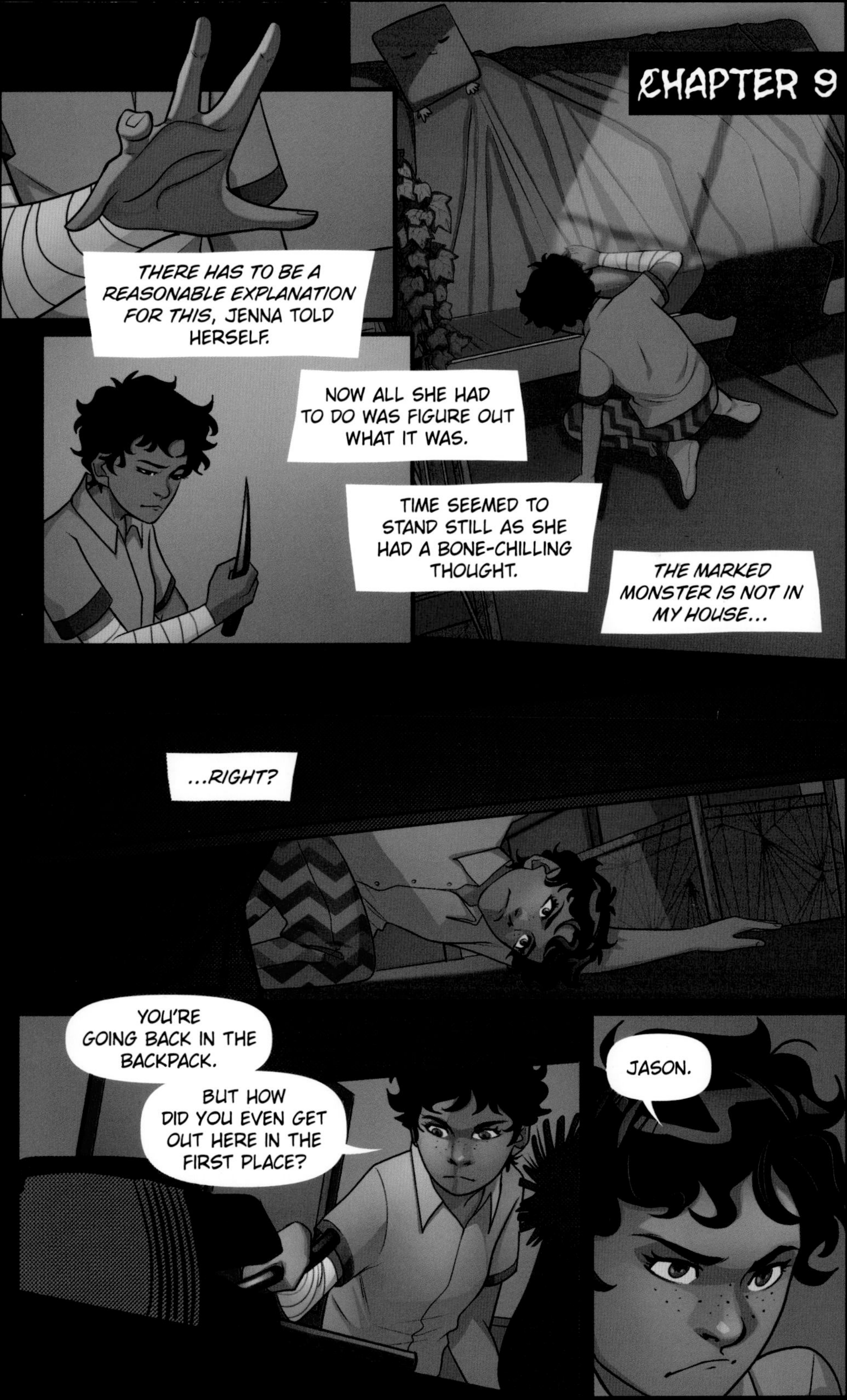
CHAPTER 9
THERE HAS TO BE A REASONABLE EXPLANATION FOR THIS, JENNA TOLD HERSELF.
NOW ALL SHE HAD TO DO WAS FIGURE OUT WHAT IT WAS.
TIME SEEMED TO STAND STILL AS SHE HAD A BONE-CHILLING THOUGHT.
THE MARKED MONSTER IS NOT IN MY HOUSE...
...RIGHT?
YOU'RE GOING BACK IN THE BACKPACK.
BUT HOW DID YOU EVEN GET OUT HERE IN THE FIRST PLACE?
JASON.

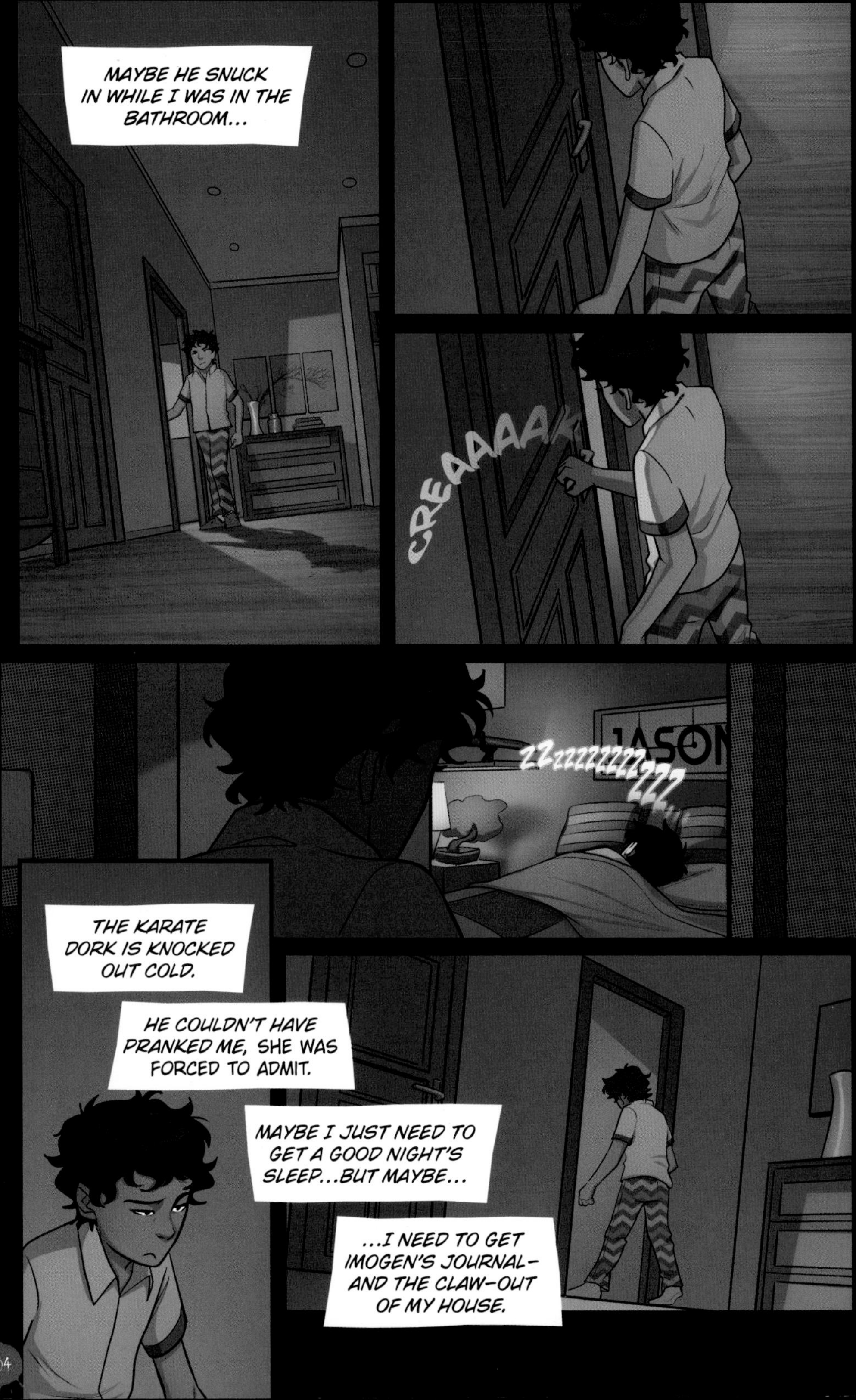
MAYBE HE SNUCK IN WHILE I WAS IN THE BATHROOM...
CREAAAAK
JASON
ZZZZZZZZZZZZZZ...
THE KARATE DORK IS KNOCKED OUT COLD.
HE COULDN'T HAVE PRANKED ME, SHE WAS FORCED TO ADMIT.
MAYBE I JUST NEED TO GET A GOOD NIGHT'S SLEEP...BUT MAYBE...
...I NEED TO GET IMOGEN'S JOURNAL—AND THE CLAW—OUT OF MY HOUSE.

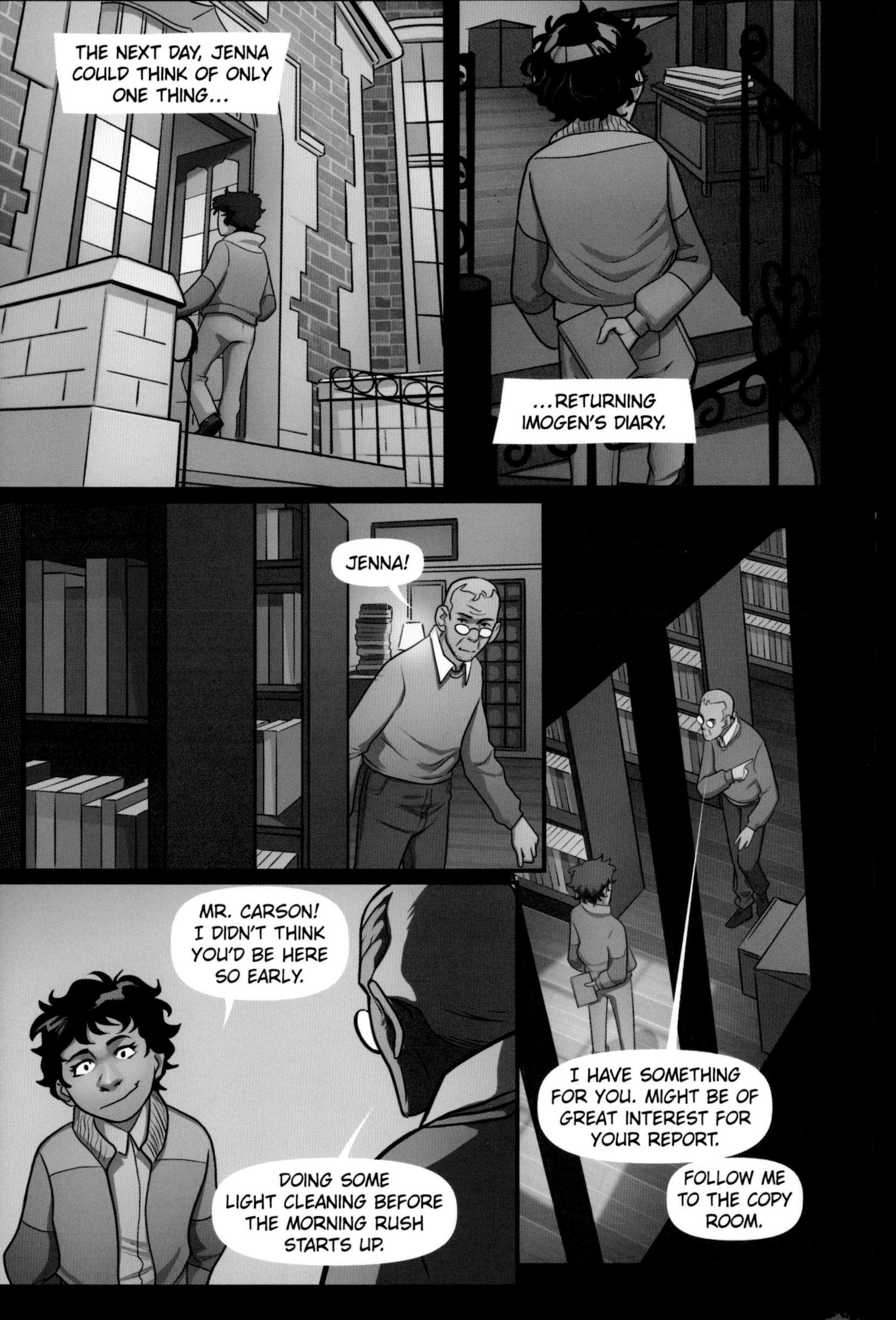
THE NEXT DAY, JENNA COULD THINK OF ONLY ONE THING...
...RETURNING IMOGEN'S DIARY.
JENNA!
MR. CARSON! I DIDN'T THINK YOU'D BE HERE SO EARLY.
DOING SOME LIGHT CLEANING BEFORE THE MORNING RUSH STARTS UP.
I HAVE SOMETHING FOR YOU. MIGHT BE OF GREAT INTEREST FOR YOUR REPORT.
FOLLOW ME TO THE COPY ROOM.

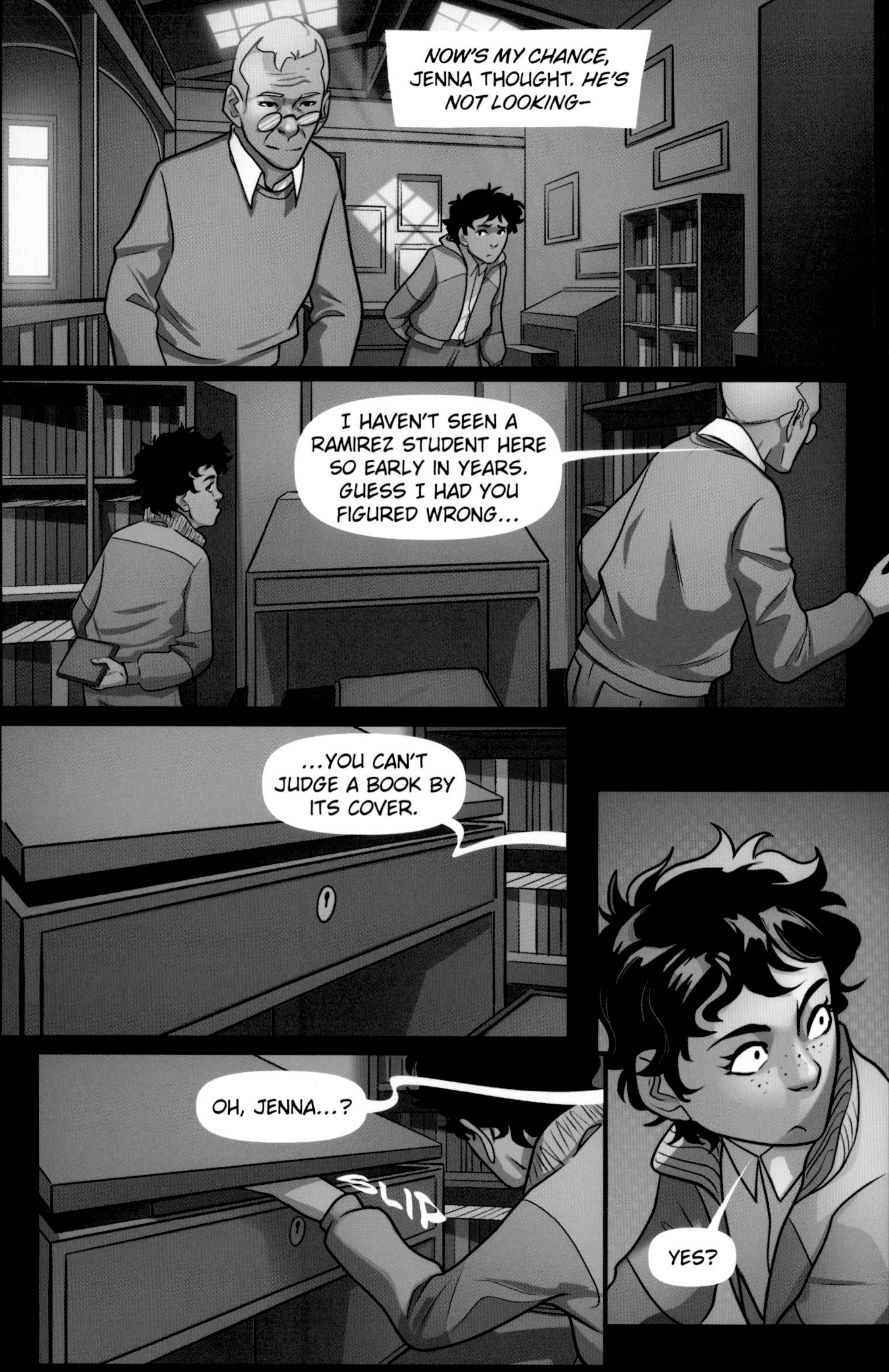
NOW'S MY CHANCE, JENNA THOUGHT. HE'S NOT LOOKING–
I HAVEN'T SEEN A RAMIREZ STUDENT HERE SO EARLY IN YEARS. GUESS I HAD YOU FIGURED WRONG...
...YOU CAN'T JUDGE A BOOK BY ITS COVER.
OH, JENNA...?
SLIP
YES?

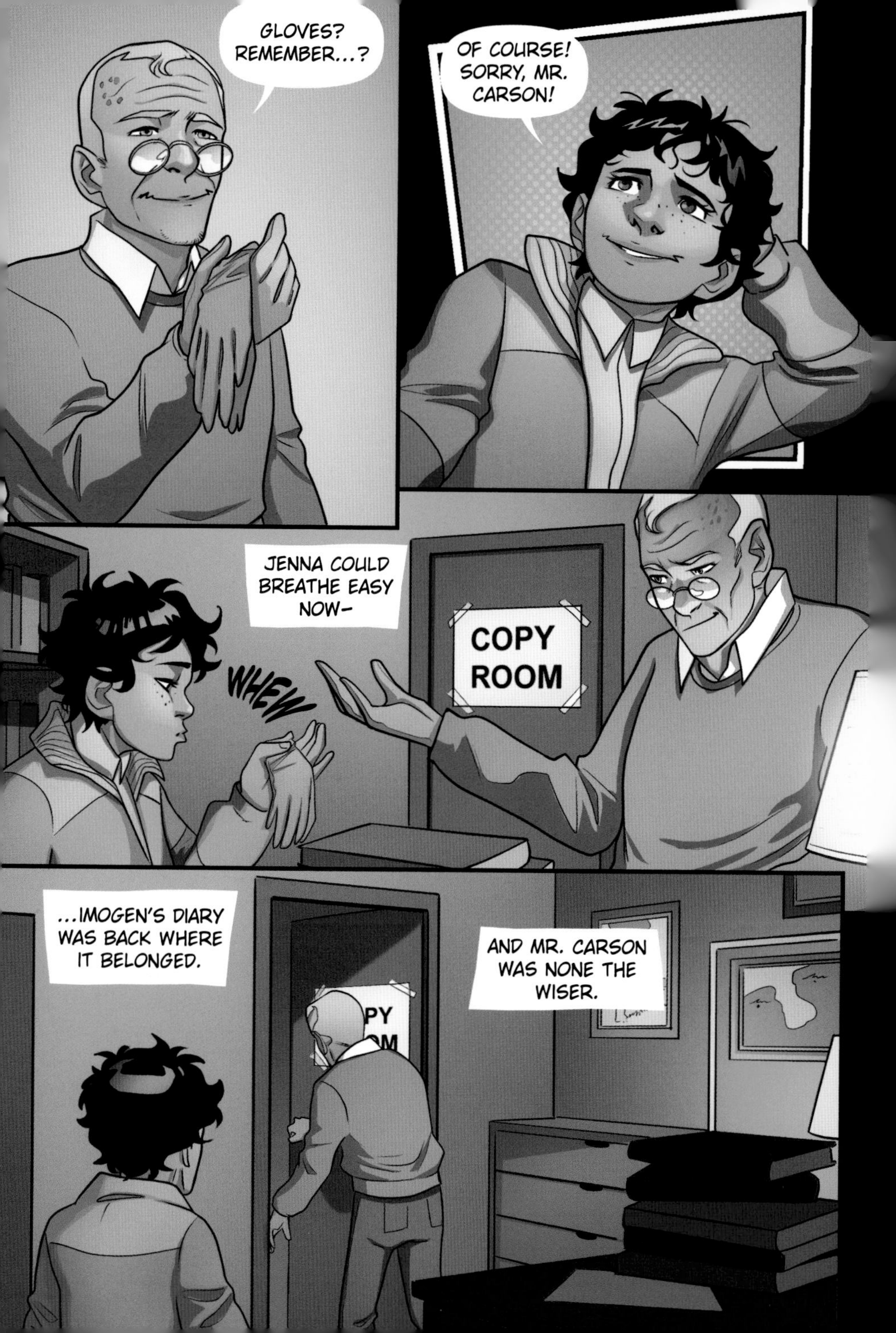
GLOVES? REMEMBER...?
OF COURSE! SORRY, MR. CARSON!
JENNA COULD BREATHE EASY NOW–
COPY ROOM
WHEW
...IMOGEN'S DIARY WAS BACK WHERE IT BELONGED.
AND MR. CARSON WAS NONE THE WISER.

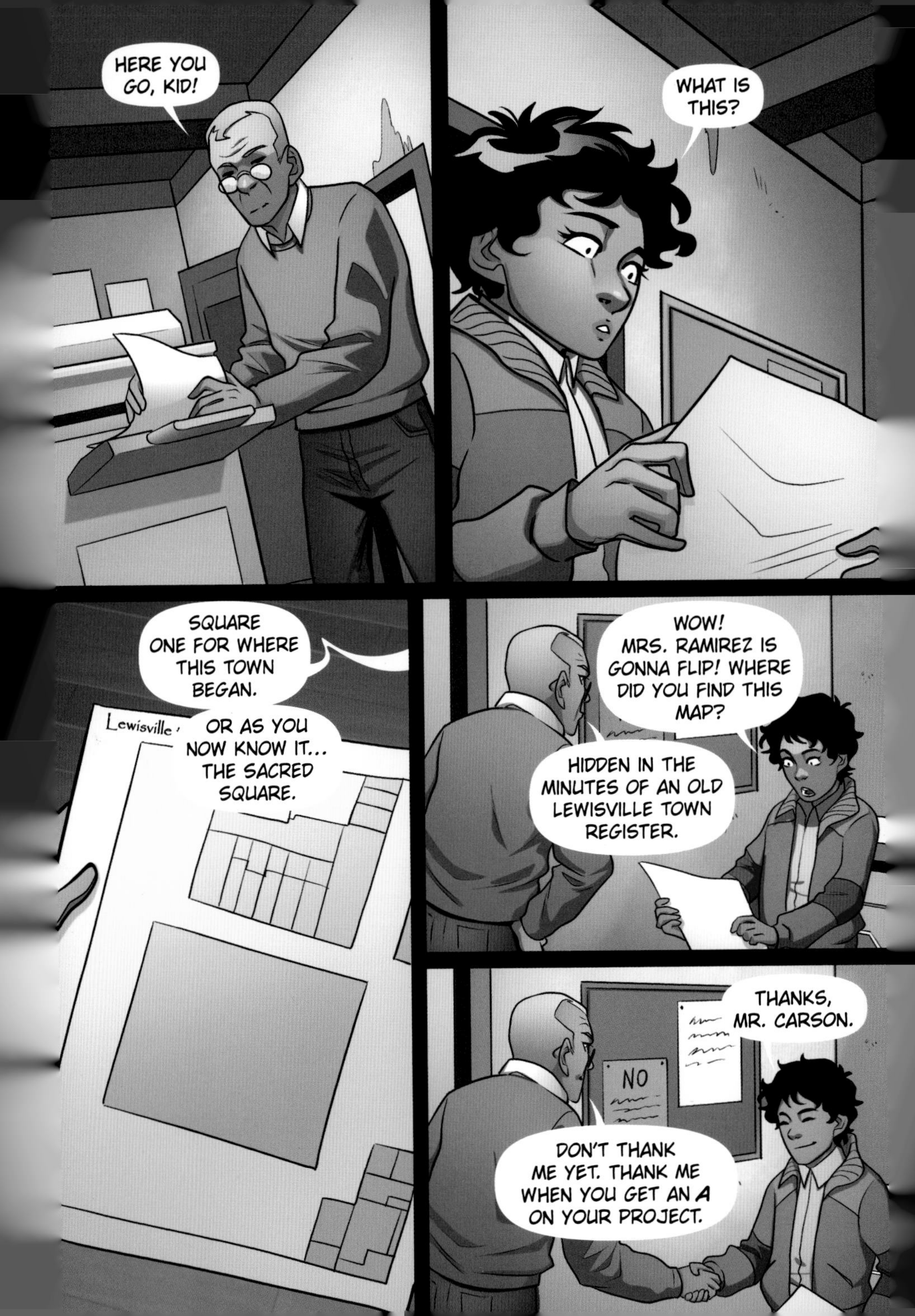
HERE YOU GO, KID!
WHAT IS THIS?
SQUARE ONE FOR WHERE THIS TOWN BEGAN.
Lewisville
OR AS YOU NOW KNOW IT... THE SACRED SQUARE.
WOW! MRS. RAMIREZ IS GONNA FLIP! WHERE DID YOU FIND THIS MAP?
HIDDEN IN THE MINUTES OF AN OLD LEWISVILLE TOWN REGISTER.
THANKS, MR. CARSON.
NO
DON'T THANK ME YET. THANK ME WHEN YOU GET AN A ON YOUR PROJECT.

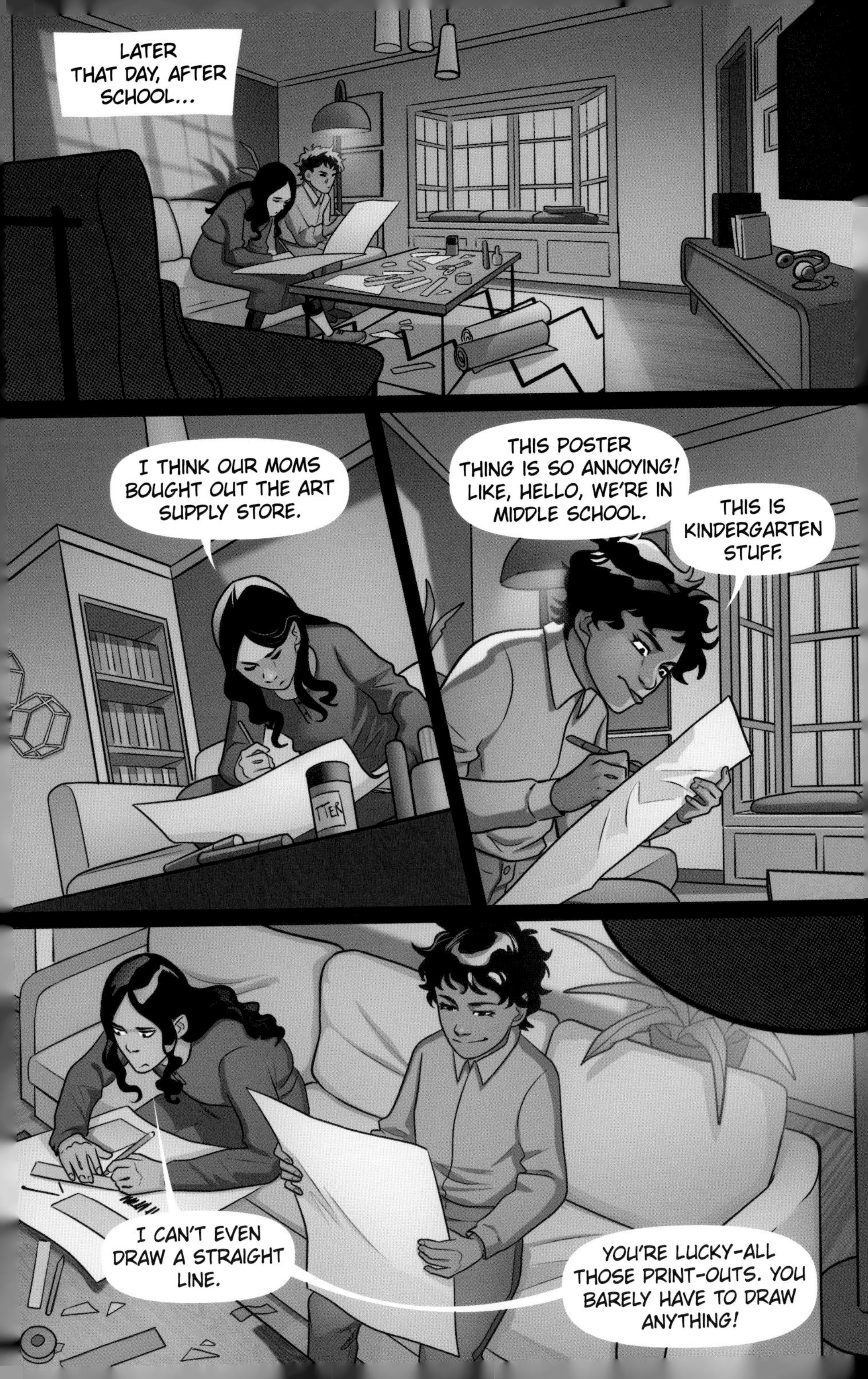
LATER THAT DAY, AFTER SCHOOL...
I THINK OUR MOMS BOUGHT OUT THE ART SUPPLY STORE.
THIS POSTER THING IS SO ANNOYING! LIKE, HELLO, WE'RE IN MIDDLE SCHOOL.
THIS IS KINDERGARTEN STUFF.
I CAN'T EVEN DRAW A STRAIGHT LINE.
YOU'RE LUCKY-ALL THOSE PRINT-OUTS. YOU BARELY HAVE TO DRAW ANYTHING!

The Marked Monster
Marking Lewisville's Legacy

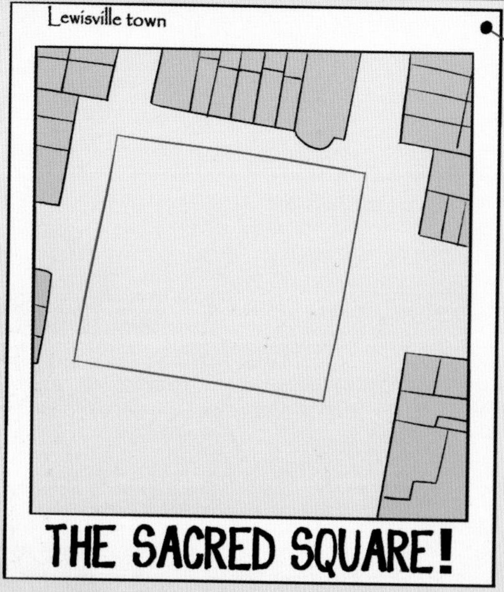
Lewisville town
THE SACRED SQUARE!

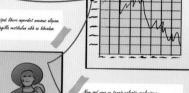

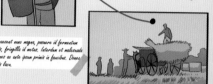

Cras volutpat libero imperdiet maximus aliquam. Morbi fringilla vestibulum nibh ac bibendum.

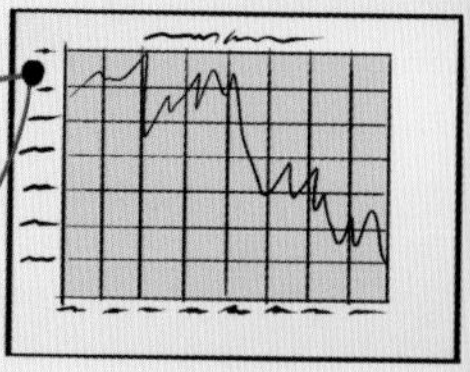

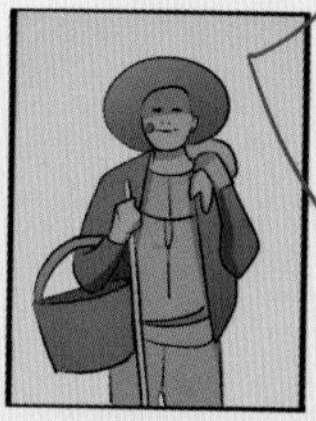

Nam sed urna ac turpis molestie scelerisque non id odio. Praesent efficitur ex vitae porttitor pretium. Nulla hendrerit consequat purus consequat imperdiet.

Praesent nunc magna, posuere id fermentum quis, fringilla id metus. Interdum et malesuada fames ac ante ipsum primis in faucibus. Donec quis lacu.

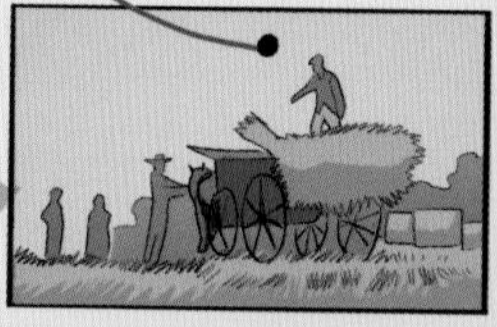

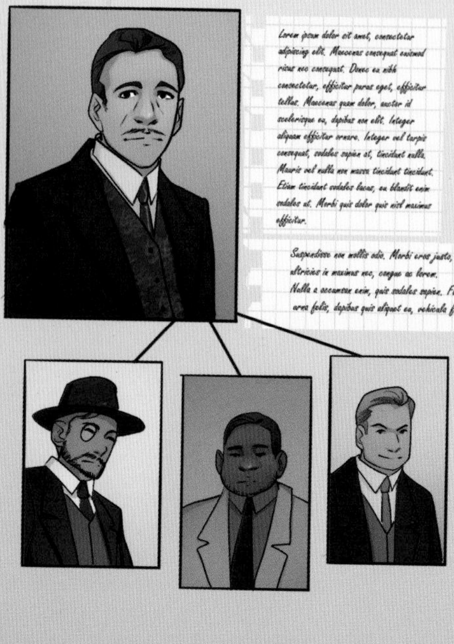

Lorem ipsum dolor sit amet, consectetur adipiscing elit. Maecenas consequat euismod risus nec consequat. Donec eu nibh consectetur, efficitur purus eget, efficitur tellus. Maecenas quam dolor, auctor id scelerisque eu, dapibus non elit. Integer aliquam efficitur ornare. Integer vel turpis consequat, sodales sapien at, tincidunt nulla. Mauris vel nulla non massa tincidunt tincidunt. Etiam tincidunt sodales lacus, eu blandit enim sodales at. Morbi quis dolor quis nisl maximus efficitur.

Suspendisse non mollis odio. Morbi eros justo, ultricies in maximus nec, congue ac lorem. Nulla a accumsan enim, quis sodales sapien. Fusce urna felis, dapibus quis aliquet eu, vehicula fringilla orci.

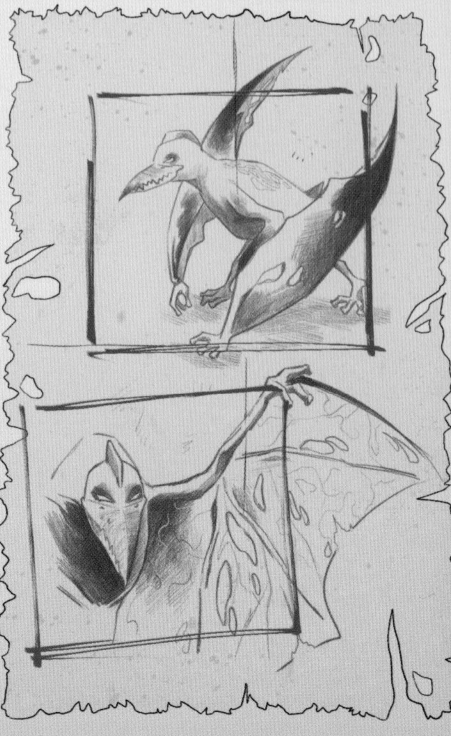

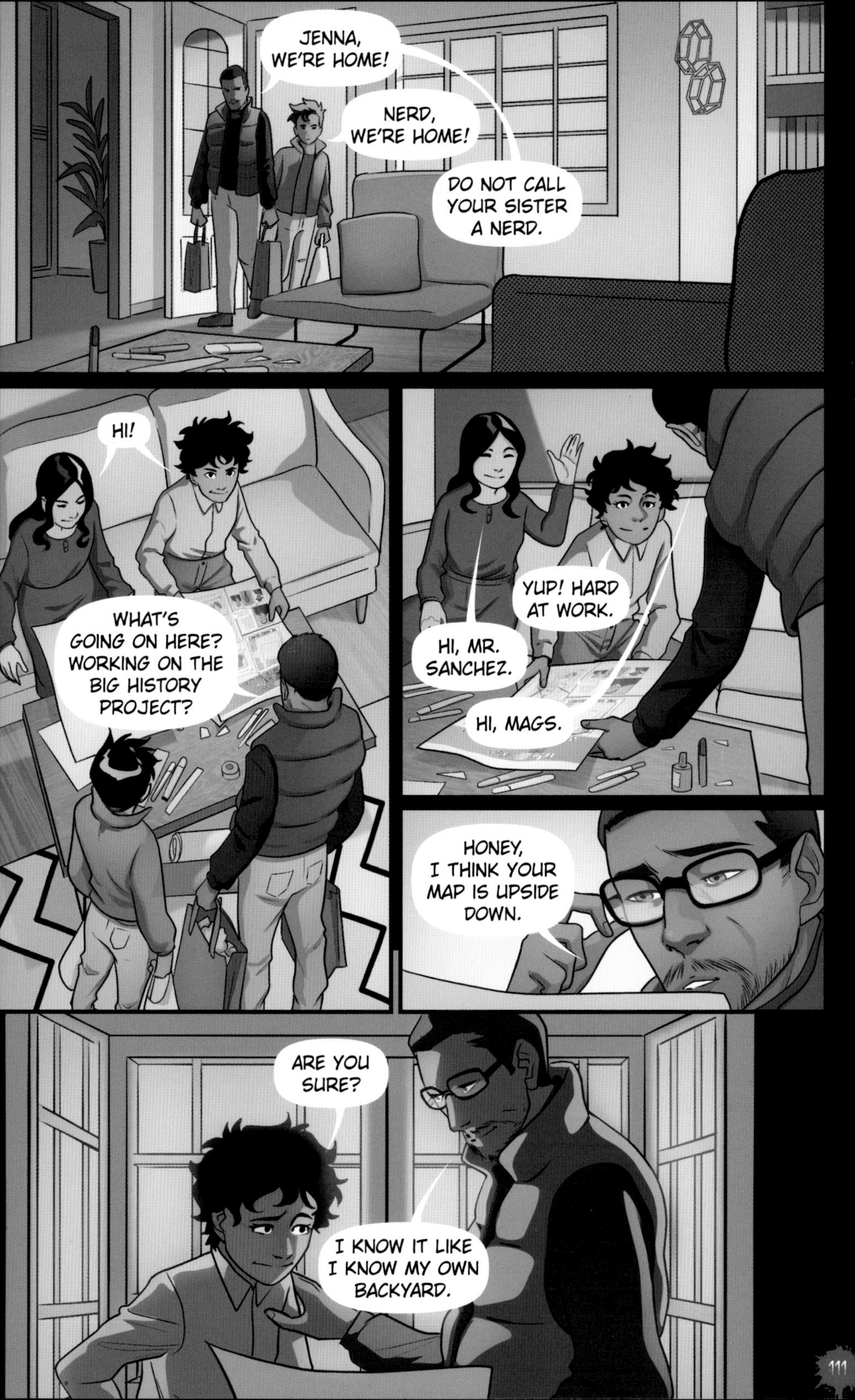
JENNA, WE'RE HOME!
NERD, WE'RE HOME!
DO NOT CALL YOUR SISTER A NERD.
HI!
WHAT'S GOING ON HERE? WORKING ON THE BIG HISTORY PROJECT?
YUP! HARD AT WORK.
HI, MR. SANCHEZ.
HI, MAGS.
HONEY, I THINK YOUR MAP IS UPSIDE DOWN.
ARE YOU SURE?
I KNOW IT LIKE I KNOW MY OWN BACKYARD.

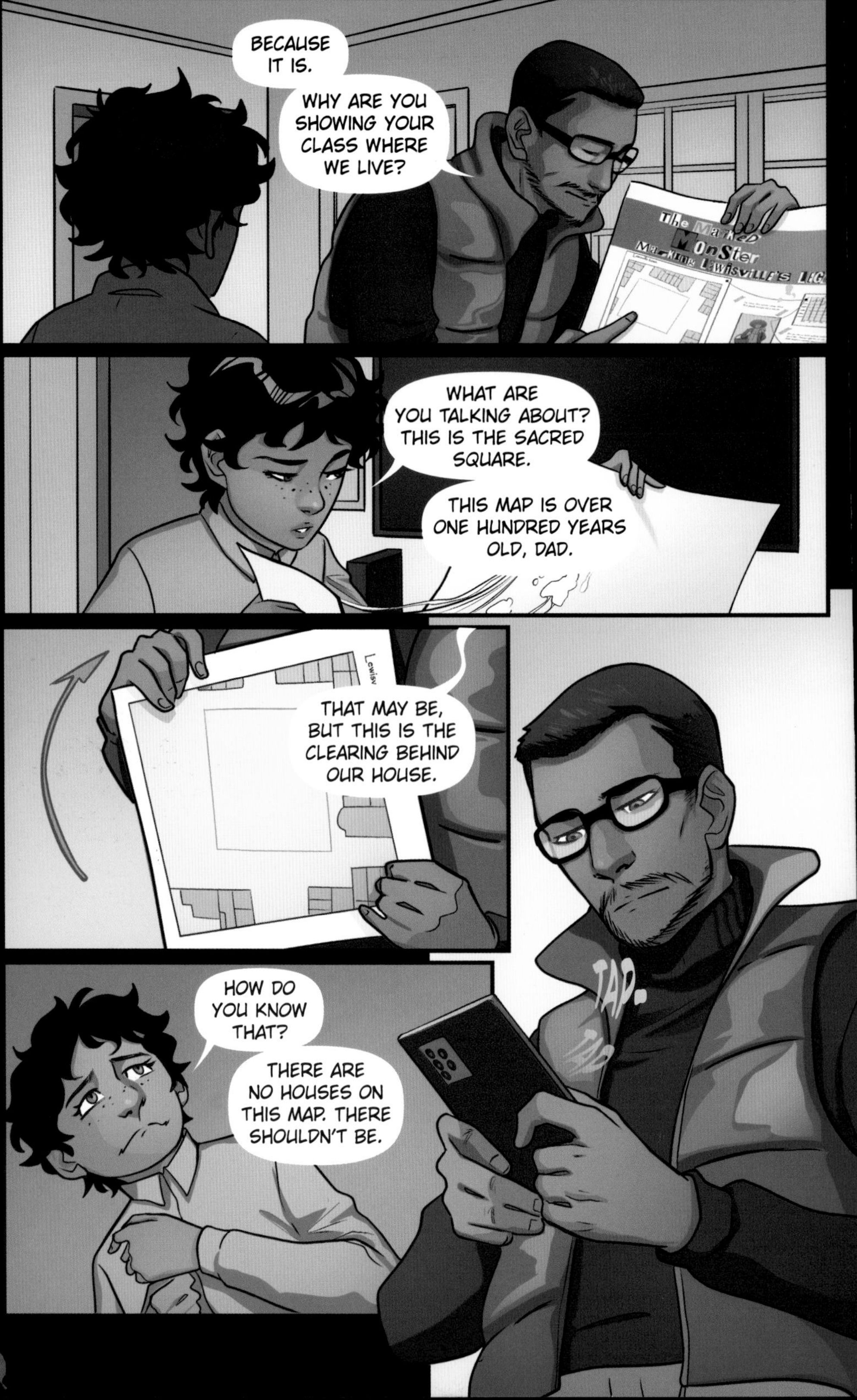
BECAUSE IT IS.
WHY ARE YOU SHOWING YOUR CLASS WHERE WE LIVE?
The Marked Monster
WHAT ARE YOU TALKING ABOUT? THIS IS THE SACRED SQUARE.
THIS MAP IS OVER ONE HUNDRED YEARS OLD, DAD.
THAT MAY BE, BUT THIS IS THE CLEARING BEHIND OUR HOUSE.
HOW DO YOU KNOW THAT?
THERE ARE NO HOUSES ON THIS MAP. THERE SHOULDN'T BE.
TAP.
TAP

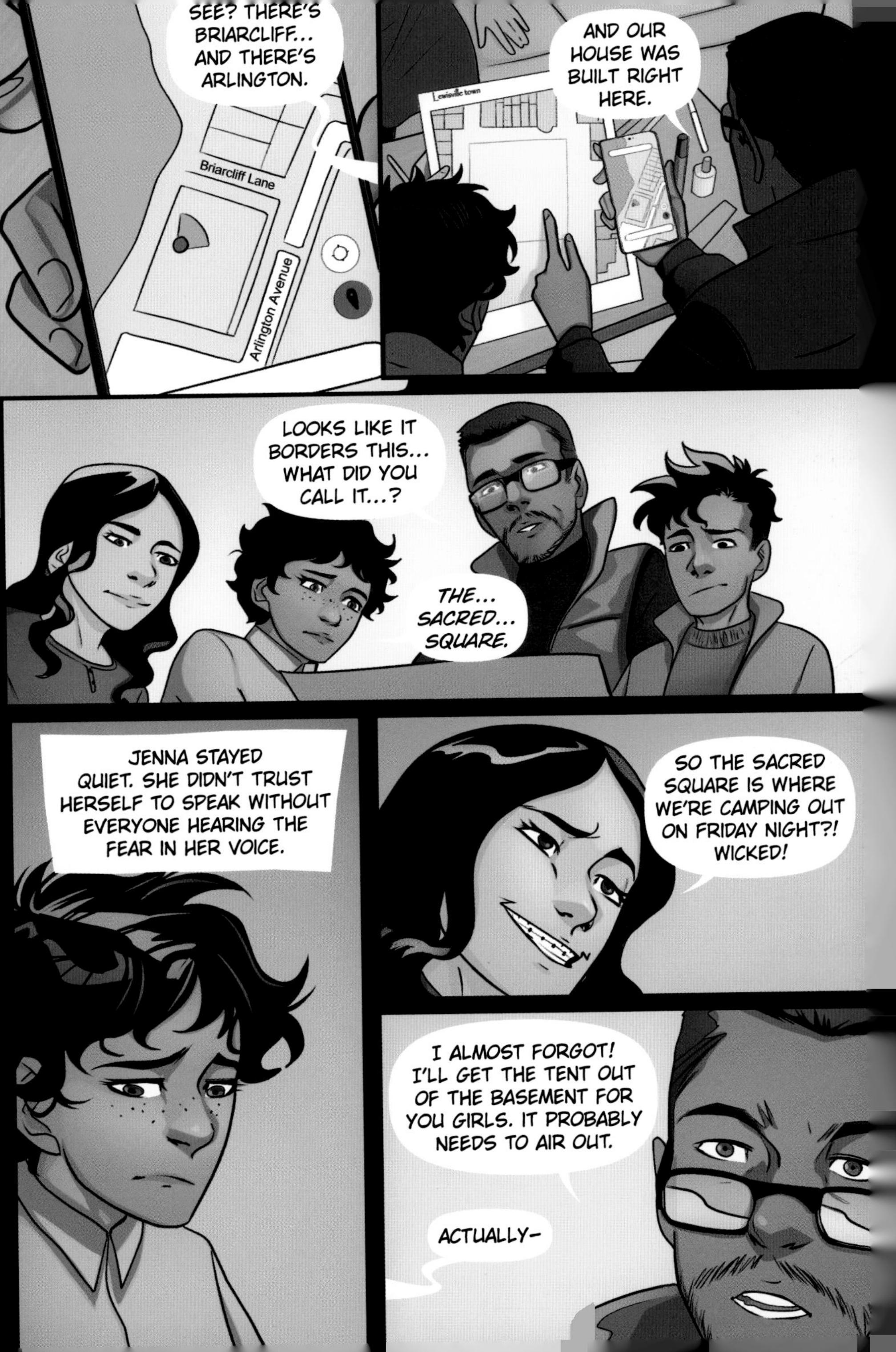
SEE? THERE'S BRIARCLIFF... AND THERE'S ARLINGTON.
Briarcliff Lane
Arlington Avenue
AND OUR HOUSE WAS BUILT RIGHT HERE.
LOOKS LIKE IT BORDERS THIS... WHAT DID YOU CALL IT...?
THE... SACRED... SQUARE.
JENNA STAYED QUIET. SHE DIDN'T TRUST HERSELF TO SPEAK WITHOUT EVERYONE HEARING THE FEAR IN HER VOICE.
SO THE SACRED SQUARE IS WHERE WE'RE CAMPING OUT ON FRIDAY NIGHT?! WICKED!
I ALMOST FORGOT! I'LL GET THE TENT OUT OF THE BASEMENT FOR YOU GIRLS. IT PROBABLY NEEDS TO AIR OUT.
ACTUALLY–

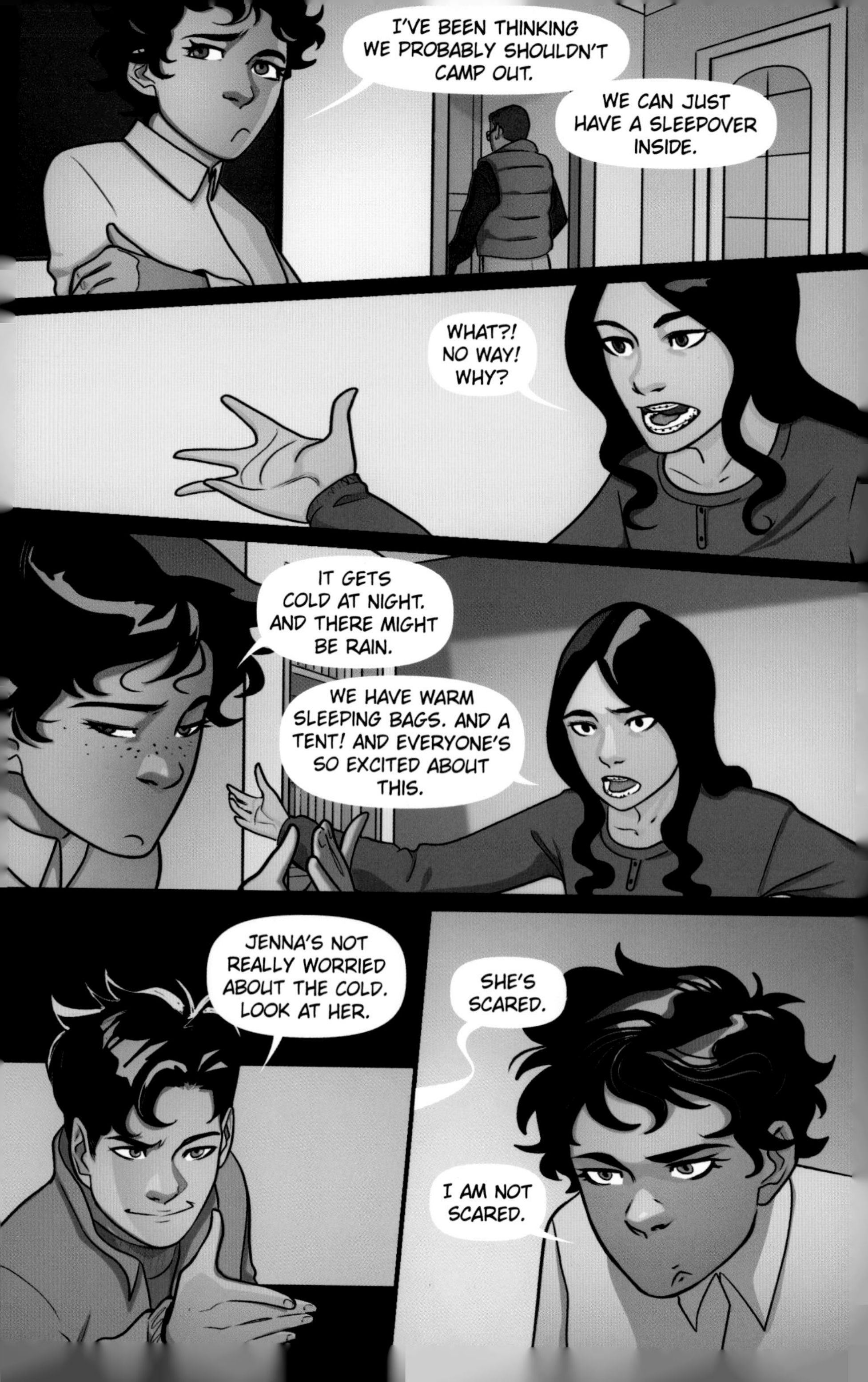
I'VE BEEN THINKING WE PROBABLY SHOULDN'T CAMP OUT.
WE CAN JUST HAVE A SLEEPOVER INSIDE.
WHAT?! NO WAY! WHY?
IT GETS COLD AT NIGHT. AND THERE MIGHT BE RAIN.
WE HAVE WARM SLEEPING BAGS. AND A TENT! AND EVERYONE'S SO EXCITED ABOUT THIS.
JENNA'S NOT REALLY WORRIED ABOUT THE COLD. LOOK AT HER.
SHE'S SCARED.
I AM NOT SCARED.

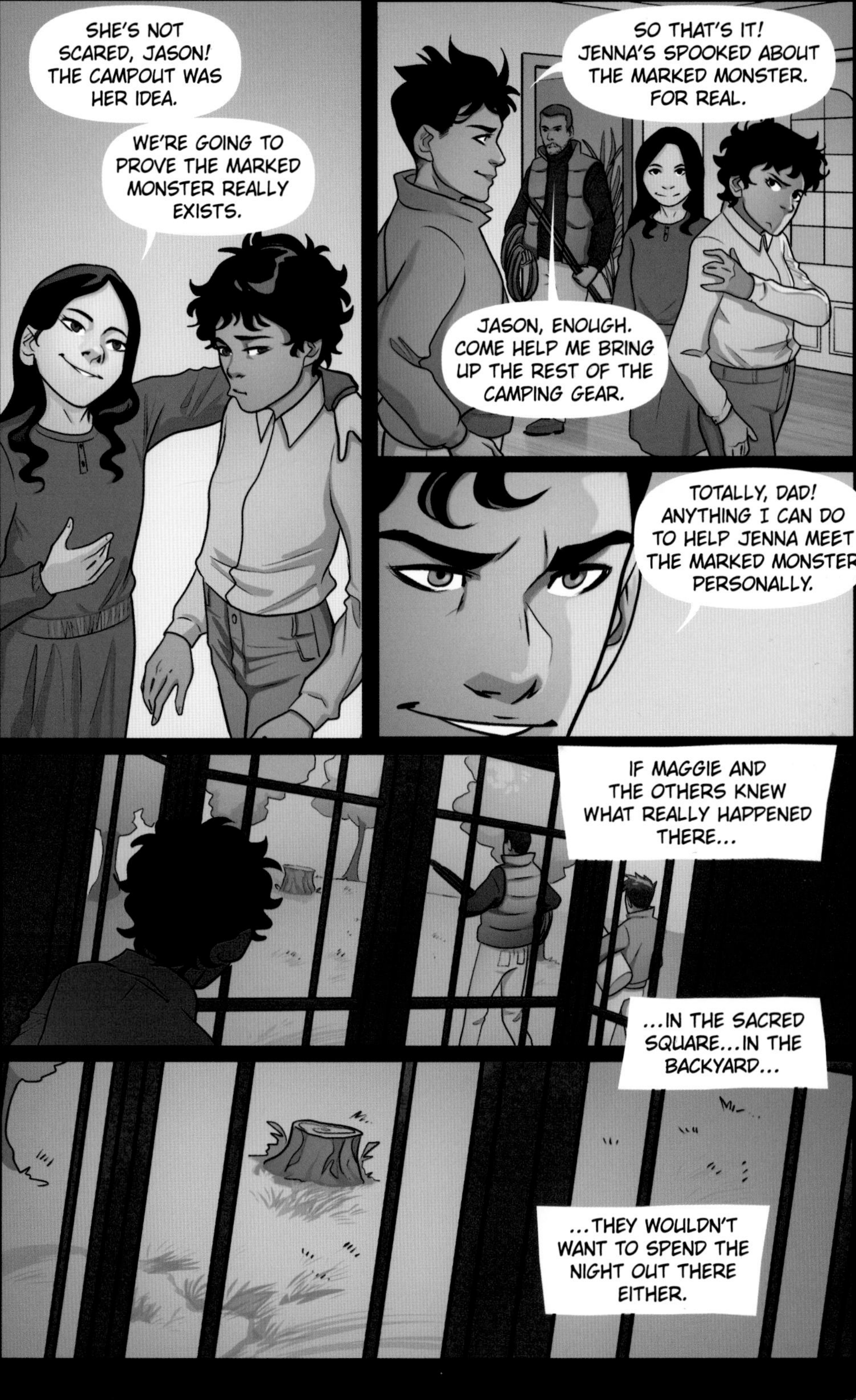
SHE'S NOT SCARED, JASON! THE CAMPOUT WAS HER IDEA.
WE'RE GOING TO PROVE THE MARKED MONSTER REALLY EXISTS.
SO THAT'S IT! JENNA'S SPOOKED ABOUT THE MARKED MONSTER. FOR REAL.
JASON, ENOUGH. COME HELP ME BRING UP THE REST OF THE CAMPING GEAR.
TOTALLY, DAD! ANYTHING I CAN DO TO HELP JENNA MEET THE MARKED MONSTER PERSONALLY.
IF MAGGIE AND THE OTHERS KNEW WHAT REALLY HAPPENED THERE...
...IN THE SACRED SQUARE...IN THE BACKYARD...
...THEY WOULDN'T WANT TO SPEND THE NIGHT OUT THERE EITHER.

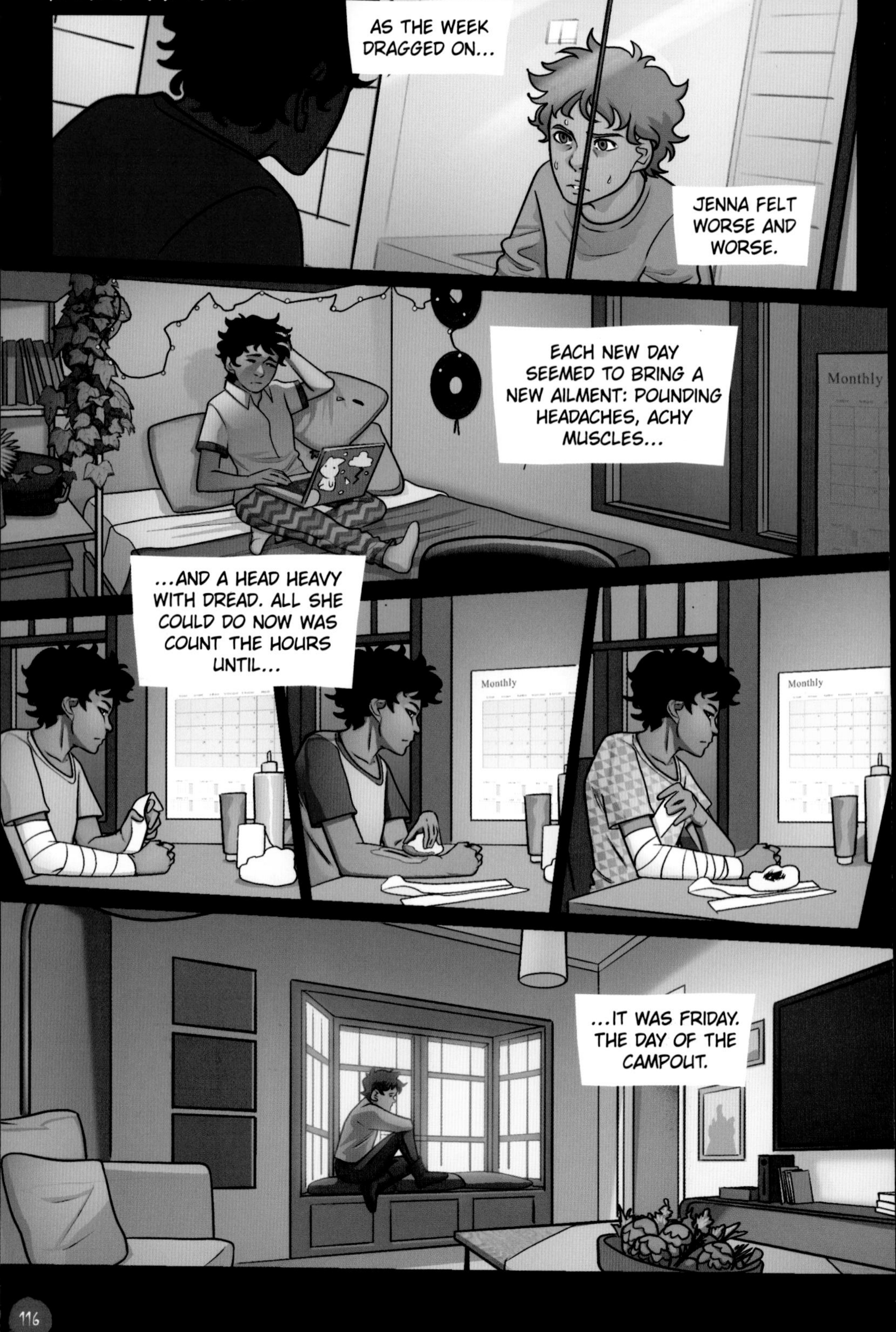
AS THE WEEK DRAGGED ON...
JENNA FELT WORSE AND WORSE.
EACH NEW DAY SEEMED TO BRING A NEW AILMENT: POUNDING HEADACHES, ACHY MUSCLES...
...AND A HEAD HEAVY WITH DREAD. ALL SHE COULD DO NOW WAS COUNT THE HOURS UNTIL...
...IT WAS FRIDAY. THE DAY OF THE CAMPOUT.

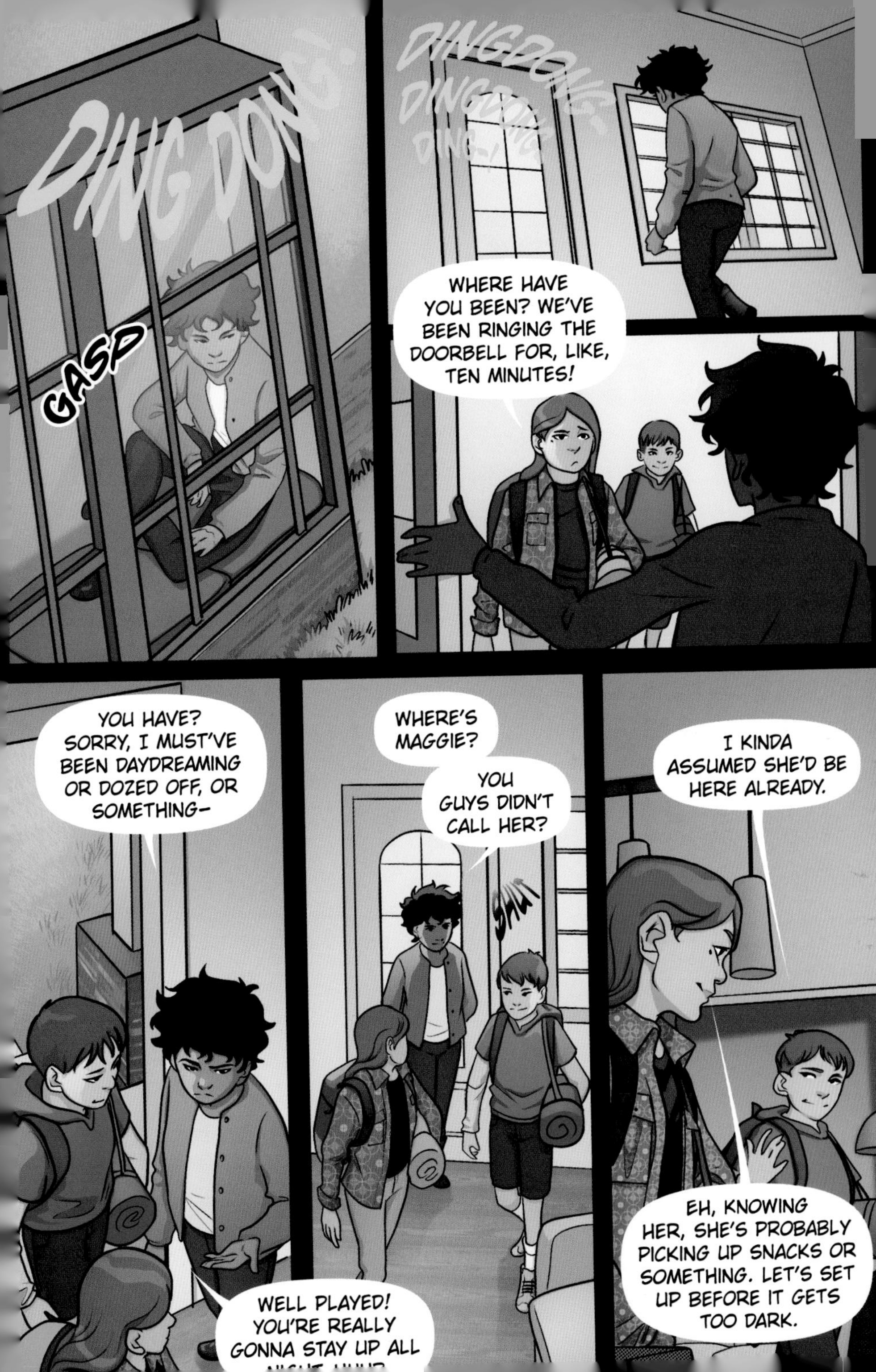
DING DONG-
GASP
DINGDONG-
DINGDONG-
DING-!
WHERE HAVE YOU BEEN? WE'VE BEEN RINGING THE DOORBELL FOR, LIKE, TEN MINUTES!
YOU HAVE? SORRY, I MUST'VE BEEN DAYDREAMING OR DOZED OFF, OR SOMETHING–
WELL PLAYED! YOU'RE REALLY GONNA STAY UP ALL
WHERE'S MAGGIE?
YOU GUYS DIDN'T CALL HER?
I KINDA ASSUMED SHE'D BE HERE ALREADY.
EH, KNOWING HER, SHE'S PROBABLY PICKING UP SNACKS OR SOMETHING. LET'S SET UP BEFORE IT GETS TOO DARK.

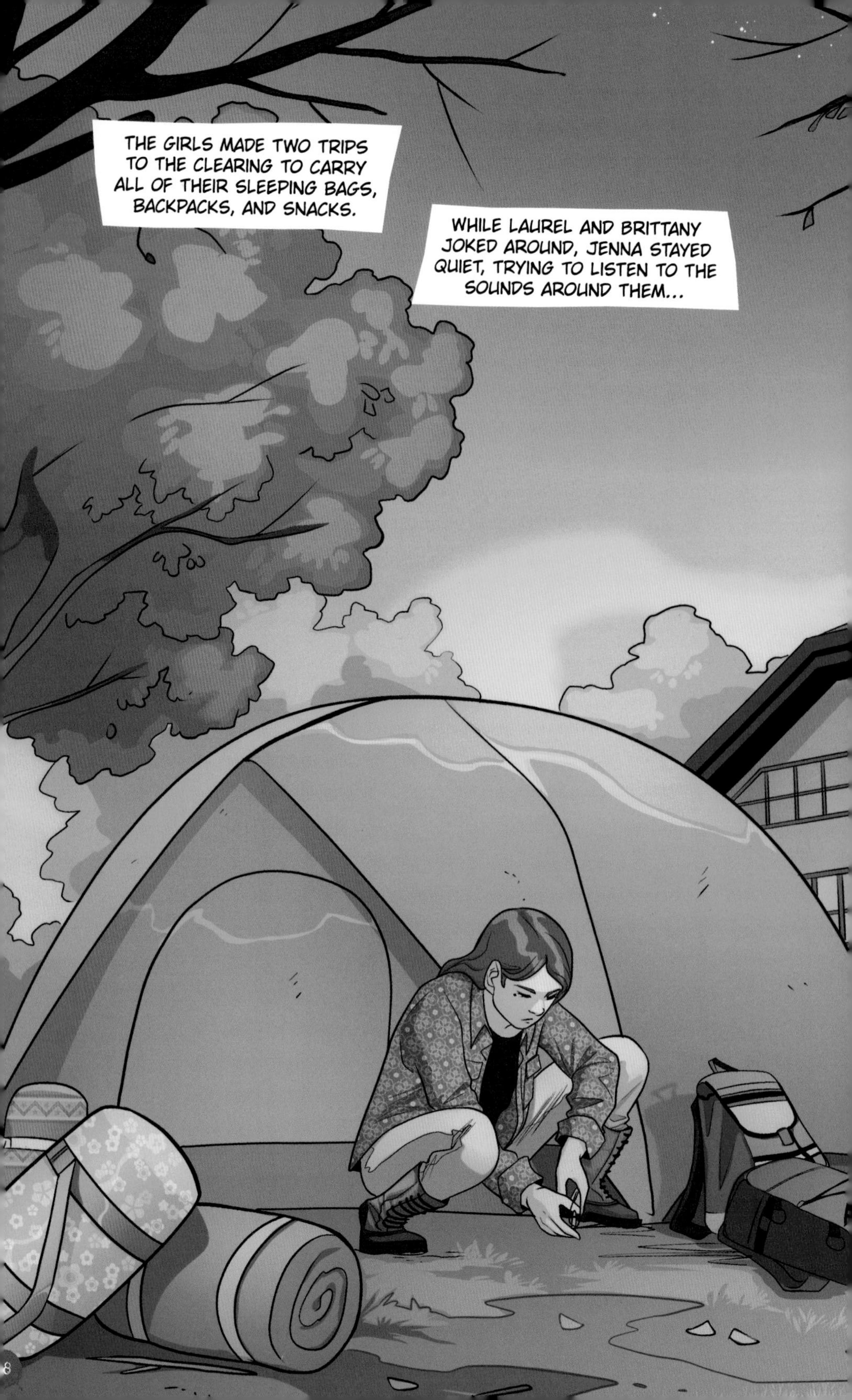
THE GIRLS MADE TWO TRIPS TO THE CLEARING TO CARRY ALL OF THEIR SLEEPING BAGS, BACKPACKS, AND SNACKS.
WHILE LAUREL AND BRITTANY JOKED AROUND, JENNA STAYED QUIET, TRYING TO LISTEN TO THE SOUNDS AROUND THEM...

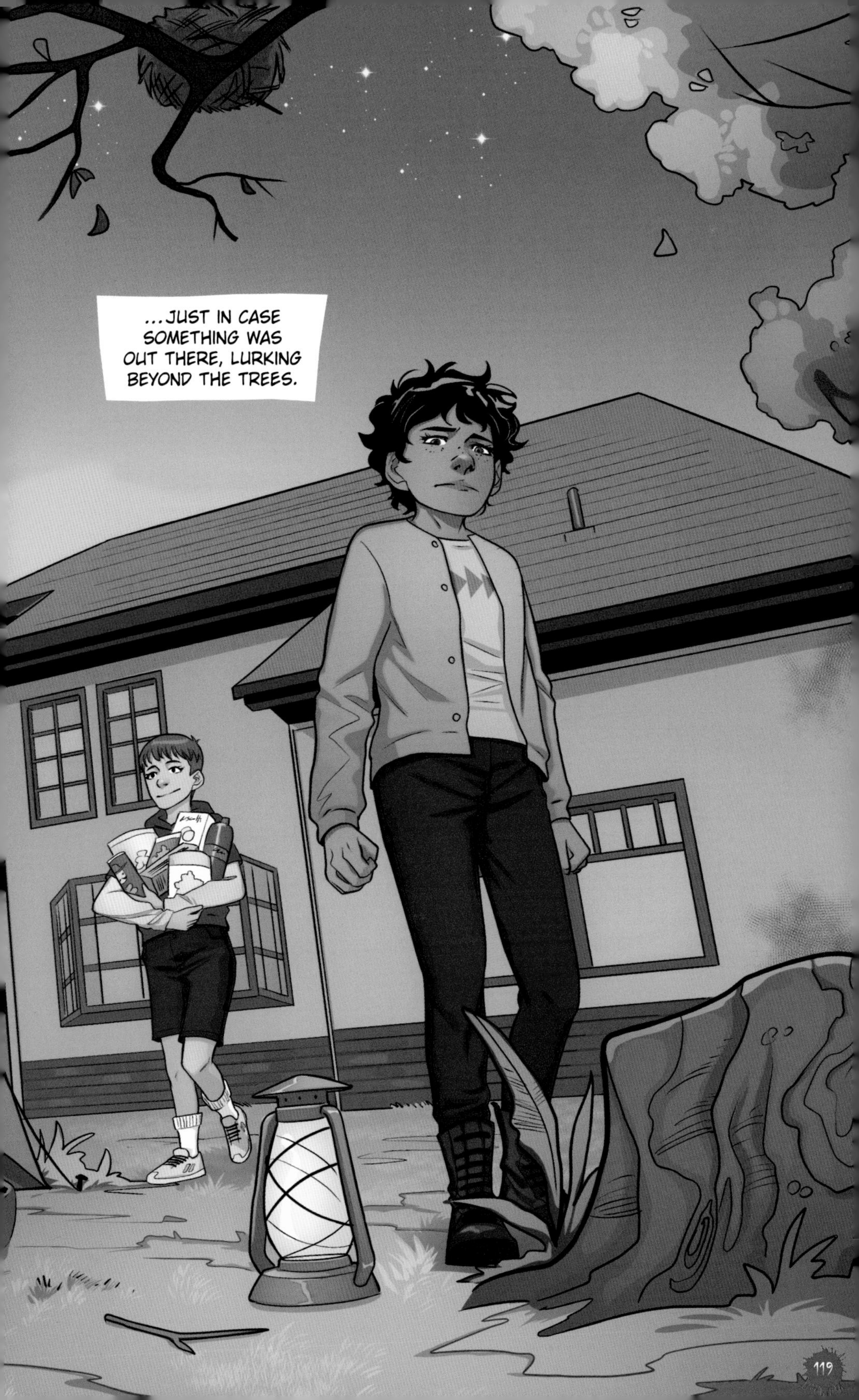
...JUST IN CASE SOMETHING WAS OUT THERE, LURKING BEYOND THE TREES.

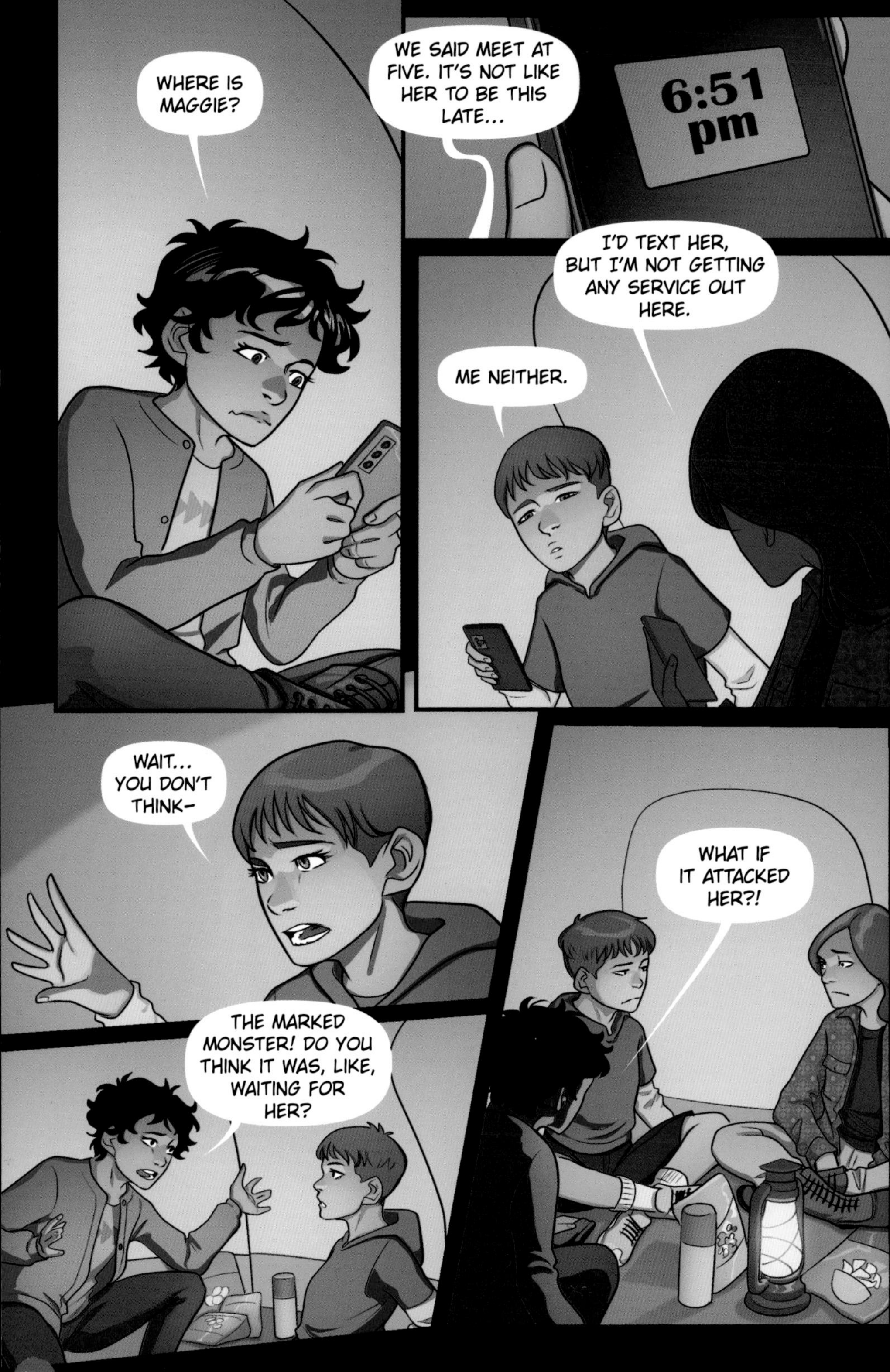
WHERE IS MAGGIE?
WE SAID MEET AT FIVE. IT'S NOT LIKE HER TO BE THIS LATE...
6:51 pm
I'D TEXT HER, BUT I'M NOT GETTING ANY SERVICE OUT HERE.
ME NEITHER.
WAIT... YOU DON'T THINK-
THE MARKED MONSTER! DO YOU THINK IT WAS, LIKE, WAITING FOR HER?
WHAT IF IT ATTACKED HER?!

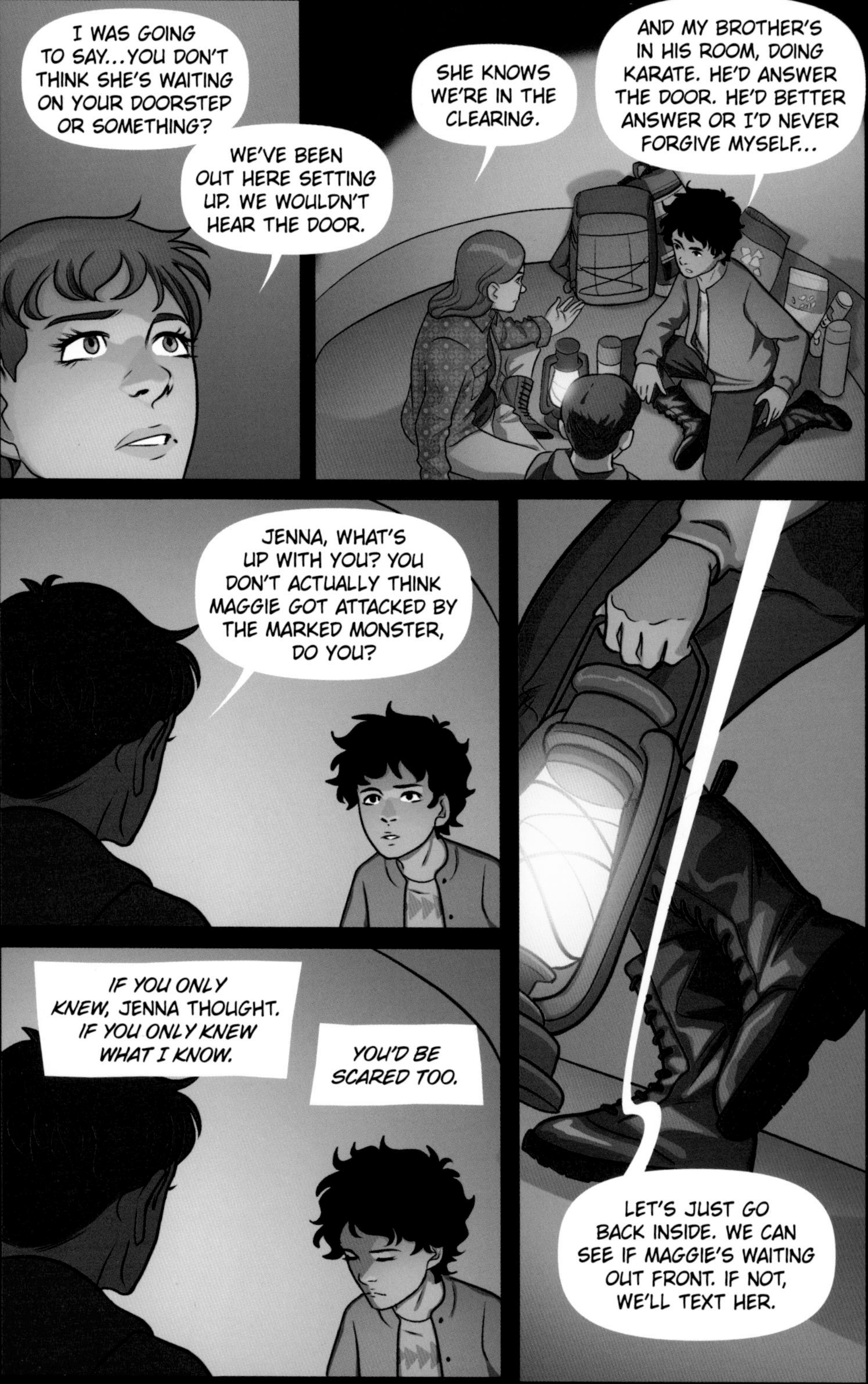
I WAS GOING TO SAY...YOU DON'T THINK SHE'S WAITING ON YOUR DOORSTEP OR SOMETHING?
WE'VE BEEN OUT HERE SETTING UP. WE WOULDN'T HEAR THE DOOR.
SHE KNOWS WE'RE IN THE CLEARING.
AND MY BROTHER'S IN HIS ROOM, DOING KARATE. HE'D ANSWER THE DOOR. HE'D BETTER ANSWER OR I'D NEVER FORGIVE MYSELF...
JENNA, WHAT'S UP WITH YOU? YOU DON'T ACTUALLY THINK MAGGIE GOT ATTACKED BY THE MARKED MONSTER, DO YOU?
IF YOU ONLY KNEW, JENNA THOUGHT. IF YOU ONLY KNEW WHAT I KNOW.
YOU'D BE SCARED TOO.
LET'S JUST GO BACK INSIDE. WE CAN SEE IF MAGGIE'S WAITING OUT FRONT. IF NOT, WE'LL TEXT HER.

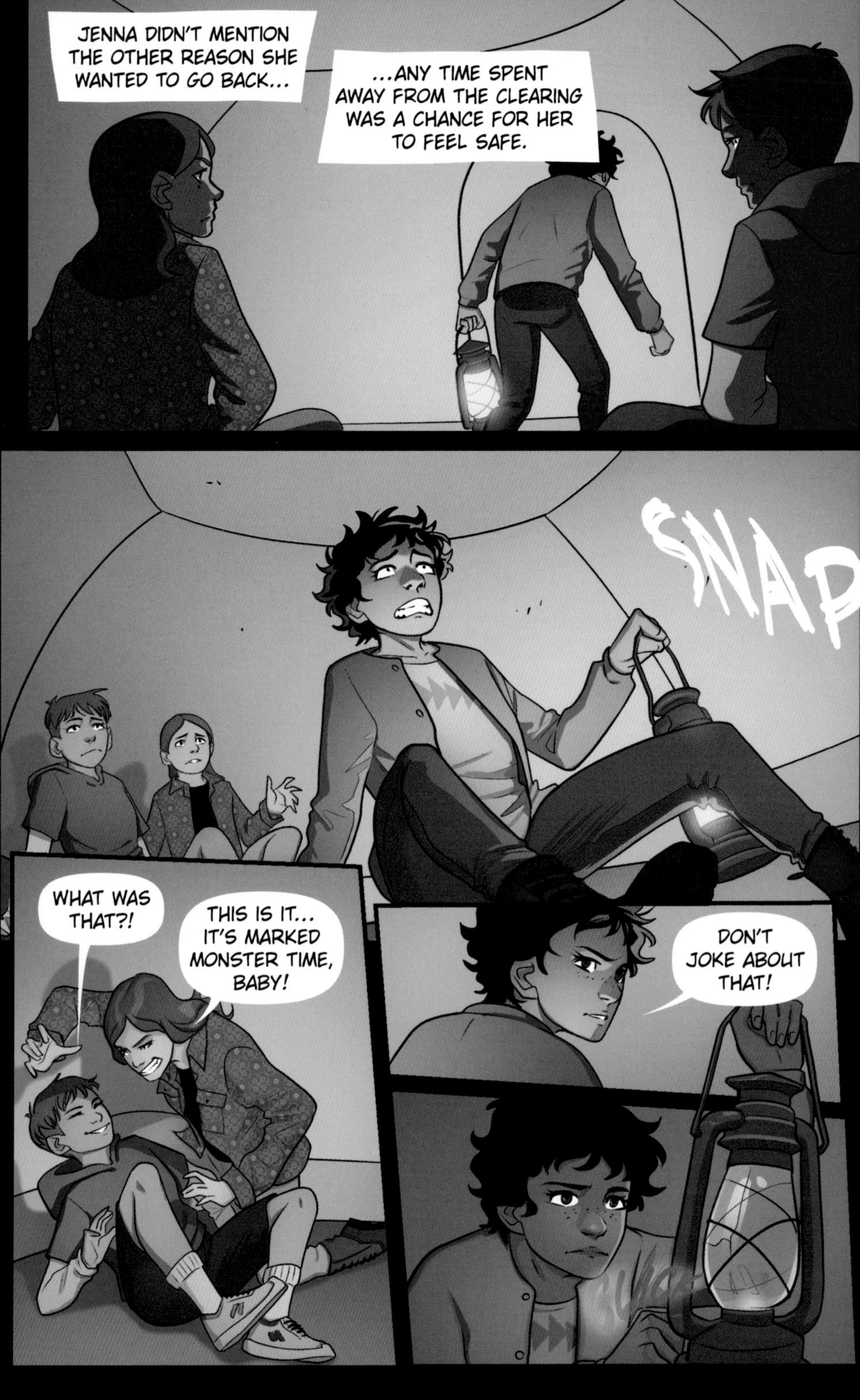
JENNA DIDN'T MENTION THE OTHER REASON SHE WANTED TO GO BACK...
...ANY TIME SPENT AWAY FROM THE CLEARING WAS A CHANCE FOR HER TO FEEL SAFE.
SNAP
WHAT WAS THAT?!
THIS IS IT... IT'S MARKED MONSTER TIME, BABY!
DON'T JOKE ABOUT THAT!

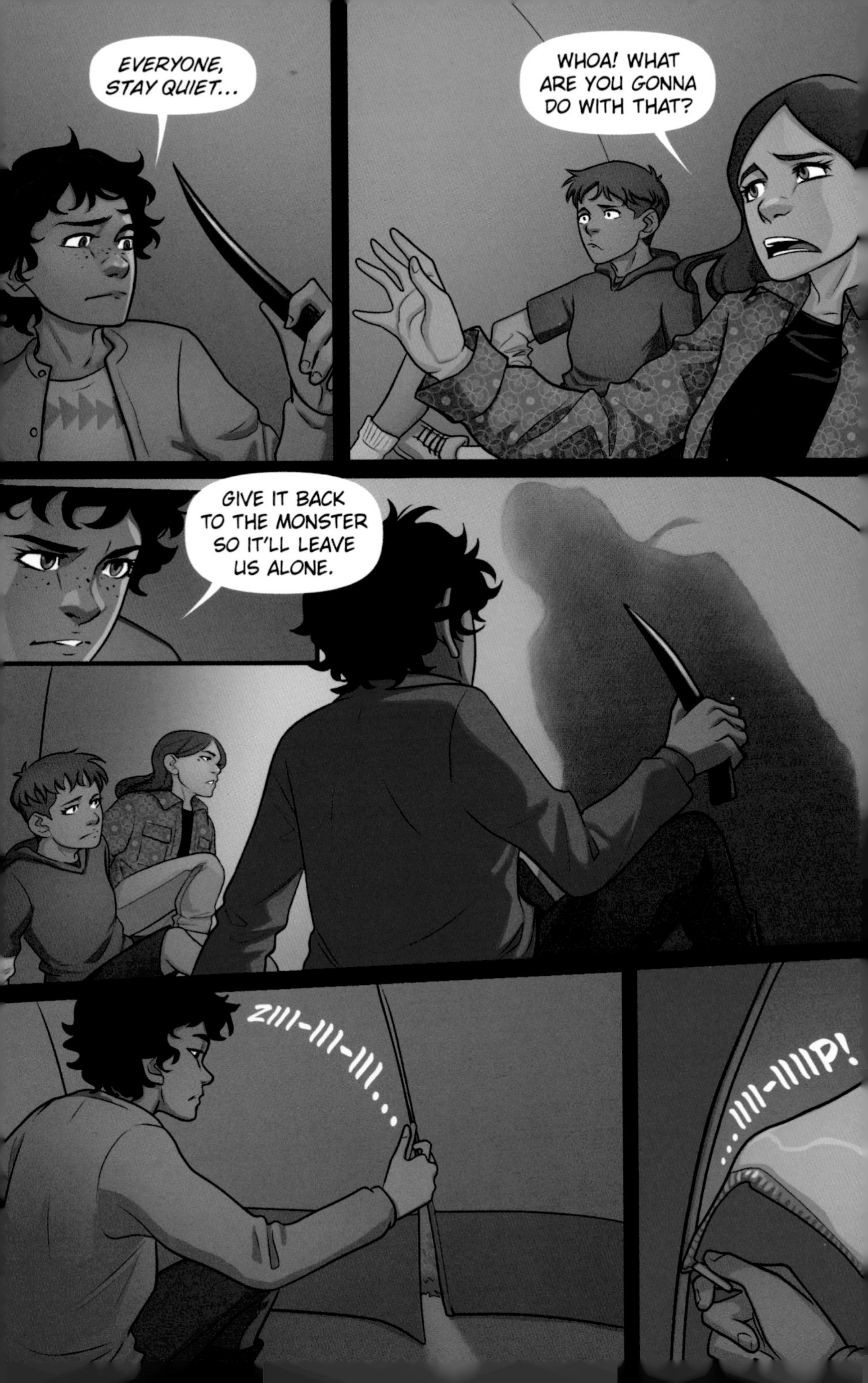
EVERYONE, STAY QUIET...
WHOA! WHAT ARE YOU GONNA DO WITH THAT?
GIVE IT BACK TO THE MONSTER SO IT'LL LEAVE US ALONE.
ZIII-III-III...
...IIII-IIIIP!

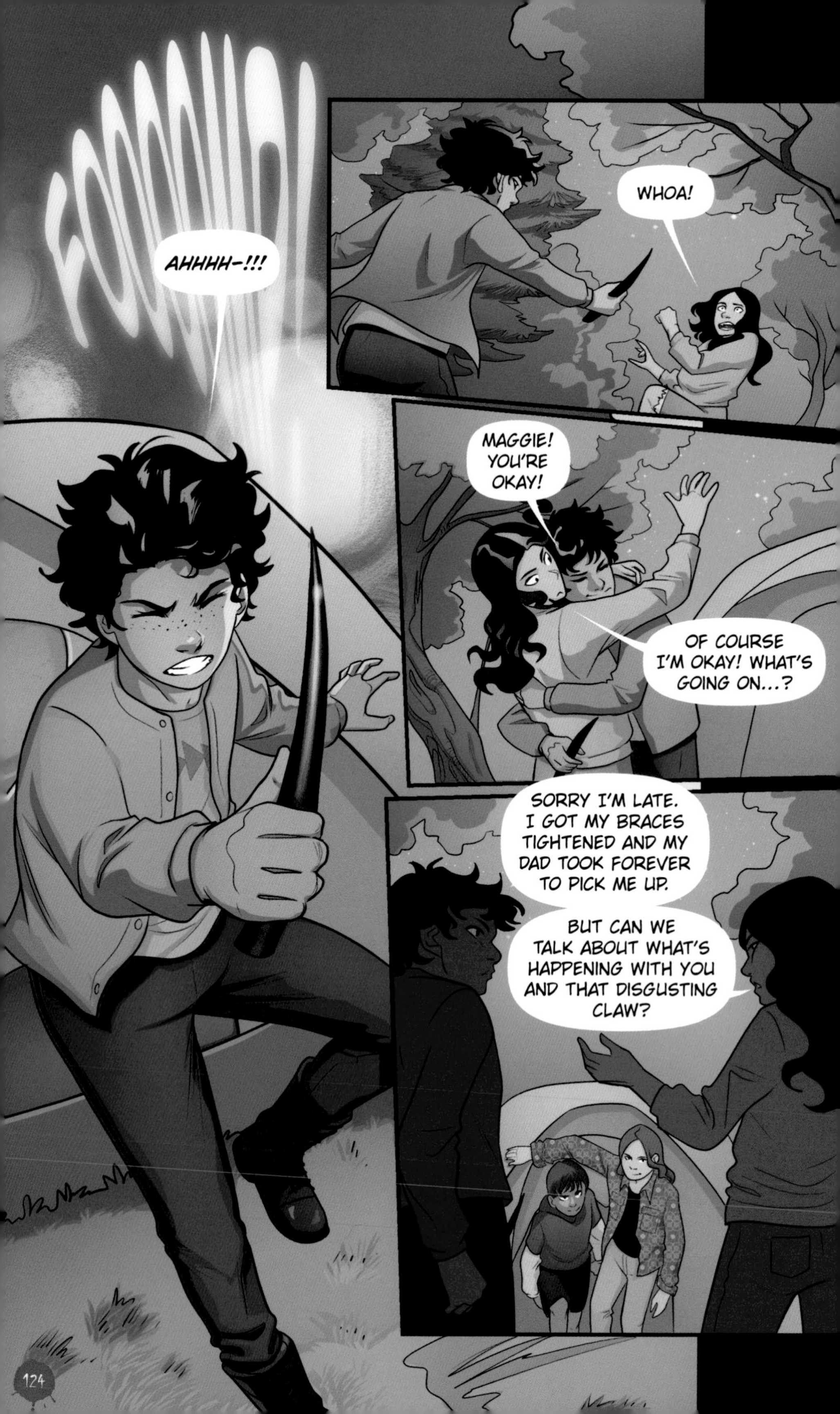
FOOOOOOP!
AHHHH-!!!
WHOA!
MAGGIE! YOU'RE OKAY!
OF COURSE I'M OKAY! WHAT'S GOING ON...?
SORRY I'M LATE. I GOT MY BRACES TIGHTENED AND MY DAD TOOK FOREVER TO PICK ME UP.
BUT CAN WE TALK ABOUT WHAT'S HAPPENING WITH YOU AND THAT DISGUSTING CLAW?

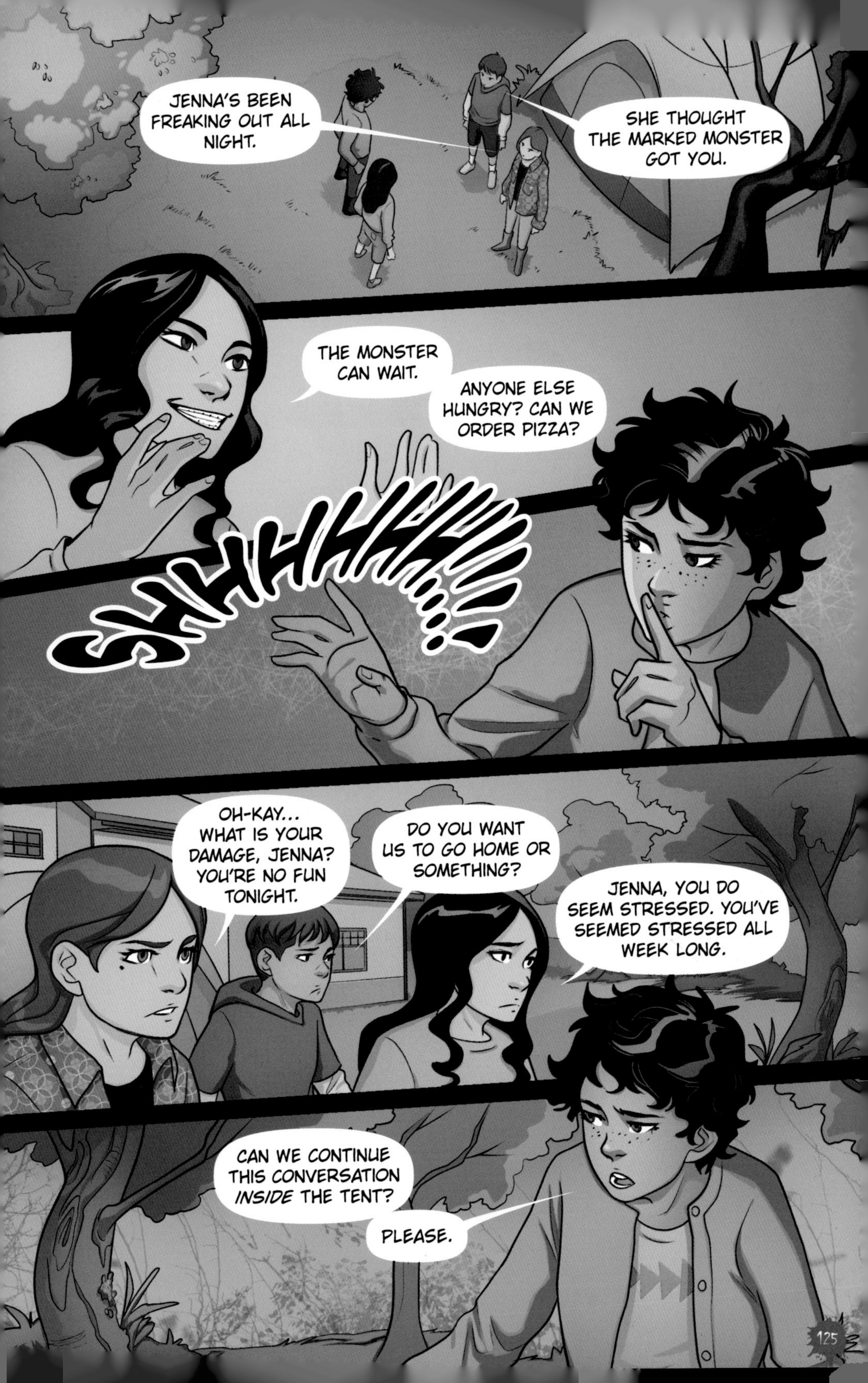

JENNA'S BEEN FREAKING OUT ALL NIGHT.
SHE THOUGHT THE MARKED MONSTER GOT YOU.
THE MONSTER CAN WAIT.
ANYONE ELSE HUNGRY? CAN WE ORDER PIZZA?
SHHHHHH!!!
OH-KAY... WHAT IS YOUR DAMAGE, JENNA? YOU'RE NO FUN TONIGHT.
DO YOU WANT US TO GO HOME OR SOMETHING?
JENNA, YOU DO SEEM STRESSED. YOU'VE SEEMED STRESSED ALL WEEK LONG.
CAN WE CONTINUE THIS CONVERSATION *INSIDE* THE TENT?
PLEASE.

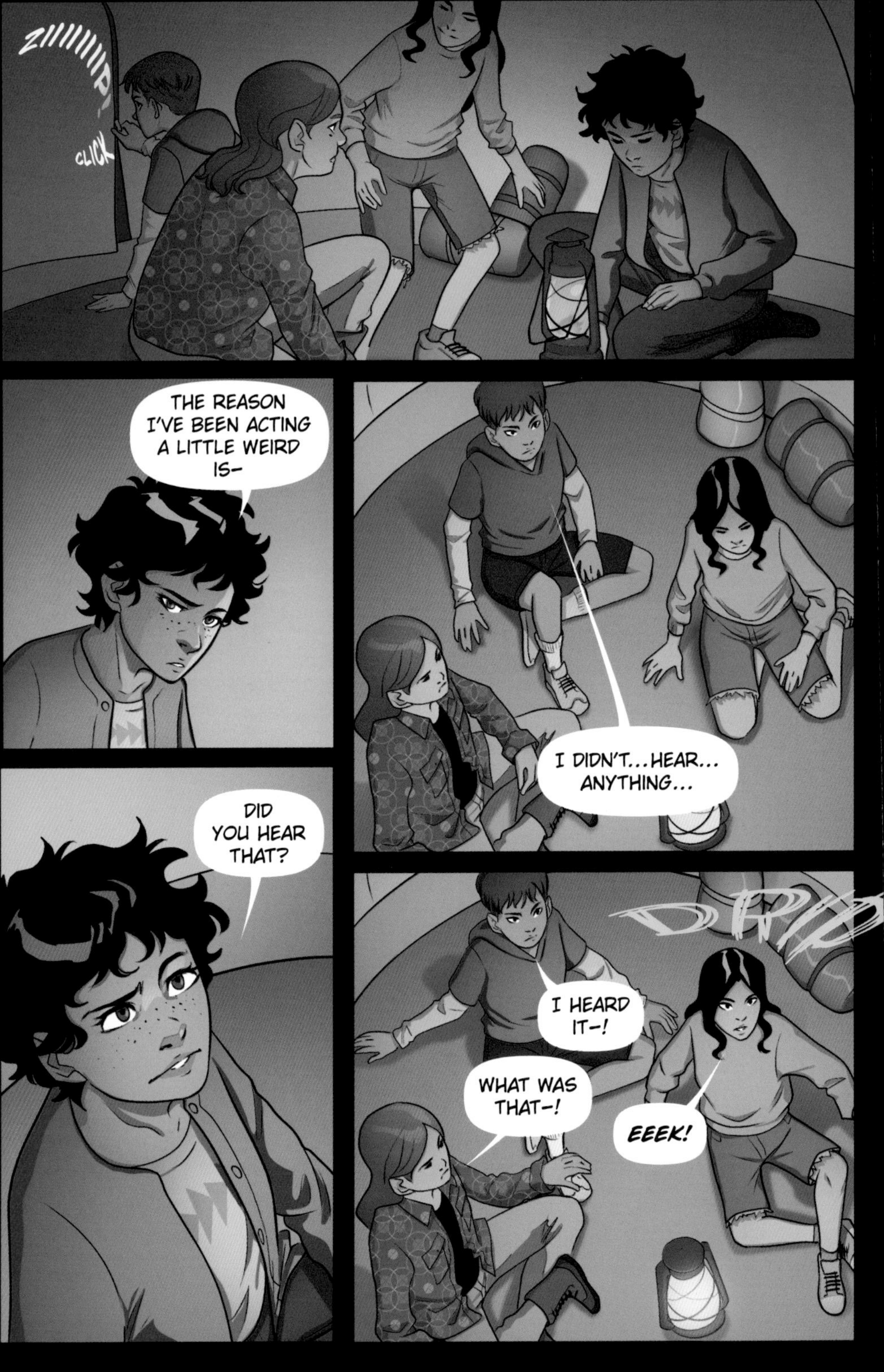
ZIIIIIIIP!
CLICK
THE REASON I'VE BEEN ACTING A LITTLE WEIRD IS–
I DIDN'T...HEAR... ANYTHING...
DID YOU HEAR THAT?
I HEARD IT–!
WHAT WAS THAT–!
EEEK!

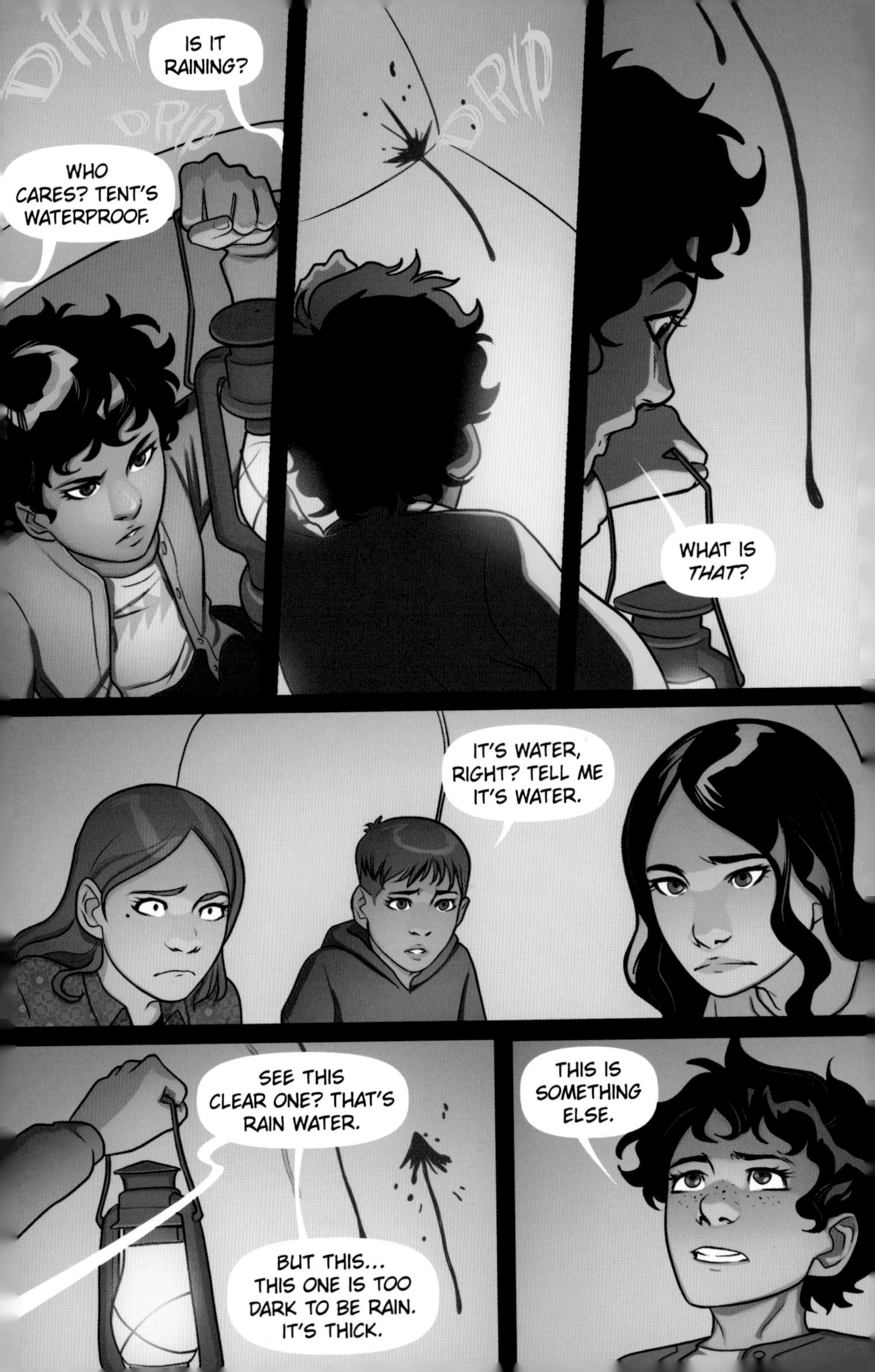
DRIP
IS IT RAINING?
DRIP
WHO CARES? TENT'S WATERPROOF.
DRIP
WHAT IS *THAT?*
IT'S WATER, RIGHT? TELL ME IT'S WATER.
SEE THIS CLEAR ONE? THAT'S RAIN WATER.
BUT THIS... THIS ONE IS TOO DARK TO BE RAIN. IT'S THICK.
THIS IS SOMETHING ELSE.

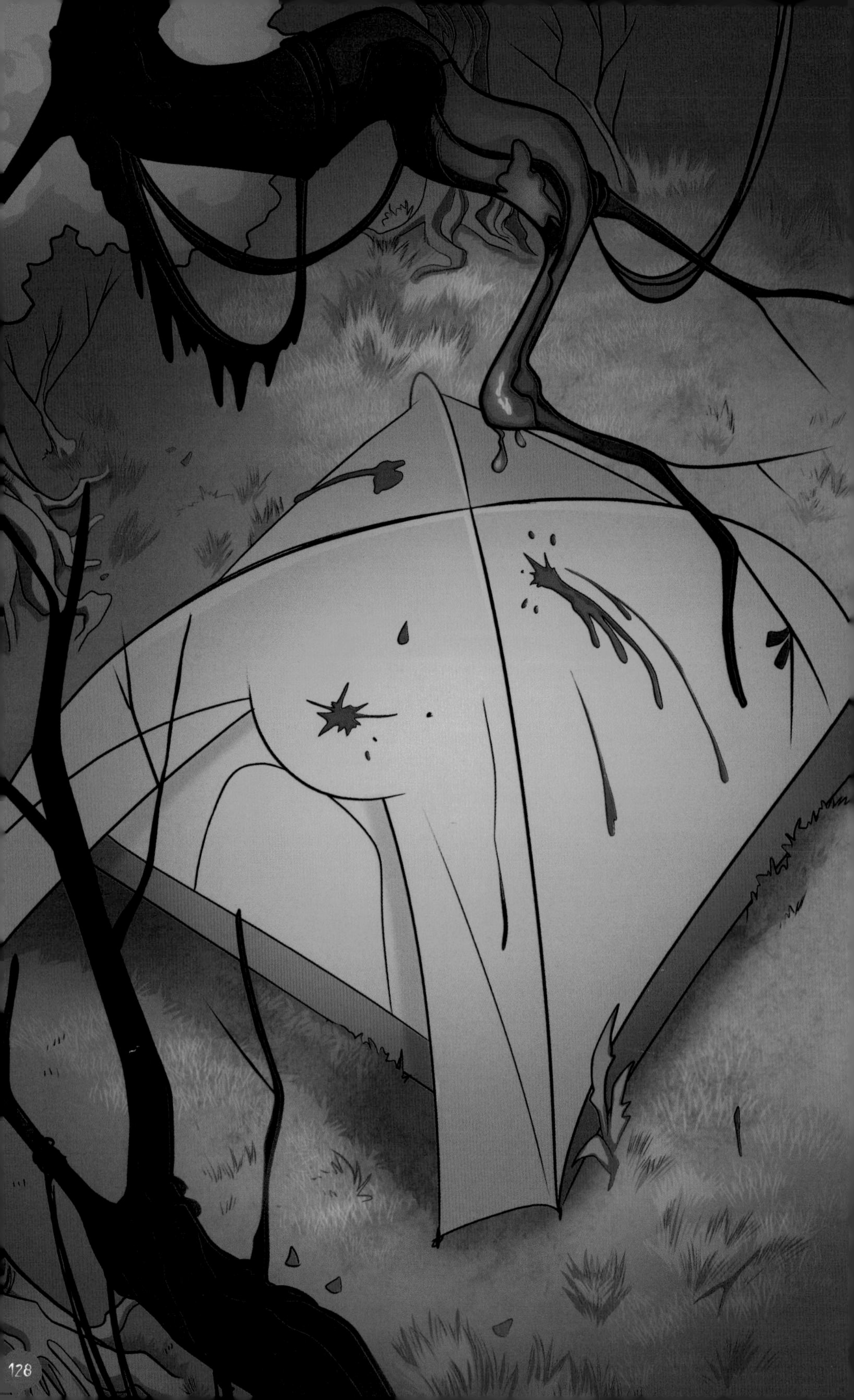

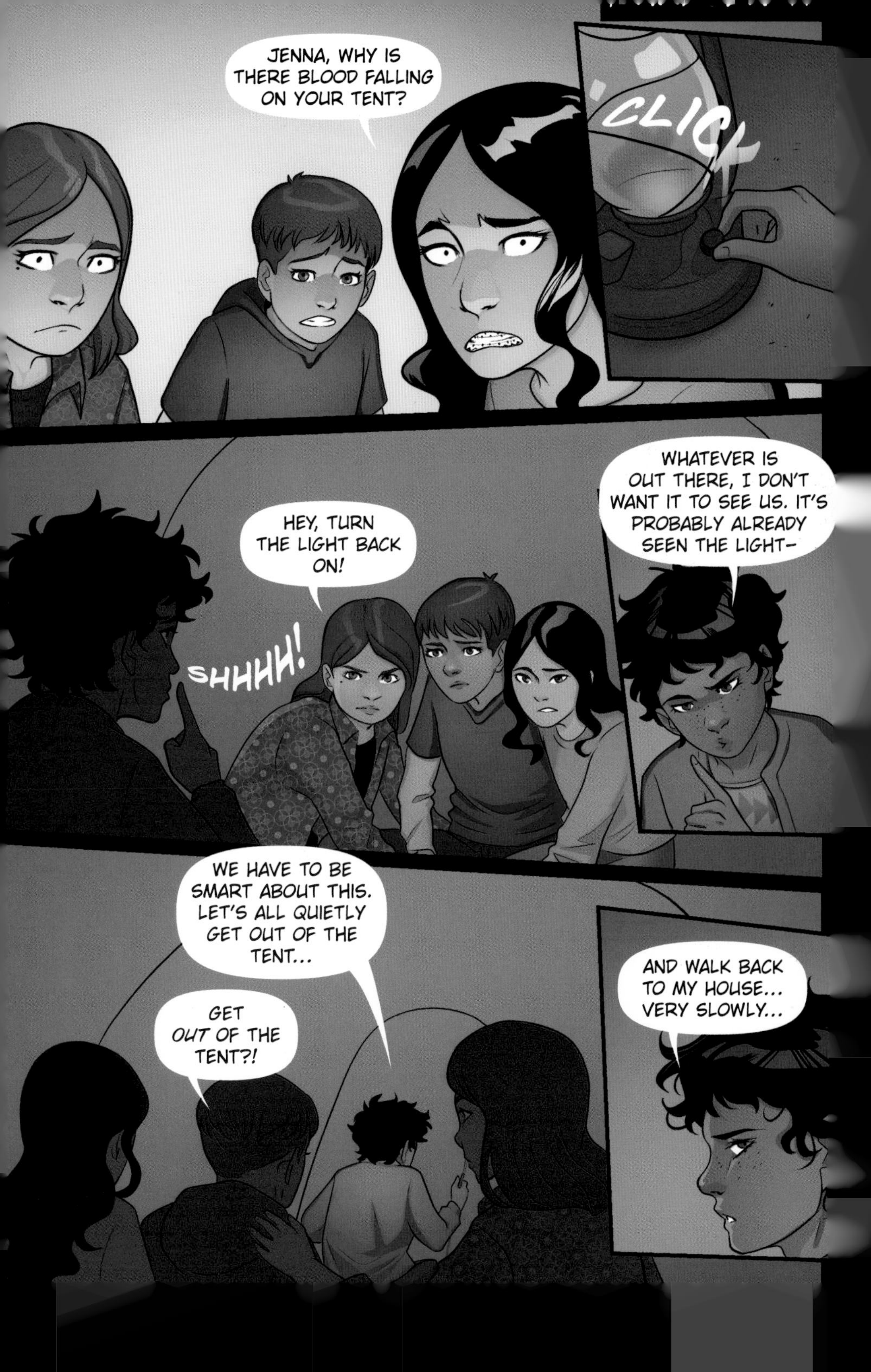
JENNA, WHY IS THERE BLOOD FALLING ON YOUR TENT?
CLICK
HEY, TURN THE LIGHT BACK ON!
SHHHH!
WHATEVER IS OUT THERE, I DON'T WANT IT TO SEE US. IT'S PROBABLY ALREADY SEEN THE LIGHT—
WE HAVE TO BE SMART ABOUT THIS. LET'S ALL QUIETLY GET OUT OF THE TENT...
GET *OUT* OF THE TENT?!
AND WALK BACK TO MY HOUSE... VERY SLOWLY...

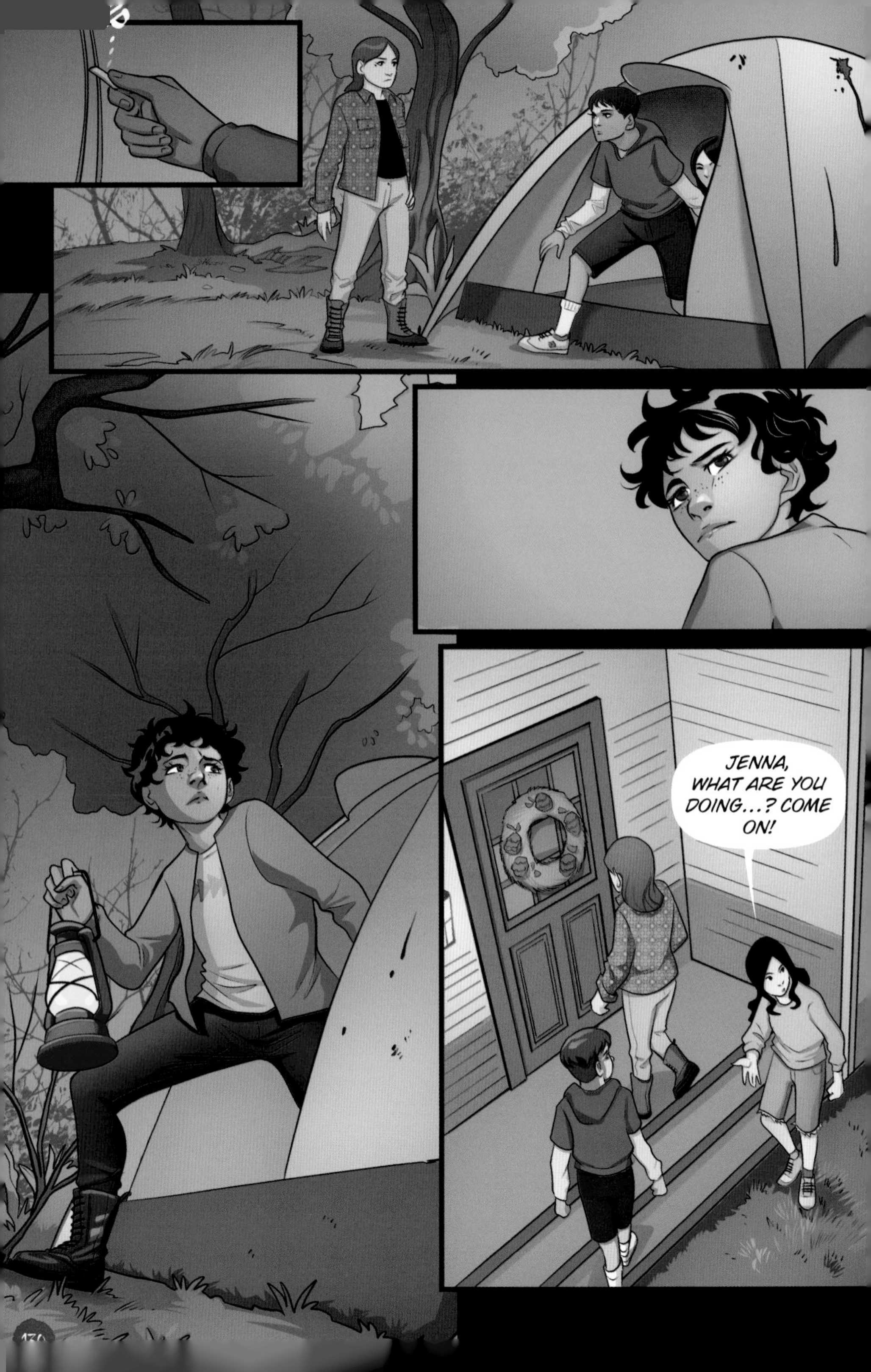
JENNA, WHAT ARE YOU DOING...? COME ON!

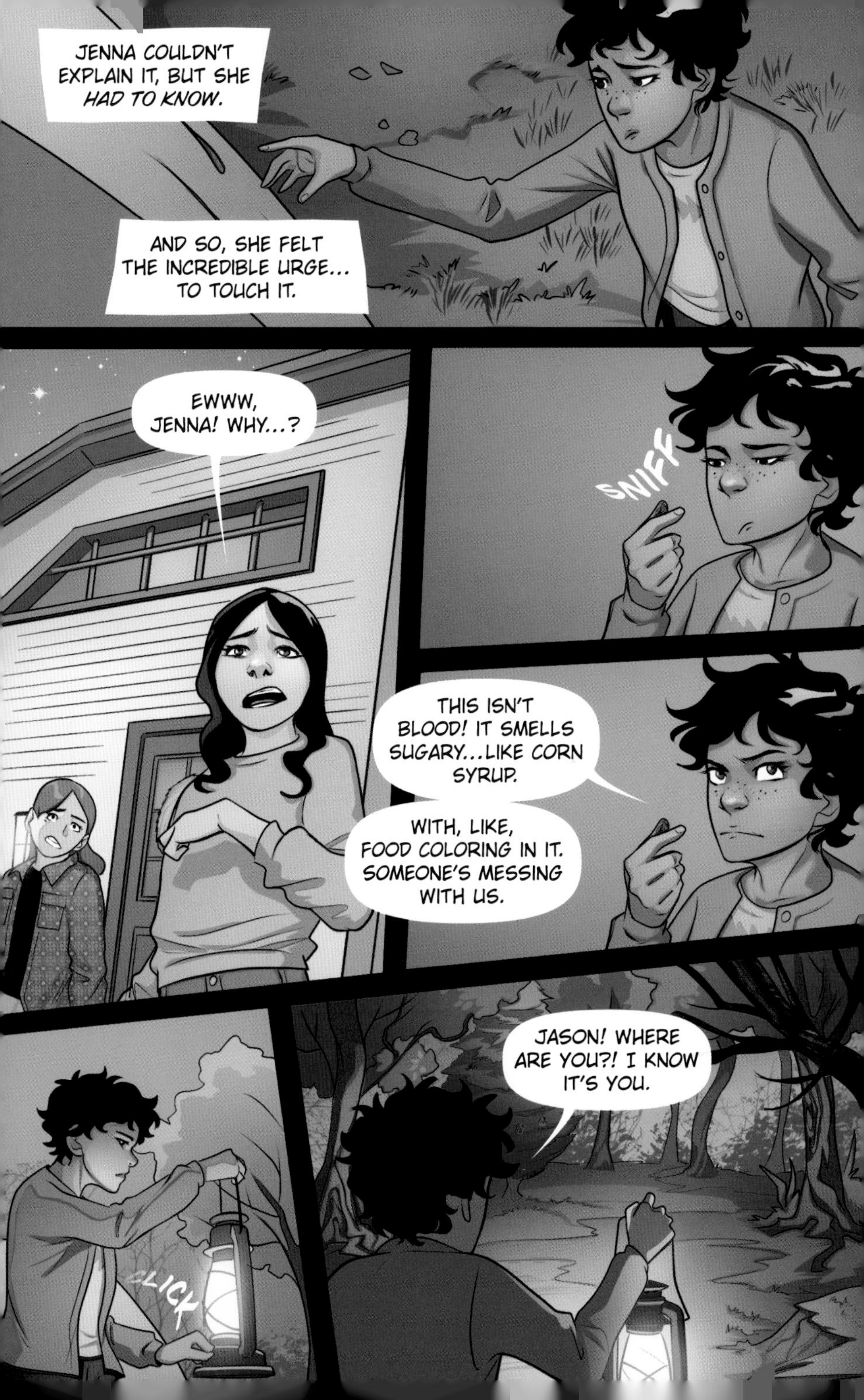
JENNA COULDN'T EXPLAIN IT, BUT SHE HAD TO KNOW.
AND SO, SHE FELT THE INCREDIBLE URGE... TO TOUCH IT.
EWWW, JENNA! WHY...?
SNIFF
THIS ISN'T BLOOD! IT SMELLS SUGARY...LIKE CORN SYRUP.
WITH, LIKE, FOOD COLORING IN IT. SOMEONE'S MESSING WITH US.
CLICK
JASON! WHERE ARE YOU?! I KNOW IT'S YOU.

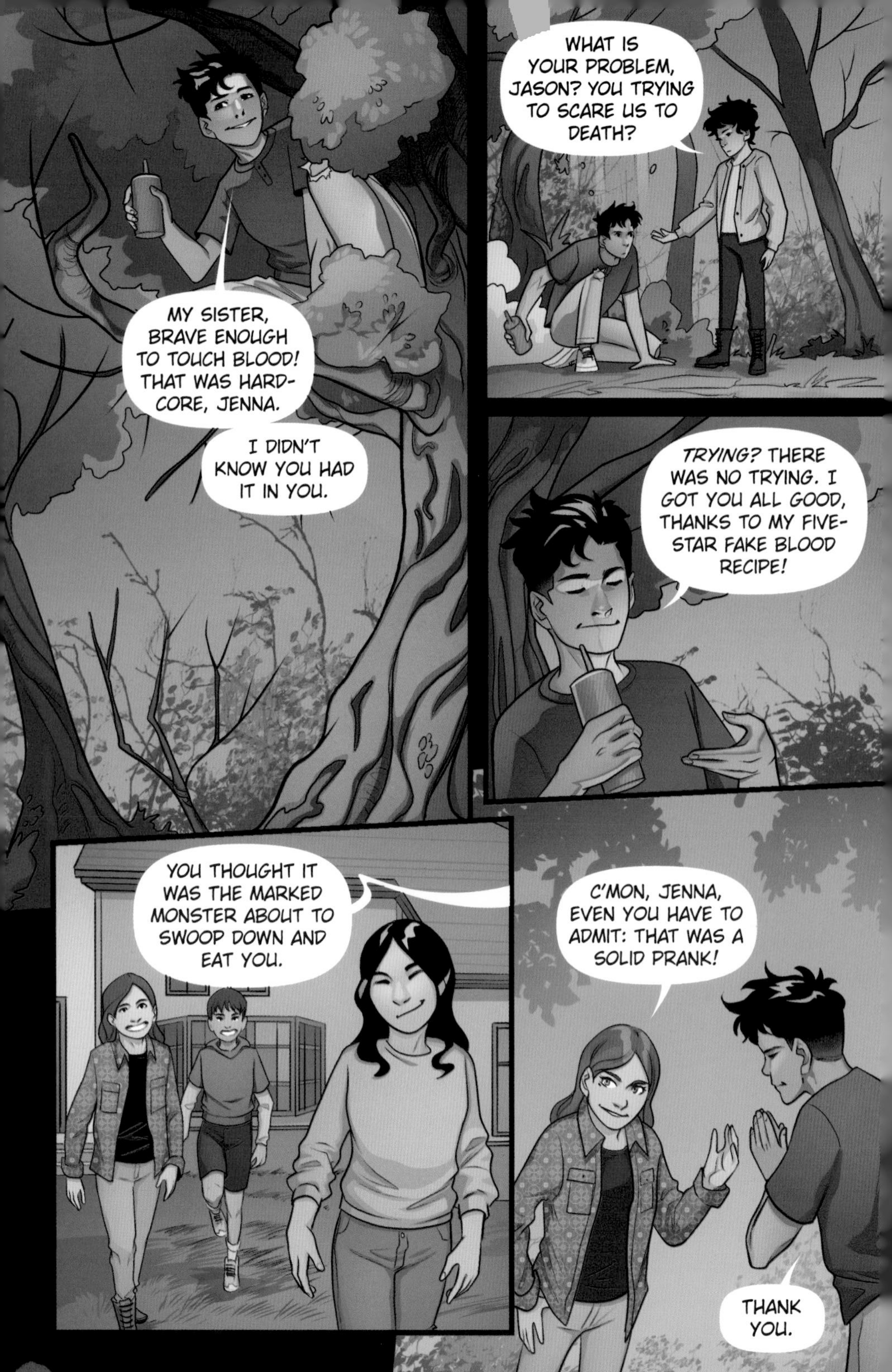
MY SISTER, BRAVE ENOUGH TO TOUCH BLOOD! THAT WAS HARD-CORE, JENNA.
I DIDN'T KNOW YOU HAD IT IN YOU.
WHAT IS YOUR PROBLEM, JASON? YOU TRYING TO SCARE US TO DEATH?
TRYING? THERE WAS NO TRYING. I GOT YOU ALL GOOD, THANKS TO MY FIVE-STAR FAKE BLOOD RECIPE!
YOU THOUGHT IT WAS THE MARKED MONSTER ABOUT TO SWOOP DOWN AND EAT YOU.
C'MON, JENNA, EVEN YOU HAVE TO ADMIT: THAT WAS A SOLID PRANK!
THANK YOU.

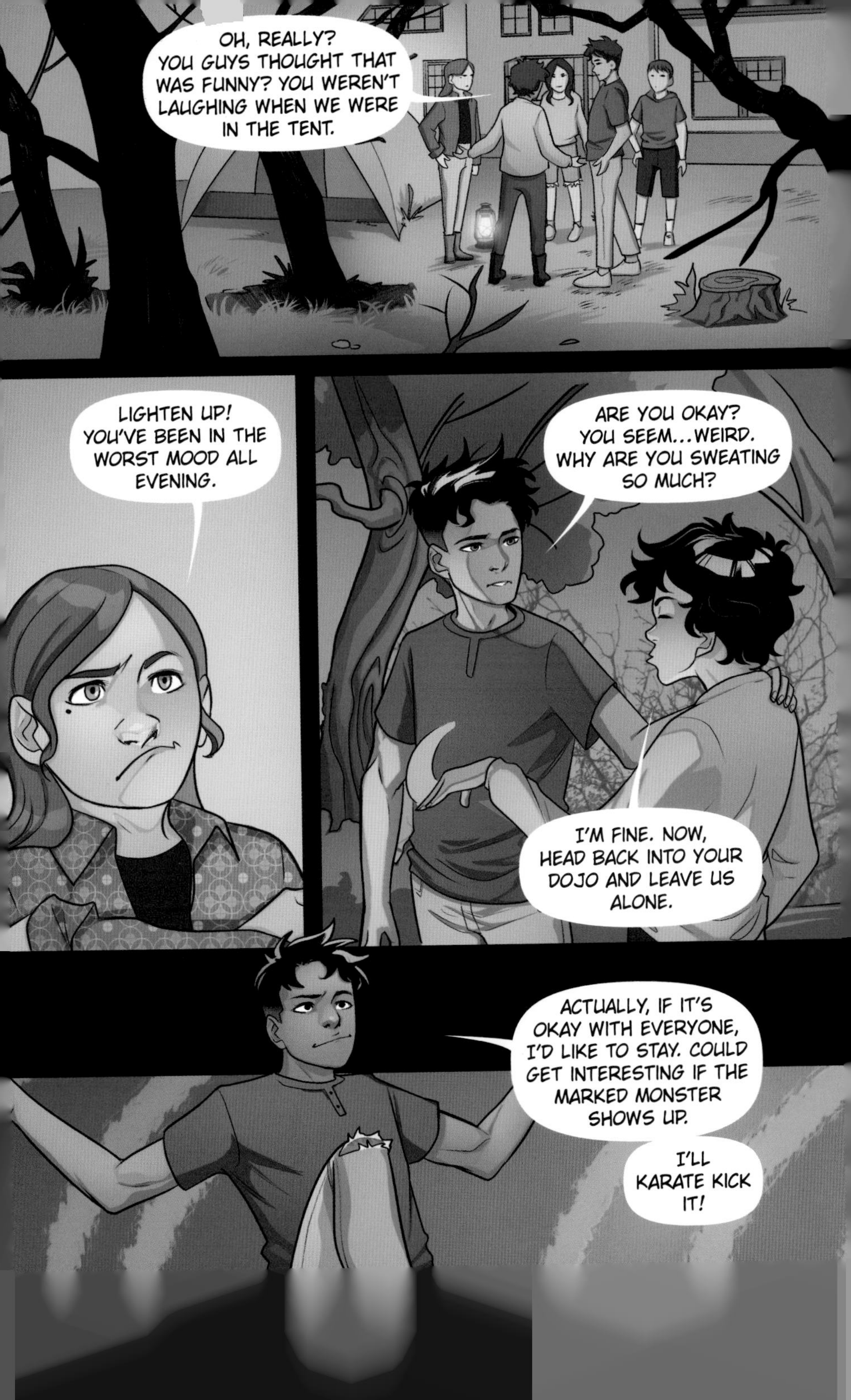
OH, REALLY? YOU GUYS THOUGHT THAT WAS FUNNY? YOU WEREN'T LAUGHING WHEN WE WERE IN THE TENT.
LIGHTEN UP! YOU'VE BEEN IN THE WORST MOOD ALL EVENING.
ARE YOU OKAY? YOU SEEM...WEIRD. WHY ARE YOU SWEATING SO MUCH?
I'M FINE. NOW, HEAD BACK INTO YOUR DOJO AND LEAVE US ALONE.
ACTUALLY, IF IT'S OKAY WITH EVERYONE, I'D LIKE TO STAY. COULD GET INTERESTING IF THE MARKED MONSTER SHOWS UP.
I'LL KARATE KICK IT!

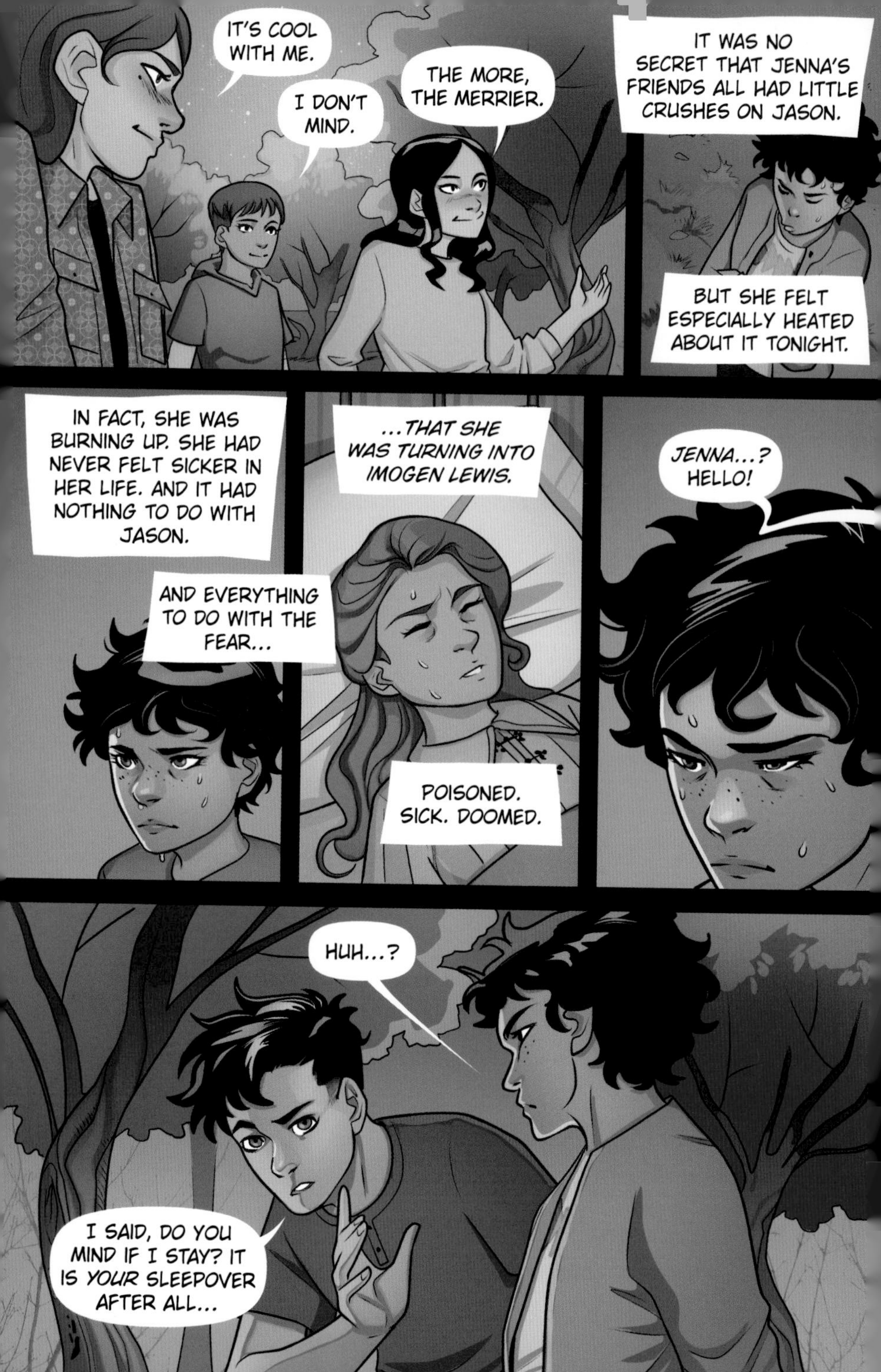
IT'S COOL WITH ME.
I DON'T MIND.
THE MORE, THE MERRIER.
IT WAS NO SECRET THAT JENNA'S FRIENDS ALL HAD LITTLE CRUSHES ON JASON.
BUT SHE FELT ESPECIALLY HEATED ABOUT IT TONIGHT.
IN FACT, SHE WAS BURNING UP. SHE HAD NEVER FELT SICKER IN HER LIFE. AND IT HAD NOTHING TO DO WITH JASON.
AND EVERYTHING TO DO WITH THE FEAR...
...THAT SHE WAS TURNING INTO IMOGEN LEWIS.
POISONED. SICK. DOOMED.
JENNA...? HELLO!
HUH...?
I SAID, DO YOU MIND IF I STAY? IT IS YOUR SLEEPOVER AFTER ALL...

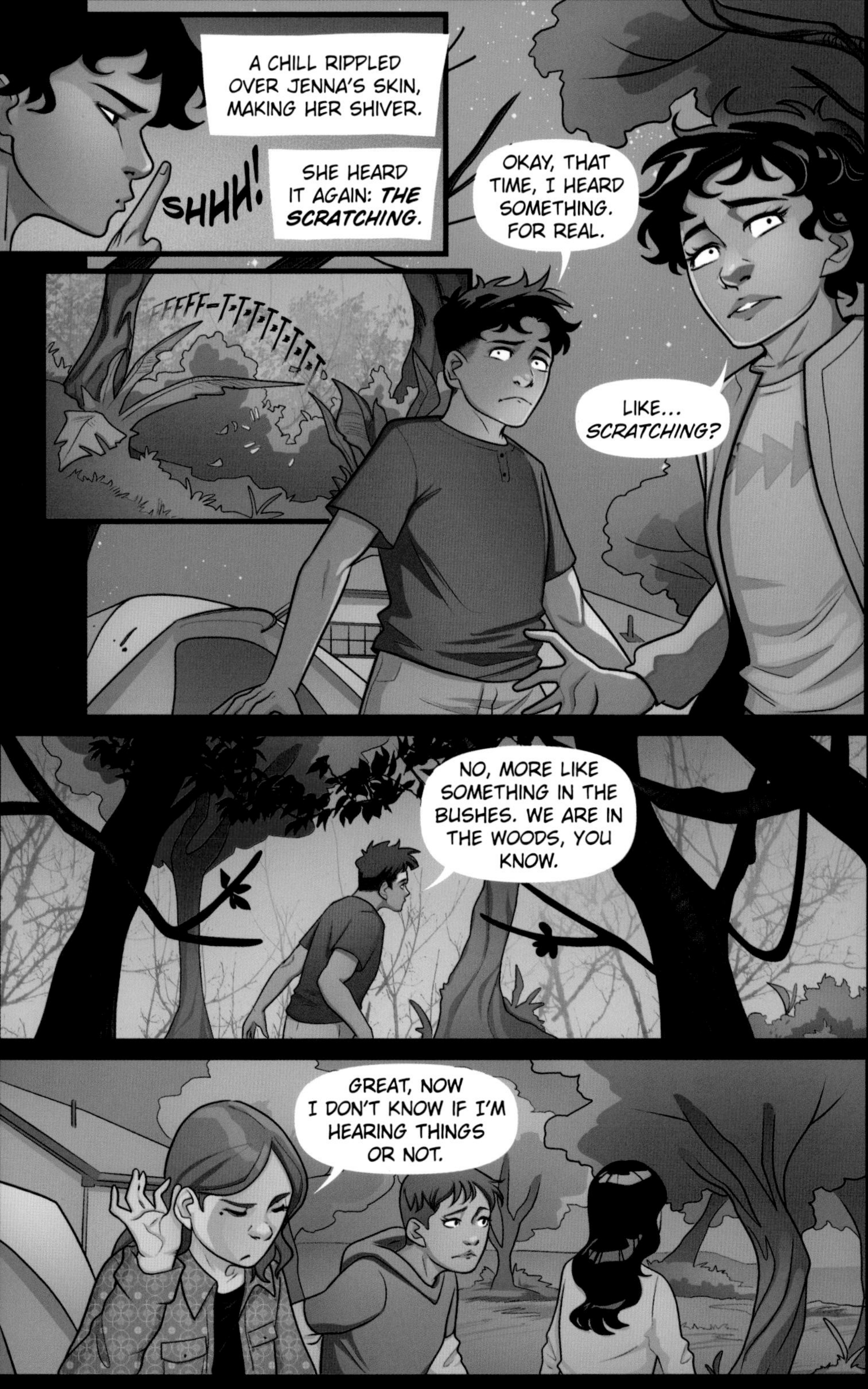
A CHILL RIPPLED OVER JENNA'S SKIN, MAKING HER SHIVER.
SHHH!
SHE HEARD IT AGAIN: ***THE SCRATCHING.***
OKAY, THAT TIME, I HEARD SOMETHING. FOR REAL.
FFFFF-T-T-T-T-T-T-T-T-T-T
LIKE... *SCRATCHING?*
NO, MORE LIKE SOMETHING IN THE BUSHES. WE ARE IN THE WOODS, YOU KNOW.
GREAT, NOW I DON'T KNOW IF I'M HEARING THINGS OR NOT.

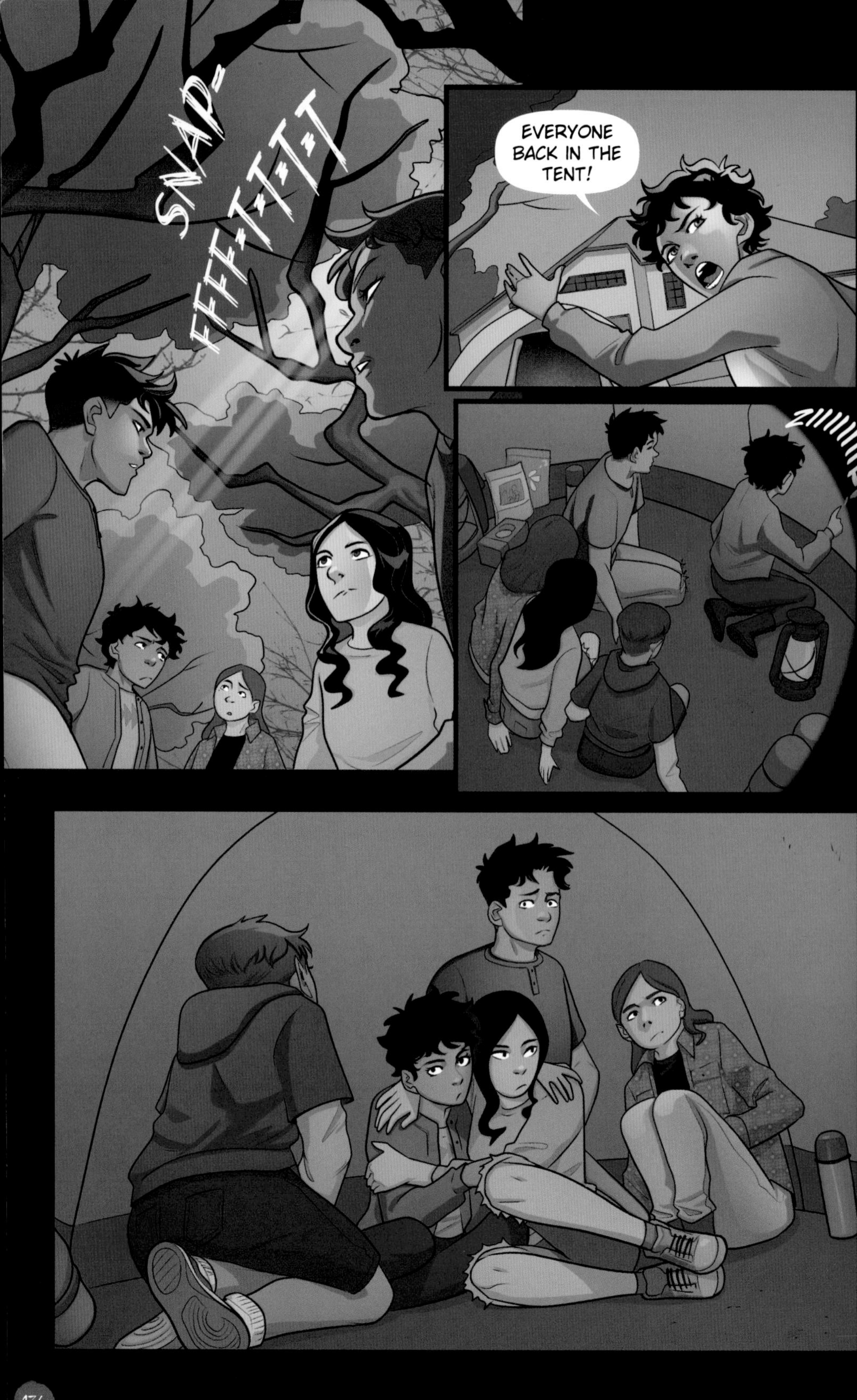
SNAP
EVERYONE BACK IN THE TENT!

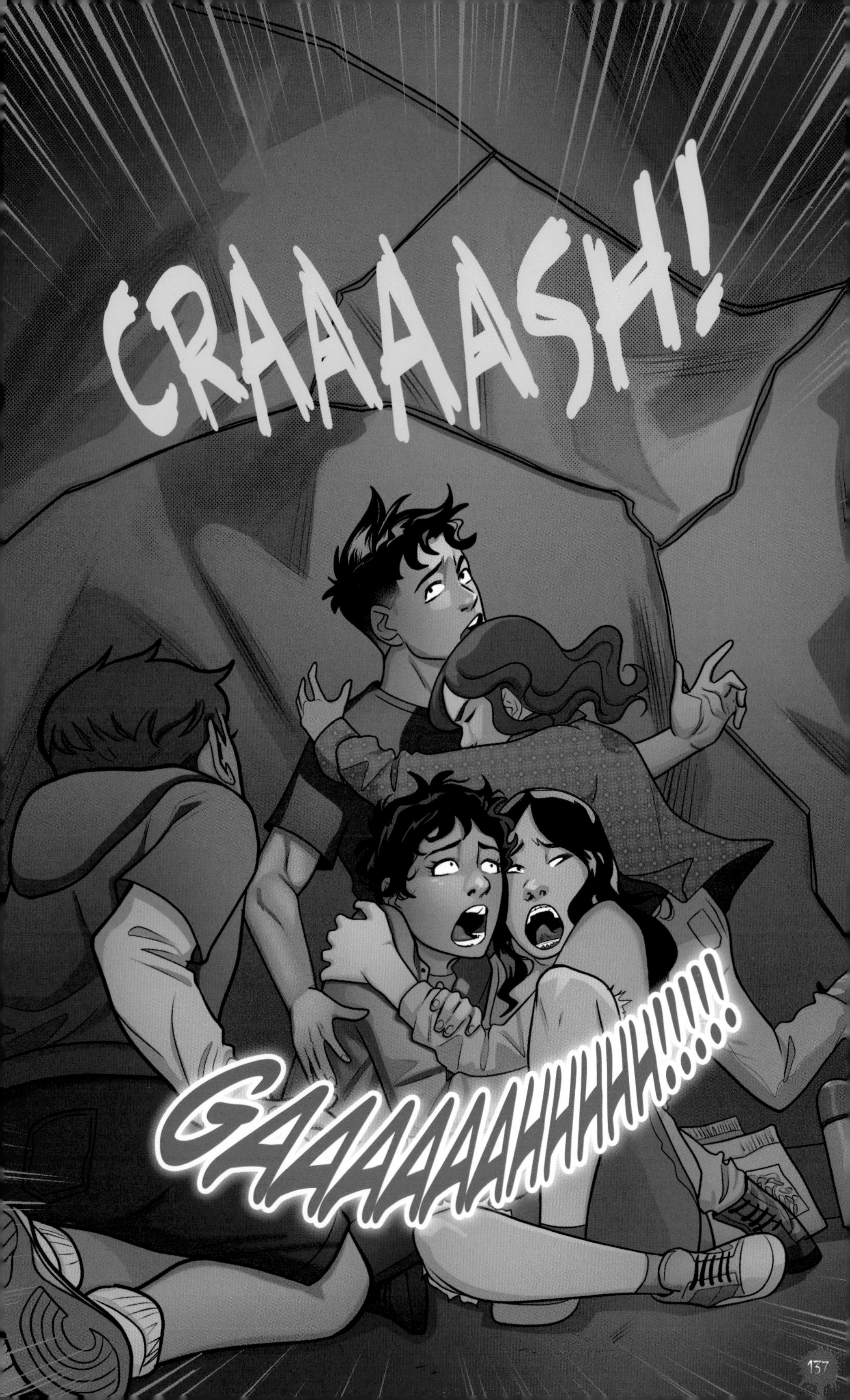
CRAAAASH!
GAAAAAHHHHH!!!!!

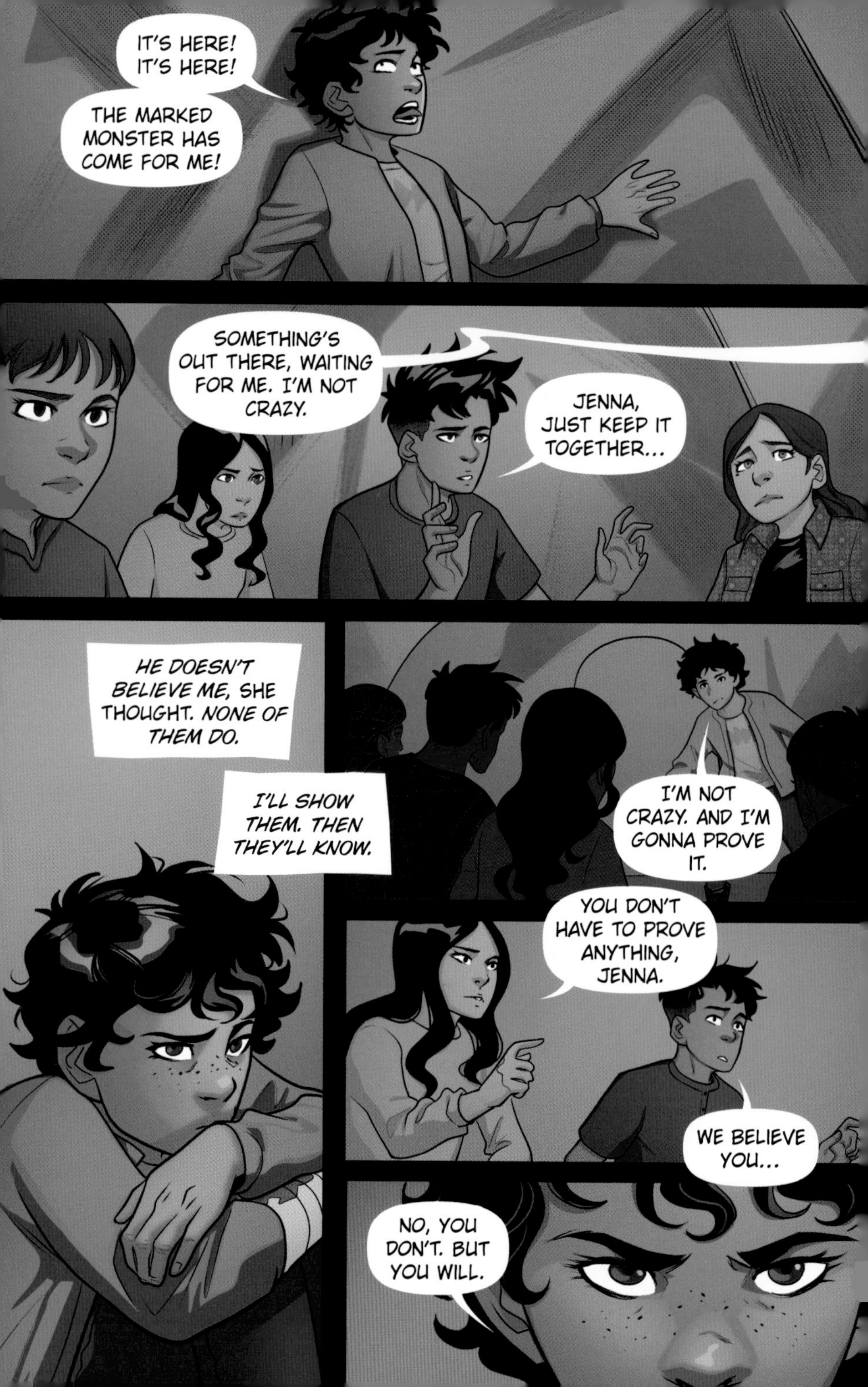
IT'S HERE! IT'S HERE!
THE MARKED MONSTER HAS COME FOR ME!
SOMETHING'S OUT THERE, WAITING FOR ME. I'M NOT CRAZY.
JENNA, JUST KEEP IT TOGETHER...
HE DOESN'T BELIEVE ME, SHE THOUGHT. NONE OF THEM DO.
I'LL SHOW THEM. THEN THEY'LL KNOW.
I'M NOT CRAZY. AND I'M GONNA PROVE IT.
YOU DON'T HAVE TO PROVE ANYTHING, JENNA.
WE BELIEVE YOU...
NO, YOU DON'T. BUT YOU WILL.

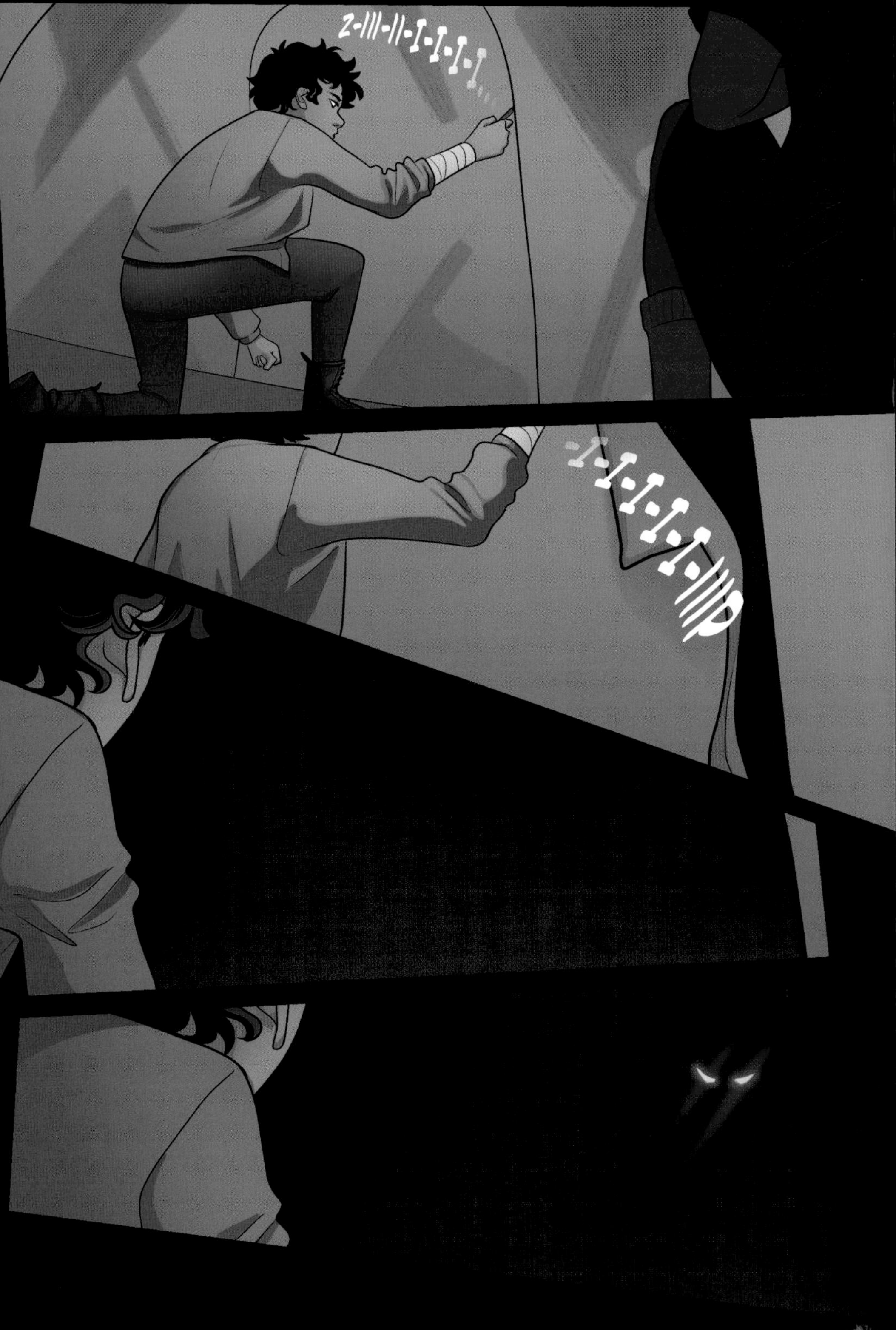

CHAPTER 12

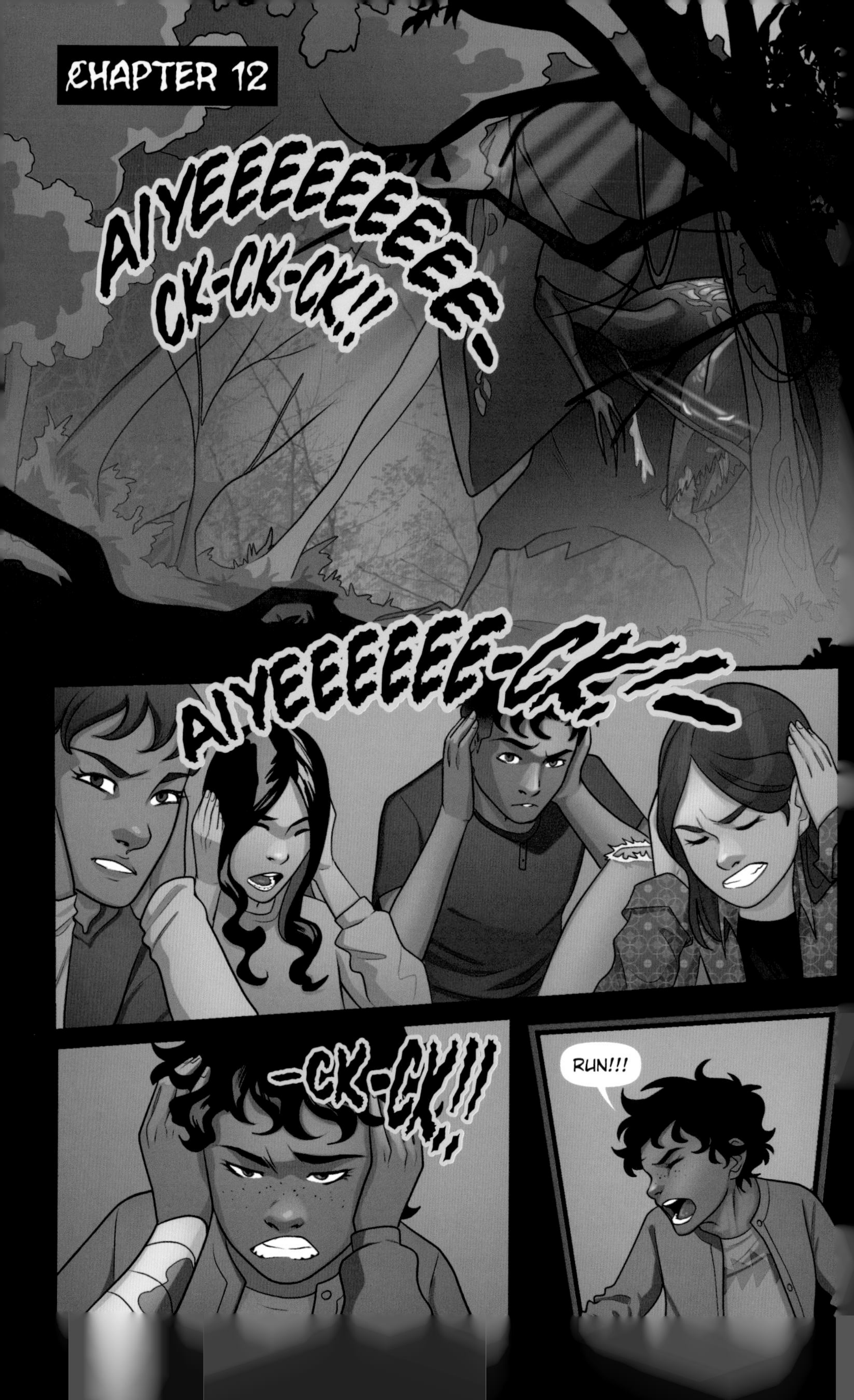

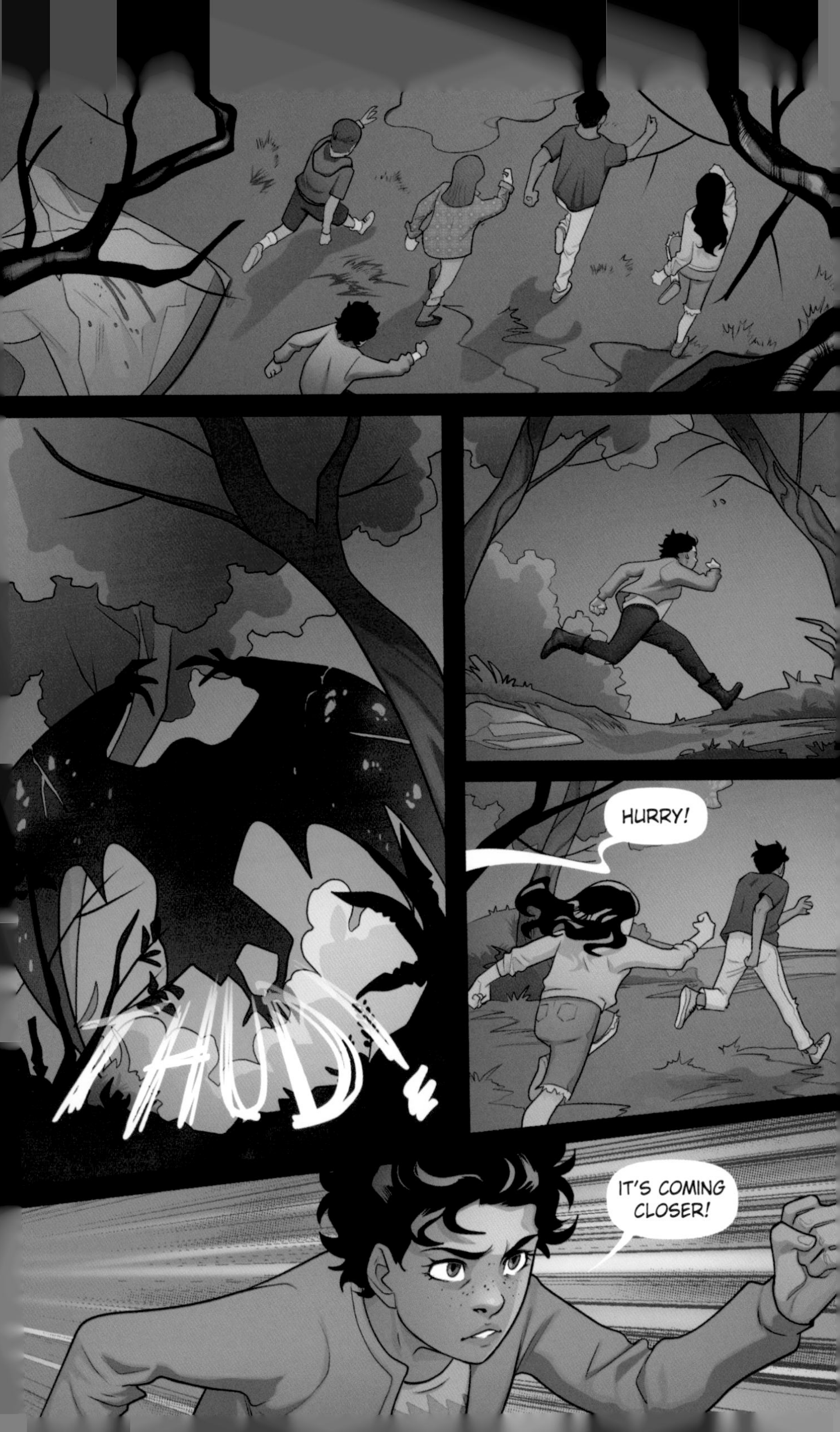
THUD
HURRY!
IT'S COMING CLOSER!

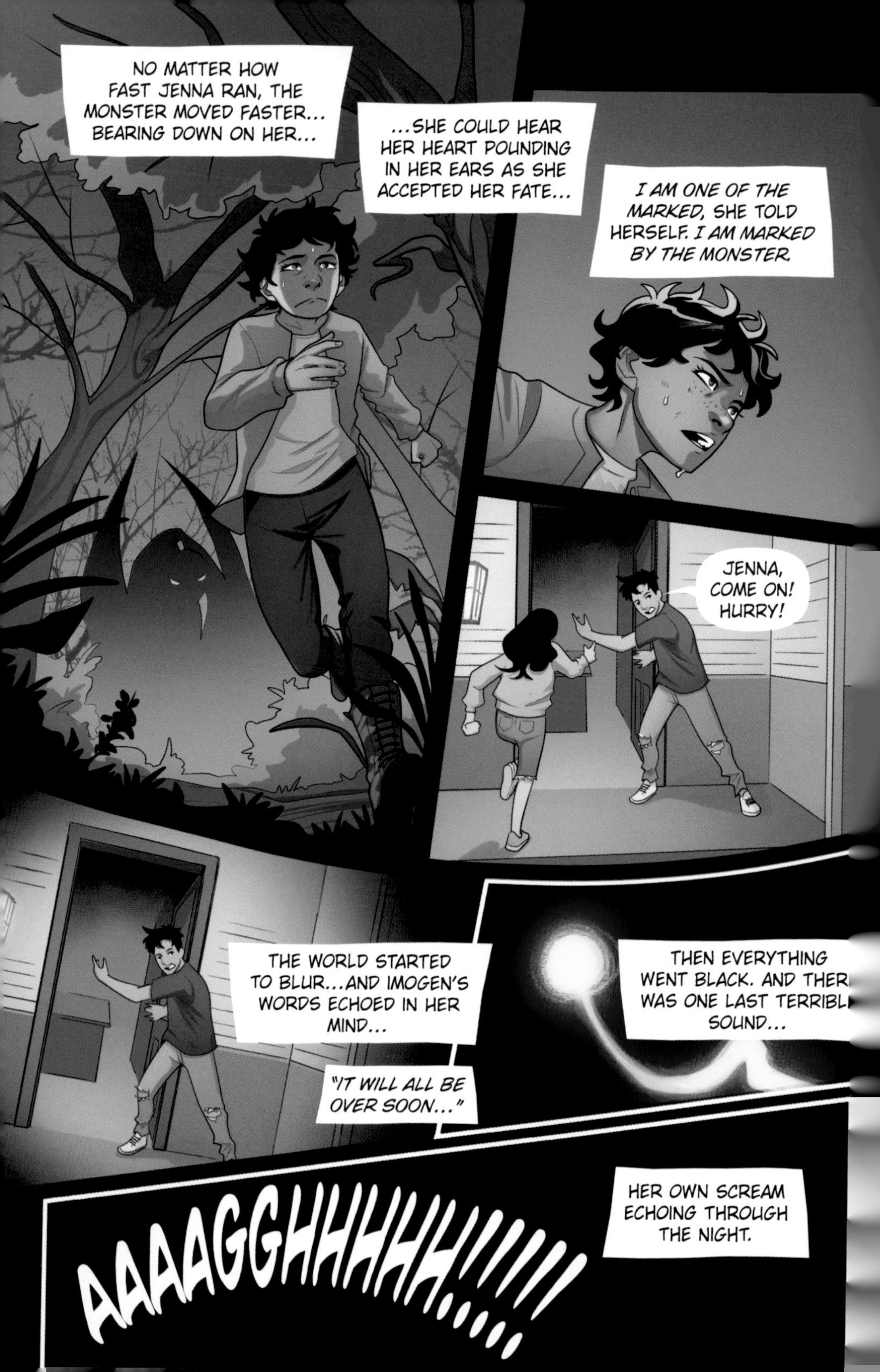
NO MATTER HOW FAST JENNA RAN, THE MONSTER MOVED FASTER... BEARING DOWN ON HER...
...SHE COULD HEAR HER HEART POUNDING IN HER EARS AS SHE ACCEPTED HER FATE...
I AM ONE OF THE MARKED, SHE TOLD HERSELF. I AM MARKED BY THE MONSTER.
JENNA, COME ON! HURRY!
THE WORLD STARTED TO BLUR...AND IMOGEN'S WORDS ECHOED IN HER MIND...
"IT WILL ALL BE OVER SOON..."
THEN EVERYTHING WENT BLACK. AND THER WAS ONE LAST TERRIBL SOUND...
AAAAGHHHHHH!!!!!
HER OWN SCREAM ECHOING THROUGH THE NIGHT.

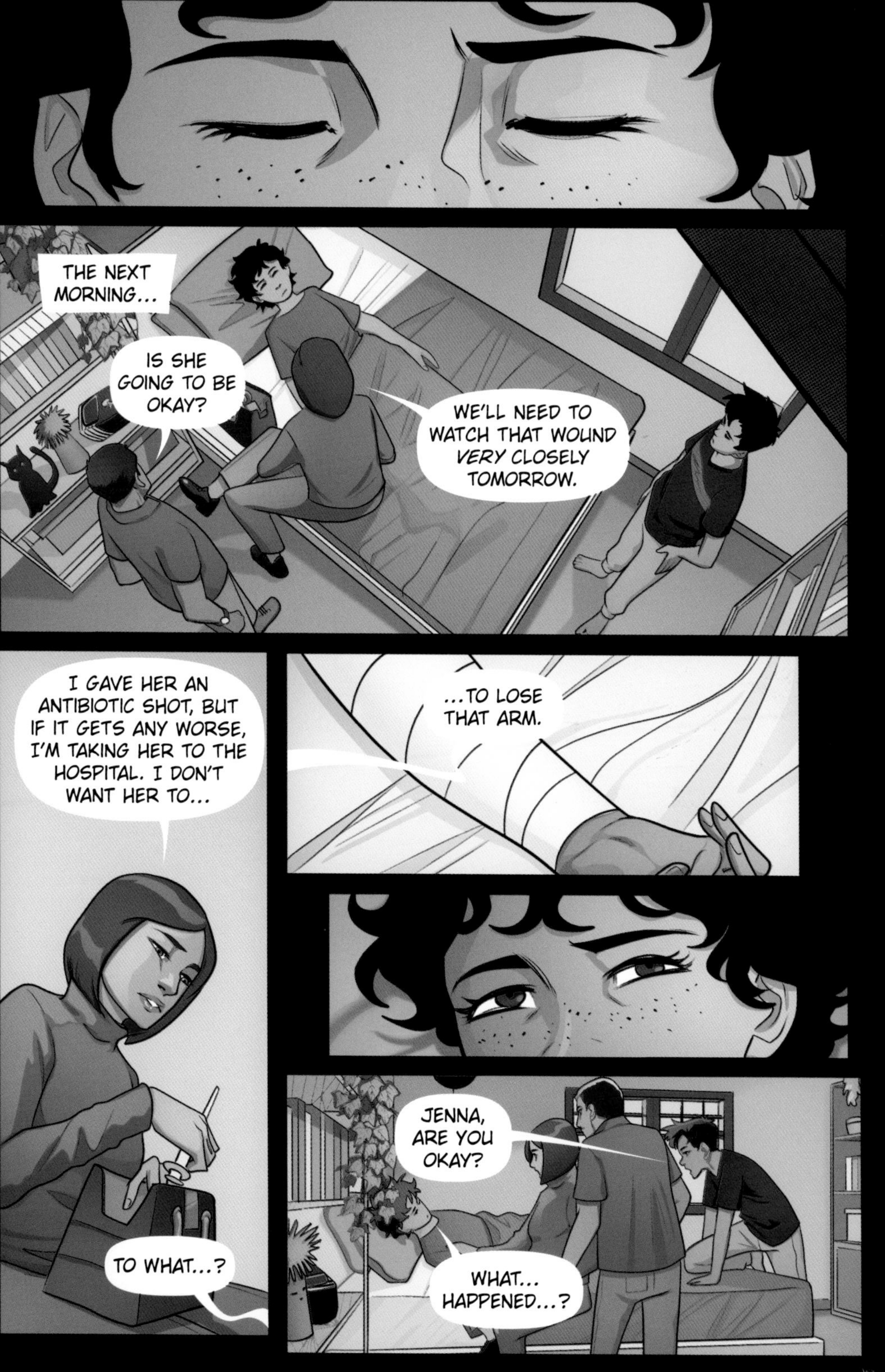
THE NEXT MORNING...
IS SHE GOING TO BE OKAY?
WE'LL NEED TO WATCH THAT WOUND *VERY* CLOSELY TOMORROW.
I GAVE HER AN ANTIBIOTIC SHOT, BUT IF IT GETS ANY WORSE, I'M TAKING HER TO THE HOSPITAL. I DON'T WANT HER TO...
...TO LOSE THAT ARM.
TO WHAT...?
JENNA, ARE YOU OKAY?
WHAT... HAPPENED...?

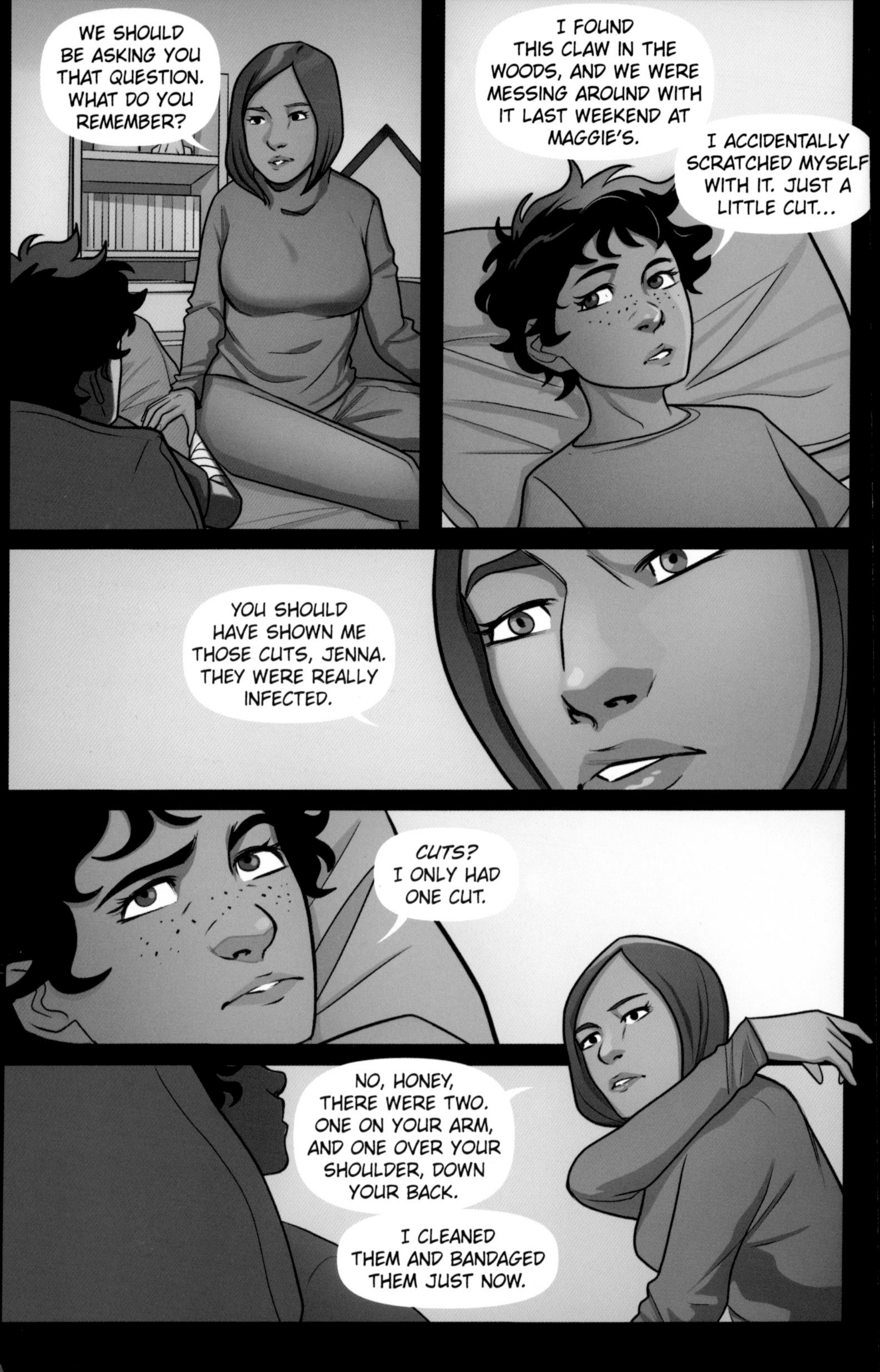
WE SHOULD BE ASKING YOU THAT QUESTION. WHAT DO YOU REMEMBER?
I FOUND THIS CLAW IN THE WOODS, AND WE WERE MESSING AROUND WITH IT LAST WEEKEND AT MAGGIE'S.
I ACCIDENTALLY SCRATCHED MYSELF WITH IT. JUST A LITTLE CUT...
YOU SHOULD HAVE SHOWN ME THOSE CUTS, JENNA. THEY WERE REALLY INFECTED.
CUTS? I ONLY HAD ONE CUT.
NO, HONEY, THERE WERE TWO. ONE ON YOUR ARM, AND ONE OVER YOUR SHOULDER, DOWN YOUR BACK.
I CLEANED THEM AND BANDAGED THEM JUST NOW.

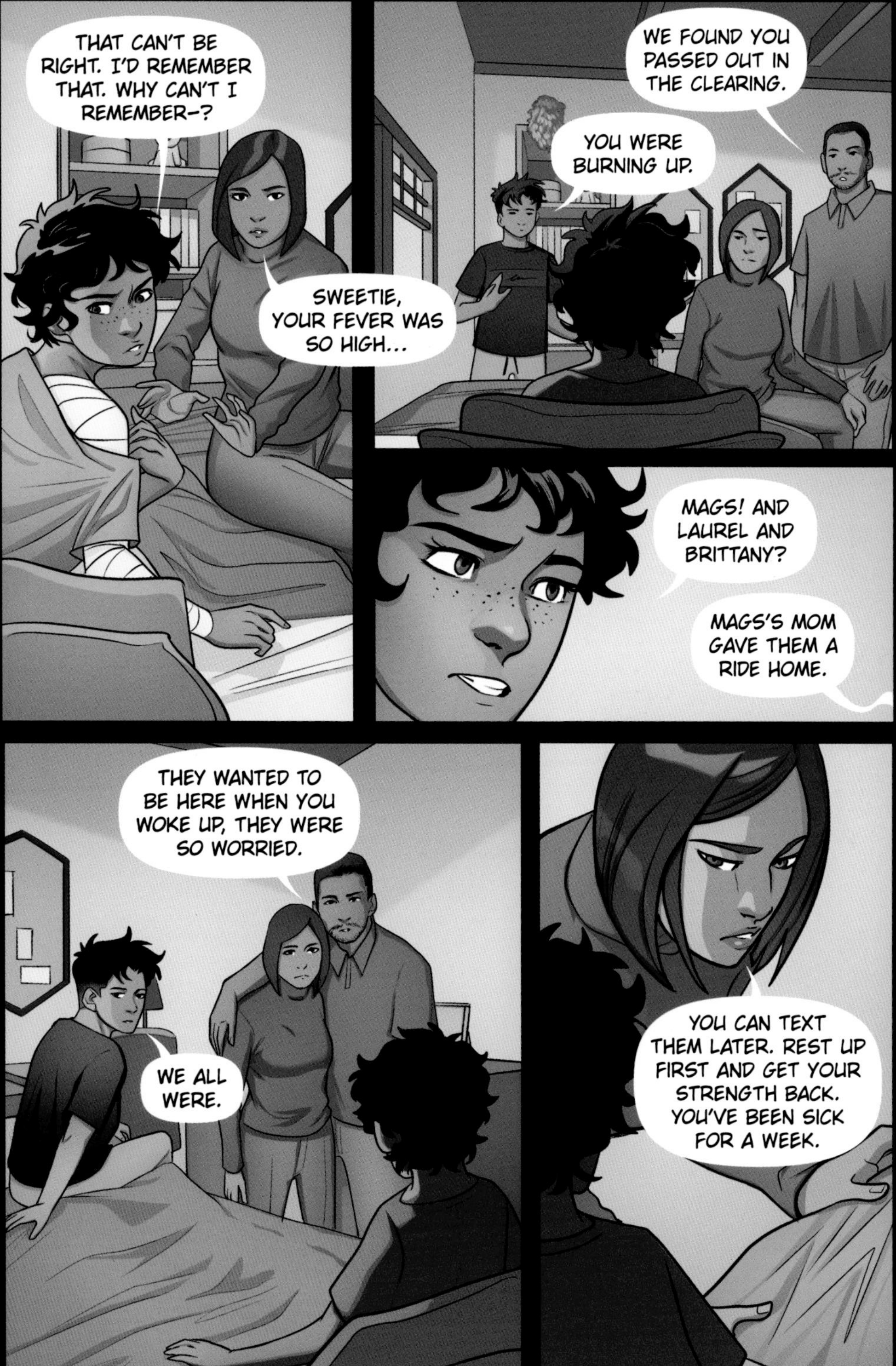
THAT CAN'T BE RIGHT. I'D REMEMBER THAT. WHY CAN'T I REMEMBER–?
SWEETIE, YOUR FEVER WAS SO HIGH...
WE FOUND YOU PASSED OUT IN THE CLEARING.
YOU WERE BURNING UP.
MAGS! AND LAUREL AND BRITTANY?
MAGS'S MOM GAVE THEM A RIDE HOME.
THEY WANTED TO BE HERE WHEN YOU WOKE UP, THEY WERE SO WORRIED.
WE ALL WERE.
YOU CAN TEXT THEM LATER. REST UP FIRST AND GET YOUR STRENGTH BACK. YOU'VE BEEN SICK FOR A WEEK.

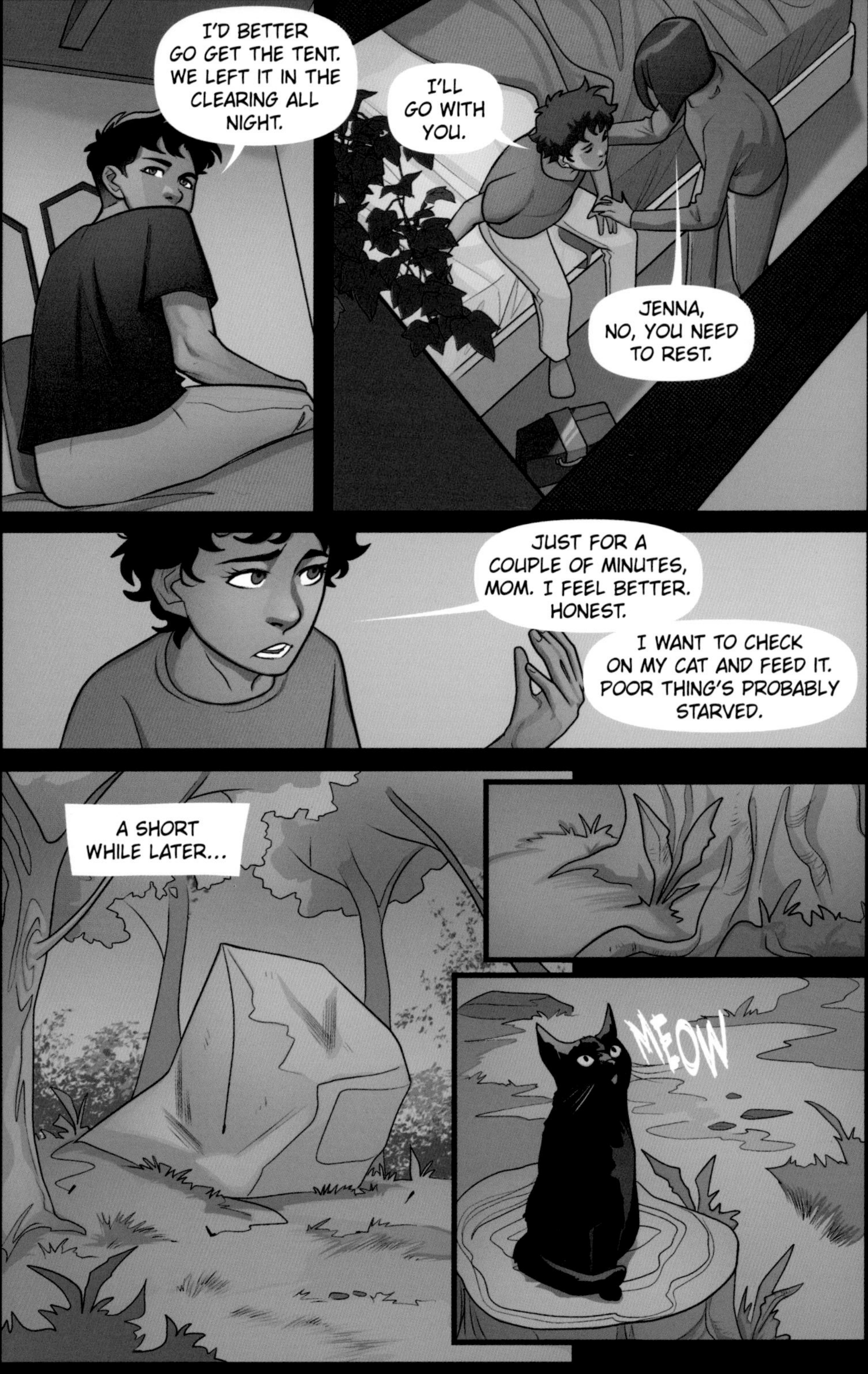
I'D BETTER GO GET THE TENT. WE LEFT IT IN THE CLEARING ALL NIGHT.
I'LL GO WITH YOU.
JENNA, NO, YOU NEED TO REST.
JUST FOR A COUPLE OF MINUTES, MOM. I FEEL BETTER. HONEST.
I WANT TO CHECK ON MY CAT AND FEED IT. POOR THING'S PROBABLY STARVED.
A SHORT WHILE LATER...
MEOW

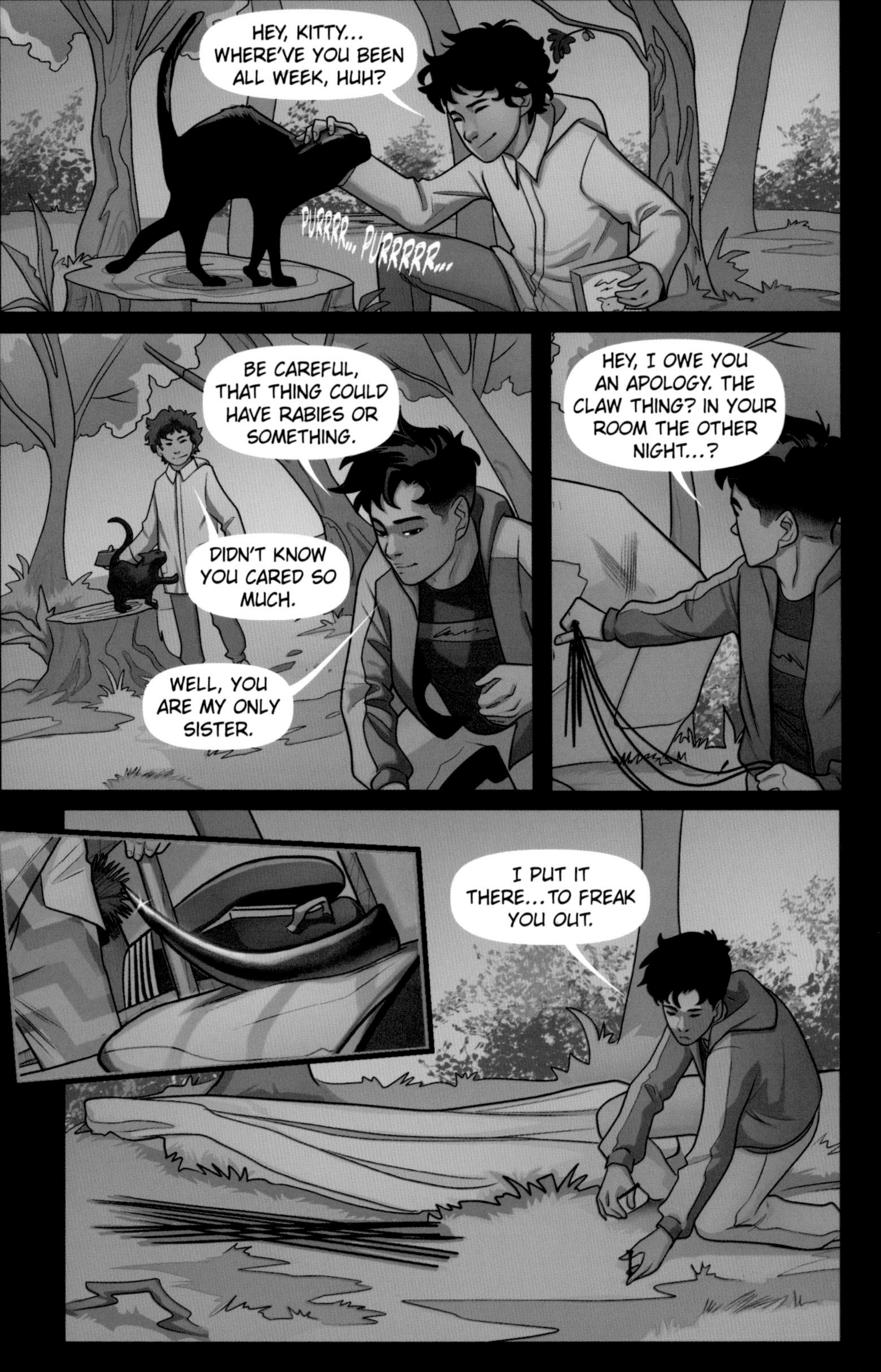
HEY, KITTY... WHERE'VE YOU BEEN ALL WEEK, HUH?
PURRRR... PURRRRR...
BE CAREFUL, THAT THING COULD HAVE RABIES OR SOMETHING.
DIDN'T KNOW YOU CARED SO MUCH.
WELL, YOU ARE MY ONLY SISTER.
HEY, I OWE YOU AN APOLOGY. THE CLAW THING? IN YOUR ROOM THE OTHER NIGHT...?
I PUT IT THERE...TO FREAK YOU OUT.

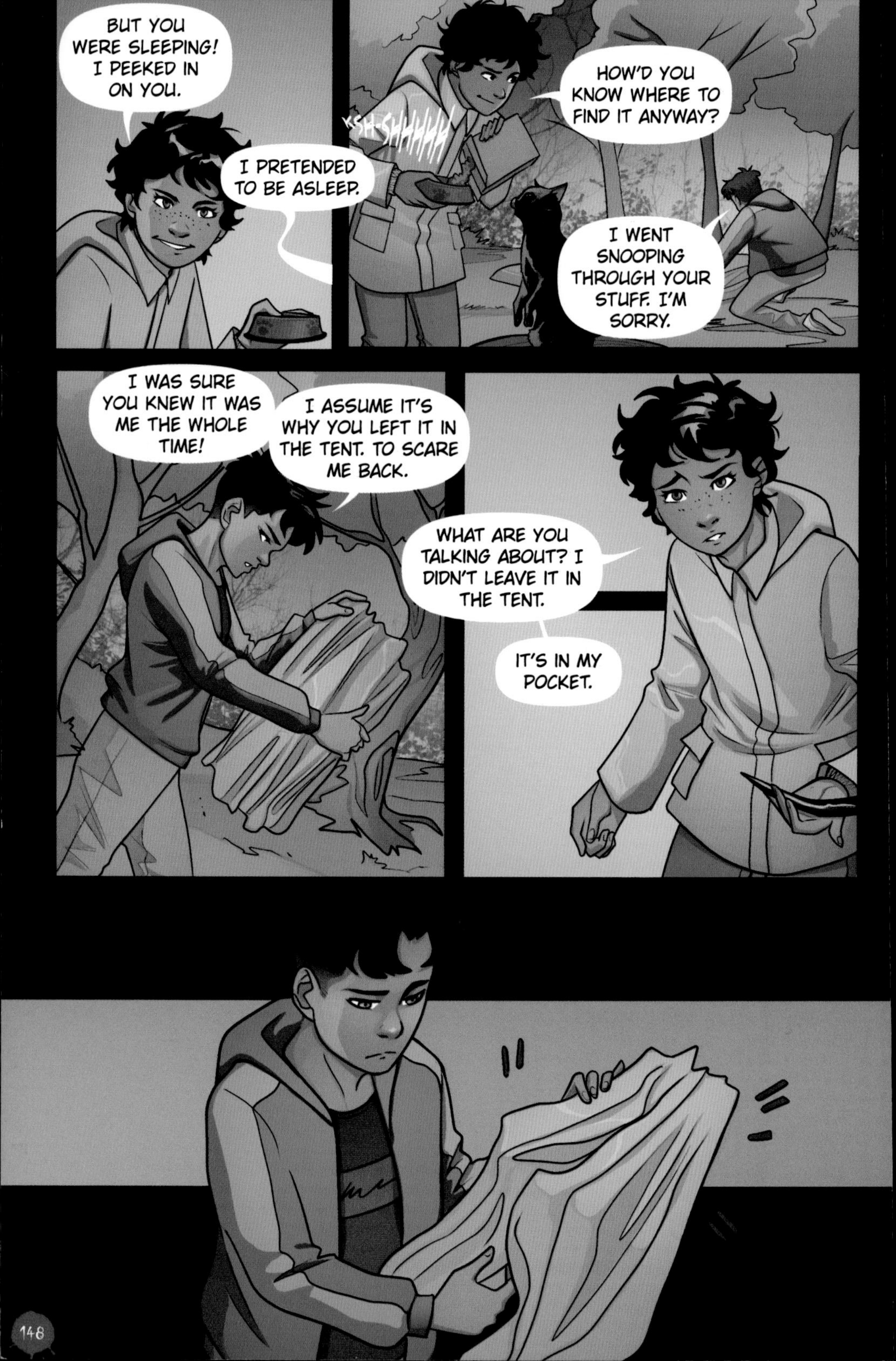

BUT YOU WERE SLEEPING! I PEEKED IN ON YOU.
I PRETENDED TO BE ASLEEP.
KSH-SHHHHH
HOW'D YOU KNOW WHERE TO FIND IT ANYWAY?
I WENT SNOOPING THROUGH YOUR STUFF. I'M SORRY.
I WAS SURE YOU KNEW IT WAS ME THE WHOLE TIME!
I ASSUME IT'S WHY YOU LEFT IT IN THE TENT. TO SCARE ME BACK.
WHAT ARE YOU TALKING ABOUT? I DIDN'T LEAVE IT IN THE TENT.
IT'S IN MY POCKET.

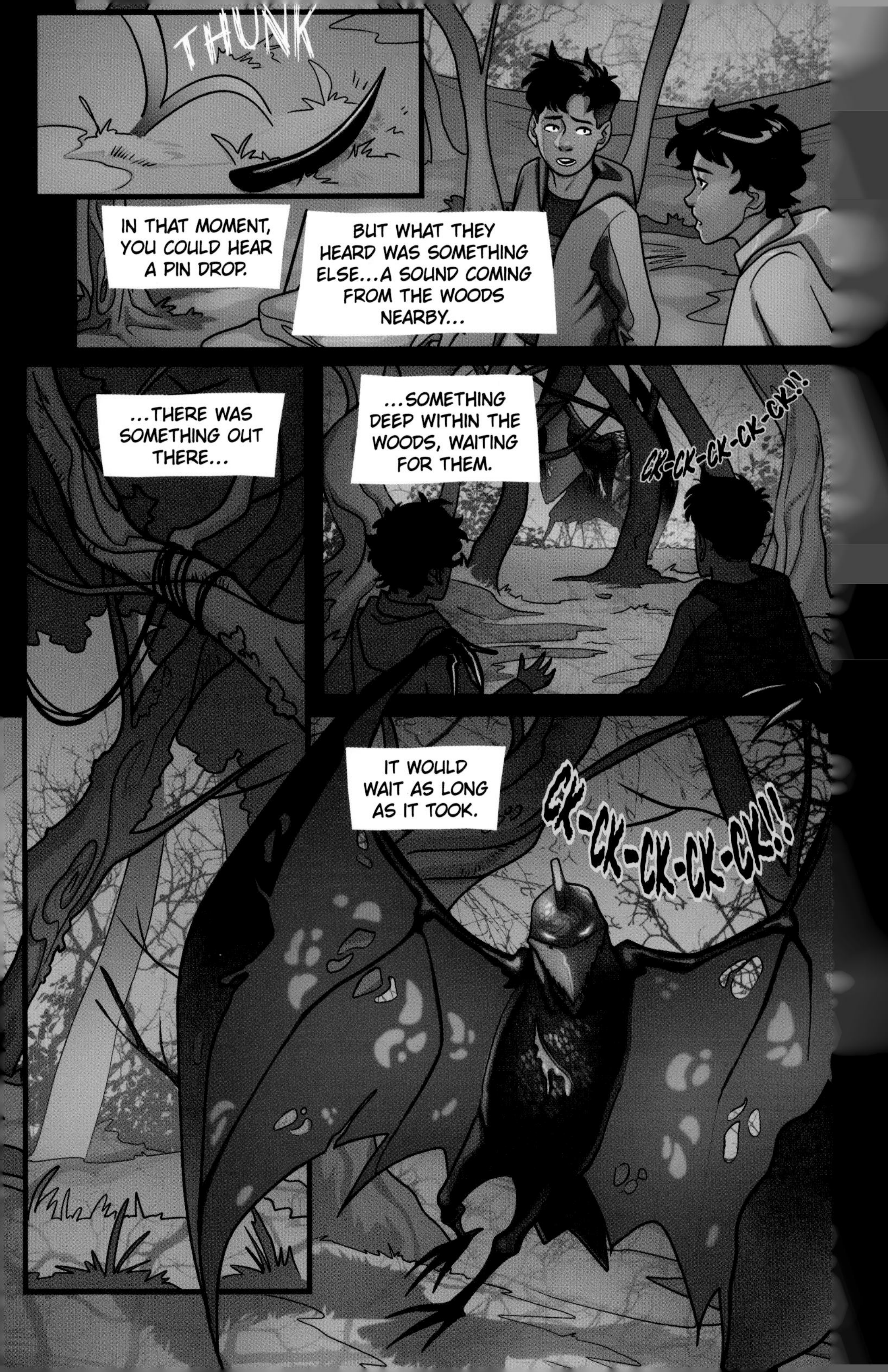
THUNK
IN THAT MOMENT, YOU COULD HEAR A PIN DROP.
BUT WHAT THEY HEARD WAS SOMETHING ELSE...A SOUND COMING FROM THE WOODS NEARBY...
...THERE WAS SOMETHING OUT THERE...
...SOMETHING DEEP WITHIN THE WOODS, WAITING FOR THEM.
CK-CK-CK-CK-CK!!
IT WOULD WAIT AS LONG AS IT TOOK.
CK-CK-CK-CK-CK!!

DO NOT FEAR—
WE HAVE ANOTHER CREEPY TALE FOR YOU!

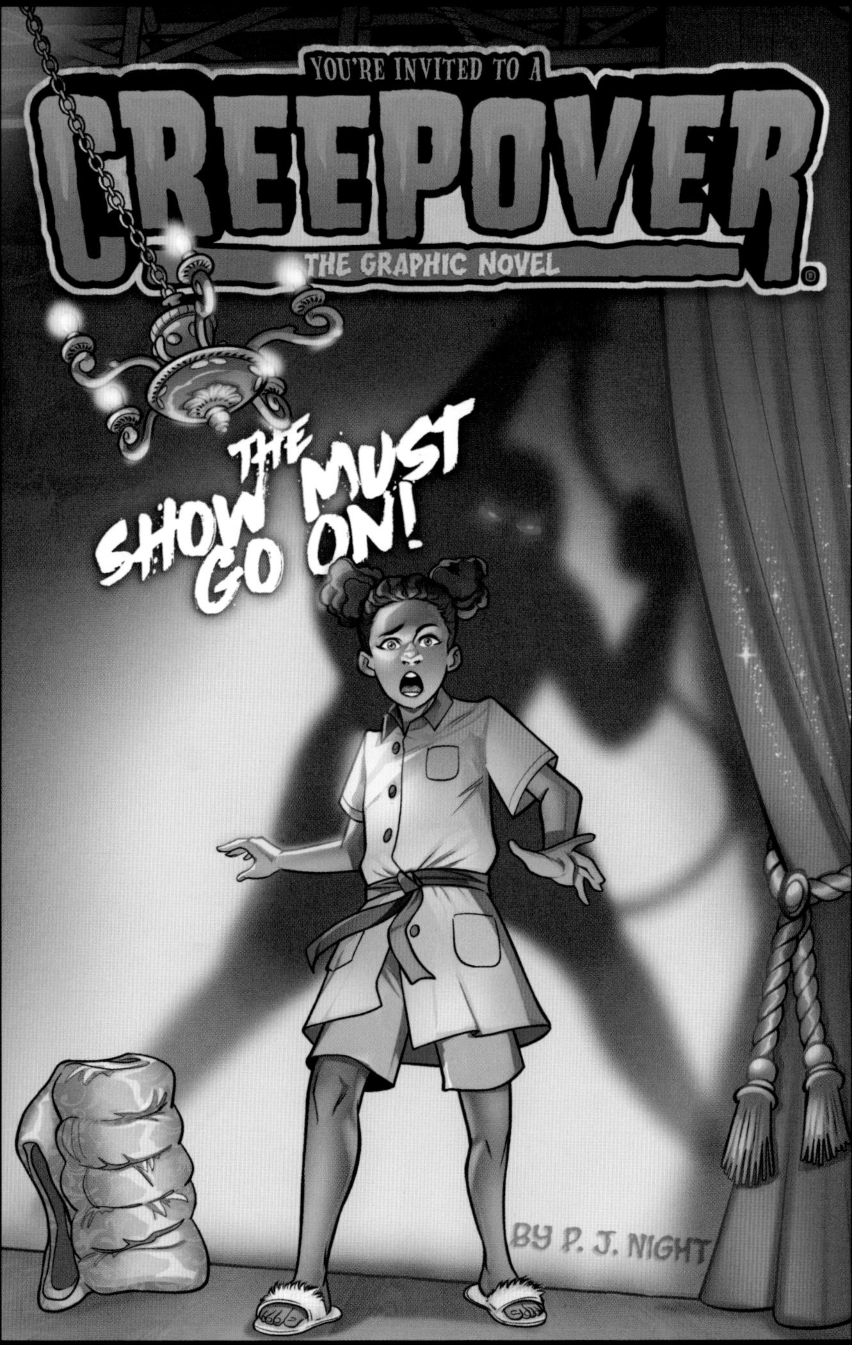

YOU'RE INVITED TO A
CREEPOVER
THE GRAPHIC NOVEL
THE SHOW MUST GO ON!
BY P. J. NIGHT

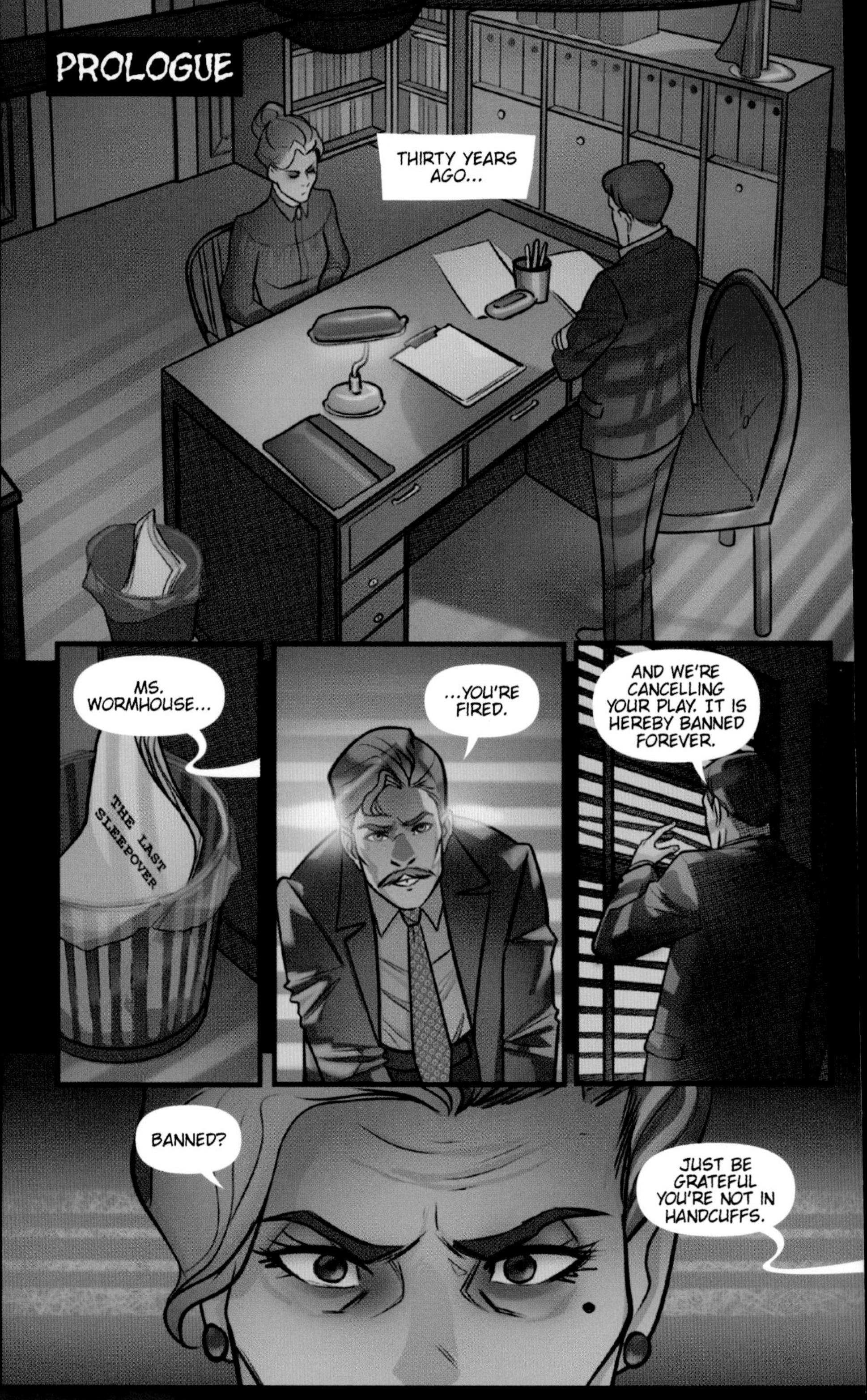
PROLOGUE
THIRTY YEARS AGO...
MS. WORMHOUSE...
THE LAST SLEEPOVER
...YOU'RE FIRED.
AND WE'RE CANCELLING YOUR PLAY. IT IS HEREBY BANNED FOREVER.
BANNED?
JUST BE GRATEFUL YOU'RE NOT IN HANDCUFFS.

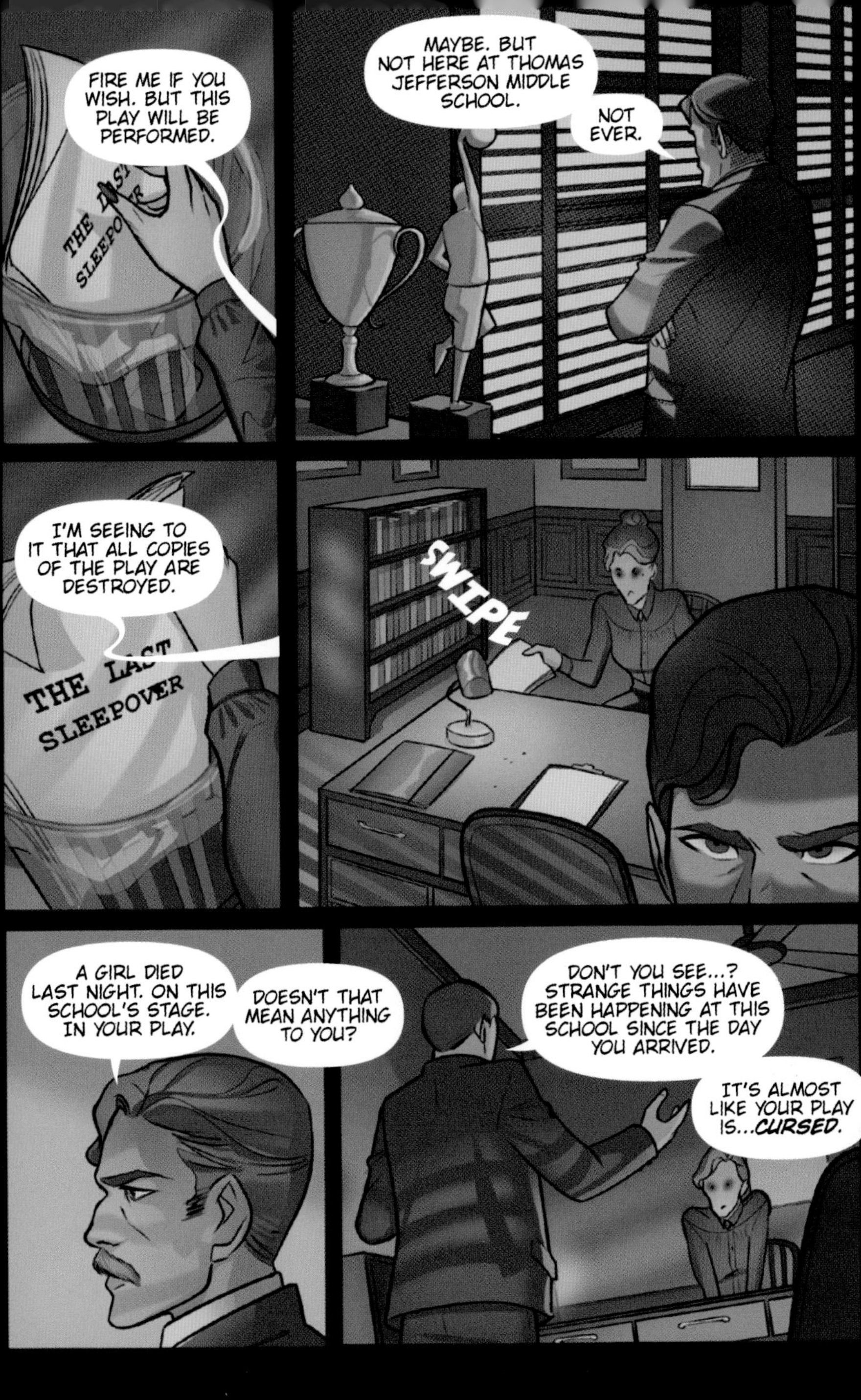
FIRE ME IF YOU WISH. BUT THIS PLAY WILL BE PERFORMED.
THE LAST SLEEPOVER
MAYBE. BUT NOT HERE AT THOMAS JEFFERSON MIDDLE SCHOOL.
NOT EVER.
I'M SEEING TO IT THAT ALL COPIES OF THE PLAY ARE DESTROYED.
THE LAST SLEEPOVER
SWIPE
A GIRL DIED LAST NIGHT. ON THIS SCHOOL'S STAGE. IN YOUR PLAY.
DOESN'T THAT MEAN ANYTHING TO YOU?
DON'T YOU SEE...? STRANGE THINGS HAVE BEEN HAPPENING AT THIS SCHOOL SINCE THE DAY YOU ARRIVED.
IT'S ALMOST LIKE YOUR PLAY IS...*CURSED*.

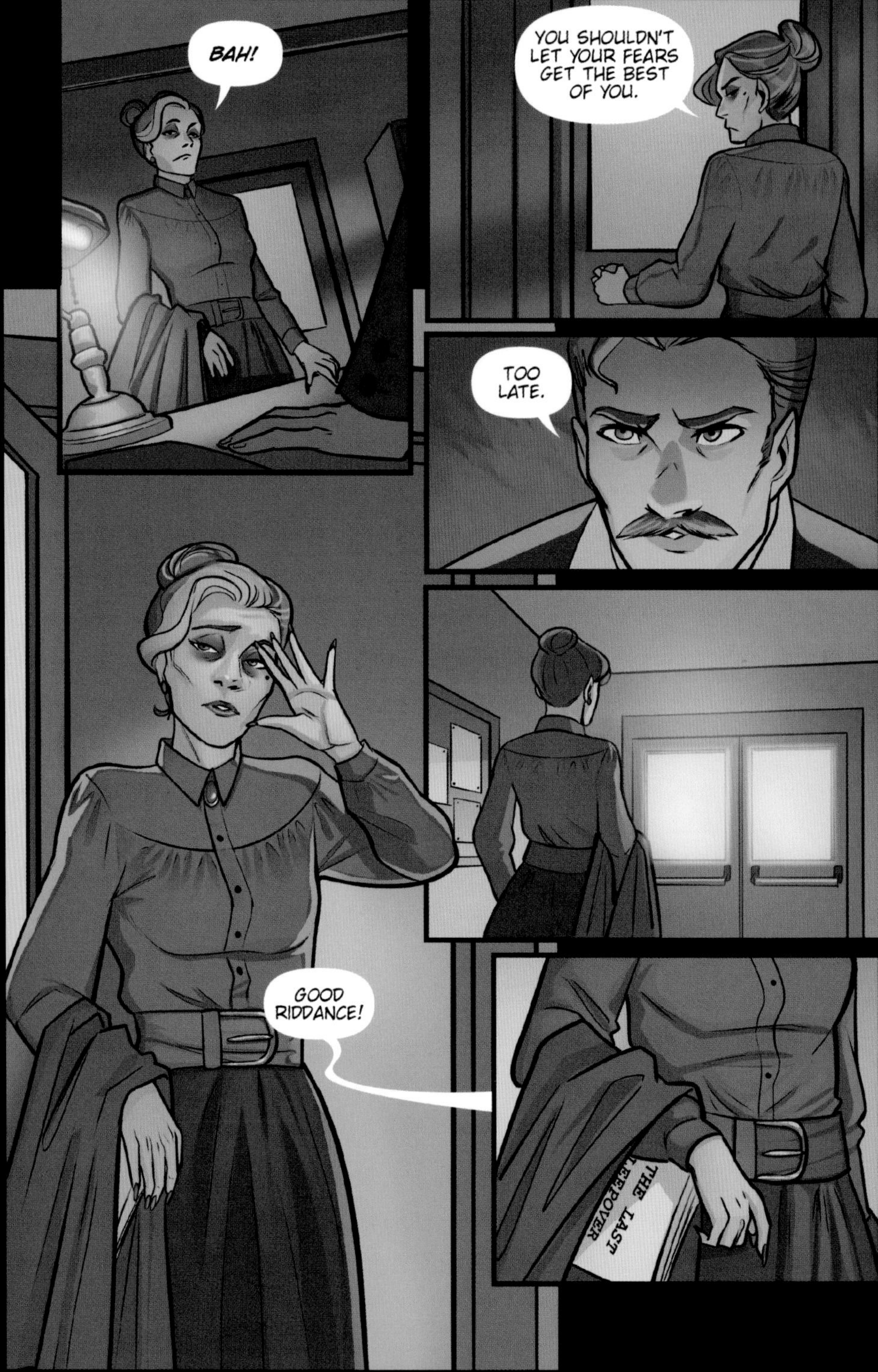
BAH!
YOU SHOULDN'T LET YOUR FEARS GET THE BEST OF YOU.
TOO LATE.
GOOD RIDDANCE!
THE LAST
LEEPOVER

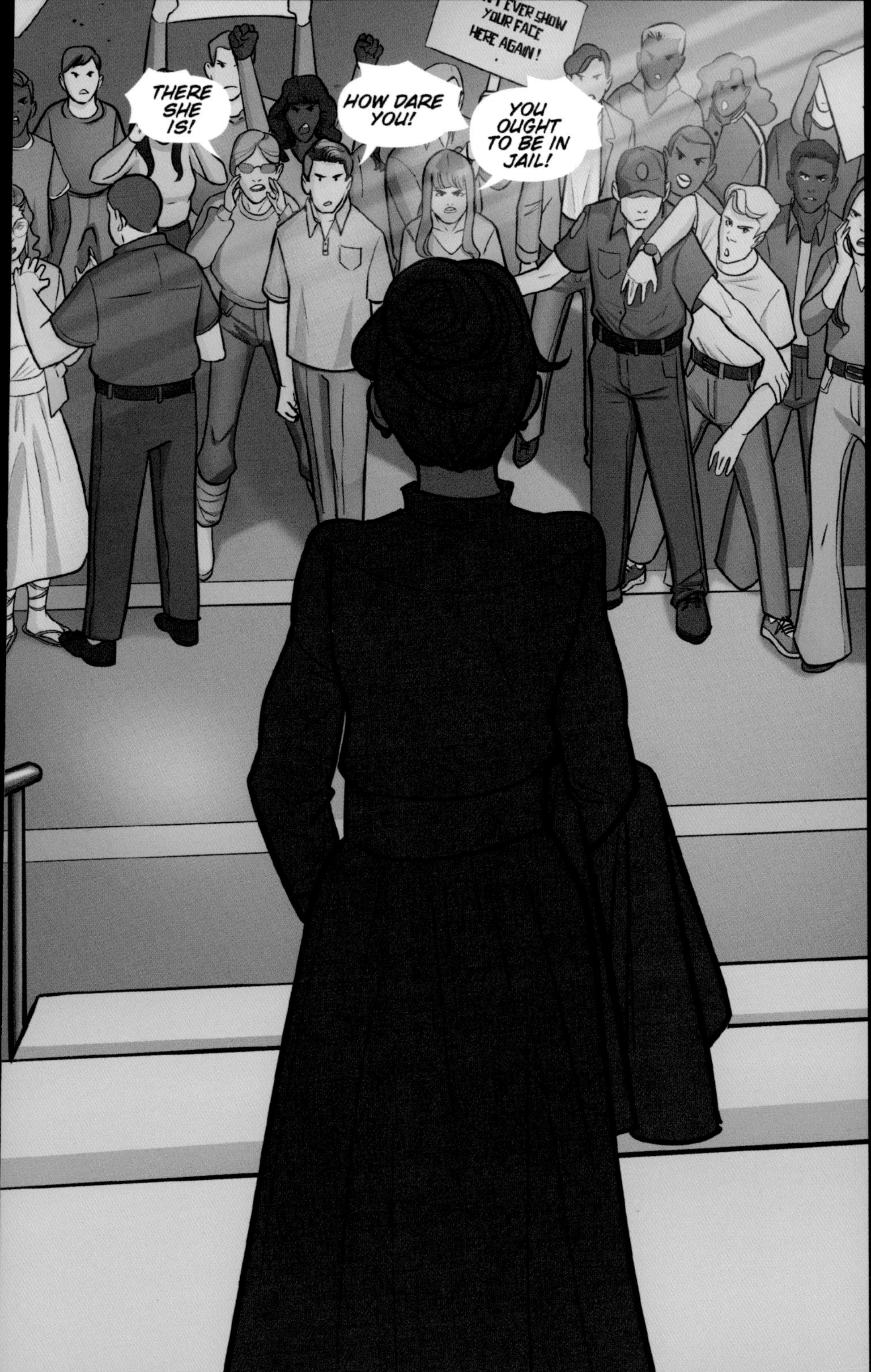
EVER SHOW YOUR FACE HERE AGAIN!
THERE SHE IS!
HOW DARE YOU!
YOU OUGHT TO BE IN JAIL!

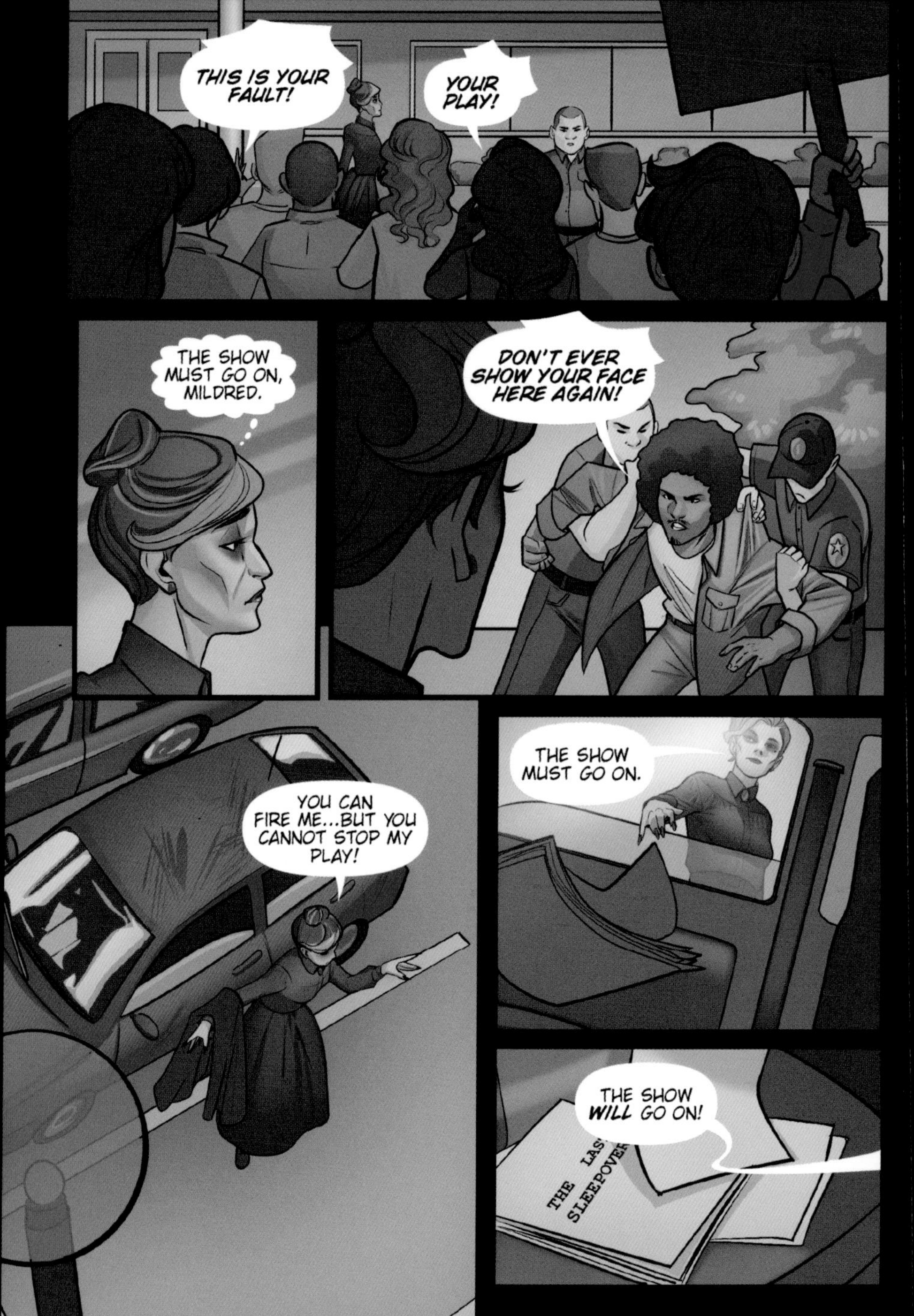
THIS IS YOUR FAULT!
YOUR PLAY!
THE SHOW MUST GO ON, MILDRED.
DON'T EVER SHOW YOUR FACE HERE AGAIN!
YOU CAN FIRE ME...BUT YOU CANNOT STOP MY PLAY!
THE SHOW MUST GO ON.
THE SHOW WILL GO ON!
THE LAS
SLEEPOVER

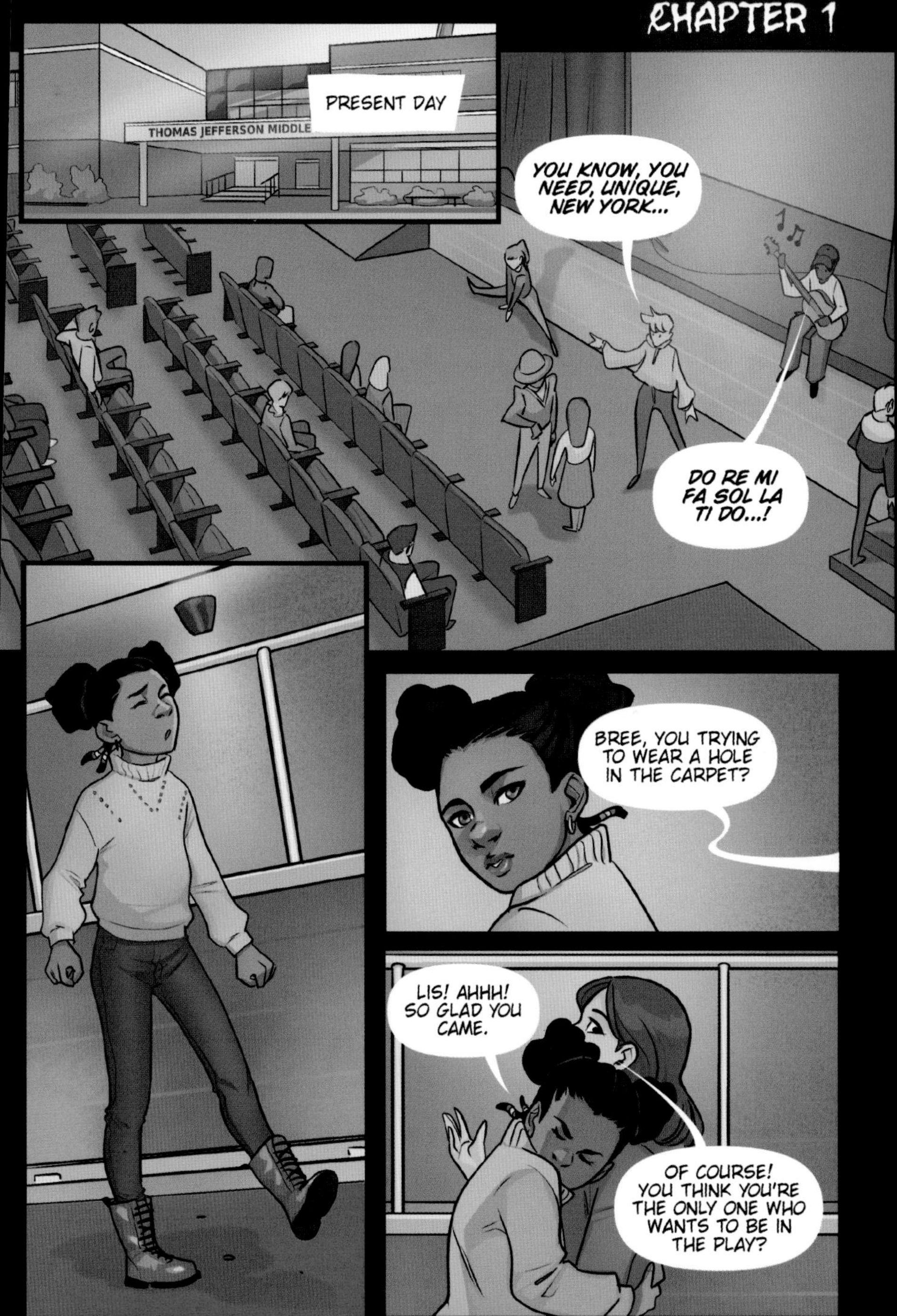
CHAPTER 1
PRESENT DAY
THOMAS JEFFERSON MIDDLE
YOU KNOW, YOU NEED, UNIQUE, NEW YORK...
DO RE MI FA SOL LA TI DO...!
BREE, YOU TRYING TO WEAR A HOLE IN THE CARPET?
LIS! AHHH! SO GLAD YOU CAME.
OF COURSE! YOU THINK YOU'RE THE ONLY ONE WHO WANTS TO BE IN THE PLAY?

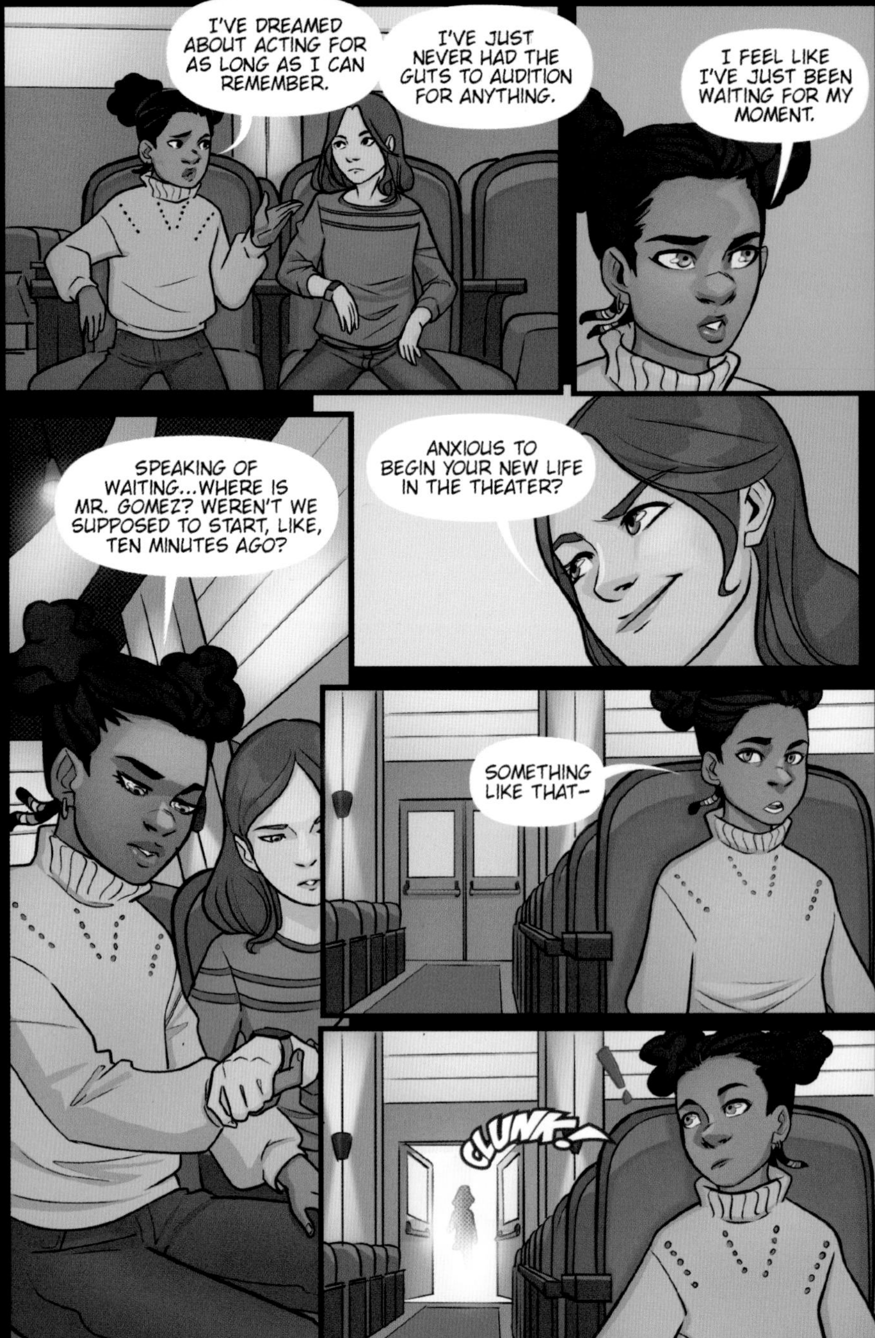
I'VE DREAMED ABOUT ACTING FOR AS LONG AS I CAN REMEMBER.
I'VE JUST NEVER HAD THE GUTS TO AUDITION FOR ANYTHING.
I FEEL LIKE I'VE JUST BEEN WAITING FOR MY MOMENT.
ANXIOUS TO BEGIN YOUR NEW LIFE IN THE THEATER?
SPEAKING OF WAITING...WHERE IS MR. GOMEZ? WEREN'T WE SUPPOSED TO START, LIKE, TEN MINUTES AGO?
SOMETHING LIKE THAT-
CLUNK!
!

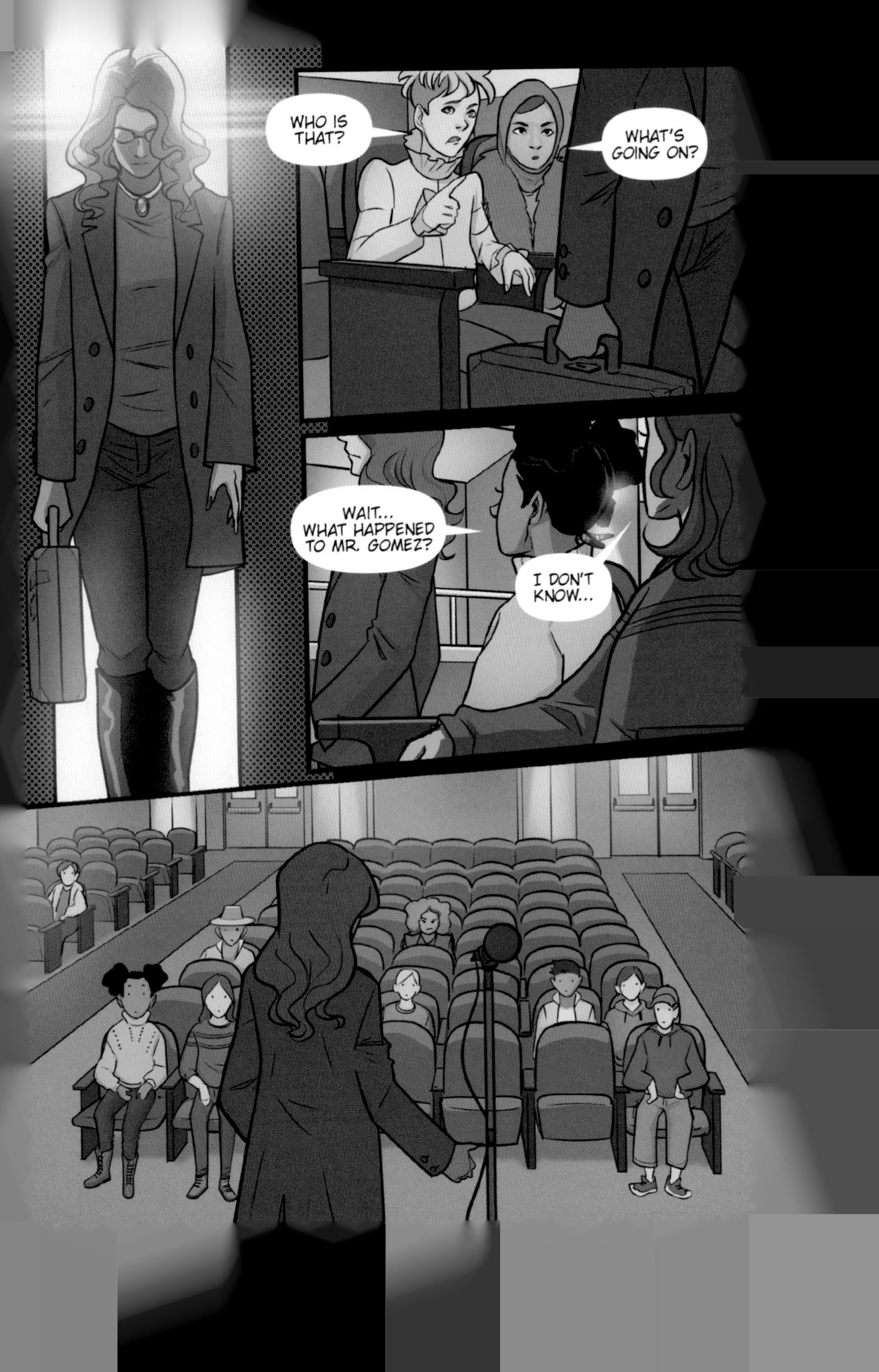
WHO IS THAT?
WHAT'S GOING ON?
WAIT... WHAT HAPPENED TO MR. GOMEZ?
I DON'T KNOW...